Preliminaries

S. Yizhar

PRELIMINARIES

TRANSLATED FROM THE HEBREW BY
Nicholas de Lange

WITH AN INTRODUCTION BY
Dan Miron

The Toby Press

Preliminaries,
English Language Edition 2007
The Toby Press LLC
POB 8531, New Milford, CT 06776-8531, USA
& POB 2455, London WIA 5WY, England

www.tobypress.com

The English translation was made possible through the
kind donation of the Rachel and Dov Gottesman Family.

Originally published in Hebrew as *Miqdamot.*
Copyright © The Estate of S. Yizhar and
Zmora Bitan Publishing House.
Published by arrangement with The Institute
for the Translation of Hebrew Literature.

Translated by Nicholas de Lange.
Translation copyright © Nicholas de Lange, 2007.
Nicholas de Lange has asserted his right to be
identified as the translator of this work.
Introduction copyright © Dan Miron, 2006.

ISBN 978 1 59264 190 1, *hardcover*

A CIP catalogue record for this title is
available from the British Library.
Printed and bound in the United States.

Introduction

A Late New Beginning

The publication of S. Yizhar's autobiographical novel *Miqda-mot* ('Preliminaries') in 1992 was a literary surprise in more ways than one. First there was the title, itself an unexpected departure, for the author's earlier titles had alternated between the straightforward (as, for example, *The Grove on the Hill*, 1947; *Midnight Convoy*, 1950) and the blatantly ironic (such as *Days of Ziklag*, 1958). In contrast, *Miqdamot* is enigmatic: The plural of the generally unused and unfamiliar noun '*miqdam*', it does not directly call to mind an image or concept. According to its dictionary definition '*miqdam*' is a technical term used in musicology and prosody, signifying either a group of unaccented syllables that introduce a line of verse that would ordinarily begin with an accented syllable, or a group of unaccented musical notes that precede the first accented note in a musical bar or musical piece. (The equivalent in English would be the equally unfamiliar term 'anacrusis'.) It was the more current Hebrew adjective '*miqdami*', meaning preliminary, announcing something which is about to come or take place, that formed most readers' impression of the meaning of the title. The novel was therefore perceived as presenting an overture, an introductory piece to be followed by other works of a similar nature. In other words, the seventy-six-year-old author was announcing the launching of a grand new literary project.

This was a double surprise. First, because this had never before been done by the author. Even his mammoth-sized *Days of Ziklag*, the longest Israeli novel to date, appeared in one piece, without any preliminary publication of some of its many sections. Secondly, and much more importantly, *Miqdamot* was published almost three full decades after what had been considered Yizhar's final collection of pieces of prose fiction, *Sipurey mishor* ('Plain Stories'). The book, which appeared in 1964, included the few pieces that the author had written after the publication of *Days of Ziklag*, and particularly the centerpiece novella, *A Story That Had Not Started*. With the publication of this novella, Yizhar, universally acknowledged as both the founding father of Israeli literature as a whole and as its chief master of prose fiction, was regarded as having exhausted his call as a writer of emotive literature. All his work, from his first extended short-story 'Ephraim Goes Back to Alfalfa' (1938) to the incisive, expressive and exhaustive novel *Days of Ziklag*, published two decades later, focused on the community of pioneers and soldiers that had laid the foundations for a new Zionist society. Everything that could be said about this society had been said at length in *Days of Ziklag*. Now, facing a new and different Israel, an Israel which had outgrown and all but forgotten its earlier idealism and sacrifices, Yizhar seemed unable to continue being its literary spokesman.

In *A Story That Had Not Started*, a wild, experimental and expressionistic piece written at an *Allegro furioso* tempo, he seemed to be taking leave of prose fiction not with a whimper but with a bang. The story viscerally exposes the mediocrity and ugliness of a contemporary middle-aged Israel while evoking again and again, in a series of repetitious cadenzas, the most traumatic event in the author's life: the death of his elder (and much idealized) brother in a gruesome accident while driving a motorcycle at full speed across railway tracks.

The accident supposedly occurred because Yizhar's brother, stung by a hornet, lost control and did not see the approaching train. However, Yizhar, even while dwelling on the threatening presence of the hornet, seems to intimate that if the death was not a suicide, it should have been one, since death in the full glory of youth and boundless freedom (symbolized by the mobility of the motorcycle) is preferable to the debasing processes of aging and decrepitude. The harsh broader significance of this parable about the dismemberment of the young Adonis could not be missed. Combined with Yizhar's decision to retire from politics (he was a member of the Israeli Knesset from 1949 to 1966, representing the ruling MAPAI party) a short time later, it seemed to add up to a voluntary withdrawal.

Leaving the arena of Israeli prose fiction to much younger writers (such as Amos Oz, A.B. Yehoshua, and Yaakov Shabtai; the last of these three he regarded as the best), Yizhar invested himself instead in semi-academic interests. He published essays on literary theory and critical analysis (in 1982 he published a magisterial dissertation-like disquisition on how 'To Read a Story'), as well as on the problems of 'value-oriented' education. His denial of the tenability of the concept and recommendation that such education should not be attempted triggered intense and heated debate. In short, there was little to prepare the public for Yizhar's comeback as a fiction writer, other than the fact that in 1989 he began re-publishing his earlier works in newly edited versions. Indeed, it is quite possible that this reworking of his earlier texts played a decisive part in rekindling the author's need for self-expression through fiction. In any case, the year 1991 was dedicated to the writing of *Preliminaries,* and then, as the title promised, came four more books that could loosely be considered sequels in quick succession: *Tzalhavim* ('Radiances', 1993), *Tzdadiyim* ('Asides', 1996), *Etzel hayam* ('By the Sea', 1996), and *Malkomiya yefefiya* ('Lovely Malcolmia', 1998). Thus the author, who by now was approaching his eightieth birthday, added a whole new wing to the formidable edifice of his fictional oeuvre.

This oeuvre can be viewed as triple tiered. Yizhar's earlier works had fallen into two main groups: the early stories written between

3

1938 and 1947, which culminated in the short novel *The Grove on the Hill*, and the stories written between 1948 and 1958, which focused on the War of 1948. The first group of stories, in which the author establishes his unique style and fictional idiom, deal primarily with the individual and collective struggles of the pioneer-settlers as they cultivate a difficult terrain even as they protect it from the growing menace of the Arab rejection of the Zionist project. These stories are set mostly in sequestered agricultural settlements with their surrounding fields and groves. The second group of stories deal exclusively with the experiences of the War of 1948—its moments of fighting and respite, the crushing fears it engendered, and the exhilarating vanquishment of such fears, the proximity of death and the yearning for life. These stories also dealt with what Yizhar viewed as the blatant injustice that the IDF inflicted upon innocent Arab villagers in the latter part of the war (what has become known as 'the Birth of the Palestinian Refugee Problem'). They catalyzed a years-long stormy public debate that was renewed with extra ferocity when one of the key stories of this phase in the author's work, 'The Story of Hirbet Hiz'ah,' was used as the basis for a short movie which questioned the morality of the settlement of Greater Israel in the 1970s.

Then, in the 1990s, Yizhar, not unlike the protagonist of his very first novella, 'went back' to hard work in his own field—not that of alfalfa but rather of emotive prose fiction—and added a third, upper story to his house of fiction. His many admiring readers were eager to discover what new fictional territory he would explore in this third period of writing. The Israeli 'literary republic' was buzzing with the question: Was Yizhar offering more of the same, or had his comeback been prodded by a new insight into Israeli society or his own role as one of its chief spokesmen and artists-educators? In short, was there a 'new' Yizhar that one would have to get used to, or was the old and much beloved storyteller from the days of the pangs and throes of the State of Israel's birth simply returning after a lengthy period of absence to an Israel that was approaching its fiftieth birthday?

2

A careful reading of *Miqdamot* yields a complex answer to this question. While the author maintains certain central elements of his narrative style, he simultaneously and perhaps, more importantly, breaks new ground, defining the distinctive narrative space of all the subsequent works he was to write in the 1990s. In order to understand this significant combination of old and new elements, one needs to be aware of the seven essential interrelated components of the author's earlier fictional world. These components were tenaciously adhered to as a single construct—in other words, Yizhar never separated between them, but rather kept them together as complementary ingredients of one narrative compound.

a) Thematically, Yizhar always focused on people in situations of strife—either with an unforgiving natural world which they struggled to domesticate (as in *On the Outskirts of the Negev* [1945], the author's first book-length novella, where a group of workers attempts to sink a well in the desert), or, more often, with an unrelenting human enemy in the framework of war. None of the author's works prior to the 1990s (with the exception of some of his children's stories) deal with situations other than those of an individual or a group of individuals pitted against an obstacle, a threat, or an opponent. By focusing on the theme of strife and struggle, Yizhar's early work conveyed the quintessence of the Zionist endeavor, which was regarded at that time as the conquest of the desert and the protection of life and home from the enemy.

b) In keeping with the focus on the Zionist struggle, Yizhar's stories were generally situated in the open spaces of Israel, particularly the parts where the southern coastal plain gradually turns desert-like and becomes the so-called

'Negev'. Almost from the very beginning, his emphasis was on wild, uninhabited spaces. Only in the very early short-stories (such as 'Ephraim Goes Back to Alfalfa' or 'A Night with No Shooting') are significant interactions allowed to take place beneath a roof, or even against the backdrop of cultivated agricultural terrain. In two of the stories dealing with the War of 1948 ('The Prisoner' and 'The Story of Hirbet Hiz'ah') such domesticated landscapes are presented as the domain of the enemy: The protagonists enter them only as conquerors and demolish or degrade all vestiges of normal human habitation. In contrast, the archetypal 'place' of Yizhar's stories is that of the wild hills and ravines which had become battlefields. Yizhar's artistic ability to convey the experience of 'being' in such spaces is overwhelming, and rendered him the greatest poet of the spatial experience in Hebrew letters.

c) This overwhelming capacity to realize being in space came at the expense of the sense of being in time, and therefore, also of the sense of history. In spite of Yizhar's extraordinary investment in the factual and detailed reproduction of historical events, such as the specific battles of the War of 1948 that he uses as background for his war stories, or the abandonment of Hulda during the 1929 riots (Hulda being the first Zionist settlement to be temporarily abandoned due to Arab attacks), which closes *The Grove on the Hill*, the stories are devoid of genuine historical essence. This lack is due to the protagonists' sketchy and limited memory, which places them in a history-less bubble. For instance, though practically all the protagonists of *The Grove on the Hill* are pioneers of the so-called Third Aliyah, who had immigrated to Palestine only six or seven years before the time-frame of the story, none of them evoke the memory of a Polish or a Ukrainian hometown, childhood experience, or the languages (Yiddish, Polish, Russian) they used to speak. This curious gap cannot be excused by the fact that they are in great danger and so are focused solely on their duties as defenders of the sequestered and besieged Jewish settlement, for this does not diminish their ability to pay attention to space and record in their minds its subtly nuanced impressions. Rather this diminution of the role of memory and the shrinkage of historical consciousness is actually the clearest manifestation of the Zionist inversion of the Jewish imagination. Where the triad of history, memory and text had reigned supreme, now place and concrete objects become the dominant realities, while time and memory become stunted and the holy text melts into the fiber of the narrative itself, permeating the author's style (which is replete with Biblical allusions) rather than representing a source for interpretative elaboration.

d) By downplaying memory and history, Yizhar placed his stories (with a couple of exceptions, most notable of which is 'The Story of Hirbet Hiz'ah') in a continuous present narrative modality: the human experience is portrayed as it is evolving. This temporal framework leads to quite a few distinctive characteristics. One is a certain amount of repetition: The strict adherence to raw experience as lived in the present inevitably results in meticulous reconstructions of slightly different variants of similar experiences that have already been described (such as sunrises and sunsets in the battlefield, the experience of being shelled by the enemy's canon, etc.). Another characteristic is the unavoidable reliance on superimposed structural time frames that are actually extrinsic to the protagonists' sense of being. Such temporal frameworks can be either 'natural' (such as a full day, from sunrise to sunset or from sunrise to sunrise) or historical (the real duration of a certain event, such as the seven days of the battle described in the twelve hundred packed pages of *Days of Ziklag*). The intrinsically significant time unit in the stories, however, is actually that of the single experienced moment, which can stretch or contract, be felt as fleeting or 'endless'.

e) The striving to capture the singular instants of experience (what Virginia Woolf refers to as 'moments of being') led Yizhar to adopt the stream of consciousness narrative modality along with its characteristic devices and techniques—mainly the so-called 'direct' interior monologue. Though he learned much from Western masters such as James Joyce, Virginia Woolf, and particularly William Faulkner, Yizhar nevertheless regarded the early twentieth-century U.N. Gnessin, who had introduced stream of consciousness narration to Hebrew fiction before it was adopted by British and American writers, as his master and model. In any case, almost all of Yizhar's works (with some exceptions such as 'The Story of Hirbet Hi'zah,' or 'Habakkuk', and, of course, the stories written for young readers) attempt to verbally evoke associative modes of thought, while lacing them with an emotive lyricism of mood and setting them within the subtly nuanced impressions of immediate physical reality. However, Yizhar's work differs from other stream of consciousness fiction in a significant way: the aforementioned weak role of memory in his stories stands in strong contrast to the central role it usually plays in such fiction. Therefore his stories, including the huge *Days of Ziklag* (the longest work written in stream of consciousness modality in any language), do not contain the sudden temporal shifts, the quick movements between the present and many pasts, that are a staple characteristic of such stream of consciousness masterpieces as Woolf's *To the Lighthouse*, Faulkner's *As I Lay Dying*, and Gnessin's *Etzel* ('Beside').

f) Yizhar's early fiction focused therefore on the individual consciousness, and often conveyed a deeply idiosyncratic view of reality, that of a protagonist who was not altogether in synch with his human environment. At the same time, however, almost all of the stories dealt with collective projects—whether peaceful (as the sinking of a well) or combative. Therefore Yizhar's individualistic and often all but anarchistic protagonists also function as fully committed members of active groups. This is the source of some of the tormenting inner conflicts that inform many of the stories. In these stories the protagonists have to fight and suppress yearnings for total freedom, have to combat the desire to break away from tasks dictated by the collective project. In its purest essence this desire for freedom finds expression in the urge to drop everything, to run away, or to roam alone and unconstrained in large and open spaces (a romantic ideal that finds its ultimate expression in the short story 'Hanimlat' ['The Runaway']). The protagonists, however, usually control such urges and accept the responsibilities they have assumed as members of the collective. Thus they 'go back to Alfalfa' or march to battle. They have to do it, because, in the final analysis, they are informed by a moral fiat.

g) Yizhar's early work, as a whole, is deeply moralistic—a feature it inherited from early twentieth-century Hebrew fiction, particularly from the work of Y.H. Brenner. However, this inherent moralist tendency creates clashes between individual and collective altogether different from the aforementioned conflicts triggered by sheer anarchism or by an aesthetic recoiling from the vulgarity of the group. In such cases the tension emanates from an incisive critique of the group's moral standards or of the means it employs for the purpose of realizing its goals. It is such conflict that informs the fierce criticism of the IDF's handling of non-combatant Palestinians in some of Yizhar's stories. For many, this moralistic aspect of Yizhar's work became the one they either vehemently rejected or with which they enthusiastically identified. For the latter the author became much more than a great writer. He was the strong and clear voice of the collective Israeli conscience.

3

Turning to *Miqdamot*, we can now trace how it resumes Yizhar's narrative art after the three-decade hiatus and further develops at least five of its quintessential emphases: the emphasis on open spaces as the setting in which people best come to know themselves and their role in the world; the emphasis on situations of strife with the elements as well as with the enemy; the use of the stream of consciousness narrative modality to best express the author's view of reality and of the core human experience; the moralist vein of critical self-assessment; the focus on an individual who stands at the fringes of a group, both part of it yet also a stranger in its midst, one who in spite of having internalized the collectivist ethos of the Zionist pioneers, cannot live in harmony with it, and at times has to assert a contradictory call—that of the lonely observer, or rather, as this book unabashedly declares, of one who is destined to become a poet, concerned with the creation of beauty rather than the achievement of utilitarian collective goals.

Open spaces form the backdrop of the novel as a whole. For in spite of the fact that more than half of *Miqdamot* takes place in Tel Aviv of the 1920s, it is the open landscapes of the still relatively empty and deserted early twentieth-century Palestine that permeate not only the many extensive descriptive passages scattered throughout the five sections of the novel, but also, more importantly, inform the development of the particular Zionist mentality which the novel follows and delineates. It is the open expanse of virgin soil, of sands, of the flaming red *Hamra* sods characteristic of the fertile borderline areas between the golden sea-coast dunes and the darker and heavier soil of the eastern mountainous ranges, that challenges both old, seasoned pioneers, such as the protagonist's father, and the children growing up in the far-flung sandy suburb of Tel Aviv. They all know that it is their generation's role to 'conquer' this 'open' land, to prove (as the father asserts in the first section, when tilling the unyielding virgin soil of a newly purchased field) that there is no such thing as land that is not arable, of land that should be left uncultivated. The more courageous and imaginative among them, such as the protagonist's all but deified older brother, dream of conquering the heaving expanse of the sea and the enormous bell-shaped blue dome of the sky as well. The protagonist himself, as the exquisite prelude to the novel so poignantly conveys, is mentally born into a still dim, primary consciousness of color and line—the basic ingredients of the painter's art—that is bestowed upon him by the sky and hills of his rustic and half-deserted birthplace. As a mere toddler he orientates himself by examining the grainy sods of the earth on which he crawls. 'He soaks up...into his inner being' the grayness and crisp and crumbling qualities of the earth's substance, that 'perhaps...some day they might do something, so that he may tell them precisely as they were' (p.49). It is the sense of 'place' he craves rather than food and drink, and perhaps it is this craving that renders him so slight, weightless, so almost devoid of bodily presence—a description repeated again and again throughout the novel. This characteristic lends him a lightness similar to that of an insect or a small bird, and enables him to easily climb the very precarious tops of the tallest trees, from which he can observe the vast distances—westward to the sea and eastward to the filmy, gaseous silhouettes of the mountains.

But this orientation towards 'place' involves strife, as the two first sections so dramatically illustrate. The open Palestinian expanse vehemently rejects the tribe of pioneers who have arrived with the purpose of 'conquering' it (Yızhar dwells on the many, perhaps too many, uses of the verb 'to conquer' so prevalent in the discourse of the Zionist pioneers), and impose upon it their own sense of rational order, pragmatism of human habitation, and national sense of belonging. It subtly undermines their pretentious plans of cultivation and exploitation, often replacing their surety of success, their fierce will and faith, with a recognition of failure. The life story of the protagonist's father, as hardened and dedicated a Zionist pioneer as any, which the novel gradually unfolds, is permeated with the consciousness of such failure.

The 'open' spaces can also attack and inflict terrible pain.
Nowhere in the Hebrew literature of the Zionist endeavor is this
more vividly illustrated than in the first section of *Miqdamot*, with
its description of the onslaught of hornets on the innocent infant
playing in the shade of a carob tree while his father is busy plowing
through the hardened crust of a piece of land that has perhaps never
before been broken by human tools. A multileveled scene, it is, first
of all, an unusually detailed, realistic depiction of a horrific event in
the life of people who choose to make the frontier their home and
raise children in the desert. In addition, it is a symbol not only of
the clash between Zionism and Palestine, but also of the unavoidable
victimization of sons by the blind idealism of the pioneering fathers,
an echo of the binding of Isaac; for, of course, the horrific poisoning of the infant is the 'response' of the desert to the father's invasive
intervention, as the father acknowledges in his guilt-ridden heart. 'As
for a man, does he not need to know his place?' he asks himself, quoting Isaiah's 'When ye come to appear before Me, who asked this of
you, to trample My courts!' (1: 12), while carrying his half-dead son
(rather like the father in Goethe's 'Erlkoenig') in search of the closest
country physician (who, even when reached, will hardly know how
to treat the boy). And isn't this attempt to invade nature, upsetting
a primeval equilibrium perfected over thousands of years, a sacrilege
of sorts, for the land belongs to the Lord, to Him only. 'She silently
turned to Him through all the emptiness and heat and little clouds
of dust, and He silently to her through all the torrid, empty skies
grey from so much arid light, until the perfect nothingness of the
skies above reaches and touches the perfect nothingness of the land
beneath, on which there is nothing. And there is only the silence
between them, and only the arrogance of our deafness prevents us
from hearing that it is not silence at all' (p. 87).

Thus the scene, functioning like most powerful symbols on
multiple levels, also serves as a political parable, which the harried
father instinctively senses. In the midst of his desperate attempt to find
medical help for his son, he remembers Isaac Epstein's groundbreaking
article 'A Hidden Problem', in which the Zionist commentator argues

that the Zionist project in Palestine was bound to bring about a collision with the Arab population of the country. The father, himself a Zionist writer and commentator (as Yizhar's father actually was), attempts to refute Epstein's pessimistic argument, listing the entire array of conventional Zionist answers to the problems formulated by Epstein (Zionism brings economic and medical benefits also to the non-Jewish inhabitants of Palestine; the country, if rationally cultivated by modern methods and machinery can absorb many Jews without harming the Arab peasants, etc.); however, in his own heart he knows that his opponent's unsettling and sobering insights are weightier by far than his own reassuring attempted rebuttal. The second section of the novel further broadens the scope of this uncomfortable awareness. Where the first section is set to the background of 1919, when Zionist activism in Palestine was just emerging from the paralysis of the war years, the second focuses on the events of May 2nd, 1921, when the Palestinian national movement staged its first organized riots, protesting the Balfour declaration and the intention of incorporating it as the essence and raison d'etre of the mandate over Palestine which the League of Nations was about to grant Great Britain. The vivid evocation of the atmosphere in a besieged Jewish enclave in Jaffa clearly points towards a future of constant strife and unrelenting clashes between Jews and Arabs in Palestine; strife and clashes that will take their toll of human lives. The chapter ends with the news that the Arab rioters have murdered the leading Hebrew writer of the time, Y.H. Brenner, who lived in a sequestered house together with some younger writers and a family of settlers in an orchard owned by Jews in the Jaffa vicinity. Thus the first two sections of *Miqdamot* fully dramatize the two aspects of strife which Yizhar's stories had dwelt on in the past: the struggle with the elements and nature on the one hand, and political/military struggle on the other.

In accordance with his earlier writing, the stream of consciousness narrative modality also clearly controls these first two sections of the novel as well as sizeable portions in the remaining three: the first section is mainly narrated through the father's direct interior monologue, while the second is a mosaic of direct and indirect interior monologues as well as other stream of consciousness devices conveying the five-year-old protagonist's associative cogitation. Though stream of consciousness is not the dominant narrative modality of the second half of the book, its devices are also employed in the last three sections, often dexterously carrying the reader from the interior monologue of one character to that of another (see, for instance, the quick cutting through the interior monologues of the depressed father, the self-confident elder brother and the alienated protagonist in the fourth section.

Of special interest is the father's interior monologue in the first section, a careful reconstruction of the specific linguistic and mental materials associated with the thinking of an idealist pioneer of the old guard. A socialist, a Tolstoyan, a Zionist of the turn of the nineteenth century dreaming of the creation of a 'new Jew' in a new Zion, the father is also an extremely well-read dilettante with insatiable intellectual curiosity and the systematic memory of a scholar, who not only remembers everything he reads but also tends to categorize every bit of information he absorbs, so as to be able to draw on it as the need arises. Thus in the middle of his frenetic attempt to save his baby son, badly stung by an entire hornets' nest, the father's mind processes every fact he knows about hornets and wasps, starting with references from the Bible, running through Talmudic and Midrashic literature, and ending with what he has read in modern German zoology textbooks. While the encyclopedic format (also known as that of the 'anatomy') is prevalent enough in stream of consciousness narratives portraying learned or pedantic characters, rarely has the encyclopedic interior monologue conveyed as poignant a tragi-comic effect as do the scholarly ruminations of the protagonist's desperate father. Adding greater complexity is the father's intrinsic conflict as a conscientious atheist and sworn rationalist who is nevertheless unable to suppress formulations of prayer and irrational supplication hailing from his religious childhood, finally succumbing to the swirl of verses from the book of Psalms which inundate his turbulent mind.

Though the use of the stream of consciousness style diminishes as the book progresses, it nonetheless remains the chief modality through which the author conveys the protagonist's sense of
alienation—or rather, if seen in the context of Yizhar's earlier work,
the ambivalence of the author's distinctive character-type who both
belongs and does not belong within the group. In *Miqdamot*, this
ambivalence is explored perhaps more thoroughly and honestly than
ever before. Rather than being an abstract quality, it is here tied to
the concrete: It is related to the protagonist's physical limitations; to
his inability to fully participate in the activities of a peer group that
takes robustness for granted and has little use for whatever does not
entail physical strength and coordination; to his extreme admiration
for and jealousy of his handsome elder brother, the ideal athlete-leader,
social mixer, girls' wet dream, and light-hearted daredevil. The novel
thus charts the protagonist's trajectory towards the total loneliness
of the final section, where he is reduced first to conduct an ongoing dialogue with a wheelbarrow, then to cultivate the friendship
of a lonely donkey, whose days of usefulness are over, and who is
therefore allowed to wander off in the company of the twelve-year-
old boy. He cannot find a single friend in the village of Rehovot, to
which his parents moved when the father lost his modest job at the
municipality of Tel Aviv as a result of the severe economic crisis of
1926-1927. Finally and predictably, the lonely boy finds his friends
on library shelves, and his place in the world of literature, the discovery of which is celebrated towards the end of the novel, when the
protagonist decides not only to become a writer himself, but also to
adopt the manner of Dickens rather than that of Dostoevsky in his
writing. But even before moving to Rehovot, while still in Tel Aviv,
and in the midst of a group of avid readers who are mentally close to
him and his interests, the protagonist nonetheless senses that his ties
with his contemporaries are tentative and tenuous. He expresses this
realization to himself in an interior monologue, his words highlight-
ing the theme of individualism in the midst of a collectivist society
as it has developed throughout Yizhar's oeuvre:

Even when they are all together there is always
one who is left on his own. And even when he is
surrounded by them there is always one who is left
on his own. And even when they all belong there is
always one who does not entirely belong. Or let's say
he belongs yet doesn't belong, or not wholly, or not all
the time, even if he is with them all the time. And not
because he likes it like this but because that's the way
it is. And even though it's sad being on your own there
is always one who doesn't entirely join in, who doesn't
entirely belong, who is always slightly not. And how
can someone like that rebuild the Land when you all
have to rebuild the Land together, and one on his own
cannot rebuild anything? Or it's as though he's only
there to watch, from the sidelines, watching, seeing,
saying nothing, but writing it down as it were in a
notebook that doesn't exist yet, and, since it is so, it's as
though all the time he is required to explain something
about himself, to make excuses or apologise, instead of
admitting, leave me alone, friends, let me be and don't
wait for me. Even though, at the same time, strangely
enough, wait for me, I'm coming too, wait for me I'm
coming too. (p. 226).

Just as this passage serves as a key to much in Yizhar's work,
as well as a guide to understanding his sense of the role of the writer
in society, many of the other motifs in *Miqdamot* shed light on
the psychological nuances of various characteristic interactions in
Yizhar stories. For example, there is a more open expression of the
mixture of attraction and repulsion, of admiration and denigration
that is triggered by the appearance of a perfectly extroverted and
virile character who can be either a bully or an all but homoerotic
object of jealous love. (Both versions are modeled after Yizhar's older
brother, or rather the various and contradictory impressions of the
brother whose early death raised him to an almost mythological level:

both the perfect beauteous youth whom the gods, in their jealousy, destroyed, and at the same time the adventurous and irresponsible Euphorion from the second part of Goethe's *Faust*.) Likewise, the dualistic attitude to sexuality in *Miqdamot*, as expressed in the counterpoint of dreamy and suppressed erotic arousal, illustrated by the protagonist's childish love for Mikha'ela (even in his dreams she appears fully covered by a soft coat) on the one hand, and its foil, his horrified discovery of sexuality in the vineyard, particularly the sight of the hairy man washing his sizeable penis after intercourse on the other, also evokes and sharpens similar dualities in earlier works, offering modes of interpretation. For example, in the context of a dualistic relationship to sexuality, it is possible to offer an explanation why Yizhar has almost never allowed his many protagonists, most of whom are young men at the peak of their sexual prowess, to entertain credible sexual fantasies that go beyond blurry, idealized encounters with 'wonderful' girls that are abstract, detached, and never sexually accessible and interested.

4

Having traced the continuity of *Miqdamot* with Yizhar's earlier work, we should now turn to its innovative side, emphasizing that the groundbreaking aspects are the dominant ones, quite overpowering their opposites. Written at the age of seventy-five, this short novel, Yizhar's 'Portrait of the Artist as a Young Boy', virtually amounts to a new beginning in the author's long artistic career. Naturally the most important new thread in transforming the entire fiber of the author's narrative manner is that of memory, the element that had been missing in his earlier works. True, memory, particularly memories of childhood and youth, had already been evoked in the author's stories for young readers, such as the extraordinarily vivid and well-crafted stories collected in *Six Summer Tales* (1950) and

Barefoot (1959), collections also made unique by the prevalence of a robust humor and upbeat mood not often evident in Yizhar's better known novellas and novels. Superficially one may even regard parts of *Miqdamot* as upgraded versions of some of these stories. The novel actually alludes explicitly to these earlier descriptions of childhood among the orchards of Rehovot, referring readers who would like more details about the experiences mentioned to the stories (see p. 262, 264). However, the similarities between *Miqdamot* and the earlier stories are illusory, as the author actually warns, albeit in a subtle and seemingly off-hand manner. The references to the earlier stories in fact amount to an indirect declaration that the author has decided to forgo those aspects of his childhood and youth that have already been covered—not for the purpose of brevity or to escape repetition (as already noted, Yizhar had never avoided repetition, to the chagrin of some of his readers), but mainly to convey that those episodes do not contain the essential 'truth' of the writer's childhood, that they are 'superfluous today...exaggerated sentimentalizing' (p. 263). Fresh and captivating as earlier presentations may have been, they emanate from a subtly doctored or cosmetically beautified view of reality.

In *Miqdamot,* childhood is mainly a time of sadness, loneliness, fear, a sense of inadequacy, and premonitions of impending disasters. All these are brought to the fore in a series of dark scenes and insights: the horrific encounter with the hornets as the infant's symbolic awakening to the toxic quality of reality and to the predominance of pain and danger; the five-year-old's tension and sense of threat when trapped in a Jaffa courtyard besieged by murderous Arab rioters; the derailing of a boy's trust in the reality of his environment by carnival masks or by a story of a leg sawn off and left in a trash can; the nine-year-old's slow but deeply unsettling realization of the failure, weakness, insufficiency and bitterness of a father who had been regarded as strong and all-knowing; the hopeless admiration for an older brother, a loved and envied role model who nonetheless can never be emulated; the endemic sense of possessing a deficient and unprepossessing physical presence, devoid of bulk, strength, and vitality in a society that elevates the physical and idealizes strength and dexterity; the overtones of sexual insufficiency which hover above the sense of one's body as a shrunken and flaccid entity—this indirectly informing the idealized, blurred and self-effacing love fantasies for a girl who never notices one's presence, and culminating discordantly in the voyeuristic scene of sexual panic in the vineyard. Dominating all else is the experience of being a mere shadow, an observer of life from the sidelines; the insufficiency of being a person who, instead of absorbing experiences for the purpose of initiating action, mentally hoards them, burying the self under an aggregate of detailed impressions for the purpose of some unclear future—a future which one's society cannot appreciate.

These dark insights are not incidental, but are the essential bedrock of the novel, allowing for *Miqdamot*'s raison d'être. For this new novel, Yizhar's sudden return to the Israeli literary scene, was to perform two vital tasks simultaneously. On the one hand, it was to elucidate the aging writer's oeuvre by supplying a key of sorts to his fictional world; on the other hand it was to deepen and expand his lifelong role as a conscientious observer and critic of the unfolding Zionist saga. In order to achieve the first task, to offer a true insight into the nature of Yizhar's art, *Miqdamot* had to be a truthful and absolutely non-idealized record of his path. It needed to draw a portrait of the boy about to become an artist that would highlight not only the strengths and the talents needed for realizing his artistic aspirations, but also the weaknesses and the deficiencies that would prod him to adopt such a mission. The vision of art that emerges through this ruthless exploration is complex, and is formed as much by the helplessness of being unable to impact reality through action as by the desire to transform raw reality through observation and expression.

In order to achieve the second task, *Miqdamot* needed to offer an incisive critique that focused not on the marginal excesses of Zionism, but rather on its actual essence. The novel therefore asks one question, repetitively and unrelentingly: Has Zionism managed to realize its core dream of creating a *place* for Jews, of inculcating in their hearts and minds a sense of being within a concrete spatial circumference, of striking roots deep into a specific piece of land? The answer to this question is buried in the many mental images and partial insights that separate, in accumulated layers, the narrator's present—i.e., the time of the writing of *Miqdamot* in the summer of 1991—from the time of the aliyah of the protagonist's father to Israel a century earlier, in 1891, a sixteen-year-old idealist carrying the Bible in one hand and the works of Lev Tolstoy in the other. The scenes from the protagonist's childhood presented in the novel are carefully selected to significantly deal with the issue of place. And what is emphasized is that the protagonist's childhood is one of wandering and dislocation (hence, each of the book's five sections evolves against the backdrop of a different location). The protagonist is never able to develop anything like a prolonged and satisfactory friendship because his family is constantly on the move (the father, who dreamt of striking roots in the land, is never allowed to do so: he loses the house he built to his creditors). Thus, the protagonist grows up without ever feeling safely ensconced in a place he belongs to, and in the middle of the realization of the Zionist dream he lives a life that is nothing less than exilic if not nomadic.

5

In order to fulfill its literary and political goals, *Miqdamot* activates memory in a manner far more complex than Yizhar's earlier work. This incorporation of memory allows the author to introduce an additional, closely related, innovation: a new sense of time. In contrast to Yizhar's standard temporality of an extended present, in this novel time is conceived as a matrix of prolonged ongoing processes, including both the slow development of the individual personality and the historical development of nation building. In other words, Yizhar's late novel breaks into a new narrative mode mainly through the use of memory— the only element of mind that his work, so deeply immersed in the reconstruction of mental activity, had, up to this point, ignored. The neglect is now compensated for, and with a vengeance.

The most obvious, albeit not necessarily the most significant, use of memory in *Miqdamot* is the vibrant reconstruction of memorable experiences and episodes, as, for example: the attack of the hornets; fear in the besieged courtyard; the taste of a first soda; the first visit to the cinema; constructing and flying an amazing kite; long lonely walks with the ass; the voyeuristic view of a vineyard worker having sexual intercourse with a half-demented girl; the first encounter with Dickens' *Pickwick Papers*. To a certain extent, these episodes are the heart of the novel. They stand on their own, and their sheer vivacity keeps the reader interested and open to the novel's more subtle elements, more profound implications.

The novel's deeper implications are conveyed through yet another use of memory—a use that is perhaps the most radical of *Miqdamot*'s departures from Yizhar's habitual style. As previously explained, Yizhar's narrative *forme maitresse* had been that of the interior monologue, through which he conveyed 'moments of being' brimming with inner life. As noted, this use of the interior monologue is still quite prevalent in the new novel, but it no longer dominates the narrative. Significantly, while the opening two sections depend heavily on this technique, the following three barely use Yizhar's characteristic stream of consciousness style. Instead, as the novel begins to gather momentum towards its closure, a new kind of narrative mode becomes prominent: narration in the future-perfect tense. This new narrative technique is a direct outgrowth of *Miqdamot*'s deepening involvement with memory.

The interior monologue, which Yizhar's earlier works use to invoke a continuous present, is also extraordinarily effective for reconstructing past experiences, giving them a vivid immediacy. It brings memory into the present, erasing the dulling effect of the passage of time and the incessant accumulation of more recent impressions. However, the retrospective nature of *Miqdamot* and its specific artistic aims demand a relation to memory that not only revitalizes past occurrences, but also includes what the Hebrew poet Yaakov Shteynberg calls, in one of his gem-like short essays, 'the memory of the future'.[1] Shteynberg insists that 'life is open-ended on both sides, the past and the future, and the voice of memory reaches us from both directions', maintaining that there 'is…a memory aimed at the future'. Interior monologue is not a narrative technique that is fully suitable for the evocation of such 'memory of the future'. In grammatical terms far drier and less evocative than those used by the poet we may argue that while interior monologue excels at transmuting the past tense into that of the present continuous, it is rarely as effective a means of transmuting the past into the future perfect tense—that tense that progressively becomes more important in the later parts of the novel. One may even claim that *Miqdamot* as a whole is a verbal and mental construct conveyed in a 'future perfect' narrative modality.

If this sounds obscure or confusing, consider that almost every element of the novel becomes fully significant and meaningful only through direct or indirect knowledge of what the future will hold—a future that is actually the past from the vantage point of the narrator telling the story in the summer of 1991. In other words, the retrospective nature of the narration implies that the future is already included in the depiction of the past. The significance of every occurrence in the novel is defined by virtue of how it will appear from the viewpoint of the distant future. Thus the opening episode of the hornet attack loses all its symbolic overtones if not read in the context of the future clash between the Zionists and the native inhabitants of Palestine, a clash that would eventually evolve into a century of unending warfare and bloodshed. The murder of Y.H. Brenner at the end of the second section has increased significance when seen in the context of Yizhar's later aspirations to follow in Brenner's footsteps, and his view of Brenner as the personification of uncompromised, pure morality. The fact that this famous writer becomes the victim of one of the first Arab-Jewish encounters in the wake of the Balfour declaration has disturbing implications for the fate of morality and impar-

---

[1] See Yaakov Shteynberg, 'Zikhron ha'atid' ('The Memory of the Future'), in *Kitvey Yaakov Shteynberg*, Vol. III, Reshimot, Tel Aviv 1937, pp. 292-294. All direct references to Steynberg in this essay are from p. 292.

tial truth in the blood-stained future of the Arab-Jewish conflict. In a similar manner, every detail concerning the protagonist's brother, even the instance of his flying the kite, is informed by the reader's and narrator's awareness of the violent death lurking in wait fifteen years hence; for the kite, pushed by the uncontrollable powers of nature, breaks its line, and, yearning for total freedom, loses itself in the desert—a symbol of the older brother's fate, as well as the fate of many other youths cut off in the prime of their exuberant existence. So too the description of the father and the destruction of his idealism, the failure of his lifelong, backbreaking struggle to become the 'new Jew'—an independent, non-exploitative and unexploited man of labor—presage the future breakdown of the socialist-Zionist dream in its highest, purest, and most humanistic form. The sad irony of this socialist idealist reduced to serving capitalism as an overseer, whose job it is to ensure that the meagerly paid workers in the orchards of Rehovot complete every last element of their quotas, reflects darkly on Israel's future. It implies that the state of Israel, in its greed and egotism, will cast the early socialist dreams aside, even as the father is cast aside and forgotten in his own lifetime.

Yizhar uses a variety of devices to create this sense of the immanent future, this narrative of future perfect modality. Most common is the seemingly random reference to what the future will bring. This device can be seen already in the first section: in the midst of the hectic description of the father's attempt to bring the sick infant to a physician, the narrator interrupts the flow of the father's pathetic interior monologue in order to inform the reader of the future of the Arab village of Mansoura. After describing how, in the narrated present, the cart must carefully circumvent the village in order to avoid getting lost in its narrow and convoluted alleys, the narrator then suddenly adds the apparently disassociated comment: 'Today there is no Mansoura and you won't find it, it has been wiped out, it no longer exists, and in its place there is just a road, eucalyptus trees, and some stone ruins' (p. 64). As the novel progresses, such sudden asides multiply, projecting the respective futures of places, landscapes and people.

Another device for such projection is the insertion of moments of prophetic foreknowledge. In the aforementioned essay 'The Memory of the Future', Shteynberg claims that one knows that the voice of memory comes from the future rather than the past when one suddenly knows the solution to a yet unformed riddle: 'There is a voice prompting hope or despair before the events that would trigger fear or joyful expectation will have taken place.' There are certain passages in *Miqdamot* that answer perfectly to this definition. An example to such anticipatory emotion can be seen in one of the novel's final episodes: the protagonist, a bored nine-year-old with nothing to do in his summer vacation, is suddenly approached by the farmer Yehuda, who urgently needs to send a horse-driven cart to one of his vineyards, as it is the end of the day, and the workers as well as the harvest of ripe grapes need to be carted back to the farm. The boy, promised a shilling for his labor, mounts the cart and begins driving, even though he has had no experience whatever with horses and cart driving. Fortunately the horse knows the way, and eventually brings the boy to his destination, where he mingles with the workers, helps them load the heavy baskets onto the cart and then joins them in their silent fatigue that closes a hard day's work. At this point, however, something quite explosive takes place in the protagonist's mind:

> But suddenly, in the midst of all the silence and non-speaking…suddenly he knows with certainty, without having any certainty, for how would he suddenly know with certainty, or who could know, and now as he moves his gaze over all those seated figures…suddenly he knows that soon, almost unnoticed, none of this will remain, neither this vineyard nor this sandy path, none of this will remain, and even Yehuda the farmer, who sent them all here to pick the late-ripening grapes from his vineyard, is not particularly attached to this vineyard or to any other vineyard, or to the muscat grapes that will make a killing on the market, or to any other grapes, or even to this particular horse or to any other horse, or to these

particular workers or any vineyard workers, and he really is not attached to any vineyard, or to any grapes or vineyard workers, not because they are not good, because they all work as hard as they can, the horse and the people, but because everything here is provisional, with no necessity to exist like this particularly, the vineyard that will be replaced by an orange grove, and the building plots that will replace the orange grove, and the houses, and this place is not like all those other places where year after year and generation after generation the olive harvest comes regularly in its season and year after year and generation after generation the time of threshing comes regularly in its season...because everything here is provisional, and that ancient cycle of the year has no binding force here, it does not enter into the bloodstream of existence here, the eternal existence of this place...but everything that there is here is temporary and they are only pretending to be farmers, only temporary vineyards and temporary orange groves, it's only temporarily that they sink in the yielding red sand or speed over the hard bare clay, they all exist but not in the blood, not firmly grounded, nothing is solid here, the vineyard has no solid basis and the late-ripening grapes for the festivals have no solid basis nor does the farmer and it is not clear if his sons will, and all the solidity of whatever seems solid here is just the ethereal solidity of existence here, and the who knows, maybe yes and maybe no, (pp. 300-301).

This negative epiphany stands at the core of the novel, condensing its essence in these few lines. *Miqdamot* opens with the father's acknowledgement that the Jewish homeland is not yet a home. Carrying the wounded boy to the doctor, he feels 'lost' in a vast 'mineral space', where he, his cart, the mules, his child and his child's mother are all 'pointless...because truth to tell there is no place here yet. Everything is still experimental. And the place that exists is precisely this vast open emptiness without anything' (p. 73). In a framing device, as the novel draws towards its close, the protagonist experiences a sudden prophetic intuition of the ultimate failure of Zionism to create an authentic Jewish place, an authentic Jewish sense of living in a real home, belonging to a specific place and to none other. Trying to barter their orientation in time for an orientation in space, the Jews who have returned to their 'home'-land are prevaricating, cheating themselves. In less than two generations they will shed their idealist dream of a new rootedness. Though they indeed 'conquer' and domesticate—i.e., make domestic, home-ly—the wilderness, they do not ultimately cultivate it as a home but rather develop it in the commercial sense of the word: buy it, sell it, make a profit on it, move from one side of it to another, leave it, come back to it, exploit it, deface and debase it, build it, destroy it. They never cease to be the nomadic merchants they have always been. This is S. Yizhar's final assessment of the great Zionist project; and it is on the basis of this negative assessment that the entire series of his late works, written and published in the 1990s, would rest. One may regard them as an elegiac leave-taking from a failed dream.

The seeds to the vision of much of Yizhar's later works, *Miqdamot* in particular, can be traced to that erratic and furious novella with which Yizhar had seemed to take leave of his role as a writer of prose fiction in 1964, *A Story That Had Not Started*. However, *Miqdamot* and the works that come in its wake cannot be understood without taking into account the developments that took place in Israeli society and, for our purpose even more importantly, in Israeli literature, between the publication of *Sipurey Mishor* in the sixties and that of the late works in the nineties. One important literary event that took place right in the middle of this interval, in 1977, a year of great political upheaval which saw Labor Zionism removed from power, and the Zionist right wing rise in its place, must be mentioned here: the publication of Yaakov Shabtai's novel *Zikhron devarim* ('Past Continuous'), a towering achievement, and the most important development in Israeli prose fiction since the publication of *Days of Ziklag* in 1958. Yizhar was one of the few who immediately understood the significance of this novel—it took years, and the help of pioneering criticism, for Shabtai's work to become widely accepted and its implications internalized. However, almost all serious Israeli novelists—including A.B. Yehoshua, Amos Oz, Yoel Hoffman, and Yuval Shimoni—were influenced by *Zikhron devarim* as well as by its sequel, *Sof davar* ('Past Perfect'), published posthumously and unfinished, three years after the untimely demise of its author in 1981. *Miqdamot* also bears the mark of the deep impact of Shabtai's masterpiece. For it was through Shabtai that what we called the future perfect narrative modality penetrated the very core of Israeli literary consciousness. It was Shabtai who devised this narrative mode, invoking it specifically to explore the decline and fall of Israel of the pioneers, as well as the gradual evaporation of the Zionist dream of creating an authentic Jewish place for an authentic new Jew, who would live primarily in concrete space rather than in historical time. For Shabtai, authentic space is represented by a small section of the city of Tel Aviv. His novel focused on the gradual dissolution of the sector of the city that was built by the socialist pioneers of the Third Aliyah to be a model Jewish town harboring an ideal modern Jewish community. The novel, astounding in its density, vividly portrays a whole tribe of now decrepit and dying pioneers in conjunction with their hedonistic descendants. It continuously shifts between the novel's present (the 1960s), the heroic past and the projected future, all time-frames coming together to form a comprehensive anatomy of the dismal failure of the pioneers' dream and of the degradation of Tel Aviv, once an authentic Jewish Zionist town, to a mere urban chaos. For Yizhar, authentic space is represented by the agricultural settlements in the southern coastal plain, surrounded by Arab villages and opening to the vast emptiness of the desert nearby. The disappearance of these once green bastions as they merged into one continuous and very congested suburban extension of Tel Aviv, is seen by him as the betrayal of the ideal of Jewish place. It is not for this essay to decide whether or to what extent Yizhar's and Shabtai's very similar indictments are morally and culturally just and deserved. It will suffice to note that these two most talented and sensitive of Israeli writers of fiction indeed did believe in their truth deeply. Shabtai's truncated career was dedicated completely to the writing of what the author believed was the last elegiac chapter in the cultural history of Zionism. Yizhar began as the great poet of the Zionist struggle; however, at the end of his long career he too took up the elegiac mode and wrote a unique autobiographical novel that is simultaneously a personal statement about being a writer in a community committed to action and a great prose threnody for a dream that has faded away.

Preliminaries

Liminary

Staring at a place

And where was the first place? The very very first? Because the first place, although there is no supporting evidence, was orange, all orange, wholly orange, very orange. Totally.

Smooth like the smoothness of silk, and there was also a casual fluttering of rich orange drapes, orange to very orange, and apparently, there is no other logical explanation, these could only have been, perhaps, a sort of lining of a tent, a very big tent, whose inside was very opulent with a rustle of very orange silk and a bellying profusion moving in lazy waves all of it orange beating in soft waves, light orange and dark orange, with every change in the light lighting the orange and all the opulence of the changes in its response, all totally silky, in that big tent, inside perhaps an army camp that was there, (English? Turkish?), and not far from the place that Mummy had come from, apparently, with the baby in her arms (where was Daddy?) or perhaps she had been invited to visit that army camp consisting of tents, and this tent, this Indian tent (why Indian? Yet apparently it was Indian: an Indian tent in a British camp?), this big, swollen tent, responding with lazy billows to the all but non-existent breeze, on that hot day, replying with a secretive rustle of silky orange to every touch of an all-but breeze, a very smooth silky orange, luminescent, poured inwards into the consciousness of that observer, who had just seen and known for the first time that he really did know, and to his innermost being that he really had just been opened to the knowledge of the existence of all this orange, all the silky ripples of orange, constantly running delicately, lightly, over the abundance of sensitive fabric that was breathing lightly, entirely full of orange brilliance, entirely orange brilliance, dull here and shiny there, as though a golden dust had also filled the expanse of that big tent, and how could the memory remember it so precisely unless it really was like that and it was really like that that he saw that breathing orange dust, breathing silently, secretly, softly, in light billows, with slight wrinkles, chased by the all-but breeze, in the bosom of one big tent, and how could he have been there unless he had been carried in his mother's arms, on her breast, perhaps at the age of two? And carried in her arms, pressed to her breast, he had then suddenly discovered the sight of the thing, the knowledge of that perfect orange, that total, perfect, universal orange, flooding everything with a confident radiant orange glow, with a whispered breath of smooth, light silk, that could be touched and perhaps even smelt, on the lining of that Indian, apparently, slightly slack tent, if that was really the correct interpretation of the movement of that perfect, radiant orange, and if all this was really correct, and if it really happened there, there was the place. And this was the place, the very first. And there was the beginning of everything, before everything that came afterwards, the beginning of heaven and earth the heat and the day and the breeze, and Mummy carrying on her breast, with Mummy's smell, this was the first place.

The spine of the hills

And then? Then there were the hills.

Not the body of the hills and their mass but the line of sky tracing the edge of their spine with that calm, necessary motion. Separating the density of the soil of the hills from the emptiness of the sky, which immediately started soaring upwards, far away, perhaps too far. A very precise, decisive, well-drawn line, with no hesitation or second attempt, tracing rounded arcs, rising and falling, and running with perfect confidence above the whole horizon of the earth's expanse, utterly simple beyond all simplicity, fine, thin, single, sharp and final, and yet, at the same time, a woolly, soft, pleasant line that seemed to be made from the touch of a cautious, fleeting mist, flowing and running in its light arcs above the roundedness of those hills, making of them all one whole profile, falling and rising lightly, not mighty hills or awesome valleys, only waves of calm fields rising and falling lightly, with all the tranquil, pure, infinite richness on the back of the expanse of the plain, like a firm line drawn by a very sharp pencil, touching and tracing the roundedness of the earth of the fields dividing them from the extent of that haughty sky, that rose up immediately and occupied the whole of the height above everything, while the earth was spread out below, so low, only up to the ankles, lost beneath all that height that cared nothing for it or its being, and in that empty warm height that turned towards itself, far above all the low compact edge that as always remained lying forgotten there below. While this line, this beautiful, indifferent line, so fine one moment and so woolly the next, ran above the whole contour of the hills, rising and falling slightly like the contour of a horse's back perhaps, or maybe that of a girl lying on her side and the tender outline from her waist to her thigh, with the same single, perfect curve recording, sensitively caressing, this roundedness, there in those gentle waves, that fell and rose all the time, with an insubstantial dreaminess, but with that same real, undeviatingly decisive materiality, and all around from side to side, as though to fill the entire expanse of that breathing earth. Were there any paths on it? Were the fields sown or harvested, or had they been reduced to stubble? Nothing, it is all obliterated by the mist and lost in it, and all the weight of the ancient earth overlaid with the dust of mist, insignificant and foggy but real and one, full and dark blue, ending precisely at this line above which was all the emptiness of that sky, the majestic arch totally empty and disappearing in the mist, and only that fine line finally separating its emptiness from the hardness of the earth—suddenly the hand felt like passing lightly, touching so slowly, almost compulsively, the whole back of this roundedness: slowly lovingly caressing, rising slowly and caressing, descending slowly as though it were the back of a young foal or a girl—to this line the fields ran with firm fullness with taut hardness, there to be cut by the lash of that one line that ran from east to west across all the immense southern distance, dividing the land from the sky, that rose immediately, too far, caring about nothing, summery to the point of emptiness, and so indifferent that there was nothing to do but to go down again under the line, into the fullness of this breathing, summer-scorched earth, that had nothing in it and on which nothing was happening now, no horse galloping no donkey plodding no camel trudging sleepily, no man and no woman, land all shaven, empty with the emptiness of late summer, with no vegetation, no grass, perhaps indeed eaten by goats or swallowed by the mist, long after the summer harvest, long before the autumn ploughing, in this full nakedness, completely prostrate, totally prone, bare with nothing on it, to the end of the low horizon that still wore no clothing, neither plants nor tips of trees nor buildings nor anything else, besides the line of curves that runs there, one bare and smooth, one whole and precise, all innocently naked from end to end, all desire of warm nakedness, thin light and dark from so much light and all fainting in the mist of dust, one chosen line, so sultry, so decisive, driving you to despair with its finality, merely rising slightly and curling slightly, like the back of a horse, like the back of a girl, like infinity.

Motion

Lines? Colours rather. And the onward movement. All the time. Unfed except by nothingness and the movement of light on a leaf. And so terribly curious was everything around without cease. People less so. And Daddy. Mummy too? Or those curves there and the continuity continuing immeasurably great. And all the time discovering all the time more. And pain. Yes. Because. And lots and lots of don't want to. And suddenly.

Waves of more all the time. A tremulous waviness rising falling breathing eternal. And then more there. And always what's it like there? And always to see more and more. Until the distant was close in all its details. And once again alone. Always. So frail. So feeble. If you only knew and still less. As though excavated inwards. And only to peep. Not sure of anything. And suddenly.

What was there threatening here? Or why did he suddenly breathe differently and as though yes it could be? Fascinated curious over there. Not so much in here. And finally alone. And suddenly.

Part one

Wasp

In the huge world, with the two poles, the equator, the five great continents, which as is well known occupy only a quarter of the surface of the globe, the remainder being always covered with water—and also within the crumbly clods of the nearby field, in an infinitesimal point among these hills, here at the edge of this plot in this field, in the shade of the trunk of the ancient carob tree, one of the solitary survivors standing spherical even if harried by dust, all the other carobs having just been planted, still clinging precariously to the lumpy soil, with the form of the irrigation dish still visible at their base, for the tender sapling to be watered once, maybe twice, as there is not enough water for more, besides the fact that it has to be carried from the bottom of the hill, from that bottomless well with a rope and a bucket, in which, for all its dark, secretive depth, the leeches are not slow to swarm and squirm, disgusting and obscene, so that it is impossible to drink without first straining the water through a piece of cloth on which there always remain some tatters of slimy moss from the depths, lying there as though in a state of utter prostration, or maybe like fish spewed up on dry land, in this patch of land that is no more than a few dunams, on the dividing line between the land that is gradually being ploughed up and that which has been hardened by time immemorial—he sits quietly, for the meantime, this infant, placed there by his father to be there a little longer, until he has completed the ploughing of the last strip or two, while he walks pressing down with all his strength on the handles of the iron plough, which is hard for it and hard for the mule and hard for the man, not deciding whether it is hard because the compacted surface of this stubborn soil has not been touched for thousands of years, if ever, and no man has touched it, or assailed its innocent wholeness or sniffed its touch, or because of the contempt of the mule which has had no part in the decision to make a field here, because there is no land that can be dismissed as not worth this effort, after the two thousand dunams that have finally been purchased, thanks to the tireless efforts of the Anglo-Palestine Company, and now the experiment of setting up the farm, as an example of conquest by Hebrew labour, is gradually being accomplished, in the most difficult of conditions, and Daddy only has to finish this one rectangle, as a final act of possession of the ground and the ploughing like a last signature on the deed of ownership, after all these troublesome toings and froings, with Turkish officials and niggardly institutions, that truly do not have a piastre to spare, and after all the running backwards and forwards of the purchasers and the go-betweens and the treasurers, and Hapoʻel Hatzaʻir and whoever else, and now here we are hammering in a post, as they say, actually redeeming another strip of land, unrecognisable for the time being, and indistinguishable from all this endless expanse, lying abandoned here to this sluggish heat, from here as far as those hills, in this expanse that folds and straightens slightly, and suddenly something, for all that, is about to begin here and to change the eternal order—despite everything.

He is so tiny in the cosmos, that without paying any particular attention you might overlook his tiny being, his lack of space in this world, it is comical to mention him and the world in the same breath, your indifferent gaze sweeps onwards without being held up by anything, because there is truly nothing at all to hold it up, certainly not his insignificance, so at once your gaze moves on, it does not even linger on this patch of land that is being ploughed, because there is nothing to linger on, it is just a speck of nothing on the slope of some rocky hillside with a few shrubs, nothing at all, it isn't clear what they are or what they are called, if they have ever had a name, with the possible existence of some wadi at the foot of the hill, more of a probability than a definite sign that it is there, before the slope changes into the rise of the next hill, an easy rise that does not stop

44

at all but simply goes on rising, and in the dusty midday air, with an imperceptible hint of a breeze, and anyone who does not need to know that he is there in the shade of the dusty carob tree, a single overgrown ancient carob tree, will ignore him and the hundreds of little things that are unseen and almost indistinguishable from the screw-beans that are scattered all around, so dusty that anyone who does not know what they are might think that they are merely more stunted acacias, as he sits there with his tiny legs tucked in, dressed in white, with his cloth shirt, trousers and hat that his mother has made him, she has no one to show off to because there is only one other woman here and she spends the whole day under a huge straw hat, working away in the vegetable garden and stubbornly insisting that she can grow tomatoes, cucumbers and corn without any water, and that constant hoeing can do what water cannot or the hopeless words she hears from passers-by, that without water nothing will grow here, and even if she protects the skin of her face from the sun with a kerchief and a straw hat she cannot protect the skin of her hands, nor does she try to, from blisters or roughness, nor can she protect her back from being broken, and there is nothing to peep out of the sleeves of his shirt or the legs of his trousers but those frail little matchstick arms and legs, legs with bare, doll-like feet and tiny ferreting hands.

With which now and with a bit of wood that makes smooth stripes on the warm clods of earth, and with those same doll-like hands that protrude from his clothes, that however narrow Mummy stitches them to fit him always end up too wide like a big hole for a little mouse, so that now from time to time Daddy has to listen out carefully, to make sure that he is still there, that he is not crying, that he has not been carried away by the slight breeze, with those thin legs, and those bare, doll-like feet on the noon-baked clods of earth, or if he is thirsty or hungry, because this child has never been hungry, and all the various sorts of food, that Mummy with all her inventiveness, skill and ingenuity, beside the stove stuffed with dry wood and thorns she has gathered, has never yet made any dish, to chew or to drink, that gave the child any desire to eat, and certainly not without stories that even at the hundredth telling make him forget and open his mouth wide, but not swallow, and even her more or less angry reprimands, come on, swallow, swallow will you, are of no avail, the more so as Daddy has to concentrate on the handles of the plough that he has to press down hard so that this iron plough does not simply scratch at the compacted crust of this ancient earth so stubborn from not being worked for several thousands of good years, and like this bloody mule, that might go on walking like this to the end of time, just as it might stop stock still and do nothing to the end of time, if you just let it, and in fact, such is the nature of everything in the world, if you just let them this hillside and the next rise will remain as they have been from time immemorial, if the whole man does not marshal all his resources against them, and all the more so the new Jew in the new Land.

There is no weight at all to any child who sits like him on the edge of the furrows that Daddy is making, just as there is no weight to any startled lizard, or to any fly flitting in the heat of the day, or a bee or a hornet, and there is only a single erased, even murmur spread all the time over everything above, all one great evenness all around, and the world does not bother to know anything about them, nor do they bother to know anything about the world, one inside the other apparently, and as though one is outside the other, and each one as though it is the totality of what there is and yet nothing of all this. And what remains? That there is one child, and there is one hot day, and there is one bee or fly or hornet and there is Daddy ploughing in a field and a field that is being ploughed and making it so that there will be a ploughed field like this in the world that did not know that such a thing is possible, and here it is happening right now.

Can he already say a few sentences? Yet they are always easier for his mother to understand than for anyone else, even now that he is two or a little less, because it's only the end of July, and what does he know, since he has nothing yet to know or to remember, and everything apparently is from the stories from later, some of them soon afterwards and others much later, but nothing apparently from the actual substance of things that you know as and when they are

46

happening, because what could he know of all the things that happened at the time, even though they are in his body, even with pain, with intolerable pain; but apparently after all they are just stories that have become family legends, even though he did, nevertheless, know something then and remember it from then, without knowing, what it is in a child that he can know or remember, something that even if it isn't the thing itself resembles the imprint of the thing, like those footprints that remain when the walkers have walked on, and on such unstable and indeterminate ground as this it is necessary now to start to tell how it is and to establish the actual substance of the things that happened with absolute accuracy, and not less, of course, within the limits of possibility.

The white cloth cap is pulled down almost over his eyes, and only they peer out, as though from a lair, and the hands too peep out as though from the lair of the sleeves that are too wide, and scrabble in the dust to grope it stroke it poke it, and its cooler crumbliness when you dig a little deeper, being half in the sun, that all the time scatters an even heat that can also be groped and stroked, and without knowing that he is the lord of all the earth within the reach of his thin hand stretched to its little limit, the soil sifted and running between the spindly fingers, and suddenly a little spider escapes and disappears, or an ant busily carrying on so many scurrying legs that do not give it any speed a large piece of chaff in the heat of the day, or he suddenly encounters a bird dropping that it is better not to taste or a round ball of dung left behind by some sheep that has passed this way, and also the whitish sticky trail left by a snail apparently, that has melted and gone and no longer exists, maybe also to grope inside some gaping totally sleepy hole, it is not clear how far it goes, or what there is in the invisible inside, or what else might suddenly spring out, and all that appears is a single oval leaf, from the carob tree, apparently, almost green, and another like it, less green, that can be folded and thrown away without flying at all, and go on moving the stick that makes a smooth line in the soil, although it is too soon to liken it to a road, because who has seen any road here or anywhere in the world.

Naturally Daddy listens all the time and looks out all the time to see how the baby is over there, and in the midst of all the effort to create and to plough he also looks all the time, and also, frankly, his heart is moved for the child, and the full extent of forty-three years that separate him from this frail thing that is sitting dressed in too-large white with a white hat coming down over his eyes, with the same soil at their feet, soil that keeps changing as he almost smiles, beneath his drooping, greying and slightly sad moustache, always, and listening how everything is still quiet there, before he finishes another strip or two here and picks him up and puts him on the back of the mule, holding him and dispelling his fear with little words of encouragement, Eh? Is that alright? And who's the tallest now? And also Don't be afraid, Daddy's looking after you, always, and other little remarks like that, and turns back to the mule that doesn't care at all about Jewish immigration or the redemption of the land, minding its own business, walking along in that indifferent way that nothing will change, and all that remains is the silence which is now filling the world, that kind of silence that if you don't make an effort to know that it's there you won't even notice at all, and you'd think there was nothing all around but one whole nothingness all around, spread out continuously over everything, from here to the western horizon that shimmers wetly, and from here to the hump of the closest hill that hotly blocks the true horizon in the invisible mountains, and with an effort you could make out also the buzzing that there always is in this empty void, things quietly buzzing, including some kind of constant grating sound of the traces of the plough when they are stretched, including some kind of grating sound of the foundations of the world as it revolves huge in space, and here and there too, if you keep listening, there is always some sort of birdlike chirp, apparently, that does not belong to any visible chirper, and not connected to anything identifiable, chirping and stopping, here and there, not very different from all the light weight of the heat that is spread over everything like some kind of fine silky cloth, spread out over everything as though it is the very substance of the air, so that above the hard earth is scattered a breath of air, that resembles nothing but is really the belly of the deep sea, and like it its outside resembles a transparent glasslike wrapping, like a totally substantial reality of the deep only finer, full of all sorts of fullnesses, light and insignificant but having their full weight.

Will he not lose patience? He is all curiosity in this place that is coming into being, and without occupying any space and without weighing down on any place; nor does the world pause for him, but revolves onwards as it is, as it revolves onwards from an ant and does not pause for it, or from the fallen leaves of the carob tree, and also those other leaves that no wind at all would suffice to stir drily upon the earth, and upon all the great earth, that from all eternity has been so hard-pressed, so grey, and anything that could have been moved from upon it has already moved years ago, centuries ago, if not millennia, and the new dry leaves, slightly concave like the half-open palm of a man's hand, rather creased, and only the break of the petiole, which is also somewhat curved and seems to be deliberately pointing to something, perhaps to another age when everything here was more joined up, when there may have been more greenery of which nothing now remains apart from this withering, and the yellow stains scattered around on the grey that prevails over everything, and perhaps pointing, daring to point, to some direction, as it were, that might lead somewhere or pointing to something that might still happen here and that we know nothing of as yet.

Daddy child dust heat and round about. Thin tiny body in a shirt and shorts that are too large for it, made by Mummy who sings as she sews and sings as she holds her work up to see, she has no one to show it to, so that it always turns out too large, and they will have to wait for the child to grow and fill out the space that is still empty now, and in the meantime with his thin arms and thin matchstick legs he moves things in the dusty ground and soaks up the frail greyness into his inner being, perhaps so that some day they might do something, so that he may tell them precisely as they were, and so that he might show them to someone who has the patience, all these things that do and don't have any substance apart from being this world from close up. And so it also happens that he does not and cannot know where he is really sitting or what is actually right there in potential that no one has yet grasped; and first of all how can he know that he is actually sitting here inside a theatre, that tiny theatre in which the greatest show on earth is being performed, the spectacle of the birth of the new Jew in the new Land, a show whose main point is the Jew working the land as a free man, independent, neither exploiting nor being exploited, and that the programme of Hapo'el Hatza'ir is being put into practice and realised here, categorically, an exploit so exciting, stimulating and thrilling that people far away, hearing of it, abandon homeland, parents, home and studies and moneymaking, and with a light haversack, in which the only heavy items are the same two books, the Bible on one side and Tolstoy on the other, stuffed among clothes that are unsuited to the climate and the work, get up and go, almost pushing away their weeping relatives, they shoulder their bag and they set off, eating up the distances by cart train and boat, until they land singing on the shore of Jaffa, that welcomes them with a jet of heat, misery and worklessness, and they quickly escape to Petach Tikva and Rishon Le-Tzion, or walk hungry but singing to the Galilee, when suddenly the rumour spreads that workers' farming communities are going to be set up in the Land, in Kinneret and at Ben Shemen and here, the Zionist Organization will pay the cost of the materials and they will earn their livelihood by their own labour. And it will be a co-operative. The curtain is going up and the thrilling show is about to begin.

A tiller of the soil, 'a natural peasant standing on his own two feet', 'a model and example to all farmers', who has only to step outside the well-known causes of despair, and here he is, taking his destiny in his own hands, and proving that there is no poor land or bad climate or unpropitious conditions in the Land, you simply get up each morning, and make it so that there should be carob trees in the Land, and fruit trees in the Land, and cultivation in the Land, and milk cows in the Land and poultry coops, and a vegetable garden to be proud of, and also pine trees, casuarinas and eucalyptuses that do not produce fruit but make a place that is pleasant to live in, and a just society, even if to begin with they have only built a single stone house in the middle for the families, with a few huts round about and tents for the unmarried men, and there are only thirty male comrades and a couple of women, but there are animated arguments until past midnight despite the hard toil that awaits from early in the morning, about where to plough and with what plough, where each mule should go and who will drive it, and what to do about the sesame patch that has not turned out well, and what A. Tzioni, the agronomist from Ben Shemen, says, and what is said about this in the German book that Daddy has brought with him to find out all about the history of farming (apart from the book by Einhorn, Isser Joseph son of Moses Einhorn, *The Science of Agriculture*, London, 5670/1910, with German and French translations of the names of the plants), and also what can be learnt from the experience of the Arab *fellah*—not that we can learn much from him here, he is the slave of the land and we are of course the friends of the land, friends for life and friends for the future.

End of the strip, just one more or two at the most. The mule walks round and round and Daddy encourages it, saying Turn there, please, turn now. Daddy never shouts at the mule, even when it is stubborn. And of course he never raises a whip against it, nor does he ever gather up the reins to hit its back and legs with the slack end, to teach it a lesson, he only speaks to it from time to time, Come on, Daddy says, or Move, he says, or occasionally, when his patience runs out, Come on, move, he says, come on, get a move on, no less. And that clumsy old mule, stretching its heavy, hairy legs, with none of the prancing grace of a horse, stamps its mighty hooves, merely plods on, turning round and round, as the traces of the plough grate and squeak, it might have got tied up in them if it were not for Daddy, urging him on to behave himself, and dragging the heavy plough backwards, while casting a hasty glance at the child to see if everything is as it should be there in the shade of that carob tree, and then returning to the start of the new furrow, planting the ploughshare into the hard crust of the unyielding earth, he will plough one more patch, two at most. In the winter, after the rain, they will plough here again, and sow lentils or beans, for their own sake and also to enrich the soil with nitrogen, as it says in his German book. And then everything will look totally different. And suddenly this field will be a rich green, the green of total renewal, and even the child will feel that a renewal has taken place in the world. What does he know today, what can he know. Here are two thousand dunams of Zionist renewal. Jewish land. A little island of rich, scientific new green surrounded by an ocean of ignorance, primitiveness and under-development, with fields of monotonously alternating exploitation, wheat followed by wheat, barley followed by barley. What about manure, fertilisers, enrichment with nitrogen, rotation and fallow years? And suddenly there will be this new green to be seen. By hostile eyes, too, perhaps, that do not like the renewal or the renewers. A hostile circle all around. Contained and not so contained, alien, Abu Shusha, al-Mansura, 'Aqir, Wadi Sarar, to the west and the south and Beyt Jiz, Dir Muhizin, to the east, Na'ana down below, not forgetting the Bedouin in Satariya. Qastina is three-hours' walk to the south, the closest Jewish settlement two or three hours westwards, apart from sleepy Ekron, an hour's walk or so to the north-west, and even the sister farm at Ben Shemen is three hours northwards. And this is how it is.

What is it like to be the child of a settler? To be the baby of someone who has decided to make the idea a reality with his own body. Or, what is it like to be Daddy, anxious always tired always and harassed up to his neck to get things done, and all the time promising Mummy that it's only the first phase that is so tough, and then everything will change for the better, while Mummy, unmollified, insists that anyone who has not tried to bring up two children, a seven-year-old and a two-year-old, in this godforsaken place doesn't know how you manage not to run away, cooking the porridge on a fire of thorns in the yard and the bread in a clay oven, and water from the well with the leeches, and still the room always spotless, and neatly ironed mats everywhere, a perfect room and when Weizmann came once on a visit where did they take him if not to her room, a pearl in the desert, and when everyone else is asleep that's when the night work begins, the holy work, by the light of the paraffin lamp with the blue lampshade, made by Mummy's own fair hands, just like everything else, of course.

He sits and writes, dipping his fine pen and in fine letters with a threadlike script he sits in the middle of the night and writes about the possibility of extending the Jewish economy to cottage industry, as it exists in many countries in the east, for instance, carpet making, such as you can find in Persia, or in Turkey, and their carpets are traded and famous worldwide. Books and newspapers that come by boat and reach him from hand to hand, in Russian, in German, and even in French or English which he can't speak but can understand, without ever learning them, simply because he set off and came to the Land in the spring of 1891, when he was only sixteen and a half, and the only education he had was from the heder, from some private lessons, and from greedily reading whatever he could get his hands on, and the only sad thing is that everything he reads he remembers precisely, and his head is full of neatly organised knowledge about everything he has come across, including bits of chemistry, biology, history and especially economics and building up a developing economy, and just ask him a question about the fate of English, French or German colonialism, in Africa, Asia or even America, and what can be learnt from this incursion of European man on these backward continents, and what do we ourselves have to learn as we renew and revitalise our old Land, which is not only ours, and not so long ago Isaac Epstein wrote a long article that caused a great stir entitled 'A Puzzling Question' about this subject in *Hashiloach* where he complains about the blindness of the Zionists to the presence of two peoples in one land, and what will happen, and Daddy sat down and wrote a long article in instalments about this for *Ha'olam* and entitled his article nothing less than 'Appearance and Reality', and he reminded his readers that the Arabs are not a single nation, and only a few of them have lived here for generations, and they do not even live peaceably with one another, but each community and each region detests the others, and most of the Land is not settled, so that we do not displace anyone when we settle in the empty sectors, just as we are doing right here in this empty area that has not been tilled, so far as is known, for hundreds or maybe thousands of years, and moreover the purchase of the land will benefit Arab agriculture on the one hand, and accelerate the movement of Arabs to the towns on the other. And finally, one must also bear in mind that there is no such thing as absolute justice, and that it is no business of ours to solve the question of the Arabs' national identity for them. This is what he sat and wrote, at night, for *Ha'olam*.

And as for the carpet making, as a home-based manufacturing industry that expands the economy beyond agriculture, first of all, they are not carpets but flatweaves (and in a footnote he lists all the possible alternatives), and that is also the title of his article in instalments in *Hapo'el Hatza'ir*, 'The Destiny of the Flatweave Industry', so what can we learn from the experience of Kormann and Rauscher, or from the experience of the Sanjak of Sarwan in Iran, or closer to home from the experience of Smyrna, which from simple raw materials but with the help of skilful handiwork produces the finest rugs in the world, except that this is not an example for us, because there women and girls work from the ages of eight to eighty, shamefully exploited, tied to their looms and forced to supply more than they can, i.e., to make 11 to 15 knots per square pique (which is 0.68 m^2) for 15 paras (1.20 roubles), and because experience has shown that what it takes the Bezalel in Jerusalem a month to produce is made in Iran in a week. And anyone who wants to know more can consult *Rustnik Finansov* for 1902, numbers 14 and 18, or the publications of the Persia Carpet Manufactory whose registered capital is ten millions! And in brief the best summary is that of Rabbi Hisdai (Talmud, Shabbat 140[b]), who says: Where vegetables go in, meat and fish will go in too.

How much longer? Mummy wakes up. What time is it? she grumbles, when are you going to bed, she mumbles, your light's disturbing me, she will turn on her side, the children are asleep, you should take care of your eyes, aren't you ever tired, when are you going to bed, it's already morning, and so forth. And it really is almost morning, and time to get up, go out, get ready, fetch, put, take, arrange, quietly, quietly, with a vague weight of guilt always, all the time, that you've done something wrong, that you weren't considerate, that it's hard to give satisfaction, specially as there is no pay for writers in *Hapo'el Hatza'ir* and *Hashiloach* and *Ha'olam*, and by the time it arrives he has already ordered books and newspapers, and what is there left. There's always someone who's not happy with him. Always doubts: what are you in fact, a peasant tilling the soil or a bookworm of a writer, building the Land with a hoe in your hand or with your pen studying humanity and society, and whether this is the final stop where one can find rest or just a stop on the way, and as Mummy suggests, we've had enough of bringing up kids in the wilderness, and we should move to the town, and start living like human beings. You don't stay young forever. There is no miraculous spring to renew your strength. How much longer will you be a hero. Mummy protests, it's easy enough for you to be a pioneer and all that, but bringing up children here, what will become of them here, and there's no one to speak a civilised word to him, and what if something suddenly happens to the child here, heaven forbid, what will you do then?

Now Daddy and the mule are coming up the near side of the field, and Daddy is driving the mule with that chirping sound that is the universal language of men and mules, *nts*, *tts*, *ts*, Daddy says to the mule, Get along there, keep it up, Daddy translates to the mule, and the mule hears and understands and flicks its bulky tail and pricks up its asinine ears, and shakes its big head up and down, making the harness jingle, and plodding on as usual, neither faster nor slower, plodding peaceably, taking no notice of impatient Zionism and the time to take the child home to its mother, and there's just this last patch left to do, and it plods on indifferently, like the revolution of the earth, such indifference as no power on earth can change, and it could go on like this all day or all year, whether it's pulling a metal plough or a wooden cart, and without varying its habit or its pulling power whether it's a patch of compacted earth that needs to be broken up or a cartload of heavy manure to improve the fields, and naturally nothing interests it less, it seems, than the beauty of the clods, for instance, as they come up behind the blade of the plough from their compacted mass and suddenly gleam in the sunlight with such a fresh odour and such a shiny look as you could never have imagined and that never ceases to amaze you and make you try to think what it reminds you of, or as though these two things are incapable of existing together, the indifference of the act of ploughing and the thrill of the outcome, and also the earth's resistance to being cut open and its opening up for renewal, and also, on the same subject, both peasant and scholar, except that the possibility of this impossible thing could not have come into being of itself, and the act of ploughing could not have taken place without Daddy's hands pressing down on the handles of the plough with bowed back with taut muscles and the pressure of the whole clenched hand that aches from the constant pressure, and against any sign of tiredness, for which there is no place and no excuse when what we are doing is ploughing this land, and all the time turning the head towards the child to see what he's up to, with a look that brings a smile, like someone furtively wiping his sweat with the back of his hand, or like someone allowing himself to take a quick break and tip the water jar towards his parched throat, something that he will not permit himself to do until the very end, when everything is really finished completed and concluded.

Who would have believed it. But really no one does believe it. A farm full of Jewish workers. A new homestead and new relationships between people. Bold ideas about co-operation and the commune. Like that first group at Kinneret, eight lads and Sara Malkin. Or that whole project of the Herzl Forest. Every Jew would pay for the planting of a tree in memory of the national hero who was cut off in his prime. How many Jews were there in the world? Each one would donate a tree. Something like ten marks (though it soon transpired that it actually cost at least thirty marks to plant one tree, and that the number of contributors, oh, it was too painful to say), and instead of eleven thousand Jewish olive trees up to last winter they have only managed two thousand, and that is nothing to boast about, apparently it isn't the right soil, apparently it isn't the right fertiliser, and apparently this isn't the right way to set about it. And the pine trees too. That's not the right way to make a plantation. And as for the carob trees, theoretically all you had to do was select healthy saplings and everything would turn out fine. And then there were the armies, first the Turkish troops and then the British troops, with their great horses, their overfed mules and all the carts and wagons and guns and tents and the soldiers tramping and trampling every good plot of land, and devouring every ear of corn and every blade of grass that was crying out for the redemption of the Land, and we ought, apparently, we ought to have planted almonds too, according to the plan, and vines on the slopes, and one thousand five hundred assorted fruit trees according to the agronomist A. Tzioni from Ben Shemen, and while they are growing we should plant intermediate crops among them. A group of workers with no boss, that was the idea. Peasants who would not exploit the work of others, and especially not foreign, i.e., Arab, labour. Natural peasants standing on their own feet and setting a living example and a model for the Jewish people. That was the idea.

Daddy writes a lot about all this. Who doesn't—everyone who is a peasant by day writes by night. And especially about, Look, a settlement will grow here, about fifty families, about eighty dunams per family, with shared labour and shared marketing, and generous mutual aid, with magnificent cows, and especially when Zalman, the 'hoer', a first-rate one at that, who has been to Latrun to learn from the monks how to make magnificent cheese, exchanges the hoeing he has been so good at for milking that he will be even better at, and when they exchange the weak Arab cows for fine cows from Damascus or Beirut, and when they bring in a bull, oh yes, a fearsome East Frisian bull, who will mount lustily and our breeding stock will become famous, and the arrogant peasants in the moshavot will see how you build up a farm, how you grow crops, how you improve what exists, according to scientific advances and the latest agrotechnical knowledge, and how you can make a decent living out of this good land—and all without exploitation, without cheap labour, without meanness and without taking any baron's largesse. No more primitive farming methods blindly aping those of the Arabs, where hundreds of dunams cannot support a single family. They will even grow vegetables here, and even the female members will have a field to exercise their talents, apart from managing the household, and there will be bees, and chickens, again, when the leghorns arrived and replaced these speckled Arab hens, and first and foremost, again, the cowsheds, the Hebrew cowsheds, and the fields of fodder, and the crop rotation, and ten times the yield, at the very least, again, of private agriculture, and a place to absorb the youth of Zion who will start to immigrate now, with a song that will only get louder, hallelujah. True there are also some who wrote about the 'debt question', and the empty coffers, here, under Zionist leadership, and also in the workers' organization, and the high price of the manure that we purchase from the Arabs, without which there can be no up-to-date agriculture, and the climate, that is never welcoming to Zionism, and is always either too much or too little, and the constant delay in any operation, whether sowing or planting or settlement of debts, and sudden mysterious sicknesses in the cows, or the saplings, or the hens, and the discord that is like a curse that cannot be shaken off, and as if that is not enough, the Jewish National Fund made plans to set up a nursery of pine trees for the Herzl Forest, and entrusted it to Berman, the contractor, who handed the work over to Arabs, and we had to demonstrate, strike, and move heaven and earth before they changed their minds and gave the work to our group, and we not only did all the work with Jewish hands but, in the end, we even uprooted and discarded everything the Arabs had planted, and planted it all again—for no extra pay—so that we wouldn't have a Herzl Forest planted by alien labour.

In the winter they will replough this patch, and then the field will be ready for sowing. They will dig holes for a new strain of olive trees, from Cyprus, and for carobs, from Crete apparently. And the group will get some new members including some women so that there will be less loneliness. And the Palestine Office will pay forty-five francs per worker per month, and the rest will come from the yield of the farm, and will be divided up equally. And to the trees in the forest they could add casuarinas, and cypresses, and maybe even an avenue of palm trees, why not. To make it look pretty. To make it look nice here. So they won't have to leave, to disperse, so it won't all end in failure. And now suddenly the mule stops, hollows its back, spreads its hindquarters and starts to piss in a great pungent yellow jet so powerful that a hole opens up underneath and starts to fill and overflow with a foamy yellow richness, until eventually tremors ripple through the beast's back and its skin, and it finishes its jet with a few decreasing bursts and eventually it shakes itself and gathers one leg behind the other, and it straightens up and waits to find out what now, whether we go on in this stupid way or whether that's enough of that and it's time to go back to the stable, to the butt of water and the manger full of oats, and it might even be set free from all these stupid harnesses and saddles, and it can roll its mighty body naked in the dust, and relish scratching its back mightily in the sand and show its huge teeth, and scratch some more and derive full enjoyment from this life, in which everything is so stupid. Meanwhile Daddy too has a pause, even though he has no time for any pause, he has to finish here, and it's turned hot too and there's the child too, and he coughs with embarrassment, and he casts a glance and a word or two that cannot reach the child from here, like a term of endearment such as We're just finishing, or I'm just coming, or some other term of endearment like that.

And suddenly, a moment of attention, and it's as if something were happening, but no, there's nothing. Only a sudden awareness of the sound of a bird, a lark? or a wild dove? Sort of three syllables, then a pause, then three syllables, then a pause. A lark? Yesterday there was a hoopoe in the yard. With a sort of fringe of feathers and black and white stripes, and a hoop-hoop-hoop, from a long beak and its way of bowing. And there's something in the Talmud, too, about the hoopoe and King Solomon, who put the fringe of feathers on the hoopoe, something like that, there was a hoopoe that made its nest on a tree stump in an orchard, something like that, why this sudden dread, as though something were not quite right, like remorse, or just tiredness, or something that should have been done but wasn't, or something similar? The big straw hat shades the green eyes and the moustache, naturally without suggesting or even knowing about a certain Vincent who painted pictures in Provence some thirty years ago (in fact in his Hadera year), a solitary man who really ploughed like him and really wore a straw hat that really shaded his green eyes and his big hands really pressing down on the handles of the plough there, in that faraway field, and with that same almost monastic gravity, only he turns his head towards the child from time to time and apparently with a smile that spreads at the sight of him, such a tiny chap, sitting there so innocently, soon they'll go home, this tiredness from going to bed late and getting up early, only so as not to give in, or give up, so that a tiller of the soil is not reduced to the level of a working beast, so that that submission does not begin, and the ease of accepting the habit of submission, and so that life in this land does not become a proof that it is impossible, that all the time, everywhere, when he was drilling in Hadera, or hoeing in Rehovot, or pruning in Rishon, or teaching at Petach Tikva, being a blacksmith, or planting in the Herzl Forest, or working the orange groves of Rehovot again, or ploughing and harvesting, picking grapes and carrying them in carts to the winepress, and all the time researching too and writing, for the *Hapo'el Hatza'ir*, for *Hashiloach*, for *Ha'olam*, for *Ha'aretz Veha'avoda*, and for *Ha'adama*, and for Brenner's *Revivim*, always signing with a disguised name, like everyone else, with various pseudonyms or initials, such as Wofsi, Ben-Israel, or B-I, or Z.S., so as not to offend against good manners or contribute to the disappearance of modesty. That was a crow just now, for certain, there's no doubt about it, just a plain grey crow.

Sting

Did he cry out? Did he hear a cry?—he can't remember but he's already at the boy's side, already he's in his arms, everything, dropped, everything, and runs, runs stumbling, runs to him, and the mule continues with the plough on its side leaping and cutting with the handle on its side, the child, what is it, my boy, what is it, but he knows already, too shocked to believe, a scorpion? a snake? no, bees?

A seething mass of golden things buzzing angrily raspingly all round and waving at them with his big hat, which you mustn't do, and with his foot kicking at them at the air, to shoo them away and to kick at them, bees, damn them, wasps, looking at the child in his arms with terror, what is it, my boy, what is it, my boy, gurgling now for lack of air and the shock of the burning pain, trying to catch some air, not to choke, with his tiny hands, and his neck, his neck, God, not screaming because he can't, now he's fainting, my boy, my boy, what is it, his hands seem to be chasing something away or explaining something, demanding something, quick quick, something that is beyond him, clenching and opening as if trying to push something away or the opposite, trying to catch something, what is it, my boy, what is it, my boy, impossible pain, deadly pain, oh no, oh no, God, run run, fear, crazed with fear, a helpless urge, and the impossible pain, and Daddy and with his hands and his kicks in the air trying to shoo them away, both of them one now, all fastened to his breast, what is it, my boy, what is it, my boy, driving them away, flying furiously, flying all around, running to run home to run, and the big hat dropped, running with heavy shoes, with no feet, and already, and calling for help too, or not calling and running, or running and calling, and Mummy now, oh God, what is it, my boy, breathing, look what I've brought you, he can breathe, how many bites here, and on the neck, and here look, red and all poisoned with venom, what is it, my boy, God what, and sometimes just one is enough, God, don't let, breathing, choking fainting so small so small, why? why?

What did he do to them that they suddenly, all against him? How can a father have sat a baby down on a wasps' nest? Aren't there always wasps near a carob tree, isn't it dangerous, isn't it, God, their nest in a hole in the ground, and when one of them stings they all attack, and who, curse them, who, what has he done to you, what, who on earth sits a baby down on a wasps' nest, you criminal, they beset me, yea they surrounded me, they beset me like bees, why, why, my boy, in the name of the Lord I cut them off, they beset me and surrounded me, what's happening now, run, to Mummy, what now, hurry to the doctor quick, quick as we can, get the cart ready, quick it's three hours to the doctor, what is it my boy, so red so swollen fainting so sobbing so, he's suffocating, oh no, God, I cut them off, they encompassed me, yea they encompassed me, and on those tiny hands too and on the legs, luckily not on the face, but yes, the eyes, oh the eyes, so much so much, what will happen, run, Mummy, get the cart ready, wrap him in a warm towel, or a cold one, how a cold one, how, quick, quick, all in a torrent, all together, in an instant, as though bursting, both together, pressed to his heart, the child, the running, the terror, to shout, to cry out, to call for help, look look, quick quick, and tell us how dangerous it is, someone who knows, say, how far, think straight, don't lose the direction, what is straight, what does he know, to Mummy, she'll know, she always does, always, in the name of the Lord, they beset me, yea they surrounded me, like a fire of thorns, what a panic she'll be in, why why, what have you done to him, I did it, little child, breathe my precious breathe, run, faster, breathe my precious, no air to breathe, on the neck a sting there, so red everywhere, the whole face the whole neck, he mustn't choke, quick, child hugged by Daddy, quick quick.

Then he knows not how Mummy is there, he is in her arms, and people, all around, how did it happen, what is it, run and harness, get moving, just get moving, quick quick, an ambulance, quick, and catch that mule and from the plough to the cart, only be quick, people, be quick, and where's the other mule, here's Mummy, in her arms already, *Mein Kind*, Mummy, *mein Kind*, wrap him in something, and she kisses him and counts where, and breathes kisses near the edge of his breaths, he is sobbing with pain, fainting, give him something to drink, everything's swollen, the face, how can it be so, choking and swollen and here all around, and Mummy more to her heart, *oy, Gott Gottenyu*, wrapping him all up and to her heart, *mein Kind*, wrapping and squeezing, and quick to the doctor, the male nurse from Ekron always comes here, or take a horse and Daddy gallop with the child in arms he and the child to the doctor, on the cart, they're all here now, and suggestions, and somebody, the main thing is the face, it may not be dangerous, only it hurts so terribly, and all kinds of experts but he is so small, lost in a faint but his tiny breathing moaning inside him, make sure the tongue is out, not to block his jaw, and some water, how all of a sudden, and why, why, and quick quick

The other mule, the female, with the second cart that went to fetch the water up from the railway station, they may be back, and the horse, who knows where the horse is, they may have taken it to the Governor's in Ramallah, they went off this morning and they'll be back soon, now there's only the mules quick and the cart, and wrap the child, cold water? warm water? only be quick, and quick it's the two mules and the cart and Mummy and Daddy, and who will look after the older boy, and run along, why haven't they harnessed yet, Daddy runs, other comrades run, that stupid mule is here but refuses the shafts, the idiot, and they push it, but it won't go, and they push it, and it just resists and complains that it's tired from the ploughing and hasn't got the strength for running, and they should let it just breathe a little and just drink some water and just maybe roll in the dust, why not, throwing its head up and from side to side so they can't get the bridle on, it backs, determined not to put up with any yoke, all whinnies of protest, in plain basic mule language, but now they've harnessed it, and now someone comes running up the hill with its partner, the she-mule from the water cart, that they've left on the track in the middle of everything and unharnessed that mule, and hurried it along too against its will, and whipped it despite its whinnies, and now they're harnessing her and she doesn't want to either, all unwilling, full of protests, and the first mule that's already harnessed doesn't want to either, and they throw in a sack of straw to sit on and the board for the driver and help Mummy up, and she wraps the child in a scarf, with the water jug next to her, and a cloth on the child's forehead, to shade his face, God how swollen it is, unrecognisable, she doesn't know where to start, swollen hurting sobbing and his eyes like a red mountain of swelling too red too terrible to look at, and Daddy is already standing up in the cart shouting Get a move on, and raising the whip, Daddy, raising and whipping, Daddy who has never whipped, and he shouts in a voice that is not his own Get along there get along with you, and now they are turning scraping, almost stumbling, swerving, and going down to the road, and only Faster you scum, faster, hurry faster, Daddy who has never whipped, and now he is gathering up the slack of the reins to whip, and whips with the whip and whips, where did he learn all this, where is it inside him all this time, and he shrieks in an unknown voice Faster you beasts, faster you scum faster, damn you, faster, and he whips, faster, he beats, faster, and he looks down at Mummy who is holding the child in her arms, to her heart, unconscious, breathing, still alive, *mein Kind*, she says to him, sobbing and stopping and sobbing and stopping and clutching him to her heart, *mein Kind*, she say, *mein teyere Kind*, she says, and quick quick

First of all they must go straight down and the shortest way to the beaten track, and then they will have to avoid Mansoura, and hurry round its edge, today there is no Mansoura and you won't find it, it has been wiped out, it no longer exists, and in its place there is just a road, eucalyptus trees, and some stone ruins, but once you had to go round the edge of it, and its dogs, and sometimes stones too, and then already in the brown dusty plain and dust-weary grasses, to gallop and gallop towards the big village, in the red-brown dust, and along the sides of the plough beyond the field of sorghum, spilling slowly down to where a hill humps gently, and from there to the empty horizon, beyond which is a shimmering haze and a totally clean sky without anything. And they bounce over the embankment of the railway line to Jerusalem and then over the tracks themselves, gleaming as though they have just been polished, scraping over the heaped coarse gravel in which the sleepers are embedded one after the other as far as the eye can see, coming from some distant part and disappearing in a great arc to another distant part, and all of them, embankment, beams and rails, seem completely artificial and forced onto these fields, but that is not important now, here's the wadi now, and they skirt it and go down onto the track through the fields and speed along it, and then they drop down into the great wadi, without avoiding it, and look out for a shallower gulley, to go down from the edge slowly, without upsetting everything, hurrying with difficulty through its marl full of pure sand looking for another gentle slope that will take them out on the other side without overturning, and the wretched mules have no desire to run all the time and hurry all the time and even when they do run they are only pretending to and have to be whipped and shouted at, and you only want to weep, and Mummy weeps, and enfolds in the scarf and to her heart the still breathing but not conscious child, whose pain is hers now, and how did it happen, to Daddy, and how could you let him, and even this not much, because everything is a rush now and confused and helpless, as though they are people abandoned in a wilderness with a child, and only to whip and hurry along there, faster, you beasts, faster, and how they don't seem to have made any progress and how the journey does not seem to have been shortened at all and they alone with the fine dust thrown up against the sun, and quick quick

Then they are approaching the village, and damn it they always get lost in the narrow alleys and among the hovels and yards and the dogs and the children and even a few stones, until some grown-up silences the motley crowd and even kindly indicates how to get out of all this, and sometimes you even have to threaten with the whip those who hang on to the back of the cart or frighten the mules with malicious laughter, and all sorts of troublemakers, until they finally escape from the hedges of prickly pear and the smoke of *tabbun* and the stench of sheep-dung, and are ready to climb up the sand at the foot of that hill, beyond which they will be able to see the roofs, and they will sink in the sand and the mules will not be able to run even if you kill them, and meanwhile they are still here on this plain, in this dust in this sunlight, and he suddenly moans, God, and Mummy turns to him, what is it *mein Kind*, and wets his lips with water, and runs her hand over his face, he is swollen and his eyes are buried in a terrible swelling, and only little breaths, with almost no pulse, and she, it hurts, it hurts terribly, and he only groans, and she, Mummy's here *mein Kind*, and he clenches, and she, not long now not long now, and he tries to swallow, perhaps, and she, it hurts, it hurts terribly, and he suddenly seems to sink, and she, not long now my child not long now, and so, and suchlike things, and quick quick

And suddenly and in spasms, as if something inside him is try-ing to escape, or he cannot cope any more, as if some refusal is work-ing inside him, some resistance from all his tiny being, and Mummy turns to him, and Daddy turns to him, the reins in his hands, his face wrinkled, his hair dusty, unshaven, his shirt sweaty, his arms big and gnarled, with straw on the backs of his big hands holding the reins, turning towards the child and all poured out and leaning, are they three people together here now, or each one alone not knowing what to do, with nothing to hold onto, and shudders go through the child, his blood is poisoned, his veins are nettle-rashed with poison, maybe right to the heart, and can he withstand it, how far has the poison got, and the terrible pain that the fainting absorbs for the time being, and prevents him shrieking, sobbing and flailing with his legs and arms, and writhing with this unbearable pain, what is pain, what makes pain pain, Daddy doesn't know, Daddy who always knows more than others and always knows because he has always read something once and he never forgets anything he has read, but Daddy does not know what pain is or what happens in someone who has a pain, and this suddenly takes him away from the presence that is fixed on the child and he slinks away for a moment towards the extra knowledge of those who know how to know. What do they know about wasp stings, about the poison, about what it does to a person, let alone a little two-year-old child, so weak and frail, and what did he do to them to drive them mad, why did they suddenly swarm on him and inject venom into him, did he touch them with his little finger in their hole, or push a stick into the hole where their nest was and their babies, where they stood guard against any invader, what is this wasp anyway, what do we know about it, it is written in the Torah 'And I shall send my hornet before me', and it says 'none of your sting, none of your honey', in *Midrash Rabbah*, apparently, who knows any more about the wasp, this gold-coloured bee, the big bee that eats bees, in the underground nest live the queen the workers and the soldiers, and these are the ones that were alarmed and came out in full force to repel the invader, what did he do to them, this invader, what was he capable of doing to them, he put in his hand by the hole, and sud-

denly Daddy recalls the tale of the maiden of Sodom who gave bread
to a poor man and when the act became known they spread honey
upon her and exposed her on the wall, and the wasps came and ate
her – is it in Tractate Sanhedrin? – that is it, apparently, Daddy has
not forgotten, good God, the wasps came and ate her, as simple as
that, what more does a man know about the wasp, the hornet, a tale
of two wasps that the Holy One, blessed be He, coupled and they
both planted their venom in a man's eye and the eye burst and he
fell from a height and died, where is it, Daddy doesn't recall, maybe
in *Tanhuma*, with the torn mottled cover, never mind, what does it
matter now, nothing matters, except Quick quick, faster, you beasts,
get along there, faster, quick quick

And there's more there, that it is permitted to kill a wasp even
on the Sabbath, there are five things you can kill on the Sabbath, the
fly in Egypt and the wasp in Nineveh, the mad dog anywhere, and
the scorpion is there too, lucky it wasn't a scorpion, lucky it wasn't a
snake, that it wasn't a viper, a place swarming with desolation, and
the scorpion in Adiabene, apparently, and the serpent in the Land
of Israel, that may be killed anywhere, a place of snakes, always, and
scorpions, a place in the world, a place lacking, a place lacking place,
and a child that grows up in a place lacking place, and to raise a toddler in a place lacking place, Mummy will never forgive him, Mummy
would be incapable of sitting a child down on a wasps' nest, is it
in Tractate Shabbat? Perhaps. It looks as though we can't stay here.
There was only one more strip left to finish and then we could go
home, and he was sitting so quietly there, and all the time, how red
he is, and so burning hot, let's hope his windpipe isn't blocked, he's
so tiny, and so many of them attacked him, why not me, they could
sting me as much as they liked, and the wasp in Nineveh, and there
are all kinds of other afflictions there, the grasshopper and the fly
apparently, and the wasp and the mosquito, that one does not need to
warn against but cries out against, if he is not mistaken, yes, behold
a man before You, my God, crying out, to You, prepared to give all,
would that I might take your place, my son, crying out, to You, and
a child, so small, look, in this sunlight, in this heat, with this rushing,

with this distance, and not an hour has passed, and everything now is just endless plain all totally empty, until the entrance to the village, with those children and dogs and all the confusion, such a remote faraway place, the male nurse comes once a week and what does he know, quinine, aspirin and dressings, and how to get a splinter out, or an ingrown toenail, what hurts a man when he has a pain, what is there in his body when he is attacked by the venom with which wasps stun their prey, and then they lay their eggs inside him so that when they hatch the larvae have rotten meat ready to hand, and the wasp in Nineveh, this bee, this wasp, the oriental one, there's the German one too, if he remembers correctly from Berahm, and from Schmeil, with the illustrations, *vespa orientalis*, the golden one, and the German wasp, such a beautiful queen, with golden bands, and its narrow waist, that begins with a hole in the ground that it finds and it builds up with a material that resembles paper, with its saliva mixed with all sorts of leftovers, and when the nest is built it simply lays its eggs and the workers take care of it and gather food, while the males are only there for the moment of insemination, a nuptial flight, or is that only bees, a nuptial flight where only one of them possesses her and falls dead out of the sky. But not wasps, they tear the bees apart. With their golden bands. To feed their young. Faster, you beasts, faster, quick quick

Bareheaded, his short hair verging on blond and in fact already greying, and covered in dust, screwing up his eyes, moustache and mouth pressed tight, he pushes the mules that cannot and will not hurry faster or otherwise than their panting walk, their quivering skin flinching from the blows of the whip, unmoved by his cries, this is how they hurry and they know no other way, and this is how they will run all day and all evening and all night if that is their lot, hurrying neither more nor less, that is all that their mulish ability can manage, there is nothing to be done. What can be done my child, Mummy says to her chick who is huddled close to her, enwrapped in her, shaded from the sun, soundlessly sobbing, and Mummy, water? some water? but he doesn't seem to be here, and she, rest a while like that, is that better for you? But he only writhes. And she, where does it hurt, *mein Kind*, where does it hurt, but he doesn't seem to be there, and she, does my little boy hurt terribly? And she goes on, Mummy's here, Mummy's here, lay your head, and to Daddy, almost screaming, why aren't we moving, why is it so slow, the child is burning the child is... are the three of them together, or each consumed with their own care, and one of them is almost here almost not, Daddy whipping now and shouting now and the mules hurrying now, as they hurried before he shouted and before he whipped, and this bare plain all around, that only stirs up these dust clouds, above which the sun is moving now and seems to be starting to decline a little, and the horizon is full of sort of watery ripples, as though who knows what, or hints, or as though there it's different, and only hurry along there, quick quick

Like a nettle rash, and terrifyingly swollen, as though there's no pulse in the pulse, only the sobbing of the pain that is beyond fainting, because he has not uttered a singly cry beyond that first, terrible one that rent the world and the air and the sunlight, and at once his voice is silenced, from the pain and the swelling, and Daddy is already at his side, already he's lifting him up, what is it, my boy, what is it, already waving them away with his hand and kicking them away with his foot, and flapping his hat, without being afraid of them, already running, where does it hurt, ruling out a snake or a scorpion and knowing already that it's them, the wasps, the damned wasps, from the hole in the ground, on which he had put his baby to sit and amuse himself while he finished this strip, the last one, oh the strip of the field of this place that doesn't exist yet, of this Co-operative Workers' Association of the Herzl Forest Project, of Hapo'el Hatza'ir. Are they three people together now (or four, with the older boy, seven years old, who had been left behind), or three one of whom is guilty and needs to explain and apologise and even promise? So long as, so long as, God, so long as, I lift up my eyes, whence my help, out of the depths I cry to You, O Lord hear my voice, let Your ears be attentive to the voice of my supplication, and in a suddenly murderous voice, Get along there, faster, you beasts, faster, quick quick

Without whipping we'll never get there, but even with the whip they don't go any faster, the cart judders and jolts, in unimportant potholes, with little leaps, and all its planks creak. No father of twenty can know what a forty-five-year-old father knows, and between him and Mummy there are fifteen years clear, and what does this child do to his heart, as he urges the mules on to the doctor and this weak, frail toddler, attacked with the full fury of a swarm of angry wasps in the heat of the day, what do we know beyond the knowledge of thoughts or verses or habits of reasoning, and how suddenly alone, totally alone, alone abandoned in all this terrible expanse, alone, and only from an unremembered place that was remembered, mumbling, Hide not Thy face from me in the day of mine affliction, hide not Thy face, if not for my sake—for his; with that submission only known by one who has experienced it, with that self-restraint, and in the only way that remains, the only one, only to do what remains, and nothing whatever remains beyond it, and even this time he does not do what would be expected, what everyone always does, he who does not know how to revolt or to speak rebelliously, he who does not get up and leave the way other people do, he whose submission is always too little and too late, and he does not get credit for it, and to the silence of his heart another pain is quietly added, forcing himself to manage somehow, and Hide not Thy face, if not for my sake—for his, now he is doubled up, Damn you, get along there, faster, you bastards, faster, quick quick

A cart hurrying along in the middle of the empty plain, a little dust in the heat, the fields of sorghum already harvested and nibbled clean, fields of stubble grazed down to the soil, and there is no shade and no tree and maybe only at the approach to the village will there be some big ball-like fig trees offering dark shade and the sweet mouldy smell of ripeness that attracts the bumble-bees and the wasps, damn them, alone in the midst of this vast empty ocean, wishing to get somewhere. *Yingele meines*, Mummy says to him, bringing her ear very close to hear the faint breathing, rearranging the damp cloth on his forehead, and hugging him close to her, what else can she do, now she sings to him almost soundlessly *oif der veg shteit ein boim*, and Daddy wipes away a tear, so they won't sense how low he is, and he has no voice left to shout at the mules. But to one side, low on the northern horizon, there shimmers all the time in the heat, erased by the haze and re-forming, the outline of the buildings of that old settlement, fainting in the heat, and sleeping the sleep of ages, and clinging to this powdery path, and you remember suddenly how hard everything is and how hard it is to keep hold, and specifically, why haven't they cut the thistles near the gate yet, and why haven't they fenced the gap near the gate yet, and why haven't they dug an outlet for the stagnant water below, all decisions taken but not implemented, and so neglect dares to gain a foothold within, and in another stride or two will reintroduce the desert that we have worked so hard to banish, at least beyond the perimeter fence, and the dry branches should have been pruned ages ago, and guilt lurks on every side, and helplessness too, and the fear of failure that always lurks nearby, combining to become an explicit reproof, joining the fear that always sits here close to the gate, and the desert all ready to come inside, soundlessly and self-evidently, as though returning to its own place.

Here is the eternal dread taking concrete form. No longer dread about what will happen, because it's already here, now it is all dread about what the doctor will say, if only they can get there, God, if only they can get there. And all the fear turns out to be well founded. All visible now, truth revealed outwardly, come and see. All real, all palpable. So exposed now, and the blow finds us exposed and defenceless. Everything has been snatched out of our hands. And what will be able to stop it? The hand is powerless to hold, one hand of a little child, tiny, falls from Mummy's hands, and one of Mummy's gentle hands gently picks it up and picks it up again, and Daddy's hands are slack now on the reins of the stubborn mules, and they hold the whip unbrandished, and his feeling is like that of a falling man seeing the hard ground below rushing up to meet him for the bursting blow. With difficulty he whispers to himself, Enough, that's enough now, enough Daddy enough. You are the father here so as not to lose control. Here, and in the country, and everything, and in general. And you are the father who has always taught that a man can only choose according to reason, and all of a sudden and these verses of psalms, or as though there was really someone up there to take care of you, and that you may have been wrong and arrogantly thrown away something you shouldn't have, and so muddled. Whereas the whole expanse of this plain is open now all around, a clean summer plain, and the horizon a clean whole circle, that seems to have been drawn with a sharp pencil with perfect accuracy, and in the middle, tiny and pointless, a cart is hurrying along and hardly making any dust.

Dust and more dust. Rising up here and there for no reason with no wind and falling back for no reason, bending back on itself. Suddenly it starts up and rushes across a field and suddenly it stops. Rising from nothing and falling back to nothing. Not needing reasons. As though it is just a shivering-fit of the earth. Attacking and stopping. And suddenly, in the heart of the plain, there are now deep pools of blue, deep blue, hovering for a moment delusively, glittering and fading away in a myriad shimmers, and everything is gigantic, so infinite and so much as though it were the sea, effortlessly, and without anything on its surface, and also without any clouds, and only an endless hugeness stretched out on its back in the world, like a world of minerals, sky, earth and dust devils, where nothing grows or lives, nor is there even a need for them, and only this little cart is hurrying lost on this mineral expanse, in this hugeness that is beyond the capacity of the observer in the cart, and hurry as it will it will change nothing nor get closer to anything or to any place; a vastness by itself effortlessly, which was not brought into being, existing only in its infinite quiddity, on a single whole expanse, a plain of God, whole, clean, and empty, in which it is hard to find any purchase or a beginning of a purchase, on which all the time important things happen that are unimportant, on which such glasslike, or almost waterlike, brilliance shimmers, dust devils suddenly frolic in flocks, and suddenly emptiness in the fullness of full emptiness, or a momentary blueness, deep as the fathomless deep, changing to a misty vapour, with all the mirages and all the shimmering brilliance, physical phenomena of the light, upon the physics of the plain, or as though someone is really doing things there with some special purpose when in truth everything, from one side to the other, is nothingness in the level, silent heat and the plain shimmering in the haze, and the earth that is revealed only as earth that is not worked and as though there were too much earth, earth vast beyond man's capacity, on which only a single cart is hurrying now, pointless and insignificant, and will hurry on to the end of all days, evenly, straight, on the plain, under the sun in the heart of the gigantic hugeness and only in that nothingness and all the time only in that nothingness.

As for a man, does he not need to know his place? Everything, even wasps? Starting from how they seek out a ready-made hole in the ground, always a ready-made hole to build their nest in, and near a carob tree, which provides them, apparently, with building mate-rial for making the nest. And then their venom and what makes it dangerous and what it does to its victim when he is so small, oh, God, such a tiny child, what does wasp venom do to a child who is stung by five, ten, a hundred? Because the area of the hole is theirs until it is built on and it is all built up, and only then will there be no wasps here, and no snakes, or any of the noxious demons of the desert, because truth to tell there is no place here yet. Everything is still experimental. And the place that exists is precisely this vast open emptiness without anything. It has not even been decided if there will be an experimental farm here, or a regular village, or a forest station, or some think a co-operative settlement and others a collective, all in indecisive language and nothing is clear yet, even thought in Kinneret they have already begun something, and everything that there is here now is always only provisional always only temporary only between two decisions, only moving towards only on the way to only in the meantime, and in the meantime even the two-storey building and a few sheds and a few fences for the mules, the horse, the two cows and the hens that run around, everything is just a temporary camp that tomorrow will be dismantled and will no longer exist, and no one knows for certain if olive trees will succeed here, or pines or casuari-nas, all they know is that something is coming into being all the time and changing all the time, and that the desert outside is stronger than the lot of them, and also the apathy of the institutions. And there is no budget, there is no long-term planning, and there is no faith in anything, and of everything they always only know a little and only too little, and who knows even what the doctor knows, when we get there, what does the doctor know, and what will happen.

What does the venom do to the cells of the body, what does it do to the corpuscles, the nerves, or the brain, or possibly the heart? What does a wasp have in its venom, is it just painful or can it kill, is it sufficient to paralyse insects like itself but insufficient for bigger creatures? And what does this swelling mean, and what about the loss of consciousness, the fainting, the feeble pulse, these convulsions, a struggle to expel the venom from the body or the weakening of resistance and the destruction of tissues? Now they will give him an injection, or drain off some fluid. I ought to suck the poison out of him—I ought to suck all the poison out of him, to leave his blood clean, a father must never be taken by surprise, and a father should never put a baby on a wasps' nest and claim afterwards that he didn't know. A child can be taken by surprise and claim he didn't know, anybody can be taken by surprise and claim he didn't know, but not a father. Incidentally, what do doctors who were trained in Vienna know about the oriental wasp here? What do they know about the diseases here, what did they once know about malaria, who knew till not long ago that it is the female mosquito that spreads it, and not the contaminated air that comes from the swamps, open the windows, air your rooms, breathe fresh air, they used to say to us, in Hadera, and the mosquitoes came in their millions, or who knew about trachoma, or whooping cough, or tuberculosis, everything is so flimsy, so frail, so fragile, and a tiny child walks about in all this, so exposed and defenceless, and only our blindness, our blessed foolishness, stops us seeing. Haim Hissin, Hillel Yaffe, and they used to wake them in the middle of the night and on a donkey or on horseback they used to hurry clutching their black bag, what does a doctor have in his black bag? And Dr Moskovitch was called out in the middle of the night to a typhus patient far away on the other side of the wadi in the pouring rain and by the time he came back the wadi had become a raging torrent that swept away the cart and the horses and the doctor, and in the morning they found his body in the mud of the river not far off.

Now suddenly Mummy says, When will we be there, and Daddy, describing an arc with his whip, Here's the village, and then it's not far, which is more of a comfort than an explicit promise, and Daddy gets to his feet, he is standing up now and waving the whip, and lashing, and now he is gathering up the slack of the reins and whipping and he is shouting at them, Come on, faster you scum, faster, faster, and they are so startled and surprised they break into a headlong uncoordinated gallop for a bit of the way until they revert to their swaying motion that resembles a trot but is not a gallop and they must make do with this and there is nothing to be done, because maybe the whipping was for Mummy to see and not to hurt hard-working animals, it's hard to tell exactly. In any case, aren't they building a new world here. Something the like of which has never been seen before. Something that, if you believe in it, you don't need any confirmation that it can really be done. Something where the trees that are not growing yet, the saplings that are hardly distinguishable from wild grasses are strengthening to become a forest that will change the appearance of the place. Species of trees that this place has never dreamed of knowing, but they are now going to paint the place with their colours, pine, cypress, acacia, weeping pepper, and even eucalyptus. Their seasons will be the natural ones of the place, and they will give it the names of its settlements, and all the old native species, prosopis, couch grass, thistles, and all the rest of those dusty weeds, and wasps too, will be unknown, and will disappear from here, they will read about them in books, and in natural history classes, and if there is water, if they find water here, and they will find it if they look, and they will look if they have faith, and they will have faith if... and the ideas that are blowing around are so big that they muddle all the facts, and the passage towards the possible muddles the possible, and faith muddles the land, and the land muddles men, and when there is no more muddle—one is suddenly alarmed. As though some threat had fallen upon us and threatened everything. What is happening here. How do we keep going. Surely in truth everything here is only games of illusion. All the calculations, the planning, it's all games of make-believe, and all the experts, what do they really know, what is true, what is really so, and suddenly, all of a sudden… Hurry, you bastards, hurry.

Mummy says, He's terribly quiet I'm frightened, and Daddy says, Here's the village, and Mummy says, He's burning hot, and she drips some water from the handkerchief into the open mouth, which also has a slight groan in it now, a sort of moaning whimper, of the crying of a child who cannot cope, and Daddy says, It's not far now, and he stands up again to whip the mules, the he-mule and the she-mule, though what does the sex of a mule matter, hairy overgrown donkeys with big rather ugly heads. And now they are in the village, and the great open infinite plain is behind them, the flat plain on which even the little dust leaves no trace, all exposed to the sun without a spot of shade or a point for a man's inflamed eyes to fix on, you would have to be crazy to see that it is beautiful, that it really is beautiful, and that they are leaving all this supremely vast and open beauty behind now almost too quickly, without a proper leave-taking, and here they are winding and twisting among the hovels and courtyards and smells of the village, sleepy in the middle of the day as though there is no one here, but a cow chewing the cud with its head in the shade of a fence and its whole body roasting in the sun until it gleams, and the fig trees full of thick dark shade and a faintly rotten smell, and the tamarisks on the village square on the spot where a threshing-floor stood until not long ago, and an old man sitting holding a stick, and then from somewhere the children, all whooping shrilly, but they soon calm down, and a woman who has come out and is shading her eyes to see better, and suddenly in her surprised eyes is reflected the image of this cart taking a sick child to the doctor. What has happened to you, is visible in her eyes, and curiosity and maybe also empathy, to judge by her face that is no longer young and the scarf that covers it, and then they lose their way hopelessly in a lane, when there is no time for mistakes, and someone volunteers to show them the way as if he knows and shares the secret of the journey, and it seems there is something that arouses compassion, and suddenly there are tears in the eyes, for a moment, and then the big house with the colourful window panes and many horses tethered to the rail as if there was some kind of meeting here, and a hedge of prickly pears with stray overripe fruit of an overdone sickly red, and in the middle of the bend stands a camel blocking the road and his master cursing him, apologising and tugging on his rope to clear the way. *Sah be-ednu*, Daddy says to him, *be-ednu yesalmo*, says the camel man, as an excited pack of dogs surrounds the cart, barking terrifyingly, it seems impossible ever to get rid of them, but already it's the end of the village, with a whole group sprawled lazily to say things lazily and to listen lazily, barely crowded into the scarce shade left by the edge of a bundle of fennel stalks set in the ceiling of a mud house, protruding so as to make a strip of shade, their wandering eyes following the cart as it approaches and as it leaves, and one of them, gathering up the folds of his robe, stands up and says *esh ma lo*, what's the matter with the child, and Daddy replies, *al-zunburiat akaluhu*, he's been eaten by the wasps, *in'alabuhu al-dabbur, ya nahs*, says the man, cursed be the father of that hornet, such misfortune, *ma tehafish*, says the man, don't be afraid, it's nothing, *wa-allah yesahel aleikum*.

Now at last on the track that goes towards the top of the hill of sand and clay from where it will be possible to see the tops of the tall eucalyptuses at the entrance to the settlement. And now, Mummy says, now we must hurry, quick quick, we must hurry now, and she wraps the child and kisses his forehead, to take his temperature, and Daddy gets up at once and stands in the cart and shouts at the mules that are sweaty and restless at the sound of his shouts and the lash of his whip, even though they know that he will soon stop and then they can return to their pretend gallop. Yet Mummy does not know that attached to a plank on the side of the cart there was hidden all the time, innocently, a rather stout stick, because you can never tell what can happen when you have to cross that village, just as it is hard to see this Daddy standing up and brandishing this stick apparently to smash the skulls of all sorts of possible attackers. A hidden question, the question of the Arabs, and that old argument between him and

Isaac Epstein has not been settled yet. The truth is, it's uncomfortable to admit it, that it's desperate, and reality will have to settle all the arguments by force some day. What will this place look like in ten years' time, and when the child is grown up and needs to cross this village what will he see here? But this land, as it is, is always a land that has scorpions in it and also snakes and wasps, and one has to learn how to live here and get used to it. And to bring up children here. And that's the way it is. For the time being.

And as for despair, it's hard to overcome it. You can only ignore it. This land is given to desperate people, said Gordon, to truly desperate people. And they all compete to see who is the most truly desperate. Aaron David Gordon competes with Yosef Haim Brenner, while he competes with Yosef Aaronovich and he competes with Jacob Rabinovich to see who is the most truly desperate. Because only desperate people really have hope. But the Jewish people is not cut out for despair, Brenner claims excitedly, and he also maintains angrily that he personally does not accept the whole Jewish people. The Jewish people, he claims, has no future. I am a pessimist, Brenner shouts, a pessimist to the core, with no concessions, and his first and last shout, he shouts: a different element! A different element! But Gordon doesn't want to hear. Another principle, yes, but without self-flagellation, he says, and in the Land of Israel you cannot build anything frivolously or with romantic naiveté, but only from a desperate stand on the last frontier: the stand of the last camp, what a beautiful expression, the last camp, that of the most truly desperate. Those whom you cannot seduce with soothing words, to whom you cannot sell illusions as though they were reality. Because Brenner, after all the despair, has another magic word, mystery, he says, something that reason does not know, something that is beyond reason, mystery, yes, and the hope that defies logic, and that is beyond the laws of history, because on the side of the laws of logic, he says, there is no future. It is only because of mystery, because of what is not clear and not assured, that the whole account is still not settled; and yet only with mystery the account will not be settled, either. And the name of this mystery is of course: nevertheless. Oh, God. It's easy to say. Even despair has become a slogan with us. And what is left? Only sadness. Which is so sad.

Give us individuals, wrote Aaron David Gordon, give us desperate individuals. Because desperate people make the best fighters. People who do not expect redemption to come to them, but are themselves the redeemers. And here in the sand are Mummy and Daddy hurrying to the doctor, praying they will arrive while the child is still alive, and Daddy is even reciting verses of psalms that he remembers, that come to him of their own accord without his asking and without his knowing why not, and Mummy shades the child from the sun with a scarf, and sings to him soundlessly, On the hill there stands a tree, from the faraway homeland, when she was a young girl with her parents and her brothers and sisters and everything was still strong and stable, with forests and forest berries and the smell of the forest, and songs of Zion, and as she sings she strokes a feverish little head fainting breathing with difficulty with a swollen face so you can't see the eyes and only the hint of a moan escaping painfully from dry lips, and it is not even clear what the doctor will know, not because he is not a good doctor but because what do doctors know about wasps and their venom or about what happens to someone when they plant their savage sting in him and maliciously inject their poison and into such a tiny body, into his neck and into his temples, and into his eyes and into his little arms and legs so far as they were exposed below the line of the clothes, and who can count how many stings, a whole swarm of wasps in a furious rage against this body that is all but choking, all swollen and poisoned—when will we get there.

What is known about a wasp's sting, except that it hurts terribly, and can be dangerous, especially for children, asthmatics and people with weak hearts or lungs. What can be done to soothe them, if not to save them? Cold dressings, or warm dressings? A little alcohol, a glass of brandy? What do we know about a wasp's sting, except for all sorts of old wives' tales, all sorts of witches and witchdoctors and well-meaning people who want to help. And what does a toxicologist know about poisons, except that they hurt and can sometimes be dangerous? And what does a specialist on the human body know of the effects of a sting or of the action of the poison on the body? And what is pain anyway? What is a pain? What is it that makes a pain painful? What is it that hurts when a man has a pain? Is it the nerves, the blood, the muscles, or the four humours, white, black red and green? Or is it the soul that hurts? Or maybe a pain is nothing but the body's cry for help, a way of saying that something has happened that the body can't stand? Those wasps were alarmed in their underground nest, the first one alerts the others, and then in their accustomed order they hurl themselves on whatever threatens them, and they know where to sting so that it will really hurt, and from sting to sting their strength increases while that of their victim diminishes—who knows what would have happened if Daddy had not arrived at once and snatched up the child and chased them away in their buzzing throng, and then his escape with the child in his arms, little child, my child. And already they are climbing the sandy rise, and the make-believe trot has turned into a walk, and a walk that is getting harder and sinking in deeper.

If Daddy had read what this redactor has found and read of medical research on the wasp and its sting (e.g., M. Seyfers, 'General reactions to bee and wasp stings', *Harefuah*, vol. 56 no. 12, June 1959; or A. Kessler, 'Bee and wasp stings', *Harefuah*, vol. 89 no. 12, December 1975; or the same Dr A. Kessler, 'Bee, wasp, mosquito and ant stings', *Family Doctor*, vol. 7 no. 1, 1977), he would have been appalled and he would not have understood much of what they were talking about. That the sting causes a sensitisation to a certain antigen, and it causes a type of phylactic reaction, which can cause anaphylactic shock, by means of formic acid, haemolysine, hystamine and serotonin, and that the albuminic substances of which the venom is composed do not cause an allergic but a toxic reaction, and that the reactions to insects of the order Hymenoptera are blotchy rashes resembling nettle-rash (urticaria), swelling of the throat and the lymph glands under the armpits, a sensation of suffocation, welts and wheals, hoarseness, asthmatic breathing, dizziness, nausea, vomiting, abdominal cramps, with palpitations, hypotension, sweating, foggy vision, loss of consciousness, and even, in the most serious cases, anaphylactic shock, temperatures of 104° and over, and convulsions, especially in children. And that the worst stings are those in the face, around the eyes (a terrifying sight, the doctor writes, concealing nothing), and the most dangerous of all is a sting in the mouth, the throat, the tongue, the palate—hurry to hospital for treatment, subcutaneous injection, extract the sting from the tissue without spilling the rest of the venom inwards, apply an antiphlogistic dressing (like that?), give an antineuralgic tablet, or to such a pill of ezophranel or ephedrine, or alternatively pyrobenzamine, although sometimes it is preferable to clamp off the relevant artery quickly and give an intramuscular injection of an antihistamine or a soluble steroid, or even inject calcium intravenously, and if there is no rapid response to the first or second injection then quickly administer oxygen and an intravenous drip of noradrenaline. What does it all mean? Who can understand a word of it? Who in the summer of 1918 had any of these things? Who had ever heard of such advice and procedures? They were laughing at us. And how come we did not all die?

Was there any doctor for hundreds of miles around who knew any of this or who could understand what he was supposed to do? Daddy read a lot in German and Russian and remembered everything he read, but had he ever heard any of this or could he have understood it? Was there a doctor here who had heard that the general reaction to the venom is a manifestation of sensitivity to albumin, and that consequently anyone who is at risk should take prophylactic measures? And if there is no swelling of the lymph glands, and if the albumin in the venom has not caused fierce anaphylactic reactions, and if there is no loss of consciousness, then is it safe to conclude that the patient is out of danger? Provided the stings have not blocked the airways, heaven help us! Or would he have been relieved to learn that the reaction of someone who has been stung as many as twenty times is still only classified as 'extensive local reaction', which is not terrible, and that even if the general impression is quite bad, including vomiting and fever, it still does not constitute a 'serious therapeutic problem', and that all sorts of rashes, wheals, swellings and dizziness will all clear up of their own accord, thank God. All on condition that the phenomena on the skin are not accompanied by phenomena in the respiratory or circulatory systems or the nervous system or the muscles, in which case there is no time to be lost, to the nearest hospital, and quick, and administer the most tried and tested drug of all, adrenalin, or in the most serious cases, a drip, an infusion of ACTH, an intravenous injection of calcium, it is always preferable of course for sensitive subjects to have been previously immunised, but, on the other hand, anyone who had been stung before is liable to experience a more serious reaction: a previous sting always intensifies the adverse reaction. So you see, you who have been stung—you have been warned.

Doctor

Almighty God. It is only a matter of luck that people are still alive. Terror all around. And it may be lucky too that they do not know so much. And if Daddy does not know, although everyone always turns to him if they need a date in history or a place in geography or a correct spelling, or the meaning of 'gross national product', and he ponders and remembers and gives carefully checked answers, and when he doesn't know, he asks for some time and late at night he looks it up and then he knows, and if he doesn't know who else here does? Some might laugh whenever Daddy uses obscure or obsolete expressions, but then Ben-Yehudah's Hebrew dictionary has not been finished yet, and none of the later dictionaries, by Gur or Even-Shoshan, exist, and even if there is a copy of the *Arukh* it is not complete, and there is the sea of the Talmud, or as much of it as is stored in his memory, and a lot of the Bible, especially Isaiah, and he uses an asterisk at the bottom of every article to share with his readers, in small print, his hesitations as to whether it is proper to use this expression, at any rate, he apologises, as a temporary measure. But now the track had turned to powdery sand, and the wheels are sinking in deep, the mules straining their muscles and their backs sinking from the effort to pull, so that Daddy gets down from the cart to relieve the strain, and even pushes at the side of the cart to help, and not only is there no more trotting but soon they will have to stop for a moment to let them catch their breath and pant and toss their heavy asinine heads exaggeratedly and shake their harnesses with a jangle of chains and buckles, while the deep sand waits quietly, deep here from the breaking up of the desiccated clay and the decomposition of the colloids that maintain the cohesion of its particles, to hell with its particles, to hell with the colloids, to hell with all clay soils. Enough, Daddy roars, get along now, he roars and brandishes the whip so that the whistle of it will get them moving again, and so that Mummy will hear the whistle of the whip, and at once they summon up their strength with a great stir, straining their muscles, bending their backs and pulling without noticing Daddy who is pulling alongside them, roaring at them, and sinking his shoes in the sand and straining his muscles, bending his back to push, together, he roars at them, his patience will soon run out, together, forward, together, he pushes at the side of the cart, breathlessly, really pushing and really roaring terribly and seemingly waving the whip, and in another moment they all come to a standstill again, out of breath, and they need to catch their breath for a moment and rest for a moment. What is there to do. And now of course they also have a need to spread their legs, bend their backs, and piss, right now, the he-mule in his way and the she-mule in her way. What is there to do. A hole opens up in the sand beneath them full of foamy yellow stuff, but now they have more spirit to pull, and soon they will be out of this clean, this yellow, this yielding powder, that glistens in this sunlight. Another twenty or thirty strides and the denser clay will show through, and they will be able to trudge over it to the top of this hill, all bare, all shiny, all covered in dried-up halfa grass, all covered in white snails that look like blossoms. And is this soil not ideally suited to citrus groves, is it not just made for citrus groves, splendidly perfect for groves of the Jaffa shamuti, for vines shall not

83

save nor shall almonds save nor even tobacco which has begun to be spoken about lately, as though from tobacco shall salvation come to Zion and Judah shall dwell securely: it is citrus groves that should be planted here, and wells dug, and hushhash planted first and then after a year graft with noble, fine, juicy, thin-skinned Jaffa stock. And now just one more effort, Daddy explains to Mummy and to the mules, just one more effort and we'll be out of the sand, forward, Daddy roars, get a move on, he roars, and he does not rest until they are really out of it and the ground underfoot is once more dry and firm, and he climbs back in, encouraged, and gives an encouraged look at the child under Mummy's scarf, and you can see now how she's sitting crying without saying a word.

Encouraging—what encouragement. Suddenly everything is so tight. Bereft of any chance. Don't cry Mummy, you want to say. Or to scream at the mules. But there is no strength for anything except letting things roll on as they will. Who promised that there would be citrus groves, who promised that they would arrive safely. Who promised anything. Only everything open so open all around only everything scorched and battered by the sun, and only to the west, at the edge of the west, are there some wet-looking shimmers, which actually do make you feel good, or even seem to offer comfort, or something, if comfort is possible. Only Daddy must not give in to weakness, if Daddy lets up for a moment, if he gives in to weakness too, everything will be swept away. As though it were only waiting for this. In a moment they will begin to see the eucalyptus trees on the edge of the settlement, and even before that, to the side, the big old *jumez* will appear, to the east, which is the scriptural sycamore, and anyone who comes under its shade is immediately repelled by the sickly-sweet smell of its rotting fruit, a totally strange tree, and at once on the slope beyond the eucalyptus trees you can see the buildings of the settlement, and Mummy will see for sure that we are doing everything, everything that can be done, to get there quickly, and what is there to be done. Are he and Mummy together or are they each on their own? Mummy always knows before it occurs to him. She has a sense like that, to know. However hard you try you can never know things first, things that she knows of her own accord, as though she had them straight from the mouth of the world. And he and she are two, it follows that they do not move things along in the same way. Maybe a man thinks like this and a woman like that. He like this and she like that. Who knows.

Take the queen wasp, for example, who is the mother of them all. At first she is one on her own. And one day in the spring she wakes up and finds the beginning of a hole in the ground, and immediately she gets busy deepening it a little, and she kneads a kind of paper from spittle and residues, and from this she makes the first cell of the nest and she lays an egg in it, then she makes another cell and lays another egg, and when there are enough cells and enough eggs she waits for them to hatch and she feeds them with whatever prey she can catch, spiders, flies, and especially bees that she hunts right in the hive, and with their dismembered masticated corpses she nourishes her hidden larvae so that they will grow quickly within the summer, and as soon as they have grown they start to make cells and look for food for the larvae that will hatch, and when they have grown they feed them on flower nectar and stolen honey, while she is free just to lay eggs. And she is the mother of them all, she hunts, she robs, she slays, she builds, she rears, tenderly she tends her larvae, it is not she but the warm earth that incubates them for her, and there are even some species of wasps where the queen lays her egg inside the body of a spider that she has hunted and paralysed with her venom, so that when the larva hatches it has a juicy corpse ready to devour, and there are some species where she is so crafty that she lays inside a strange egg, and when the host larva hatches the intruder hatches too and eats it. Hexagonal cell after hexagonal cell in the recesses of the warm earth, in a multi-celled grey cluster, and the workers are also the guardians, and since they are not made to lay eggs their egg duct changes into a sting for injecting venom, and at the moment of stinging some of the venom is sprayed into the air, sufficient to attract other guardians from the nest straight to the site of the provocative scent, and they are not like the bee, whose sting breaks off when it stings and kills it, they, beautiful seething and buzzing terrifying and girded with their magnificent golden waistbands, from the seventh segment of their oval abdomen they unsheath their sac of venom whole, and sting and sting again, aiming for the very same spot where they have already stung, to load it with more and more concentrated venom, more and more, until they paralyse or kill their victim, God help us, miserable, wretched army of idiots that do not notice or see whom they have stung here.

And what is it like? As though you are suddenly seized by a realisation that maybe it was a fundamental mistake. That maybe this land doesn't want us at all, really. Because we came here to make changes that it doesn't want. It doesn't want any Herzl Forest. It doesn't want any citrus groves on a sandy clay hill. It doesn't want the sandy clay to change at all, but to be left as it is, including this miserable halfa, and for this dried-up halfa covered in white snails to continue to cover the hillside, with all kinds of miserable thistles, that may be centaurea, and that is precisely what it wants there to be here, halfa and centaurea, to leave them be, and this is precisely the beauty that we are incapable of comprehending: that what has been created here over a thousand years or perhaps two thousand is wiser, more right and true, and even more beautiful than anything that might occur to the impatient minds of all those who have come to change everything here only because they have strength, a lot of strength, and limited intelligence or none at all, even though they might have read every kind of book in the world. The wisdom of a short day only knows how to destroy the wisdom of a thousand slow years, and even the plain behind ought to remain huge and empty, without anything on it, hardly even any dust, only it alone, gigantic, open and empty, without anything on it, no tree no shade and no road, only perhaps a few flocks of sheep here or herds of goats there scattered unnoticed, swallowed up in the total infinity, or perhaps also a low-built Arab village, that changes nothing in it and does not compel it to change in any way, and on which the passage of time leaves no traces, and it is always a plain all exposed to the sun, to all the sun, and nothing changes in it and it doesn't want them to come and start making changes, because one change leads to another, until nothing remains of this this that is here and that is so wonderfully wrought to be just so, and that it is right for it to remain just so, without any change, because what there is is entirely whole and even, and that no one should start travelling along roads here, no carts hurrying along, no one absently undoing something and doing things to compel this place to become something it would be a pity for it to become.

Who asked this of you, to trample My courts? saith the Lord, in Isaiah. The insolence of strangers, coming here to pull down what has been completely fixed for a thousand, two thousand or three thousand years, a single, vast, whole, empty land, so beautiful in her even, perfect, total emptiness, only she and He, the land and God, she silently turned to Him through all the emptiness and heat and little clouds of dust, and He silently to her through all the torrid, empty skies grey from so much arid light; until the perfect nothingness of the skies above reaches and touches the perfect nothingness of the land beneath, on which there is nothing. And there is only the silence between them, and only the arrogance of our deafness prevents us from hearing that it is not silence at all. When you begin to upset that sempiternal equilibrium, that has been preserved intact for thousands of years, you never know where you will end up—when you start by destroying everything that has managed to endure intact for a thousand thousand years, after a thousand thousand years have so precisely shaped its perfect perfection, detail upon detail, and ended up finally achieving this great, ultimate, even perfection that contains nothing but a nothingness that is so simple and perfect and warm and full. This perfect emptiness, this complete completeness, this delicate equilibrium of which it is hard to say how far it is miraculous, this emptiness that is full to its end—as against the shattering of this whole at the hands of impatient, insolent, indecent people, for all sorts of beginnings and all sorts of wounds, irreversible ones, and for all sorts of scrabblings and scratchings, and dragging in all sorts of things that do not belong here, forcing them, to grow here and be built here, and change the place with all sorts of things that do not belong and compelling the place to come to an end and to go or to submit, without knowing at all how it is that they can no longer hear here the perfect silence, or how they have lost forever this utter emptiness, without paying any attention to a single sign of protest: all sorts of droughts, or on the contrary all sorts of floods, and all sorts of rejection of new trees, and all other kinds of failures, and with all kinds of stings and scorpions and serpents, with all kinds of resistance to the strangers come to change, with such insolence and arrogance, with the necessary stinging of anyone who tries to push in where he has no right to push in, be this stranger as little as he may, and free of all malice and totally innocent, and be it his father who is ploughing full of faith, innocently sitting his child down on the quiet earth that tolerates its wound seemingly without protest, one innocent father and one innocent child dressed in white clothes that his mother made for him, a little too big.

Yes, but on the other hand. The other hand? On the other hand it's us. And we are here, hurrying to the doctor's. And there's only another half an hour to go or less. There's the eucalyptus grove already. We'll be there soon, Daddy says to Mummy, who looks up shading her eyes with her hand and still not believing, she has been told too many times, too many times people have tried to reassure her, we're nearly there, she can see nothing yet. Only sadness now. And every one alone. And why for instance did they go and plant eucalyptuses here, of all places, there is no swamp here, and there is no poor soil, and it's not clear what they were thinking of when they planted them, because after all there is no tree here without someone thinking there ought to be, without someone digging and bringing and planting and without hollowing out an irrigation dish and watering, trees don't just grow here, and someone always needs to persist with every individual tree until it establishes itself and grows, someone always has to wear himself out over every tree until it establishes itself and grows. The little child is tired. Worn out, and breathing so faintly that you can only hear if you bend over and press an ear to him, and his tiny hand and his tiny foot like a doll's foot. Such sadness.

Together, get a move on, Daddy shouts, waving the whip. The grove is fairly sparse. Not too much shade, and not too much grove. But there is always something encouraging about the smell of eucalyptus, even in the blades of dry leaves that carpet the sand. These eucalyptuses are not the heroic ones of *In the Hadera Forest* or *The Carters' Jubilee,* they are meagre, tired and feeble. Maybe they are going to make them into poles, for support. Maybe they mark the limit of one plot. Only here and there are some fine smooth trunks, like a beautiful nudity. Oh, yes. Alarmed, he quickly digresses. And why is it always eucalyptuses, there are other trees. The war is over now and everything will start to change, and quickly. After the Turks it will be possible to do things. And it seems Mummy won't let us stay here and we'll have to move. She's had enough of raising children in the desert, she says, she's fed up cooking over thorns in an outdoor oven. She's fed up with two pails of water a day, full of leeches. She's had enough of the boredom, of living crowded four to a single room, with six more families in the stone building, and he sits up late at night writing and won't put the light out. And his silence is not a strong point in arguments, he is defeated almost from the outset. Little boy. Hardly breathing. How could he have been so irresponsible as to sit him on a wasps' nest. Arguments about whether to leave for Kinneret, for the kibbutz, or whether to go straight to the heart of the Valley to set up a moshav, a co-operative village. For his part he likes the moshav better, because there is more private ownership, and because if you invest more you get more back, and with the two boys at his side he'd be able to have a go, and enough of this wandering from place to place every couple of years, to a new experiment, an agricultural workers' co-operative.

Between Old Jaffa and a new development, in Neve Shalom probably, or Neve Tzedek. Probably there. It's sad, sad for a man. More dragged along than going of his own accord. And you're not a child any longer, Mummy says to him, so stop drifting. You're not the unknown hero, always at the disposal of the people, constantly moving from one front to another, and dragging your family from one temporary location to the next, as if they were nothing more than suitcases. Suddenly, for a moment, he is smitten by weakness and a feeling that everything is tired now, and there is no strength for anything. One whole moment. Then, slowly, and then more, you raise your eyes again, and without anything changing, you know that the moment has passed even though a new moment has not yet come. Then, imperceptibly, as happens sometimes, he becomes aware that he is soundlessly humming some melody, a soundless sobbing, some *ya bam bim bam*, some kind of Hasidic tune from long ago, twenty-six years Daddy has been here, with one gap, yet he's still there, where he was in his first sixteen years, with that old *bim bam*, so heart-wrenching, yet so antiquated and stupid, and the moment you realise you stop in embarrassment, peer around to see if anyone has noticed, aware of how inappropriate and wrong it is for this time, and embarrassing, even though this snatch of song has not melted away or dried up, it is still soundlessly sobbingly sobbing away inside him, he does not touch and no one will touch this thing of his that is inside his innermost inside, this *ya bam bim bam oy yo yo oy* of his. Daddy has an ear for music, he does not sing out of tune, even when he occasionally unconsciously clenches his throat and wails *Aïda* or *Carmen* to himself, even though he has never been to the opera, because he was sixteen and a half when he left little Rotmistrivka in Ukraine, Kherson District, with Tolstoy in one hand and the Bible in the other and the thrill of rebirth in his heart, straight for the swamps of Hadera, that at first were thought to be fine soil and eternally green, and even when the malaria broke out they did not make any connection between its horrors and the bites of the little mosquitoes. The bites were so small and the hour was so great, and moreover the results exceeded all expectations and changed their lives, and from Hadera in a panic to Zikhron and from Zikhron for a while to Jaffa, and from Jaffa, when the repeated bouts of fever had almost got the better of him and he was little more than an overheated rattling skeleton, back to Russia in shame and explaining apologetically that it was just to cleanse his blood of the malaria, and also to study ironwork and farriery, naturally so as to make a useful contribution here, and as soon as possible from Yekaterinoslav, Kherson District, in 1904, back to Jaffa again, for the population census in Jaffa, a heroic exploit that he accomplished single-handed, then back to the vineyards of Rehovot, and from Rehovot to an iron works in Petach

Tikvah, then a temporary post as a teacher, and also an assistant in a kindergarten, then back to the vineyard, always with a hoe, always with a pruning-hook, and late at night at any old table writing till deep in the night, when the black sky outside became huge and open to man and everything was so open before him.

Because if asked he would have replied unhesitatingly, leave me alone the lot of you and just give me a table to write on in the night, or, leave me alone the lot of you and just let me work in the fields in the day, but if they had really asked him he would have hesitated to reply as much. Who was he to demand so much for himself or to make himself the centre of importance. He would find himself some other time, some later time, maybe when they were all in bed, or outside in the yard if it was too difficult indoors, a lodge in a garden of cucumbers, or on his lap if there was no table, by the light of a candle, by the light of the dawn, by the light of the sunset if there was no alternative. But even leave me alone was beyond him. Who was he to put on airs and ask so much for himself. Besides which it was forbidden and Daddy could not ask for anything for himself but only defer to those before him, and Daddy could not complain or ask or grumble. Daddy was there to do whatever was too hard for the others. That's enough, now hurry up, he roared, hurry you beasts, hurry up or I'll beat you, he said waving his whip in the air. Incidentally, who is the doctor in the settlement now that Dr Moskovitch drowned in that river last winter—a new doctor has taken his place, who is probably general practitioner, surgeon, obstetrician, tooth-puller and nurse to every gloomy heart, and even if he does not know exactly what the pain is or what exactly albumin, enzymes and toxins do to a body that has been bitten or stung, he has seen many things in his life, he has treated many people who have been bitten or stung or wounded, so that even if he can't explain everything in terms of chains of albumins and enzymes and even if he does not have all those injections and drips he does have the means to bring some relief and if he sees that the condition is serious he can decide to wait for the train from Egypt to come in the morning on its way to Lydda and Jerusalem, and then straight to Bikkur Holim Hospital or Misgav Ladakh, or the

Scottish Hospital or the French Nuns, hurry up and take the child urgently, and they will do whatever needs to be done for this little child, the poor, thin, bitten, stung, poisoned, suffering little child, who has fainted with pain, luckily for him perhaps because had he not fainted the pain might have torn him apart.

We're almost there now, almost there in the quarter of the poor exploited Yemenites, in their wretched, huddled houses on the edge of the settlement, very soon they will be trotting down the main street, very soon and now suddenly Mummy too, Look, he's opening his eyes, Mummy suddenly says, look, what is it, my child, what is it, he's opening his eyes, she says, and the baby wriggles in her arms and starts to groan pitifully, wriggles and can't find a position, and suddenly cries aloud, for half a moment, openly, brokenly, unrestrainedly, and again he wriggles and groans, and buries himself in Mummy's bosom, in a different clasp, as though in a new embrace, seeming to seek her breast, clinging blindly, with such a primordial need he wails and sobs and you cannot see his eyes but only his frail shoulders, which jerk convulsively, like someone shrugging off everything else and being pushed towards the most necessary thing, perhaps like the head of a baby being born, being pushed out into the necessary thing before him, hard though it may be, towards the necessity of its birth and there is no way back now. And Mummy is entirely with him and entirely merged with him and he is part of her and she is wholly with him, and with one hand she presses his head firmly against her, with infinite gentleness and with infinite firmness, as though this is how it is and he is now the most necessary thing of all, while with the other hand she seems to turn herself towards him, towards his seeking head, towards his sobbing that expresses his one desire, and it would not have been in the least surprising if in another moment she did what was right and necessary, unbuttoned her shirt and untied what she wore underneath, making room for her hand to get inside and press with gentle fingers, as only a woman can, that full white hidden thing, long since forbidden for him to see as he has long since been weaned, whose whiteness, smell and abundance are so fresh in him, and beyond all and with the same magnetic necessity, offers him, as he huddles against her with a sob, choked and lost in all his poisons, and with an explicit demand to be joined to her and to her life and to her gift of life and the memory of the warm white sweet flow, than which nothing is more right nothing is more healing and nothing more full of life.

Give ear to my prayer that goes not out of my lips, Daddy says soundlessly, with his lips, indeed without his lips because not a line is moving in his sun-eaten, bareheaded, Van Goghian face, the reins in his big straw-strewn, fast-holding hands, Incline Your ear to me, Daddy says without uttering a sound, guard him as the apple of Your eye, Daddy says, adapting for the need of the moment the words of Psalm 17, in the shadow of Your wings, Daddy says, adapting, because this is from the heart, a psalm of David, Daddy says, And hear O Lord, and hearken to me, Daddy says, and he does not wipe away tears with his fingers, the wind dries them and the sun dries them, and the road is opening up and soon, really very soon. Very soon they will enter through the walls of *debesh*, which is merely hardened, burnt limestone, white walls coated with pinkish whitewash, rising to shoulder-height so that one neighbour can chat to another face to face, and behind appear the small houses with their pointed red-tiled hats, with their mulberry trees pruned in a ball shape, some of them plastered in ochre and others left bare in the same rough brown *debesh* stone, and all with a Washingtonia palm on either side of the gate, and with green wooden shutters whose slats can revolve to shut out the blinding midday sun, and in front there is always some girl standing suddenly in some garden with a rubber hose watering lightly, freely, all kinds of summer flowers that are there, blooming openly, richly, in yellows and browns, soaking up water, drenched with water, merry with water, and on the wide dirt road between the houses they arrive like people coming from the great desert, and enter awkwardly with the clomping of their clumsy rustic mules, straight out of their vast hot desert that they have come from and that is still in them, and people here and there stop and ask anxiously what's happened, and people point the way to the doctor's house, and some even accompany them, while others merely accompany them with their eyes, and now here is the doctor's house and the doctor is at home and is coming out towards them, and Mummy is already and in tears, and Daddy's throat is choking, and he takes the little boy and clasps him to his breast, and the swollen child's eyes are closed, he has nothing left but an exhausted sobbing, and Daddy reaches out to help Mummy down from the cart, and for a single instant now in the midst of alighting, of helping down, they are all clasped together by this one arm, Mummy and the child in his clasping arm, and then Daddy finds his strength and in the most confident voice he can muster he says to the doctor who is coming out towards them, Wasps, Daddy says in a voice he does not recognise, wasps, Daddy says to sum it all up, and as though he only now grasps the enormity of the calamity that has struck them—an entire wasps' nest—he describes soundlessly, unable to endure any more, and they are all standing here in front of the doctor so exposed, so destitute, Mummy and the child, and Daddy and Mummy, and Daddy and Mummy and their child, all before him.

And the doctor takes the child, with those hairy arms and those bear-like hands of his, with which he can extract a deeply-embedded splinter, apply iodine, or prise out an ingrown toenail, and always with a cheerful mien and a promise that everything will turn out all right and for the best, and without a hint of panic—If he is not dead—the doctor says, to them and to all the crowd round about—then he will live, the doctor says very knowledgeably, pushing his glasses up on his forehead with that bear-like hand, either smiling at them or lost in thought.

Part two

Iron bar

There is unease. On every side unease. You can feel it. People crowded together all the time. Not talking aloud. A shadow over everything, it's unclear what, just a shadow over everything. And unease.

A large square courtyard, surrounded by a covered arcade and the doors of the apartments, and in the middle of the courtyard the round well, into which, when they first arrived, he threw his hat into some dark, frightening depth, and ahead the brown wooden gate is closed and only occasionally someone comes in through the small wicket, they open up and then close it quickly behind him, and it is quiet again. And nothing. They only listen. And nothing is clear. Only there is unease.

Or as though there were a faint smoke suspended over everything, creeping slowly and enfolding it in unease, or as though there were a stench enfolding them all the time quietly—it doesn't make them cough but it's unpleasant to breathe and they listen hard all the time, only listen. And the unease worsens.

Nobody says anything. But it's clear that it's coming from Jaffa. And that Jaffa now is a big black forest that is getting closer, and now it is actually here. Is the gate strong enough? There's a roaring outside and what can stop it? Where is there to hide? Nobody says anything.

It is not Shabbat today but no one has gone to work. Daddy went out and came back quickly, now he's gone out again. To fetch milk for the children, he said, the milkman, Mummy told him, didn't deliver any milk today for the children. So Daddy took the tall milk pan with its lid in one hand, and found an iron bar that he picked up in his other hand, and went to fetch milk for the children. On the third street from here. Towards the sea. In the milkman's courtyard with the big mulberry tree, and the two filthy cows and masses of chickens, and the donkey on which he does his rounds with two large milk-churns and measures the milk out in a jug with the measures incised on it, pouring milk to the brim, and the milk has this kind of smell, and it bubbles and froths, as though it has come straight from the milking, and he is not back yet.

Pressed into himself like a little bundle, in the corner between the door of the apartment and the wall of the arcade, seeming absorbed in his game, but in reality all his back straining for the gate, with only a need croaking in his tummy that all this should be over. At the last minute you can always jump into the well and hide in its depth, cling to its damp round wall like a frog and wait for it to be over. There is a wooden lid on top that you can cover the mouth with. It will be dark and closed and safe there and no one will know where he is, only he mustn't fall into the water, which gives you a cold feeling in your tummy, and in your legs, specially when you remember how the sides of the well are covered with revolting slippery green slime, and how the man came and fished for the hat he'd thrown in with a bent hook attached to a string and in the end he caught it and hauled it up triumphantly except that what he pulled up was just a mouldy piece of sacking.

What have we done to them? Why are they angry with us? Have we taken something away from them? It's hard to know anything. No one is saying anything. Just waiting, and nothing is certain, nothing. Something strong terrible and savage is stalking around free outside, we are shut in here waiting and out there it is free and roaring and strong, all-powerful, coming and going. Daddy is not back yet. He went to fetch milk for the children clutching an iron bar. Unease. Unease on every side.

Sometimes on the seashore, not far away—you only cross a few streets, and only the big houses, and only those courtyards of the Arabs, with the little houses, underneath the big houses of Jaffa, and at once you come to the damp sand and the beach and the sea comes all sun-struck, and the white crests of the waves run towards you in rows, broken and full rows, and all the blazing sky, and the stains of the black rocks with the throngs of seagulls flying, and the smell of seaweed, and the attractive terrifying depth—you bend down and take off your white sandals to dig in the sand and make a canal and make a wall and make houses and buildings, and strengthen it all with sea-shells and by patting it with your hand, when suddenly a wave comes up from the sea and washes it all away with a single lick and it totters and all falls down, and then it comes back with a wide lick, it licks and flows with a murmur and as it goes back it takes all the walls and ramparts and little houses and big houses and canals, and nothing can stop it or resist it or remain standing, even if you build it up to your own height and reinforce it and strengthen it with all your strength and with shells and bits of wood and stones, everything will still be easily carried out to sea and swept off and flattened and erased and end up as smooth as though there was nothing there, and apparently there is nothing in the world that can stop any evil.

What's going on here. Unease between the columns of the arcade that surrounds the courtyard, shading the apartments beneath it, one door for the two rooms and another for the little kitchen, with the paraffin stoves, the pots and pans and the big pitcher, the *jarra*, always kept full of well water, Mummy's gleaming copper mortar, and the table covered with flower-patterned oil-cloth, where Mummy sings as she works, all sorts of *With joyful heart I sing of flowers in the spring*, or Yiddish effusions that are incomprehensible apart from soulful longing, the two rooms sparsely furnished but spotlessly clean, with lots of cushions on the bed, little cushions piled on big cushions on the bed, and on the walls pictures of her father and mother and brother and sisters (Duvid, Hinde and Dvoirenyu) and her grandfather and great-grandfather, all sitting calmly, with the forest behind them, the one, real, famous, serene forest, the heavy black forest, with the most respected members of the family sitting of course in the front row and the others, also loved to tears, standing behind them, some with hats and long beards, others bare-headed and stylishly dressed, one hand tucked into the front of their buttoned-up coat, and now everyone is outside in this arcade, waiting, crowded together, uneasy, whispering and not knowing what. Every two doors an apartment and all the square courtyard doors and all waiting for something, not knowing, uneasy, and Daddy is still not back.

In the corner between the door of the apartment and the wall of the arcade, that is where he begins, and at once he's off and away—all he needs is some object to serve as the hard thing in the game, some broken utensil, a bit of something that has come to pieces or been picked up absent-mindedly, provided it has something to hold onto, to turn into a locomotive—and at once they disappear into the distance, to places that he knows in detail, perhaps from the books he has read—because he can read already, he has been reading since the day he was born, whatever comes to hand, without asking if he understands or what he understands, reading and rereading, everything, including the name of the printer, not just the numbers of *Moledet for Young People* edited by J. Fichman but also whatever Daddy happens to have on his desk, including *Hashiloach* edited by Dr J. Klausner, *Ha'olam* edited by M. Kleinman, and *Ma'abarot urevivim* edited by Y.H. Brenner, including Ahad Ha'am's *At the Crossroads* and Lilienblum's *The Way to Bring in the Saved*, not promising that he has understood everything in them but only that his eyes have not skipped a single word, and some words he will remember while others he will let sink in, and wait for the day when he will retrieve them from where he has stored them, and some make him burst out surprisingly in the laughter of a lonely child who suddenly laughs among the junk he is playing with in a corner of the arcade, a laugh that has no companion; nor does he skip over the green copies of *Hasadeh* edited by A.L. Jaffe or the fat numbers of *Ha'omer* edited by S. Ben-Tzion and certainly not the parts of *Sefer Ha'agadah* edited by H.N. Bialik and Y.H. Ravnitzky that lie around the place in tattered bundles, and if you just prompt him and give him the opening words he will continue the story of how Rabbi Shimon ben Shetach took a donkey from an Ishmaelite, or 'Once the month of Adar was almost ended and the rains had not fallen...', or the tale of the two men who had a wager as to which of them could provoke Hillel to anger, like a row of pearls whose string has broken. It was even said that while Mummy was breastfeeding him he was already reading Ahad Ha'am's *Truth from the Land of Israel*, but he is no longer a little child, as his skinniness may indicate: it is after Passover now and by the autumn he will be five, and if left to himself he will crouch on the bed with his legs under his tummy and his head in his hands, his eyes racing from line to line, and it is a waste of time to talk to him, the written words rise up and make things that are more real than any real things.

The most beautiful thing is the lettering in some books, those published by Shtiebel, for example, or the prayer book, where the letters are stretched to complete the lines, some with longer tails or elongated necks or sharpened stings, making everything prettier if not necessarily easier to understand, and like bulbs the words are buried to a certain depth waiting to shoot up when their time comes, and when you shake him suddenly out of his book he looks up with startled eyes, not knowing what you want from him and why he has to come back to the dreariness all around.

Someone has come in through the wicket. Not Daddy. Waiting to know increases the unease. Why hasn't Daddy. Nobody knows whether they should get indoors or go on standing around like this, or pack some things and get out, further away, it's too hard to go on. The courtyard is not a fortress and the wooden gate when it comes to it cannot withstand a push. They have no firearms or batons, and only Daddy went out this morning with an iron bar in his hand to fetch some milk for the children. Suddenly it may be necessary to, it's not clear what, or it is clear but no one has the courage to know. Sometimes when they don't turn up to fetch him from kindergarten, or his older brother forgets he was supposed to pick him up, he dares to come home on his own; after all, it is only three or four streets, and this is his finest hour: the way gets longer on its own even without any detours, and now you can slowly see everything precisely, how the plaster is peeling from this building revealing the *debesh* stones beneath and causing a specific fear of collapse, and also a recognition that even the weak can endure and not fall, and how the peeling wall gathers great stains of colour as though it were a big rich picture, or how a little rivulet of foul water snakes over the dirt road, from that courtyard, and if another bucket of water is not poured out quickly it will dry up like a thirsty tongue in the desert, or how on a waste plot a castor oil plant shows off its green and red and how a bird perches on it pecking at its big hooked seeds, and here a lady comes out of a gateway, first one foot crossing the raised threshold then the other, and finally all her heavy rustling skirts and she groans as she comes out, and gathers herself up with her pretty hat and her impressive necklace, and she opens a flowery parasol over her head and sails away with it all, big black handbag swaying rhythmically, and how there is something so ridiculous about it all that you burst out laughing without being able to explain why or needing to explain. And the most fascinating thing of course is this low wall made of limestone full of holes so big that you can put a small sandal-shod foot into one of them, and straighten yourself up on it until your head is above the top of the wall, and there, oh, there below cradled in this trench runs the railway line and that is where the train goes, and if his luck is in it may go by right now, and the most wonderful thing will happen, almost close enough to touch.

For what in the world is more beautiful than a train journey? And this is the precise point where it begins to slow down before entering Jaffa station, its terminus, or the contrary, it's here that it ends the laborious beginning from Jaffa and it can start to pick up speed as it hurries on to the next station, Tel Aviv, chuffing and panting, puffing steam at every gasp, and the black smoke from its chimney, that Daddy calls a funnel, trails in a row of loops that no one has eyes enough to follow all the way to the end, and the steam envelops and covers you for a moment, puffing to left and to right, in coils and chunks that no sooner resemble balls than they dissolve and float away damply, while other stronger balls puff up, burst and dissolve, as carriage after carriage rushes past, casting a beam of light between each one and the next, the other side of the line revealed in a flash and vanishing behind the mass of the next carriage, and finally on the balcony at the back of the last little carriage stands a man holding a green flag and a red flag, ready to wave either, but meanwhile he only waves a greeting to you, and smiles at you, unbelievably, he is really waving to you.

You cannot understand anything just from listening to a story, even if it is the most beautiful story there is. How powerful and power-breathing is that black engine, powerfully drawing the whole tail of the train behind it, with the driver's head at his window and the fireman shovelling coal, lit with a hellish light; and perhaps you have to stand like this, with your sandals in a hole in the wall and the train within reach of your hand, and you are with it, squealing and panting and puffing out steam and smoke like it, both so hot and furious and strong and splendid, to appreciate how wonderful this all is, and how exciting it is to get all the details right: how for example the driving rod of the engine is swallowed up and then spewed out from that metal sleeve, that is not yet called a piston, and if we do use the term we shall be anachronistically inventing a word that does not yet exist in Hebrew and putting it into the mouth of a four-year-old who cannot yet even say what he is able to say, while that rod is ejected, swallowed up, ejected again, and the whole point of the boiler that is almost bursting with power is to eject and swallow the rod that turns the big wheel, and the three other wheels with it, all joined together, rising together and descending together, and all the time the straight line of the driving rod runs backwards and forwards, becoming a circular line that turns as it rises and falls, do you get it? No, because you are too small, but you already know that that's exactly the secret of the engine, and yours too, and if that George Stevenson whom you read about in the issue of *La'am* that is sent out free to subscribers to *Hapo'el Hatza'ir* had not invented the steam engine in his day you would have done so, there's no doubt about it, so much so that you almost crow triumphantly, imagine. A pity, a child can't explain properly or say things properly, but he has no doubt that what he can see now is the seed of everything that is beautiful—the way the movement of a straight line is converted into a circular motion—so that if they could all feel what he is feeling now they would join hands and sing.

It's hard to tell everything, and you always think that, one day, when I'm big, perhaps, I'll be able to tell it as it ought to be told. And perhaps, really, this is the opportunity that has been postponed, and one ought to take a deep breath and tell it in full, without leaving anything out, all the splendour of the story of the straight driving rod that turns into circular motion that causes the revolution of the wheels of the engine that speeds along pulling all the train, until it brakes in Jaffa, but not before, whistling and hooting two or three times, a howling sound that no one in the world can imitate as he does, until there in Jaffa station everything stops and stands still, and, just in case, at the end of the line they've built a barrier made of heavy beams supported on more heavy beams to stop anyone that forgets to brake, so that the speeding train should not career crazily right into the sea, with the full pressure of the steam in its boiler and the full heat of its momentum straight into the water, in a wild, mad rush and God preserve us from what will happen when this fast-moving, blazing thing penetrates the excited dark water and dives inwards, when all the time above it is just calm, clear water, unaware of what is inside it, and suddenly everything explodes and a tower of water rises up and nothing is left of the world—he will never manage to tell what he ought to tell, and the story of the wonders of the points, when the rails change tracks, for instance, by means of the lever that a man struggles to move, even though they have fixed a heavy metal ring at the head of it, even with one leg stretched out behind him pushing with his last strength, until with an almost-jump he succeeds at last and turns it the other way, and the rails shift from this side to that and the train can now change tracks; or for instance the story of how the engine is moved from the main line to a branch line and how there is a huge turntable there, built inside a circular ditch, and when the engine enters it, not suspecting what they are about to do to it, the driver gets off and another man comes round the other side, and on their own the two of them easily revolve the turntable that the heavy, smoking engine is on, until it faces round from Jaffa to Jerusalem, and then the driver climbs on board again, oh God, onto his panting engine, and he whistles once, and he easily turns a sort of wheel and he easily pushes a lever in front of him and the engine starts moving with all its power and gets off the turntable as gently as a lamb, straight onto the track all ready for the journey to Jerusalem.

What should he do with all these stories that fill his belly and interest no one and that no one has any patience for, like for instance the story of those iron pads shaped like cymbals between the carriages, and how they absorb the shock of the impact in the giant spring that is secreted in their sleeve, or the story with all its precise details of the moment the engine gets going, how it starts moving, sometimes with an easy transition from a standstill into movement and sometimes, suddenly, with a commotion of excessive power, a hundred times more than is needed, that makes the wheels turn on the spot, with an ear-splitting squeal, as though to test its power or remind you how powerful it is, and with a clash of the cymbal-shaped shock-absorbers the train shifts with an unnecessary din; apparently the time to tell it all will never come, to complete the story of the splendour of the train when it rushes along the winding track, leaning into the bend, one shoulder higher than the other, and seemingly all is lost, and the time never comes to tell properly the supreme beauty that he saw once and absorbed into himself, nobody wants to hear and nobody cares, and you are nothing but a nuisance, you had better shut up, there is nobody in the world to tell anything to. And that's the way it is.

Only this, how once under the Shloosh Bridge when you were standing on it looking down, suddenly it came rushing along and when the engine was right beneath you the steam came into you and inflated you, entered your trousers and puffed you up and filled you and flooded you with such a warm excitement from the pressure of the unruly steam, and you were suddenly filled and ballooned, warm, damp, and bloated, and the bridge trembled beneath you with the rhythmic rattle of the speeding train hurrying past on its way to Jaffa, filling with jets of steam and smoke the quiet little houses on either side of the track that suddenly went wild and swelled up with the noisy wild swelling whiteness, while up on the bridge you sang excitedly like a captain on his bridge, everything is yours now even the wonderful speed, and the magic of this whole thing becoming real and possible, even if no one in the world wants to hear a word about it.

It is clear that Mummy is frightened. She is moving, she is no longer in the middle of them all, she doesn't say doesn't know doesn't interrupt others. Daddy has not returned and there are only rumours all the time that outside somewhere an ugly mob is gathering. Where are the police, someone asks, and Where's the British army, he wants to know, and They say the Arab policemen have also joined the troublemakers, somebody knows, and The district Governor, says one who knows what's what, and the High Commissioner, he protests, our brother Sir Herbert, he protests, but there is no patience for him or his protests, and there is no one to contradict him not because this is already old hat, but because it's clear that there is no one on our side. And where is the Shomer, where is the Haganah, and what have we got, someone asks too much. You can see that Mummy is really frightened. Perhaps we should get out of here, nobody says it but you can see that's what they're thinking, make a dash for the Herzliya Gymnasium in Tel Aviv, and its extensive cellars not far from here, less than half an hour away—what are we waiting for, it can't be long now, and when all is said and done Mummy never liked Jaffa anyway, ever since she arrived in July 1908 with her brother Joseph, when they landed excitedly from the boat that had brought them ashore from the ship, amidst the shouting and the crowds and the jostling and belongings flying down the side of the ship into the boat below, and among all those frightening big black rocks, and to the shore; and even before we had managed to grasp that here we were in the land of our ancestors, and that this was our homeland, the longed-for Land, and that those were our brothers who cherished the soil of our Land, we were already surrounded by the jostling and shouting, the stench and the filth, and through the doorway of Haim-Baruch's inn, already in a hurry to escape, to find a cart that would take us while it was still daylight straight to the vineyards of Rehovot and the fresh air of its orange groves, freed from all these frightening Arabs, their crowds, their din, their filth, even though every morning it was they who filled the young settlement, the courtyards, the vineyards and the orange groves, to leave each evening and return to their homes, out of bounds, far away, and we had no contact with them, until the morning when they come back again in their crowds to the market and return to the courtyards of the houses crying their wares in Arabic Yiddish, their vegetables, their fruit and their eggs, you had to bargain with them firmly and in a medley of words of which the commonest was 'go away', and you had to beat the price down to a quarter if not an eighth, because you can't believe a word an Arab says, least of all when they swear—the only language they understand is deceit; and after they pushed themselves in and left no place for Jewish labourers to work, one fine day they suddenly got together in their masses and attacked the settlement in a wild screaming mob with ululating women ready to loot and plunder, a terrible, savage, uncivilized, murderous mob, until finally after shots and shouts and the intervention of mediators they returned home, and the world was saved, the settlement like a small island surrounded by a sea of Arabs, like a world of darkness around the little light.

Because who knew about the Arabs where she came from. Nobody had ever talked about them, and in the midst of the constant discussions, lectures and arguments back there in the Volhynian forest on the bank of the River Styr, which flowed slowly with a contented, shady calm, and received quietly and almost indifferently the most powerful of the songs of the homeland, and the finest of the proofs that only in our own land could we find our homeland; they, the Arabs, were never there, in any place or in any argument, in any considerations and certainly not in any songs, they simply did not exist—just as in the shadowy forest there were neither camels nor donkeys nor any of these prickly wild shrubs, although actually there were wild shrubs in the songs, and these very shrubs, so they sang, we would uproot when we returned to our land and tilled our fields, well-watered Zionist dream, and we would plant new trees brought from overseas. Moreover, since the end of the war, Mummy had been making plans to bring her brother Duvid and her sisters

Hinde and Dvoirenyu here, and her mother too, who would be the grandma and be called the Bobbeh when she came, and they would open a restaurant or a sewing workshop and a proper life would begin in our land, because all we want is peace, Mummy insisted, we just want to build the homeland, and what do they want from us, all those desert Arabs, what have we done to them, apart from bringing them medicine, enlightenment and a culture of cleanliness. That wooden gate is all that divides us from them. Almighty God.

A rumour is going around now. Someone who has just entered through the wicket gate that was opened and immediately closed behind him. They listen and their faces change. They listen and fall silent. The corners of their mouths turn down. They do not know what they can do. They listen and seem not to understand. And even when they have all understood there is nothing more to say. And it goes on doing the rounds, the thing that was said, that 'they've butchered the cobbler', not denied, not understood, except that it is terrible. The Georgian cobbler who used to sit on the street corner further down towards the sea. What is 'Georgian' what is 'butchered'. And he always had some nails in his mouth and he hammered them into the sole that rested on a last held between his knees. There's a book—is it *Baron Munchausen?*—where there is a weird picture of some people who are carrying their cut-off heads, their necks smooth and headless. Is that what it means to be butchered? Will they sew the heads back on again afterwards? Or is it like chickens when Mummy has plucked them and you can't bear to look? And what is it like to be 'wounded'? What happens to the 'wounded'? They lie on the ground and the blood flows out of them like from a tap, and people tend them and bring them food from the houses, and collect loaves of bread for them from house to house, and yesterday there was a hollow crust among them, as though bread that you don't eat is good for the wounded. And where is Daddy? Now his older brother appears and Mummy tells him off, where have you been and what are you up to now, he and the boys of his age, all nine or ten, all ragged and barefoot clutching huge chunks of bread and jam in all manner of states; there is no way of telling that they have not taken wing and circled the courtyard that is closed with the big brown closed, lying gate, have been out in the streets, running from alley to alley, they may even have seen that butchered cobbler, and in another moment they may vanish again and who knows where they will fly in their ragged barefoot band, his older brother and his ragged band like a flight of birds, who, if they are not playing in the street with a ball made of rags, are playing with a pair of sticks, using the big one to hit the smaller one that is sharpened at both ends, and if they are not playing marbles and his brother is the champion they are playing fivestones which is more of a girls' game and his brother is the second best; and now without fear, anxiety or caution they are flying from a rooftop to a wall between houses and from a street corner to the lintel of a gate and see everything and sometimes they even throw a few stones and escape like flying birds.

His older brother has never been fascinated by the train travelling in its hollowed-out cradle—a train is just a train—although occasionally he and his flock of birds slip on board a train at Tel Aviv and disembark merrily in Jaffa, without paying a penny, and he has never taken the time to build sandcastles on the beach, but he leaps into the water and swims far out to sea like a young dolphin, he has never been caught reading *Hashiloach* down to the printer's name and date of publication, or the worn copy of *Sefer Ha'agadah*, or even *Munchausen*; his older brother is a whinnying colt outside, he has never been alone on his own, he always runs around with the others, flying with his splendid mane, he has never pushed away Mummy's cooking, he always licks his plate and asks for more, to the evident delight of Mummy whose eyes devour her adored son, while she adds a little sweet wine and plenty of sugar to the younger's semolina so that he will not refuse it as well with I'm not hungry—he is so lean and skinny and insubstantial, nothing but a pair of staring eyes and his mother's sorrow. More than once has Mummy repeated to him, in moments of despair, the story of how last summer when he had fallen seriously ill (dysentery?) and the local doctor did not know what to say, and there was nothing left of him but a little smell of his loose diarrhoea, they took him to Jerusalem in the train, they anxious about a hospital and he fascinated by the train journey, when they got to Ramleh station, and the engine was detached from the train and taken to be filled with water from a big canvas hose that emerged from a big iron pipe with a circular stopper that the man turned and opened while the other man on the neck of the engine guided the tube into the boiler that drank and drank without stopping, preparing and filling copiously what would later be turned into thick white steam, there in the middle of Ramleh station that was full of people jostling to get off or on with bundles and baskets and Arabs shouting and Arab women dressed in black with masses of coins hanging on their faces and tearful children pressed to them, and a sickening smell of tobacco and an unwashed stench, in the midst of all this he had disappeared, that thread of a boy who almost snapped, he was so skinny and lean, and the train would soon hoot and move off and the child was not there, until Daddy had a flash of inspiration and rushed over to the place where they were watering the engine from an iron pipe the end of which was inside a canvas hose the end of which was inside the engine, and at its feet unnoticed and wide-eyed the small child stood, not replying to Where did you go to, or Why didn't you say, or We were looking for you everywhere, or The train almost left without you, he only replied to Daddy's hug when he stopped speaking with a little hug of his own, and through all the bundles and pushing and the stench of tobacco Daddy pushed a way for them to Mummy in tears and all hugging each other being jostled and climbing up and resuming their places in the carriage, and there standing on the bench and not taking up any place on any bench he stood with his eyes fixed on the track only he would never have anyone to tell about what he had seen and nobody in the world would ever be interested in hearing anything. And when they got to the Hadassah Hospital in Jerusalem, Mummy told him, the doctors did not know what to tell her and the nurses would only nod, and they did not stroke the child's head because he was so horrible, so thin, so smelly, and he was nothing but eyes, and one day the head doctor said to her, Mummy said, Madam, the head doctor said, you are still young, you can have more children, strong healthy ones, while this weakling… the doctor said indicating the child, and she could not finish telling what the doctor had said to her because she was already sobbing and stammering in her tears, and the story never ended. Mummy is very emotional, and now as she feeds him one spoonful of 'something new and really tasty' that she has made for him specially, and he just holds the contents of the spoon in his mouth without swallowing, and she says to him 'swallow my little horror' and she is sorry she said horror so she says 'swallow my little *kvatchuk*' and she is sorry she said *kvatchuk*, and even though she is sorry and regretful both words are swallowed up by him, and then sometimes she brings a damp letter she has just written, and she is so moved when she reads him what she has written, in a voice that starts out almost singing and ends up almost sobbing, 'Fly oh fly my missive,' she reads, 'sing my words to my heart's desire'—that is how they used to write then, and that is what she read to him in a singsong, sending to each of her heart's desires greetings and longing, hugs and kisses, from a heart as full as a vase is full of flowers—and so that the child will not be cut off from what she lost when she left behind the forest and the river she draws for him on the oilcloth on the empty kitchen table three clear dots that are the triangle at the heart of the world: here is Bromel, here is Luck, and here is Brestchke, Volhynia District, she tells him, all of them on the River Styr or its tributaries, all in the dark forest, members of her family live in all of them and everyone she knew made a living from those wonderful, calm, sweet forests, until she cannot refrain from picking the child up, he weighs nothing at all, and hugging him and squeezing him firmly but gently to her heart, and kissing him noisily.

Glass

All of a sudden the wicket opened and a lot of people entered all at once in a jostling mass, and Daddy was there too, clutching the milk pan in one hand and the iron bar in the other. They had been held up at the entrance to the neighbourhood and could not get back. Difficult things were going on all the time, not only the crowd from Jaffa but also the Arab policemen, and the British mounted police, and witnesses had seen how, instead of firing on the savage mob, policemen had stood directing them this way, and how a few people who had tried to escape were not allowed to get away, and there were a lot of casualties already, killed and wounded, and they were being taken into town, to the Herzliya Gymnasium; the shops at the entrance to Jaffa were being looted and robbed in broad daylight; to the south among the orange groves crowds of peasants had been seen assembling, with rifles, axes, sticks, clubs, pitchforks, singing and jostling, a dense mass of maybe hundreds of people, and screaming, ululating women, and there was no barricade to stop them, just a single detachment of British soldiers who fired in the air and held them up for a while, but in another moment they would break through and it was not clear what could stop them. And this was no small local disturbance, here on the edge of Jaffa—there were outbreaks all over the country, as though it were all organised centrally, and as though the English government had not made up its mind yet, and some kind of defence or guard was being organised in Tel Aviv and they would come and help soon, or something like that, it wasn't clear yet. It looked as if it was a full-scale war and the Arabs had decided to get rid of the Jews who lived near them and put an end to Zionism, and all the time they were being incited vigorously, and if the British police vans didn't arrive soon or the mounted police or our friends from the Haganah— it was unclear what would happen. That was the way it was.

There was also some shooting from the direction of the sea, people said. And near the Saraya, Government House, in Jaffa, hundreds of Arabs had gathered with sticks studded with nails, they said, shouting that the Jews had started it, the Communists had started it, the Zionists had started it, and the Government was not taking any action against the Jews, and that they were going to march on Tel Aviv now; and they also said that on the other side of the German Colony many people had been seen dragging looted household objects; and from the el-Dir Market rose the smoke of burning shops, and all the big shops in Boustros Street had been closed, and no one could come or go, there was great fear; and there was one man who related how he had been rescued from there by the skin of his teeth, how he had escaped into the Governor's house, how they had brought the injured there, and inside he had seen women and children, and screaming, and crying, and then he had gone to the French Hospital, where there were already some wounded, and the situation was getting more serious all the time, another man said, no longer in a whisper, and it was getting worse by the minute, the man said. And the rumour that the cobbler had been butchered with a knife was correct. And it was true that as soon as the police had cleared the Jews off the streets the Arabs had burst in and they seemed to be in league with one another, and it was true that Arab policemen had fired on the Jews, just as it was true that it would have been enough for a single British policeman to fire in the air and the whole crowd would have stopped, true too that help might come, they were hoping it would come soon, and messengers had been sent at the risk of their lives—it was all true.

He knew Boustros Street, wide, quiet, dignified, built of impressive stone, with those shops that extended back endlessly, full of fathomless treasures, splendid merchandise piled up far into their endless depths, so that everything there was in the world beyond the sea also existed here, in stout barrels, strong packing cases, fragrant new sacks, and such splendid abundance that even when you walked past outside you felt impressed, when you peeped into the lit-up part inside, calm and imposing, and saw the dignified table covered in polished copper, and heavy, dignified men with or without a hookah, with or without a tarbush, you huddled against Daddy for protection and you walked on away from this too-much, this calmly stored-up abundance, into the dark depths, in the heavy peacefulness of those wholesale goods, that had issued forth from the bowels of heavy ships, and would go forth carried on the humps of mighty camels, in chests that despite their weight held a mysterious secret, that may have clung to them from the darkness in which they were stored, and suddenly

Boustros Street was the real centre of the whole world, and perhaps even the temple of real treasures, which he would never attain and which were not here for his sake, or even for Daddy's: they were only here as unsummoned witnesses to this weighty substance that was not for them and felt nothing for them, even when someone here was fascinated by the unknown beauty that was not destined for him, neither the calm nor the confidence nor the abundance and power nor the perfect serenity that could not be harmed by anything in the world or by any worldly upheaval—although, see for yourself, who could have imagined what would become of this Boustros Street, or what would be left of it today.

Daddy called Mummy indoors to talk in Russian so that the children would not understand and even closed the door behind them. But the child from his corner, where he was playing with a bit of junk, saw and heard everything behind his back, what he understood and even more what he did not understand. There was something that grown-ups did not dare know, grown-up though they were. But he was completely swept away by the clear knowledge that everything was collapsing and was about to fall. And nothing would help, not Mummy or Daddy or anyone else, because that was the way it was and there was nothing to be done about it. And even though he was so small and wouldn't start school till next year he knew that this was the way it was. And even if he was a child who could float in the air and could easily fly away, they couldn't trick him or tell him stories, although they always did, especially to overcome his resistance and push a spoon into his mouth. Something inside him could always tell when they tried to evade the knowledge that all was lost, to pretend that it wasn't so. Nothing that he could explain. And even when Daddy and Mummy had a row sometimes, and Daddy stayed quiet while Mummy attacked, and afterwards they said it was nothing, they were only joking, or when Mummy told him seriously that if you didn't eat your soul went scavenging among the pots at night, and it was so frightening that he opened his mouth and swallowed the lot, and only threw it up afterwards, something inside him, even though he wanted everything to turn out well, knew that it wasn't true, and that it was just to calm him, and actually it wasn't like that at all. And really it was all lost. Even though he did not know this word or another word for lost. Or that God is the last hope. Only God.

But God was not in the house. Daddy didn't talk about Him, Mummy mentioned Him often but not truly, and his older brother hadn't even begun to think about Him. Daddy knew some prayers and he sang, very very quietly, sobbing *ya-ba-bim-bam* tunes, and Mummy, who did not have a good ear, also sang all sorts of gushing songs from back home, that quickly merged into various heart-wrenching songs in Russian, embroidered with strong tear-jerking words, but even then God was not in the house. And yet He was the last hope. When it was hard to go to sleep or when you woke up in the middle of the night and everything was so frightening that you were scared to breathe, and the ceiling creaked, and you were not sure if they had all gone away and left you all alone in the world, and you strained to hear if there were any sounds of breathing in the room (and once he heard rapid breathing, almost sighs, from Daddy apparently, and Mummy whispered sh-sh-sh, the child will hear), when a moment fell like a deep well that you fell into, and there was nothing to do except scream if it weren't for the choking, then there was nothing else left, and he turned and spoke to God, and told Him that He was his last hope, and that if He didn't intervene now—everything was lost. With that very word. Everything would be lost. Only God did not reply, He did not answer, He did not speak, He did not comfort, did not say Sleep now My child, or Go back to sleep, it's only a bad dream, or come down and straighten the blanket or stroke his hair. But He heard. That was certain. Because if you God don't hear, he used to say to Him at these hopeless moments, then everything is lost. And when everything that people know how to do is ended and you reach the point where no one knows anything, and your hands are completely empty—who is left then if not you God, and only You are the last hope.

Tam teidel, tam teidel, tam tam, Daddy used to sing shyly, one of his Hasidic sing-songs, and in a kind of ecstasy, under his moustache, that hid many things, and much shyness, but not his sad smile, or his emotion, as he sang in a sing-song and with pure devotion, when he thought he was alone and no one could see him, stopping suddenly when he was caught by surprise. And Daddy would take him on the festivals to the local synagogue, hand in hand, both in their best clothes, and there he would wrap himself in his faded prayer shawl, and even showed others the place in the prayer book, and everything there was tiresome and endless and boring and unreal, and Daddy read in correct Hebrew what the others round about deformed with their chanting, pretending, almost as though they were in disguise, and at the end they walked home in a leisurely fashion, as though they were just passing the time, because that was the way it was done, but God was not there. He was just a little boy who understood nothing, but he knew that there was something here that was not right. Both in going to synagogue and in what there was all the time between this neighbourhood and Jaffa. And even when nothing happened between the Jews and the Arabs, all the time something was happening that they tried to hide and not tell the truth about and not to admit that something was not turning out right. Wasn't this our place? Wasn't it their place? Were we intruders? Were they intruders?

Someone came in through the wicket, and recounted breath-lessly how he had been in town and seen Arabs running around with sticks, and they had almost caught him, he had barely managed to escape, and he had seen how the injured were taken into the Governor's house and the Governor himself bent over them and nursed them and dressed their wounds, and then he went with some Major John who had picked up a rifle and they went together to the pioneers' house where eleven, yes eleven, corpses had been laid out, he had seen them with his own eyes, all new immigrants straight from the boats, and a lot of injured—as he spoke they gave him something to drink but he couldn't—and they had only found a doctor with difficulty, and they had taken some of the wounded to the French Hospital, and there wasn't a doctor there either, then the Governor gave them an army lorry to take them to Tel Aviv, and they said that there was a commotion in Tel Aviv too, nobody knew what, and they also said that a lot of soldiers were being hurried in from Sarafend, and that they might get the situation under control, if they wanted to, but that it still wasn't isn't clear what the English really want, and they also said that there were some Arab policemen who had torn off their brass numbers so they could not be identified, and they were led by a fat policeman, with two stripes on his sleeve, and everyone who was in the know said that even the porters and the sailors had been organized; and they also said that it was some pioneers from Hungary who were working blowing up rocks on the seashore who had repulsed the attack from Jamal Pasha Street; and they also said there was fear in the settlements because of the impending Muslim festival of Nebi Saleh, in Ramleh, and that there were several Jews who were trapped in Abu Kabir among the citrus groves and it was hard to reach them.

Mummy and Daddy went outside and Mummy offered everyone her homemade lemonade, pouring out one glass after another, in silence, as they all watched the big closed wooden gate. It was already two o'clock in the afternoon. It must be the same in the next-door courtyard, and all over the neighbourhood—the gates were closed, and there too they saw that it was two o'clock and there too they did not know exactly what to do now. The wicket opened again and they let in a man who could tell them exactly what had happened at the pioneers' house, because he had just escaped from there and run for dear life. At half past twelve, he said, they had seen bands of Arabs gathering around the building, so they had closed the big gate, but the Arabs had started throwing stones into the courtyard. Then they decided to dismantle the iron bars in the big gate and use them against the approaching crowd. The building was surrounded by now and the shouting was terrifying, but they had stopped the first Arabs who tried to break in and beat them with the bars and they stopped, howling with pain, and then the whole crowd stopped for a moment, but then the stone-throwing resumed from both sides, and some brave lads decided to go out of the courtyard and attack the rioters with the iron bars, and the Arabs were taken by surprise and stopped again, and there was still a gap between the two sides, with only shouts flying across from one side to the other. Then some

Arab policemen arrived, and they thought they would restore order; no one had been injured yet; but then the policemen entered the courtyard and handed out bombs to the Arabs and they themselves started firing at close range and threw a bomb into the building, and then there were two killed and several injured, and the crowd broke in and started looting and stealing and destroying and butchering, and then they escaped and went upstairs to the first floor where they shut themselves in well, not knowing what would happen now, and then, finally, a British police patrol arrived, and scattered the mob by firing, and then they went down and gathered up the dead bodies and the wounded and then it was too much to take, the man said, and he started to sob.

The neighbourhood was arranged around courtyards and all of them were shut and barred. The narrow streets that separated the courtyards were desolate, and anyone who had to go outside ran like a madman. The neighbourhood bore the names Neve Shalom, 'Abode of Peace', or Neve Tzedek, 'Abode of Justice', but where was the abode, where was the peace, where was the justice? The beautiful names looked at the neighbourhood and it looked at them. But sometimes when they didn't turn up on time to fetch him from kindergarten, or when his older brother was asked to fetch him and forgot because he was too busy with more urgent matters, the younger brother could slip out like a shadow and go outside on his own, and Miss Yehudit, the teacher, was too busy to notice that a little bird had escaped from her nest, and he celebrated the gift of freedom quietly and walked slowly and freely along the narrow streets, freely observing things without hurrying over anything. He was not interested in the inhabitants or the owners of the houses but in the truly important thing, how each building stood, plastered in pale and peeling ochre, or how the shabby sandstone blocks peered out, seemingly made to gather shabbiness, and that secret, sad wonder hidden between the peeling wall and the closed shutter, tired with dust, and he also knew the alleycats, and he watched out for certain dogs, and once he saw where a rat went to hide, and he went down on his skinny knees to discover from close up what a column of ants was like and where it was going, and unlike his brother he never leaped and crushed a stray brown cockroach feeling its way with its delicate antennae, swept away by white washing water with a smell of Arab soap, and if he had leaped on it to crush it what would have happened to that cockroach that they called a *juk?*

The kindergarten was also the teachers' training college, of which Daddy was the secretary. It was a big building with endless rooms and storeys, maybe three with a tiled roof, and some palm trees and lemon trees, and there were always people coming and going, young people, and teachers with neatly-trimmed beards, straw hats, ties and walking sticks, all plump and respectable, all pillars of culture, and suddenly here coming towards you was Mr Nisan Turov or Mr Yishai Adler or Mr Yehiel Yehieli, well-dressed and distinguished-looking, and you made way for them in the narrow alley, pressing your back deferentially against the wall and saying nothing until they had passed, and occasionally you could even see Dr Matmon-Cohen, who had one day put up a notice on the wall of the synagogue announcing that he was opening a middle school for boys and girls, and that was how he founded the Herzliya Gymnasium, walking arm in arm with Mrs Matmon carrying a pretty parasol with sunflowers, and you could also see the teachers of the Takhkemoni religious school, always dressed in black, walking past, as well as the boys and girls who began to run and shout only when they were a safe distance away, and beyond the college on one side you came to the bridge over the railway line, and the other way to the disused factory, and on the other side to the engine works and the foundry that belonged to Wagner the German, and beyond that extended the main street that was dangerous to walk along even for Daddy, and that even Daddy avoided.

It was easy to skirt the disused factory, but it was not easy to ignore it, because it was terrible. Once it had been a factory but since it went out of use it had stood empty and derelict. Three floors and lots of windows, all of them smashed, perhaps by stones thrown by the big brother and his gang or by an Arab gang, or perhaps of their own accord, out of despair. Could there be anything worse than the windows of abandoned buildings with their smashed panes. Those window panes that once used to let in the light, set in wide frames, shattered to sharp slivers, pointed like tearing claws, bent, menacing, and what remained of them stood dusty and shabby as though all the spiders had hunted all the flies and left behind only a smeared tissue of spiders' filth, smeared like a terrible, malignant sickness, hard to say what exactly, something desolate, dismal and smashed, smashed bad, smashed ugly, without hope, to touch is to be cut, a cut is incurable, urging you to run away and forget you had seen these sick panes, except that you were trapped and you couldn't run away and it was shameful to run away, and even if you did run away and you didn't see, you'd still see it in your dreams.

He would never be able to escape from those panes of glass, from the sight of those smashed things, the desolation that moaned from their fragments, the frailty that was too weak to withstand, the desperate way they were smashed, abandoned but unable to care, dusty with a dingy yellow smeared on like grease, like some kind of curse, plates of mouldy glass that ultimately you could not escape and whose maliciously curved talons would catch you, curved, dusty and sharp, they would find you and trap you and wound you and give you blood poisoning, dangerous, gloomy fragments, terrifying and dreary, something all finished that yet persisted, that didn't care that it was finished and irritating, so that even a child could tell that it was a vision of failure, those old window panes, malicious and envenomed, frames with nothing behind them, when not long ago the great factory was alive here, and people wandered around opening and closing windows, washing and wiping the panes, until one day failure fell, maybe nobody bought the product, maybe they couldn't manufacture it cheaply enough, because one day they all went away never to return, and there was nobody left to carry on, and days and years went by, and nobody returned or tried again, and everything began to collapse, topple and break, from within and without, all the doors were broken down, and whatever was there was taken, and whatever was left was smashed, and all that was left was a memorial to failure, and the panes or glass or whatever it was broke in the windows and became grim sickly slivers, like a sort of leprosy, and from within arose an intolerable dreary emptiness, that howled yawning with slivers of glass, and despair could be heard scraping at the smashed panes like a gloomy ghost.

When Daddy told about what had been and how it had been, he sometimes told about such things that had begun and not finished and about failures, always. About Stein's pump factory and iron foundry, for instance, here just on the other side of the bridge, which provided water for the citrus groves, or Dizengoff's bottle factory in Tantura near Atlit, which provided containers for the rivers of wine that would be produced at Zikhron Yaakov and Rishon Le-Tzion, or the cork factory here in Neve Tzedek, which provided corks to cork the wine that rejoiced Jewish hearts and the oil that would be made in the He'atid factory owned by Vilbushevitz in Ben Shemen, to provide joyous oil for Jews and soap and cosmetics from the abundance of olive groves in the fertile Herzl Forest, and all these were great ideas based on well-worked-out calculations, all full of living, working Zionism, all of them giving great hopes to a poor nation that it would finally get itself a real foundation and a solid economy—yet all had failed, each one on its own, each for its own reasons, and all were shut down never to be reopened, and turned into desolate ruins, the He'atid factory in Ben Shemen a ruin, the bottle factory in Tantura a ruin, the iron foundry a ruin, and all the workers were sacked, all the managers packed their bags and vanished, and not a few of them embarked on those ships not far away on the other side of the rocks in the sea, and the ships hooted and blew out smoke and vanished beyond the horizon to the west, the last to vanish being the mast because everyone knows that the earth is completely curved.

And how about Zionism? And the forests of oil-giving olives? If every Jew bought the equivalent of a single tree then millions of trees would be planted and make mountains of fruit and rivers of oil, and there would be a fully-equipped factory for oil, soap and cosmetics, and they would have the choicest grapes that would make mountains of fruit and rivers of wine, that would only have to be collected in barrels and bottles, and they would cork them with the corks that would be all ready here and stick on the pretty labels that had already been designed at the Bezalel Academy, and everything was a hundred per cent OK and the barrel factory was already up and running, the bottle factory was already up and running, and the cork factory, and every one of the seventeen million Jews that there were in the world apparently, the majority in Russia and Poland and the minority in the Seven Seas, would be queuing every Friday to buy Jewish wine for kiddush and Zionist oil for anointing, and on Friday evening they would welcome the Sabbath by singing devoutly 'On the day on the day on the day of Sabbath two he-lambs of the first year without blemish, and two tenth parts of an ephah of fine flour for an offering, mingled with oil', and 'the drink-offering thereof is one fourth part of a hin' (the hin being exactly six litres!), and the candles glow and the *Shekhinah*, the divine Presence, wipes away a pure tear—not to mention bathing on Friday with soap and cosmetics from Hod Hasharon—and all so solid and the future of Zionism so well based and so assured and unquestionable, totally well grounded and seriously thought out in all its details, and the labour all well organised and dedicated, only suddenly something went mad, ran out of control, got muddled, went wrong, and suddenly there was failure. Total failure. And that was the end.

It took an effort not to be drawn into the interior of that terrible building. Into that yawning terror, into that seductive abandonment, that tempted you even to reach out and touch a single mouldy piece of glass. It seemed plausible that a witch had taken up residence there. Even outside, broken glass lay here and there, sickly repugnant, lying unconcernedly. To dare perhaps to pick one up. To listen to its sound. And that scraping sound the wind made as it passed between those sick shards of glass, the most desperate grating sound in the world. And it was not clear how one could escape from here, or to believe that there was a different world in the world. Without the whistling of the wind in the pieces of broken glass. He forcibly uprooted his feet and started to run away, and the little basket, with the embroidered napkin that was freshly ironed this morning and that enfolded the two slices of bread with butter and lots of halvah between them—he had secret relations with a dog that loved butter and halvah, and he had practised showing Miss Yehudit the teacher how he wiped his mouth with the napkin as though he had enjoyed himself—was swinging on his arm now light and empty, until suddenly Mummy, who was getting anxious, came running down the lane towards him wrapped in whatever she could hastily snatch up, full of reproaches and recriminations, Thank God mingled with outpoured wrath, but she did not hit him, why should she, she just picked him up with his sandals and his little basket, and just kissed him noisily, not realising how in an instant she had destroyed everything and all that freedom. And that was the way it was.

Mummy is not the only one who is afraid. Everybody in the arcade is frightened. Nobody can say exactly. And Mummy wants her chicks close to her now. She wants them to eat something and to drink something too. But the older brother has already taken care of himself, as usual, and with a concentrated look on his handsome face and his thick brown hair tumbling down over his forehead, with a faint whistle from between his teeth, as only he can do in the neighbourhood, he is cutting a handsome slice from the loaf, spreading it with a handsome layer of butter from the chunk that is floating in water so it will not melt, and with his handsome fingers he is handsomely peeling a young cucumber and slicing it lengthwise, laying each slice on the buttered bread and sprinkling it with a good pinch of salt, and after wiping his fingers on his trousers he fills a carefully washed glass with the remains of the milk, that is still fresh and frothy, and while he stuffs his mouth with bread with one hand he wets his muzzle with milk with the other, looking good and making his mother happy, like a beautiful young animal eating well with a youthful appetite, and Mummy runs her open hand through his tumbling hair as though to comb it with her fingers. Mummy is so anxious for him, that the gods will not be jealous and do something, her fear is apparently unfounded, but even so she trembles in the depth of her heart for this handsome youth, and remember that he was born on the 17th of Tammuz, the day Jerusalem was breached (and it was not long ago that she baked him his birthday cake), and if he was born on the 17th of Tammuz it is obvious that he was conceived on Yom Kippur, and right away she had wept before Daddy, saying that they had done something that was forbidden and that she only hoped the gods would not punish them. It was wrong of them to have got carried away and done that on such a holy day.

On the round rim of the well, on the edge of their behinds, uncomfortable as everyone really is right now, three people sit, with two or three more standing over them to hear, and Daddy, who is listened to because he knows more about Jaffa, even though more than fifteen years have passed since the census that he conducted with the help of the caretaker of the school and one of our Sephardi brethren who was able to find ways into the hearts of the Sephardi population who were terrified of the evil eye that accompanies any census, ever since the census of King David whose direct descendants they are, and eventually published it all in S. Ben-Tzion's journal *Ha'omer*, since when no one speaks about Jaffa without first consulting *The Jewish Population of Jaffa*, 1905, 108 pp., and marvelling at how one man carried off such an exploit on his own, and they are sitting on the edge of the well, twisted, uncomfortable as everyone round about is, and the child cannot hear everything they are saying and cannot understand everything he hears, but he can hear clearly that they are afraid, Daddy too, and the others even more so, and they do not know what to do, sitting uncomfortably on a quarter of a buttock with no more patience for anything, their big hands empty, and no help appearing from the outside. If they come from Tel Aviv or from Sarafend, if the British Governor decides to intervene, or if they should wait till nightfall and leave, and suddenly it seems to become clear how vulnerable we all are here and how, not to mince words, foreign we really are, and how unwanted, and they ask Daddy what it was like in his day in the *moshava* of Rehovot or in Petach Tikva when the mobs broke in there, and surely mobs have always been breaking in, there have always been attacks everywhere, not to revert to the hated word 'pogroms', how did those confrontations end, did they manage with just sticks and spade handles, or was it necessary to have firearms, and was it only when you fired and wounded and killed some of them that they began to retreat, not without getting entangled afterwards in lawsuits, blood vengeance, arrests, fines and bribes, and all the rest of it, and eventually with feigned reconciliation, and how did they manage to hoard firearms in the settlements, and how is it that here they don't have a single pistol, and even those who volunteered for the British army didn't hold onto them when they were demobilised, and why are they sitting here like idiots, and it isn't clear what's going on in Tel Aviv, and Daddy tries to answer frankly, but what does he know apart from stories from bygone times, while what is happening here now at a quarter to three in the afternoon on the second of May how should he know, or what will happen here by nightfall, or in the next quarter of an hour, just as there was no way of telling if these are just stray riots for some reason or another that will go away, or stirred up by some incitement that will die down, or because of the weakness of the British administration that hasn't made its mind up yet, or because of the hostility of the police who instead of stopping the rioters are leading them, or if these riots will never end but will turn into endless wars, and if only they had some arms here just to fire a few shots if only into the air, then everything would change in an instant, even though everything here is much more serious, and there are two tribes, two nations, two peoples confronting each other here, and it's either us or them, and there will never be calm here, there will never be peace, they can't stand each other, they can't tolerate each other, they can't put up with each other, there's only a thin skin barely covering the mouth of the raging volcano. Go, the earth cries here, get out of here shouts the place, go away, scream the streets, off with you, screech the alleys, away with the lot of you, and *Allahu akbar*.

It is becoming increasingly clear that something has to be done, and there is no point, no patience, no solution in sitting here with twisted buttocks on the edge of the well waiting, with silences and mutterings and reminiscences and a sense of shame and we can't go on like this. We ought to go outside and ask in the neighbouring streets, perhaps we should go to Tel Aviv, or go out with iron bars to the Governor's residence, or simply take those bars and go on the rampage and enlist the men from the neighbouring courtyards that are huddled wall to wall, all shut up now behind their wooden gates, some of which have been reinforced with wire, several well-tied layers, and get out there with tens or even hundreds of men and attack the mob on the other side of the neighbourhood, take them by surprise while they are still hesitating for some unknown reason and not rushing into our neighbourhood, or they may have gone home to eat or they may be busy looting, or they may have changed direction, just not to sit blindly like this waiting like this just not to sit gloomily passively helplessly, pick up and go out and not be Diaspora Jews but pick up and go out and do something, it's high time, but first find out what's happening.

That's why they get up from sitting uncomfortably on the rim of the well, dusting the seats of their trousers with the backs of their hands, and rallying all the others, men women and children, get some hush, and it emerges that three will go outside to find out what's happening, and Daddy too because he knows the place better than anyone else and has experience, and Daddy does not forget to take the milk pan and the iron bar and the other two take wooden beams because there are no more iron bars, and baskets because the bread has run out too, and first of all they'll run to the next courtyard and carefully, and from there they will run further on, while here it is best to close the big gate well, and could everyone please go into their rooms, and not congregate, and the scouts will try their best to come back soon with news. Mummy is not happy, she thinks that younger men than Daddy should do the running, but she knows that there is no one here who knows more than Daddy, everything there is to know about Jaffa, even though this knowledge does not hold back her tears, she stands silently saying nothing, just blowing her nose, just hugging with one arm the older brother, who left to himself would take wing and come back at once with all the news that was needed, and more than needed, and with the other arm the younger brother who is trying to guess in his little heart and has no idea how all this will end. And that's the way it is.

Masks

Go indoors and rest a little, go indoors and sleep a little, go indoors and eat or drink something, all suggestions that are blighted as soon as they are spoken and there is no patience for anything, there is nothing to do to make the time pass faster, only Mummy's fear is now exposed and plain to see. But the child gets up and goes indoors, barefoot and small, has some difficulty opening the door, and straight to the windowsill where the dewy *librik*, the pitcher whose water is always cool, though not without a faint smell of mould, and which his brother picks up (it is covered by a fine cloth with snail-like things sewn round its edge to stretch it over the mouth of the pitcher against flies, ants and other creepy-crawlies), tips it, raises it, and pours a fine jet of water straight into his mouth and drinks like a camel, whereas he when he tries to imitate him always misses and splashes all around and almost chokes and coughs a lot for the small amount of water that he manages to drink, that is just about all that has entered his mouth all day, and now he frantically drags the stool that Mummy calls the *tabouret* over and climbs up on it, one knee first and then two bare feet, examines the pile of magazines that Daddy keeps piled up there (and Mummy is always complaining that it's just a dust-trap that attracts cockroaches and is a danger to the geranium that lives in a pot in the shade of the pile with its single sparse flower on a little ironed mat, and Daddy always promises her that he will sort them all out soon and even have them bound and force them into the overcrowded bookcase), wrenches out several magazines from the bottom of the pile, and soon finds what he is looking for in an issue of *Hapo'el Hatza'ir* from 1913 whose price is still marked clearly: 4 matlik, 12 kop., 30 centimes, 6 cents, the equivalent of 8 Egyptian piastres at today's prices, and he soon also finds the advertisement he was seeking, that might save the situation where all those grown-ups have given up hope. There is a man who has a big store full of excellent wares, as described in the advertisement and illustrated in the picture that accompanies it, a choice of clocks and watches with

Hebrew numerals, jewellery, spectacles (on medical prescription, it says), and also electric torches (by means of which a man can see without being seen, it says), all at reasonable prices, and also mandolins, violins, flutes and other musical instruments, all at Mr Yitzhak Salzmann's store in Jaffa, opposite the Russian Consulate, and he delivers to all settlements and towns in the country, by post, and only afterwards, right at the bottom, Just arrived: a wide range of Browning and Webley automatic pistols and various other systems (what is that?), with all types of ammunition, also hunting guns, there is a wide range, so why not go there, why not run now straight to Mr Salzmann and take all the guns from his big store, and fire some shots right away from the various systems of pistols and the hunting guns at the crowd and in the air, and they will scatter in every direction and the whole thing will be over, and then they can give everything back to Mr Salzmann, and pay him for the spent cartridges.

The only worry is that now in 1921 nothing may be left of the things that Mr Salzmann had in his blessed store in 1913, because there have been no similar advertisements since, and also even if he has got guns, would Daddy shoot and kill a living Arab? Daddy can't stand this, and even now with the iron bar surely he only intends to frighten not to kill, just to scare them off by waving the bar and shouting *yallah yallah*, and not really hit anyone, if he knows his Daddy. He himself would not even be able to look at those wounded people. He wouldn't dare to see their severed heads lying next to them on a cushion with all the bare flesh, crushed and bleeding, as you see with horror at the butcher's, and with the terrible hole in the middle, and that congealed blood, and all that white and that red that makes you want to throw up, and they just lie there quietly waiting for the doctor to come and sew the heads back on, and it's hard for them even to scream with pain, how could he bear to see it, he'd have to run away or faint, with all those dried-up fluids and the dried blood, and maybe the doctor won't succeed and they'll die, and they'll bury their bodies in the earth with their heads separately on a cushion by their side, so you can't even think about it. And the terrible smell of the hospital with all its terrible smells. And it stinks of fear here.

Everything under the arcade stinks of fear now. The men who are standing still and those who are wandering around too, the talking and the silences and the looks towards the gate. They don't even pretend it's not fear any more. Even his corner doesn't protect him any more. And it didn't begin just now. One day suddenly. When those three came. Not long ago. And suddenly three were standing over him. Tall as the ceiling. Dressed in something loud and noisy with a lot of red, but that wasn't what was too terrible to stand. Their faces, their faces, that was just too much to bear, those faces, there was nothing else like them in the world, there couldn't be, something impossible to bear, he could only scream, or run away, if he weren't paralysed. It's impossible to describe what they looked like, it hit your vision so you couldn't see, that unbearable thing, which was the sight of their faces, not just the colour, but the whole face seemed to be back-to-front, to have been deformed or reversed, or you can't say what, but how all of a sudden and then they stood over him, huge and terrifying, all three of them, encircling him, making a savage guttural gurgling sound, an unbearable sound that no human beings could make, something that if it came on you you would have nothing to do but not to exist any more but just be wiped off the face of the earth.

He will never be able to go back to what he was before, he will never be able to remember what he was before, but only from that suddenly and onwards, and how suddenly and he was no longer one child on his own sitting quietly over his bit of junk, making it travel from Jaffa to Jerusalem, suddenly the suddenly fell upon him and stopped everything and surrounded it on every side, making a terrible noise, it's impossible for a thing like that to be possible, and it's impossible for a thing like that to exist in the world, and if it is possible everything is lost, and if monsters like these are possible and stand over you and roar at you, then that creature in the sea is also possible, that you know how some day it will silently emerge, and snatch you in its filthy jaws, and close on you with its teeth, and carry you off held in its mouth, and it will start to close its fangs and crunch you, and you will be crunched in its mouth, and it will feed you to its drooling offspring too, with its dead glassy eyes, and that's the end, and the sooner it's over the better because there is no more strength for anything. Oh, God.

Three terrible things stood over him gurgling, and only afterwards when they came to pick him up from the ground shrieking soundlessly and sobbing lifelessly, and tried to tell him that it was nothing at all and they were just masks and today was Purim, and they had only gurgled to disguise their real voices, and to collect Purim gifts with laughter and clowning, they were just friends of his brother's, Yigal and Go'el and Yiga'el, with their freckled faces and Mummy's creams and colours that they had smeared on themselves and Grandma's rags that they had dressed up in, and even after they cuddled and kissed him and told him it was nothing and he'd just had a fright and there was no need to be so alarmed by what was just masks after all, and he shouldn't be foolish enough to think they were really like this, they'd fetch them over, since they had run away in a panic because they thought they'd killed him from panic, and he'd be able to see that it was nothing and it was just a Purim prank after all and just for fun, but he only screamed no no and no, and didn't want to see them, didn't want, didn't want, and just buried himself under the bedclothes, with just his feet flailing, and no one could do anything and perhaps, as Daddy suggested, it was best to give him something to drink and let him calm down slowly, such an excitable child, Daddy said, isn't it terrible to be so sensitive, Mummy said, and she also said, no my child and no my sweet, and look Mummy's here and Daddy's here, and it's nothing, it's only Purim, but nothing calmed him down and the world was lost, a world in which there were such monsters and they were possible, simply possible, and the sea monster too that had started to gnaw at him and he heard how he was being crunched like a nut in its drooling mouth and its protruding dead eyes, and how at the same instant you could see what it looked like from the outside as it crunched you and from the inside how you were being crunched in its mouth.

It's clear that they were not just children dressed up for Purim. It's clear that they were real creatures and there is no doubt about it.

They should stop telling him stories to calm him down. And there was no doubt about what he had seen or about the impossible that suddenly turned into possible, and if they wanted him to believe them they had to believe him. How can the impossible suddenly become possible? How can yes become no, how can a lie become the truth? Suddenly there they had been standing over you huge and terrifying totally impossible but as true as true, and they were all just trying to gloss over what you knew now for all your life, and why didn't they all leave you alone and go away.

Tired now. Everyone is tired now. Everyone is stressed and exhausted. Four apartments on the front of the arcade and three on each side, and one beside the big gate, and all the residents are outside now, some round the well and some here and there in scattered groups and only the children running about, although with some restraint, and they do not snatch this child away from his corner, because they are playing real games and he is playing at make believe and let's pretend, with himself and the lump of wood that it's enough to move from here to there and that's a journey from Jaffa to Jerusalem, and how can you tell the difference between what is really real and what only pretends to be real. Is Yigal with his freckles real, or was it his horrible disguise that was real, was the disguise on Yigal on the outside or was Yigal in the disguise on the inside? The more so as it wasn't a disguise. It was no good their trying to tell him stories. And the truth is that everyone is alone. A child on his own. And a Daddy on his own too. And the neighbourhood on its own. And all the Jews on their own. God too.

There are always conversations round the well. People are always trying to perch awkwardly on the rim that is too narrow to sit on comfortably. Not loudly or confidently, only with repeated glances towards the gate. I don't have any problems with the ordinary Arabs in the street, someone says. They are being stirred up, another agrees, stirred up all the time, and in the mosques, he says, they frighten them, the man explains, that we'll drive them out and take their place, he says, that we have secret plans, the other agrees with him, to get the better of them, especially now, says the man, when the world is changing, and the English are coming instead of the Turks, and everything is different, explains the man, and maybe they're allowed now and they're testing our strength, and they're permitted to loot in broad daylight and plunder, agrees the man, and they won't do anything to them, the man knows, and they tell them that Islam is threatened too and they stir them up, the man adds, and in the end, to come to our land, and even here in our homeland there are pogroms, another man standing over them exclaims excitedly, even here? He spreads his hands out, and they nod at him, and from those filthy sods too, he can't get any rest. Nobody can get any rest. They just sit on the rim of the well, awkwardly. And the well, like the river, always hears words and speeches, speeches and silences, and says nothing, not even that it's already heard all this often and endlessly, both the speeches and the silences, always awkwardly on its narrow rim, maybe because it is exactly in the middle of the courtyard, maybe because there is no bench in the courtyard, or maybe because it contains, deep down, ancient water, so it's as if they are really on the bank of some river, that knows more and remembers from way back, one speaking and another answering, one speaking and the other saying nothing, and nothing remains of all that except as usual, what's going to happen, what's going to happen.

They're all outside, in this arcade. They're too impatient to stay indoors. And everyone's hot, and the gate doesn't open. It's as though they're in a cage. And they all have butterflies in their stomachs. Mummy is here there and everywhere, talking to these now and then those. Suddenly she can't see the child. He isn't in his corner. She goes inside but he's not there. She comes out but he's not outside, he's not anywhere. She doesn't believe and she still doesn't ask, but there's just a terrible dread, she goes around among them all and she still doesn't ask, because how on earth and where could he have got to, that little boy, the gate's been closed the whole time, and he doesn't know how to leap over the wall yet like his older brother, who's sleeping the sleep of the just now indoors, with a big picture book propped up on his nose, like every time he starts to read; she goes outside again and leans against the wall again, and the wave of pent-up sobbing cannot be restrained any more, and from group to group she goes, and she still doesn't ask and only peers into corners, and among the children running around from corner to corner, and he's not among them, and suddenly she turns with dread to the well, but there are only two or three people there perched awkwardly on the edge of their buttocks, explaining to each other how the Arabs, and what will happen, he couldn't have jumped between them into the well, how on earth, and indoors again but he's not there and maybe she should wake the sleeper, it all seems like a terrible impossible dream and now she unties her long black hair, Mummy's hair, and winds it round one hand while with the other she fixes it with pins tight around her head, she knows how to do it with her fingers and get it right even at the back of her head without looking, as Mummy always does.

Now she starts running around among them all and she even asks if they have seen, and they all get nervous. Feverishly they start peering everywhere, checking in all the apartments in case perhaps, and she is wringing her fingers, and only stops to think calmly and not go out of her mind. Whispers run round the courtyard but the gate as usual is only closed only brown only hot only boring. He was always crouched down in that corner of his, alone with that bit of junk he found and that he's made into an engine apparently, to judge by his make-believe whistles and chuffing, what could have got into his head, and where was she, his Mummy, although on the other hand, he was born wrapped in the caul, which is surely a sign and an exceptional omen, for good luck in life of course, and that no harm could befall him, of course, only those children who were running around have stopped in alarm and they are also looking in their own way, and all of a sudden, yes he's squeezed between them, between the people sitting on the rim of the well, there's someone else there, someone as thin as a line, listening without talking, to those who know more than he does, peering from between them down into the depths of the well, and the darkness within, and one of those sitting awkwardly on the edge hears now and smiles and stops Mummy whose tears cannot be stopped and whose sobs cannot be restrained, with one hand on the head of the child who is pressed to him, all of him less than a single thin line, and with the other hand the man takes Mummy's hand, Here, he says to her, take him, take your son, something far far away maybe from the depths of the well and as though these very words have already been spoken before.

Mummy hugs him, she hugs him hard, and weeps aloud, and others shed a tear or two, Mummy presses him to her breast, and there's no Where did you get to, or Why didn't you say, I've been looking for you everywhere, or *Mein Kind*, she just to her breast hard and with her arms hard, she just tries to stop her tears and her sobs, she just says at last Come, I'll give you something to eat you haven't eaten all day. That's all she can say at the moment, and what he can say at this moment is just Enough, Mummy, down, down from your arms now. He doesn't say that it was all because he had to, because no memory would remain of everything that was said there on the edge of the well if he didn't soak it up and if he wasn't able to repeat it and tell it one day. On the other hand, there was a sort of stirring in the courtyard, as they all remembered that they really hadn't eaten anything all day, and perhaps after all they should have a bite to eat and something to drink. And several women went indoors to see if there was a tomato or a cucumber, or a piece of bread, or something to drink with a bit of lemon or something, and soon the afternoon breeze might come from the sea, even though the big gate was shutting out the outside world and the breeze, and it was also as though, suddenly, they could hear voices from outside, or a movement or something, and suddenly there was a frantic hammering on the wicket, they opened up and someone dashed in, out of breath and bleeding, he was wounded.

It's nothing serious, he says breathlessly, it's nothing he says, at the end of the street opposite Shmuelevitch's house, they tried to break through there, but we didn't let them, with sticks and shouts we stood there across the street, he tells breathlessly, and they stopped, and we are standing there, and now we need everyone who can to take a stick or a beam or something and come with me quick, we've got to stop them there, and fast, these wounds are nothing, now they're trying to break into Barnett Street, and we've got to stop them there, and someone's gone to get help from Tel Aviv, so who's coming? He is panting and has difficulty drinking the water they give him, and he's standing at the gate, and only lets them wash off the blood, and someone just tries to bandage his arm with a torn sheet, and three or four with sticks have already joined him, and now another joins him, but his wife clings to him, Not you, you're ill, he shakes himself free and stoops at the wicket and runs after them, and others peer after them through the wicket until they disappear round the bend, and they close the gate and are alone now, as though they have been duped.

Is Daddy there, at the barricade? It feels narrow and crowded and small and pointless here now, as though they're imprisoned. It's dreary now and everything is a pity and unnecessary and terrible and pointless. Even the fear can be felt now as though it's too hot and sweat trickles down your back. Nobody speaks and they shouldn't speak, and Mummy who is still wandering here and there, going indoors, coming out again and leaning against a column in the arcade, looking for the child with her eyes, and seeing him with his eyes fixed on the roof, where a dove is landing on the tiles, how she curves her body, flexing her wings to stop against the wind, spreading her tail wide to stop, stretching her legs forward for the landing, coming down and taking a step, and already she is totally terrestrial, the transformation of flying to walking seems to enfold no wonder, she hops along as though this were all her nature, and straight afterwards her mate lands too, stops, folds his wings, and croons to her lovingly.

Where is the Georgian cobbler now, where are the man and the woman who were lying dead on the ground at the pioneers' house, where are all the people they found dead there afterwards, all new immigrants who arrived yesterday and could not yet tell their right hand from their left, and suddenly they have been murdered. Now there is movement in the courtyard, they are discussing whether to pack their bags, in case they need to leave suddenly for Tel Aviv, or to run away in a hurry. Or if somebody shouldn't go to the next-door courtyard to find out what. The children have almost all been gathered in that corner, they are tired and don't know what, nobody knows what. The thin walls and the wooden gate are all there is now to protect the children. Recklessness. The whole idea of a Jewish neighbourhood next to Arab Jaffa, living from each other by day and separating at night, the enlightened, the clean, the cultured, the builders of the Land on this side and the natives, the backward, the filthy, who have caused the desolation of the land on that side. Not just Jews (Daddy calls them 'our brethren') against Muslims (whom Daddy calls 'Mohammedans'), not just immigrants against indigenous people, not just the progressive against the primitive, Europeans against Asiatics, but as if it were as simple as that, as if they could sort out their differences peacefully here of their own accord, without a wall between them, without iron gates between them, without weapons for the day of reckoning—what is this: naivety, folly, or criminal behaviour? Mummy is looking for someone to talk to. It's hard to be alone. And it's hard to talk. And the truth is that until it happened no one gave it a thought. Or if they did they didn't say anything, or if they did they didn't talk seriously. On the contrary, Daddy used to say, and he even wrote it in his *Hapo'el Hatza'ir*, that the longer we live together, Jews and Arabs, the more this neighbourhood will do good things, and acquire good habits, and the best fence there is, Daddy said, quoting someone or other, is good neighbourliness. And it sounded wonderful.

She, who was born and raised far away and has been here for twelve years, with all her heart and her dreams and all her loved ones still on the River Styr in Volhynia in the dark forests, and some ignorant Arab woman who was born and raised here and her parents and grandparents were born in this place, and the alleys of Jaffa have been the whole of her world for generations, are they really of the same worth and can they really have the same rights, and can all their fear of each other somehow be transformed simply into good neighbourliness with no fences? And is there a place for my children and her children where they can play together without a high wall separating them? Is that naive, foolish, or criminal? And the shouts we can hear now, not far away at all, and suddenly, God, shots too, and more shots, what's going on? Should we get indoors? What if a stray bullet hits somebody now, and the fear seems to have recovered its strength, the suffocating panic and nausea. They stand and listen, trying to guess where, or who is firing, and where from and who has been hit. And no one knows anything. Imprisoned in blindness. More hammering on the wicket gate, and they open up and two rush in, one with a lot of blood, and the other, A tourniquet, he says, shouting quietly, quick, he says breathlessly, and the first man is completely pale, and somebody, that same woman who knows, again tearing that sheet, is leaning over him and looking after him, telling them to fetch water, please, and fast, and the other man can talk now, It's there, he says, in Barnett Street, he says, the boys from Tel Aviv have arrived and they are returning fire, and it may help, he says, and Scissors too, says the woman, cut the trousers all round, and she bandages the leg tightly above the knee, and the blood is quickly soaked up, the red stains everything, she has a piece of wood and she twists and tightens the tourniquet with all her strength, and the man is pale or fainting and they recognise him, he's a man from the next courtyard but one, lay him down now, and send for his wife or somebody, and what else is happening there? And who else did he see, and has anyone else been injured? It's lucky the boys from Tel Aviv have come, the second man says, thanks God, he says, at last, and with pistols, and they say some British soldiers are on their way and they say they saw them towards the market, because they heard some lorries there, and it'll be enough if they fire their heavy machine-guns for all the attackers to withdraw, and it's high time, he says, because it's been more than two hours now, and all the time, right on the other side of the street, the shops have been broken into and they are looting and stealing in broad daylight, and that may be what slowed their attack, the looting fever, he explains, drinking some water. And he wipes his sweat away, and the injured man needs to be got to the doctor in Tel Aviv at once. And who has seen Daddy? And what's happening in the direction of the market? And they also say, the man has more to say, that the disturbances broke out everywhere at the same moment, and in Tel Aviv they don't know where to send help first. And they say that in

Abu Kabir to the north, in some house among the orange groves, they are trying to rescue a Jewish family and some other people who live with them there, and they say that Brenner is there too, but it's hard to get a military escort and an automobile, and they're bringing in the injured from all the surrounding areas and there are many dead, more than thirty, he says, and they don't believe, more than thirty? And it's not over yet and he has to run now and get back and they must get a doctor to this man, who is deathly pale, and gurgling and groaning.

Tempted to go and look at the wounded man, but terribly frightened. More shots and then more, and they listen, and it's hard. Now it's really afternoon outside. It's already past four o'clock. And today is not going to be a good day. And it's not just any old day, it's a day they will remember forever. A day people will never stop talking about. It doesn't matter that it's hot, and that there's no breeze from the sea, and nothing matters now, and no one knows when the gate that was closed yesterday will be opened again, or who will come back though it whole. They don't know, they simply don't know and all day long they simply don't know. All day long they are simply waiting to know. Lucky is the man who is already in the evening hours now, and can look back and see us now in the afternoon not knowing anything of what he knows. He knows how it ends, and he knows what happens to Daddy, and how and when he will return home. If only that man who knows already would reveal what he knows, so that this terrible pressure in the tummy would go away. And God, too, knows, because after all everything happens according to His word. And nothing will happen to Daddy. He will come back, Daddy always comes back in the end, with the milk pan in one hand and the iron bar in the other, because Daddy is a good man, and has never hit anybody, with any iron or with any bar. He'll be back soon. I promise you.

Too many things are happening outside all the time. As though we had to finish it all in a single day. They are already talking about dozens killed, and huge numbers wounded. They are talking a lot together about everything, and all together, but they don't manage to know the pain of a single man, nor who nor what his name is, nor who at home will wait for him in vain. Frantic hammering on the gate, and the throat constricts, now they've come with a stretcher to take away the wounded man and move him to Tel Aviv, and the automobile is waiting with more wounded, and they don't know much about the shooting or the situation, they have difficulty taking him and getting out with the stretcher and there's lots of blood all over it. If there is anybody here who knows how to pray and who knows the right prayer they should start praying right now, but if He up there can see what it's like down here why does He need to wait for a prayer to start doing something, surely He can see? Daddy will come back, there's no doubt about it. Because we can't do without Daddy. Because without Daddy everything will be over, and it won't be worth staying if he isn't here and if there is someone who knows what will happen and who knows what everyone will know when the sun has set I'm asking him to tell me, just me, I won't tell anybody, if there is someone who knows now what God has decided will happen, because surely nothing happens in the world without Him deciding it will happen, and only we don't know anything, and we don't have the strength to wait to know what will happen.

Daddy never says anything. Daddy always gives in. Daddy always gets pushed aside. Daddy thinks that everyone else comes first. Work comes first, Mummy comes first, the children come first, and the land comes first, after he gave in and left the land, and the experimental farm, and didn't join his comrades who went off to build Nahalal, that he had spoken and written so much about, and had so wanted for himself and his two sons to be peasants in this new Nahalal that they are building there now out of the swamps and the heavy soil, they could almost have had their own field and their own plantation and their own cowshed, their own little house, together with his good friends Aharon Ben-Barak and David Ben-Yishai and Natan Hofshi, the vegetarian, and he would not have to pull up his roots and wander every year or two from one place to another from one conquest to another from redeeming one wilderness to redeeming another, but settle down finally with his sons on their own land under their own roof, under the giant mulberry trees that Mummy didn't want because they attract flies and filth, just as Mummy didn't want Nahalal and she'd had enough of living in the desert, of bringing up children like little Arabs, not seeing people or going to lectures or going to hear the baritone Har-Melekh accompanied on the piano by Hopenko, or hearing Mossensohn lecture on the biblical prophets or Bistritzki's lecture on the problem of our modern culture, in the hall of the Herzliya Gymnasium, or Brenner's lectures on *Mendele Mokher Sefarim*, which he had published as *Towards Self-Esteem* in three parts, and which A. D. Gordon had not been satisfied with and had written against explaining why he disagreed, and on Saturday afternoons they debated with Aaronovich and Rabinovitch about who was right, and at the Hebrew theatre they were putting on *Hasia the Orphan Girl*, which apparently had some good moments, and in Jaffa opposite the Kaminitz Hotel Mrs Atlas had just opened her ladies' fashion shop, and it was beginning to be a real city, and then to get her brother Duvid and her sisters Hinde and Dvoirenyu here, and her mother who would be a grandmother for the boys and they would call her the Bobbeh, and then at the festivals they could all sit together round a single table spread with a big white cloth and wine and fish and every delicacy, they would finally be able to sing in perfect tranquillity *and purify our hearts to serve You to serve You to serve You in truth, in truth and peace,* and her eyes filled with tears at the thought.

Daddy always gives in. And he goes out early in the morning, because he gets up early, and before he leaves he gets breakfast ready, puts a kettle on the paraffin stove, makes sure they are all well covered in their beds, and creeps out of the house quietly, always quietly, so as not to disturb, this Daddy, to the Women's Teachers' College, he sits there at a desk, working on account books, faithfully adding up columns of figures, and at the end of the year when they all have their picture taken he does not go outside to have his picture taken because he is too shy, so now there is no picture of him on the wall, standing in the second row on the left, or the third row at the end, or four rows above Mr Turov or to the right of Mr Azariahu, who sit proudly in the front row with neatly groomed beards, their faces beaming with culture and dignity, but with an ill-at-ease, crooked smile he peers out of the pictures of the committee of *Hapo'el Hatza'ir*, an indistinct face in the shadow of the heads crowded together in the foreground, so that at the bottom, among the names of all those historic personages, the publishers of the Yearbook have added a request to all those whose names have been omitted for some reason to write to the editors and identify themselves, Post Office Box such-and-such, and even his great articles are not signed with his name but always with a pseudonym, and only S. Ben-Tzion, in *Ha'omer*, almost by force, made him sign his name, in full, because this is science, he said reproachfully, because it was a huge task he had done by himself, he argued with Daddy, and because in the future nobody will be able to know about Jaffa without reading and studying what you have written here, and in the universities, he almost shouted, they will examine students on this material, and nobody will take an unsigned article seriously, or one that is signed with some kind of Ben Israel or B.I. or even Z.S.

Is it possible to talk to someone who does not answer? Everyone is silent because they have nothing. And because there's no one who does have anything. They are all alone and each one is alone. Not just the little child. And no one has anyone to tell him or to listen to him. As though a ring of solitude has closed in round each of them. And soon there will be more hammering on the gate and another man or two will burst in and again they'll say something that is nothing and then they'll run off again, and again they'll be left here with nothing. Who has it worse, those who are standing there in the middle of the firing and the dead and wounded or those who are shut up here to wait and be rent by anxiety fear and nothingness. Because what they feel here now is that they are just bursting. And everyone is standing or sitting or wandering around and is just bursting. It's as if we have been abandoned and there is nothing, this is all there is left, so small and so forsaken. It's hard to say precisely how it's hard but it is terribly hard. Even Mummy who is always involved with others is alone now, and only the older brother is always not alone, and if he's not asleep he is always involved with the others, but even this courtyard which is always involved with the others is alone now, and perhaps only after many years have passed, when he is grown up and knows things from many books that he has read too much, one day he will stop when he suddenly reads things he has long known but couldn't say because he was too small, but he really knew them precisely when he was still uncorrupted. And as though a chrysalis of blind feeling suddenly opens and spreads wings that were prepared long since, after a long time, forty years or more, he suddenly comes across words that he could not say when he was little, but if he had known them he would have used these very words, and continuously since then, Our Father in heaven, so he found in a book one day late in his life, in a moment of silence when a man stands solitary and abandoned, he read in a book, when he does not receive Your voice and imagines that You have abandoned him and that he is abandoned, that moment, he read, is but an instant of silence in the midst of a conversation. Only an instant of silence in the midst of our conversation, he read later what he knew before, many years ago, and exactly so.

Hammering on the gate again and some people come in. Something is changing outside and it seems it's about to be decided, they can report, and they are from the next-door courtyard, where they have an attic from which you can see more. They'll be coming from Tel Aviv soon, they say, and the British army is coming too, they say, those soldiers with shorts down to their knees and cork hats and above all with those beautiful dark rifles and thick polished leather ammunition belts worn slantwise across their bodies, and their red faces, the faces of children who have been thrown somewhere they don't belong, because one way or another it can't last much longer, they can report, and they've burnt a lot of shops and looted a lot of goods, they say, and two stretchers were carried earlier to the automobile that arrived from the city and picked them up and sped off. And another group from the Haganah, with rifles, is being organised to come openly, they can report, and it all sounds as though you have to believe them. And they have brought two watermelons with them that they thought might be welcome here, and they believe that they are red and good. And that's all for now. They look at each other, as though there is something more to be said, and they nod at each other, and say nothing, and they stoop as they go through the wicket gate and try to smile broadly despite everything, and they are gone, and we are left with the watermelons. And Mummy suddenly stirs into action, she fetches a knife, and puts on an apron, and puts one of the two down on the rim of the well, one hand on top of it and with the other she cuts into it and splits it open, happy to be up and doing something, and no sooner has she finished slicing it than an attentive circle has formed around her to know how red it is, and they all utter a collective sigh now a sort of broad ahhh at the sight of the beautiful inside of the watermelon that now gapes with a real bleeding red, reminding them of something that they dispel with a slight laugh, and slice after slice Mummy cuts and spears on the tip of the knife and offers to each of them with bright eyes, There you are, she says, bless and eat, and on the rim of the well in the end only a little watery red trickles slowly, and the skins, Mummy admonishes—in the bin!

Hammering on the gate and they start coming in one after the other. Two lorries came, they tell, and stooped up the street, and each one had a machine-gun on its roof, a Browning says one expert, and with the two machine-guns with a series of wonderful barks over their heads the whole thing suddenly stopped, as though both sides were just waiting for this, God, how easy, how easy, they say, just two rounds of barking, fairly softly at that, and it's all over, and if they'd come two or three hours ago, all the dead in the pioneers' house and all the slaughter of those new immigrants, so innocent and terrified and before they'd realised what was going on they were already butchered, and all the looting and the pillage, and as if they were really just waiting for the two sides to tire themselves out, they say, and then they came and with one barking round of insultingly brief fire it was all over. Not quite over yet though because they haven't dispersed yet. But they say a detachment of cavalry is on its way here now and they will send them all scurrying home, they may even catch the looters red-handed, and those Arab policemen, who were the leaders of the

rioters, But where was our Haganah, our own defence force? someone asks, and why do we have to be dependent on the generosity of
the English, he says rightly, and as though they're above everything,
and it's only after these natives finish rioting that they come along
and send them all packing, those English, those *goyim*, those over-
lords, he says rightly.

You'll see that they'll make no distinction between the Arabs
and the Jews, and they'll treat the killers and the killed, the robbers
and the robbed all alike, the attackers and the defenders. They'll haul
all of us before the judge together like so many thieves. A man who
has just come in, exhausted, is speaking. And another man who came
in after him is saying, as though continuing what he has been saying
outside, that We should never rely on strangers to protect us, with the
humiliation of having to prove ourselves in the right, and We should
know how to treat the wounded, adds another man, so they don't die
on the way, and Arms and arms, the man says, and The behaviour
of the Arab policemen, other voices add as though continuing from
outside, and a woman runs up to one man and throws herself on
him and hugs him, pressing herself to him and touching his clothes,
kissing him, and he holds her tight and says Good good, good good,
he says, holding her tight, from now on it'll be good, he holds her
very tight, and a woman goes through the crowd searching, asking if
they've seen, and a child is suddenly thrown in the air and his father
catches him with a shout and throws him up again and another shout,
and suddenly there is a hail of gunfire streaming suddenly and slicing
the air, and gut-wrenching panic, and it seems it's not quite over yet,
or maybe this is just how they urge on the stragglers to clear the
street where the looting was, by Barnett Street, on the way to Jaffa,
as a cowherd urges straggling cattle, *ta'i ta'i ta'i*, the cowherd scolds
his herd and hurls his stick at a stray cow who understands and with
a ridiculous gallop and an exaggerated swirl of her udders goes off
to join her obedient comrades. People are rushing in now, fleeing
the bullets apparently, another too, but still no Daddy, and they
report that a gang that came from the direction of the railway lines,
and tried to break into the warehouses taking advantage of the last

minute—it seemed the English hadn't noticed them—were spotted and they opened fire splendidly and they ran away and scattered, and they say that Mordechai the Bulgarian was killed defending the entrance to the neighbourhood, a young man of maybe twenty, and his friend who was stabbed has died of his wounds, a young man of twenty-three or so, they say, and they say that there are more than thirty killed, God preserve them, and they say.

In the night they will all meet, the killed, terribly tired, not recognising each other, coming from everywhere, endlessly sad, and they do not know what they are doing here in this place, only that it is dark for them, and frightening for them, and terribly alone. And also it's completely new for them to be killed and they don't know exactly what to do. And suddenly Daddy too comes in, with the milk pan in one hand and the iron bar in the other, very tired apparently, and without a word he hands Mummy the milk pan and hugs her, without a word, and something trembles in his face as though he is holding something back, and without a word he puts the iron bar down and rests it against the wall, and he picks the child up and hugs him and his throat is quivering, and not a word, and he lays his big tired hand on the head of the older brother who has already gone to test the iron bar and his strength with it, that bar that no one knows if Daddy has used, or if there is anyone in the world who has ever received it on his head with all Daddy's pent-up force, who seems to have gone off and forced a way for himself with the iron bar smashing heads to fetch milk for his children, and now with these big, strong, empty hands, he stands there and it is clear that he wants to say one thing, quietly, only he is not sure of his voice, that he can say quietly what cannot be said, and Brenner too, Daddy says now, Brenner too, says Daddy, and his voice breaks, he cannot, Brenner too, says Daddy, oh Brenner, says Daddy.

Part three

A leg in the dustbin

Here is Nahalat Binyamin Street and here is Montefiore Street, the second building from the corner, three floors, the first floor.

Montefiore Street is not fully built yet, but just opposite on the corner of Nahalat Binyamin Street a new coffee house has just opened that some call the Kiosk, all spanking new and sparkling bright, and in the middle there is a sparkling frothy soda machine, and the man in the apron takes a shiny long glass in one hand and a magic bottle in the other and he pours in a measure of red or green or yellow syrup and when the amount is right he points the glass at the sparkling tap and shoots a frothy gush of soda into it, raising and lowering the glass as it fills to show how the magic trick works, inclining his expert head, and then this high priest gives the froth a moment to settle and shoots another jet in to take the place of the deceptive froth and fill the glass, turns off the tap, waits another moment, to show the whole effect and to reveal that there is no trickery, then artistically puts the full glass down on the marble counter, pushing it slightly towards the customer who is startled, fascinated, lost for words, and even forgets to feel in his pocket for the half-piastre if he is not one of those who prepare the money in advance and stare in amazement, drumming with the pierced coin on the moist marble, on which there is sometimes a wasp struggling briefly after the sweetness that is melting there before being flicked away by the magician's damp cloth, and for every sip of colourful cold fizzy sweetness taken by the happy drinker—if he is not one of those even luckier drinkers who have been fortunate enough to receive a kind of straw to suck up the paradisiac liquid, which as soon as you put it in tricks you into thinking it has been broken at an angle—the crowd of fascinated onlookers, who lack the requisite half-piastre, stare straight into his throat to watch it going down and to envy his good luck, although on the other hand there are always passers-by on Nahalat Binyamin Street who pause for half a moment with an embarrassed snicker, or perhaps it is because the wet pavement is shiny and slippery, and immediately find the courage to announce that they are not happy at all, because it begins like this, but it's the thin end of the wedge, just see what will become of our young people from now on, what a dissolute degenerate generation will emerge, and at such an apocalyptic and difficult time, and they are lent some support by the great din that bursts suddenly from the throat of the big gramophone with a powerful, outrageous tune that the man in the apron unleashes powerfully all along Nahalat Binyamin Street, totally terrifying the drawn curtains in the windows of those seekers of peace and quiet who have chosen to settle here of all places, not to put up any more with the noise of Jaffa, while the colourful horn of the gramophone, striped in red and blue and shiny silver, only mocks them and gleefully blares tunes the like of which has never been heard before, as the man turns it from side to side with relish and remarks, So, what do you say to this wonderful foxtrot, although those standing round in a circle understand nothing of what he is saying, or what they are supposed to say, and even if you make a detour and turn into modest Montefiore Street, you will be stopped at once by the sight of the sorcerer's apprentice, bent over a sort of brass-bound wooden barrel that he spins with all his strength with a handle as he ladles in more chunks of powdery ice and churns an ice cream capable of watering the mouth of the most extreme ascetic and totally enchanting the watching child.

They call him 'youngster' now, not because he is a young man or because his body has filled out so that he no longer floats like a feather in any breeze that blows; he is only six and is still in the first year at school. Perhaps it is because he is not a kindergarten child any more and does not need to be taken to school (although he does not willingly agree to be left alone in the evening, and they have to promise solemnly what time they will come back, and a dark dread descends upon him even when he does give in and agree), and also because now they live in the city and not in a remote suburb of Jaffa, and in Nahalat Binyamin Street the world is quiet and calm reigns everywhere, including Montefiore Street, the second building on the right when you are facing the sea, to the left of which on the corner that same Kiosk Coffee House opens onto the street with its sparkling frothy soda machine and all its magical wonders and the pavement in front of it constantly sprinkled by the sorcerer's apprentice until it is like a distorting mirror reflecting the sparkling soda machine and the gramophone horn like a gigantic noisy sea-shell, and also reflecting a quivering image of the feet of passers-by who pause to take a closer look, and everything dissolves in the damp of the pavement into a clash of strong colours mingling at their feet, with the frothy sparkling and the colourful syrups, and the red-white of the awning that has opened to give shade from the sun, as long as it is shady and cool and pleasant and interesting and new and proclaiming new joys, hallelujah!

And so every morning with his little basket and his canvas satchel that Mummy made for him and that isn't heavy at all although it cuts into his shoulders because Mummy made the straps too narrow, thinking of the narrowness of his shoulders rather than the weight he would have to carry, overcoming all the new sights in Allenby Street so as not to be late, he hurries to the head of the street that comes out right by the railway crossing, which has a special keeper, who comes out of his little box at precisely the right time, ready to swing the barrier down by turning a big wheel, with a peaked cap on his head and holding two flags, one green and one red, and the people stop and the diligence stops and a man on a donkey stops, and children from all sorts of places and especially those who have been thrown out of classes at school, all of them hanging on the lowered barrier whose dangling slats are still swaying from the effort of the descent, and the engine suddenly arrives like the Sovereign of the Universe, full of power blackness steam speed distance and flight and filling the world till no space remains, the carriages trailing like a tail, the wheels pounding in a three-beat rhythm, and the ground trembling and rumbling, and you always catch for a quarter of a second the face of a passenger who looks out and also catches for a quarter of a second the looks of those looking at him, and something of some saying that has not been said and will not be said remains unrealised, until the last carriage has passed and it is all past, so fast, as though the meaning of life has passed, and you are left alone and terribly ground-bound, and the man turns the wheel and raises the barrier, takes off his peaked cap, picks up his flags, wipes his bald head with a big handkerchief, and then it transpires that after all he's just a man called Haim, and nothing special.

In front of the school is a mighty sycamore tree, and all the climbers and even those who are no climbers are always clinging to some height or other on it, but in time it will disappear completely and no longer exist, this giant tree, and the boys' school will also be moved away from here one day and resettled in Ahad Ha'am Street under the name of Boys' School A, apparently, and this building will become the seat of the Histadrut Executive Committee, which is pronounced as though it were one word, and then it will be turned into the *Davar* newspaper, and Berl Katznelson will come here, and Zalman Rubashov, and many others, all of them serious men with serious responsibilities, and from one of the rooms the secret Haganah will run everything, and then they will leave too and everything will be demolished and replaced by the Central Department Store, apparently, on Allenby street, and nothing special, and even the railway will exist no more and no more trains will pass.

It was easy to get to school, but he doesn't remember much about what happened there, or what he did, or what the teacher said, or who exactly she was, or what she could teach a child who already knew how to read and write, except perhaps how to sit quietly, and that was just plain unfair because there was no one quieter than he was, and not to daydream, and that was just right, and to cover pages in drawings with coloured pencils, and there was always an engine hurtling onwards in a splendour of smoke and steam, in breaktime it was impossible to find him anywhere because he was always up at the top of the sycamore tree, hovering on the thinnest and most delicate of branches quite safely, because he was lighter than any branch, as light as light could be, both to be the first to see the train arrive and also to watch from above the children running around beneath and not to be running around with them, and it was also easy to go home from school at the end of lessons, even if you did have to rein yourself in and not stop in front of all the countless novelties that accumulated in the street day by day. And even his older brother was already in Year 6 and no longer had to look after his younger brother, but was completely free during the wonderful breaks between the dreary lessons, apart from Daddy's threats when Mummy insisted repeatedly that he had to reprimand the boy and the year was passing and he would remain an uncultured ignoramus, and the note that he had to bring home from his teacher to testify that he had not flown away from all the bother of lessons and evaporated, or that he had come to the lessons but had not done his homework, even though he knew that there was not much connection between Daddy's reprimands and the things he threatened to do, although all of a sudden, in extreme cases, even Daddy could do something terrible, all the more terrible because it was Daddy who did it—although not without Mummy watching from the sidelines and goading him on to do it—like that time when his brother won a huge number of glass marbles, maybe as many as a thousand, and then it came out that he had won them instead of attending Scripture and nature study and free composition classes, and Daddy snatched the pretty bag the brother had made from colourful scraps of cloth, so strong and splendid, and closed with rubber bands, and ran straight to the toilet (that Daddy called the throne room) with it, and hurled the bag with the thousand marbles that the boy had won and that he knew individually into the bowl, and pulled the chain so hard it nearly broke, and the elder brother fell down on the floor in a paroxysm as though he had been smitten by God. And the rest is best left unsaid.

But when classes are finally over, and the wonderful after-school time arrives, you can always tell them at home that there was an extra lesson, or you have been to an extra gardening class and dug in the sand, or have been rehearsing the end-of-year play, *Daniel and Belshazzar*, or *Jephthah and his Daughter*, or *Trumpeldor, in Galilee, in Tel Hai*, or that you have been putting up posters on shops saying 'HEBREW, SPEAK HEBREW', or any other plausible excuse, and then the whole fun-loving, long-legged gang are free to kick a rag ball around exactly as they have recently seen a team of British gunners from Sarafend play against a team of British police from Jaffa right here, on this empty sandy plot of land, how they kicked a real ball between the posts that their Arab had put up for them in the sand, red shirts and socks versus green ones, sinking into the deep sand that had no pretensions to be a football pitch, kicking with all their strength in the soft sand at their real, inflated ball, going all red, even the greens went red and wet with sweat and shiny with wet, surrounded, apart from their Arab, by lots of Jewish kids burning with envy and aflame with curiosity and with the little English they had calling a penalty *pendel* and a half-back *haff-beck*, and screaming *gol* whenever one side scored, and everything about them was so foreign, so fascinating, so magical, because there is no Maccabi or Maccabi Tel Aviv yet, or Maccabi versus Hakoach, and there is no name of a single football star yet, no brilliant player, except perhaps the brothers Asaph and Amihud who are almost heroes, only they never play with nothing players like us and they and their friends don't play in the sand but were invited and taken in an automobile to the real pitch in Sarafend and there they had a good time, they had it easy, and they smoked English cigarettes with that aroma of theirs, and drank the bitter English drinks, and even spoke English, even as their famous father sat hidden away in his home in Gruzenberg Street for days on end compiling the great Hebrew Dictionary. Nobody imagined then that it was not from them but from us, from the older brother, that a great football player would emerge, a splendid player whose name would be praised in all the Judaean settlements as the fearless right-back of Maccabi Yehuda, whose kicking smashed the opponents' goal and at the same time, in a different way, broke the hearts of the girls of Judaea and its settlements, with his blue-and-white shirt, his chestnut hair and his lithe body of a young god, and his endless generosity as

he bought them sodas and invited one of them to go to the pictures
with him, Rivka, Bilha or Rochale, whose elegant photographs with
dedications in the prettiest, most slanting, girlish handwriting the
younger brother looked at, and after the show, but what happened
after the show the younger brother did not know, nor did he imagine
that anything special might take place afterwards between his brother
and one of them in the darkened gardens, all he knew was that his
brother's glory shone on him too, and they pointed him out as he
passed, thin, light and lean, remarking in reverent tones, there's his
brother's brother, and in this way he went from nothing to being
respected.

And so, even with his small footsteps, the youngster arrives
from school to his home in Montefiore Street in a short while, even
if in that short while he goes from one side of the world to the other,
and at home everything is still new, and on the upper floor a man
does not have what a man sitting in the entrance to his home at
ground level has. If Daddy had not, thanks to the intervention of
his brother Uncle David, who lived in Yehuda Hallevi Street, right
next to the railway line and the level crossing gate in Herzl Street,
which did not lift but opened sideways, and what fantastic luck to
live right next to the railway, and when the train rushed past your
window and whistled as it approached the crossing the whole flat
filled with swirling angels, although Uncle David stopped his ears
and wailed with distress, *oy vey*, such a calamity, and the filth, and
then Daddy got his new job, and Uncle David, who was always a
devoted adherent of Mr Dizengoff, even after Mr Dizengoff relieved
him of the round sum of twenty thousand francs that Uncle David
had earned honestly in Rotmistrivka, Kherson District, in the years
of his unwilling exile after Hadera had struck him down to the very
gates of death, and he had become a qualified accountant and made
a small fortune, and returned to the Land and come running to his
trusted master Meir Dizengoff for wise advice about how to invest
the money to the benefit of both sides, his own and that of the land
that was being rebuilt, and Mr Dizengoff gave him sound advice and
said that it was lucky he had come along at this particular moment

because he himself was just setting up a bottle factory in Tantura, near Atlit, for the wine of Zikhron and Rishon, while his very good friend Leon Stein had already opened a factory here in Neve Tzedek making water pumps, for the citrus groves of Jaffa, Arab and Jewish alike, and Uncle David, whose head was as smooth and clean and shiny as a dried bean, whose hands were soft and clean, who had never touched anything that was not clean, and had always belonged to societies of good people and do-gooders, took the money he had made in foreign exile and divided it in two, half to make bottles in Tantura and half to make water pumps in Jaffa, two much-needed, well-founded and reliable industries, labouring for the rebuilding of the Land, and he looked that they should bring forth grapes, until they both, alas! brought forth wild grapes, and went bankrupt, and he lost all his money, and all he had left was the reserve he had set aside for a rainy day, and again on the advice of his trusted mentor Meir Dizengoff he went and bought a patch of sand in Ahuzat Bayit, which he drew in a lottery with seashells at Mr Weiss's pharmacy, a single plot between Yehuda Hallevi and Herzl, the second building in, right next to the railway as we have said, oh lucky man, and he built a fine spacious building, using rather expensive Hebrew labour, that would later be known as 30 Yehuda Hallevi, where the carpet seller Ben Aharon would move in on the ground floor while Uncle David and his family would live comfortably on the roomy upper floor, until later on both storeys would be demolished to make way for the splendid mass of the Bank Leumi Leyisrael.

But on the other hand, when Mr Dizengoff set up the Tel Aviv Council, which is known as the Municipality, Uncle David was given a desk and a chair from which to run the Water and Lighting Department for Tel Aviv, sixty-eight streetlamps and seven hundred and fifty-six light bulbs, some of which were powered by electricity even before Mr Rutenberg made the electricity, and they had to be switched on and off and cleaned, and the water reservoir and the two black tanks on top of the Town Hall, very strange-looking, Daddy even said like a saddle on a cow, in Rothschild Boulevard, and all the pipes and taps and leaks and rust and water purification, and the water meters and the charges for the water, which was not given away free, a lot of complicated, burdensome work, which Uncle David did assiduously although without overdoing it because you had to watch your health, too, and Uncle David got Mr Dizengoff to give Daddy a smaller desk and a smaller chair in a more remote corner, where Daddy could sit and add up columns of figures as he loved doing, adding, subtracting, multiplying and dividing and working out percentages until evening; and from right at the foot of that water reservoir, avenues were spreading this way and that with their little trees that had trouble growing because of the poor quality of the loose, clean sand, in fact they had been planted there precisely on account of the poor quality of that loose, clean sand, because in that place there had been a big valley before there was Tel Aviv and they had called in the pioneers with their famous wheelbarrows and they had shifted the hills of golden sand into that valley and filled it until the residents were afraid to build there in case the houses they build with their last savings sink into the loose sand, so they decided to plant trees to bind the shifting sand to the firm earth. So Daddy had rented this flat on the upper storey of the house in Montefiore Street, the second on the right as you face the sea; there were hardly any buildings yet on this street, and the sea breeze encountered no obstacle, and the eddies of still salty sand scampered as free as foals all the way along Montefiore Street to the water-sprinkled pavement at the corner of Nahalat Binyamin, by that new café, the Kiosk, they flew with impunity along the bed of the still unbuilt street, which still offered an uninterrupted view of the back of the Herzliya Gymnasium and the yard with the rectangular beds for the gardening lessons, the square for Mr Nishri's gymnastics lessons, and the unrestrained shouting of the boys who ran around frantically, kicking rag balls, throwing sticks and branches for want of stones, jumping and pushing and shoving as though bursting with a superabundance of energy, while the girls, those young ladies with their plaits and their embroidered dresses, huddled in groups and it was impossible to hear from here what they where whispering to each other in girlish whispers and bursting into girlish laughter from time to time, or whether all this was just on account of youthful high spirits.

157

Towards evening the Kiosk Café turns into the centre of the world, it becomes an open flower, a busy beehive, and the middle of everyone's business, brilliantly lit by three Lux lights while numerous coloured light-bulbs hang here and there, and men and women gather, receive and carry full glasses of soda, look for somewhere to sit and bump into friends, and all the time people are meeting, and the man works non-stop, and apart from his assistant there are two girls running around, serving and clearing, but everything is dominated by the gramophone music (music?), that shiny music that resembles nothing previously known, and there is no tune or melody or song, no one knows what is playing because it has never been seen, and the sound comes from the records brought by the man from the Kiosk who does so many things simultaneously, pouring, rinsing, giving change, wiping, talking, laughing, and changing records, in his magic box inside, with its mighty conch of a horn that bursts forth with loud sounds made by no one knows who on the trumpet, flute or ram's horn, or people imitating something or singing themselves, something so shiny, so shamelessly shouting, hiding nothing however much it hurts, saying that it is permitted to say things without fear, just boldly proclaiming all the time that it's there, and if you feel like it you can do it, no one can understand the words because they are in English, they only know, even without asking, that something is happening here that you don't know what to do with but it is something you might even have been waiting for.

It is hard to escape from the music or the din, as Daddy calls it with real pain, as they sit together on the veranda that faces the garden, slightly airless but shielded from the din, sitting hitting the mosquitoes, with a glass of lemon tea in front of them, Mummy, Daddy and a couple of their friends from way back, raising the glass and taking a sugar lump, sipping rather noisily and putting it down, tasting the grape jam that is Mummy's speciality, the men sending the pips flying with a tongue movement straight over the veranda railing, while the women politely remove them from their mouths with the tips of their fingers and deposit them on their teaspoon or saucer, and they are constantly startled by the din, they should move away, or ask the municipality to do something. But all unawares, the youngster, who is sitting at their feet on the steps seemingly not involved and only busy with some undefined things of his own, notices that Daddy's fingers, a little changed because for some time now they have held nothing thicker or heavier than his thin light pen at his work at his desk in the Town Hall, are drumming on the railing, abstractedly or concentrating, not on account of the idle chat on the veranda, and suddenly his fingers are tapping out the right rhythm, carried away by the strange new rhythm that the back of the building has not managed to dull, and with his sensitive ears he is making his head and shoulders dance without moving, and only his fingers, in an unlearnt movement, are dancing for him as though they know something that has not been heard here before, and they don't know what to do with it yet or whether it's allowed, and a moment later when he notices he clenches his fingers in a panic and looks to see if he's been spotted and gives one of his familiar sighs, *ach vey*, as though he only means to say that it's the boy's bedtime and not as though it means 'Just leave me alone', an expression that is quickly effaced to end as usual with 'I give in'. And then Mummy says that there's the doctor going to the neighbour across the way again, she must have taken a turn for the worse, maybe they'll take her to hospital, and everyone looks in that direction, by the dim light of the paraffin lamp.

Changing times, says their friend from way back, sometimes I feel like Rip van Winkle, he says with a chuckle, and he too has a moustache and a shirt with an embroidered collar because it's his nice shirt for after work, maybe I'm left over from the last century, I am a native of the last century, he says with a chuckle and they sense that the conversation on the veranda has suddenly shifted to regions that are not spoken of, or that are not even decent, as though they sense that they are in the presence of something they cannot control, and they do not know yet whether to accept it, or to reject it, like the illness of the woman next door whom the doctor comes to see, which he can't get rid of or come to terms with. What's the matter with that woman, her friend from way back asks Mummy, and They don't know, something to do with her blood, Mummy says, or her stomach, or her heart? And They're going to take her to hospital apparently, Mummy says, sensing that she is creating panic, more than she intended, and it becomes clear that between the tea and the grape jam and the idle chat on the veranda someone else has slipped in and insinuated himself here, and there is not much defence against him, or much possibility of ignoring him, or much strength to start with him, or to start to understand the hint, or to start with more dread, or another lost battle, or to start now. *Ach vey*, Daddy sighs, and again as though he means that it's past the youngster's bedtime, and Mummy says that truth to tell she should have knocked on their door to see if they needed any help, but she doesn't know them yet, and also she's afraid, she says, she doesn't know why, or something. We're all new in this building, Daddy tries to explain, and we only meet on the stairs, Daddy says, and in the street we don't recognise each other. And every flat is silent about what there is behind the closed door. In this square space between the new buildings, some on Nahalat Binyamin and some on Montefiore, with an inner courtyard in the middle with some shrubs and some grass and the dustbins and a flight of steps at the back of each wing, where people go up and down quietly and close the door behind them.

Eventually the visitors get restless and start to get ready to leave, they have a way to go to their new neighbourhood, that of all things is named after the homeless, and it's a good question where they live if they're homeless, and Daddy knows where the neighbourhood is, and he says, Hey that's quite a way, and the friend says Yes, but it keeps you fit, and they all laugh in a friendly way, Daddy belongs to Hapo'el Hatza'ir and the friend is from Po'alei Tzion and nevertheless they are friends and happy to be together, and it is the same with Mummy and her friend from way back, although Mummy feels that she has been more fortunate, she is not one of the homeless; the desert, she thinks, is behind her now, and the next step will be to build a new home of their own, to the north of the town, among the sand dunes, in a place called Tel Nordau even though there is nothing there yet and it's hard to drag yourself off to that great sandy desert with sycamore trees, vineyards, foxes and jackals, and your shoes full of sand, and the sweat and the heat and everything, although Daddy's work in the municipality will only help with the arrangements and the loan from the Development Centre, where a good friend of theirs, an expert builder, works, and he knows that the Centre is soon going to become the great national construction company Solel Boneh, just as Mummy knows that it is going to be a neighbourhood of teachers, writers and white-collar workers and therefore civilization will flourish there and transform the sand dunes into a cultural and artistic festival, with a cultural centre and a social centre, a Working Mother's Association and a Workers' Theatre, not exposing the children's souls to this vulgar kiosk or to the picture house where they put on a spectacle of lights, so she has heard, in a hall built by Abravanel and Weisser and named the Eden, of very doubtful cultural value, and who knows what it educates them for. Mummy stays behind to clear the dishes while Daddy and the youngster go downstairs to see the guests off.

This is Nahalat Binyamin, Daddy explains, you can't see in the dark but they've already put up more than forty buildings here, all occupied by respectable, prosperous Poles, who have opened shops and businesses, Not like us, says Yaacov, the friend, who had gone straight to the hoe and the plough, Yes, times have changed, says Daddy, and adds some precise information, as usual, about the residents of Nahalat Binyamin, and the future that seems assured to them, only there isn't enough light yet, because there are too few streetlamps, and it's Uncle David who is responsible for the few that there are, even though they cost a lot of money, and by the light of these few lamps the bright, shiny, jolly presence of the Kiosk Café turns into a lighthouse in a darkening gulf. A house, a yard, and a picket fence or a fence of iron posts or a wall of stepped bricks, little gardens that however much you water the sand swallows it all up, and suddenly it all resembles a kind of tranquillity that you can even smell, especially here, facing this yard, enveloped by a flowering white creeper, that turns out to be simply white roses, that are simply poly-anthus, Daddy knows, a climbing rose with abundant white flowers, and What a scent, says Tzipora, the friend, and they stand there, and it's as if there is some promise that is fulfilled here more than was expected, they stand in the shadow facing the fence that is a mass of white flowers, even taller than Daddy, his male friend is already a little stooped while she is not tall at all, and the youngster is a child, and these flowering roses climb high and their dense, fragrant, true white cloud is made up of masses of tiny white blossoms that merge into something whole and beautiful, and so they stand there in silence and you can sense how Daddy is swallowing something in his throat and maybe, if it was light, you would see just how much.

And then they take their leave, the friend who stoops because of his work and his partner who is not especially tall, but she is moved and she squeezes Daddy's hand and murmurs thanks with something that is emotional warmth rather than words. And Daddy says goodnight and he says See you soon and he says Bye bye, and the youngster says Bye, and they say goodbye again and set off for their neighbourhood of the homeless, far away in the desert of sand dunes and so long as they don't get lost and they keep going north, maybe following the stars, but Daddy trusts his friend because he's an old-timer and a lot has happened to him in the Land, while the two of them Daddy and the youngster, turn and head for home in Nahalat Binyamin, and Daddy does not reach out to hold the youngster's hand and the youngster does not reach out to hold Daddy's but both their hands reach out and they hold each other's hand, because of the silence in the dark, and the rose of the polyanthus family stays behind with its blinding whiteness but its scent trails after them for a while and wherever it is still damp from the evening watering the scent seems to return, and it is so quiet in Nahalat Binyamin that the brilliant light and the noise suddenly beat like a strange drum on the body of the quiet night, and everything is suddenly filled with more motion and din and with more rhythm and light and people who don't go straight home but seem to enjoy themselves more here.

Hand in hand Daddy and the youngster reach the corner of Nahalat Binyamin and Montefiore, and they stop on the opposite corner, not on the pavement that is sprinkled with water, the one with the tables and chairs and the throngs of people, but the one opposite, and Daddy stops, looks and sees and the youngster stops, looks and sees, and Daddy looks and thinks a thought and the youngster looks and guesses what, and just when it seems as though Daddy has seen enough and is about to press lightly on the little hand that is in his big, dry one, long schooled to hard work, and suggest that enough is enough and it may be time to head for home, to go to sleep, Daddy says something that it's hard to believe he would say, even though he has guessed already: Would you like a glass of soda? Goodness gracious, what did he just say, that Daddy? But that is just what he suddenly said, and already they are crossing the road and stepping onto the opposite pavement, the sprinkled one, and already they are inside, and already they are seeing everything from close up and nobody is getting excited that they are there, and they easily make room for them, the youngster whose hand is in his Daddy's and the Daddy with the youngster's hand in his, and here they are already close up to the counter, the light is overpowering, the brightness is overpowering, the smell of the syrups is overpowering, and the man who is always smiling bows and says straight to Daddy: And what will it be for you sir? Daddy for a moment does not know what the man said or what he should answer, it is a kind of theatrical performance he has never taken part in—and instead he bends over and puts his hands under the armpits of the youngster, who is not at all tall and takes up no room and has no weight, and lifts him up so that his chin, his head and most of him are above the marble, and he does not have enough eyes and ears to know everything that is revealed to him so powerfully and he can hardly breathe, he only hears as though from a distance and not to him what Daddy asks him quietly, What would you like to drink? There is red, there is green, and there is yellow, who can know what to choose, and finally it comes out quite clearly: A mixture, which is a surprise even to the man who is smiling, after serving drinks to a thousand customers all through this long day, here is a novelty, but Daddy with his grey moustache and his shy smile and wrinkles of suffering from Hadera to Neve Shalom, and his uncomfortable way of standing as though he has just contravened the tenets of his faith, and the youngster who only has his great big eyes, make the man consent with alacrity as though this was just what he was waiting for, Right you are, he says excitedly, but he waits for a moment because the record has just finished and he leans backwards to the magic box (the youngster from his vantage point does not miss a movement), and he changes the record for a new one he has taken out of its shiny jacket with a picture of a young black man singing with a wide open mouth and holding a strange musical instrument only you can't hear his voice in the picture, and a lot of writing in gold and red, and he puts the old record back in its cover, taking care that his hands are not wet, and then, after he has fiddled in the box and pulled some spring there, the loudspeaker outside bursts into a noisy blast, a sort of leaping music, if this is music, and an incredible shriek, that your shoulders instantly begin to move with, without meaning to and before you know, and both Daddy who is lifting and the youngster who is lifted catch themselves and resist the movement that is carrying them away and suddenly they grin at each other like two naughty boys who have been caught, and then the singer stops and some musical instrument starts wailing, and the man is beaming, It's the Charleston, he announces excitedly to someone standing in front of him who seems to have been waiting for this announcement, and the man says, It's a real bombshell, and he goes off to announce the news to the others who are waiting for the announcement, then he comes back to Daddy whose big hands are holding the youngster up to the counter and above it, Ahah, he says, what was it we wanted? We wanted a mixture, A mixture, says the man in a singsong that resembles the tune the loudspeaker is blaring out much louder, Yes, sir, yes my baby, sing the man and the loudspeaker, then he picks up a gleaming long glass and he picks up a bottle and pours a little red, and he picks up another bottle and adds a little green, and he picks up another bottle and dribbles a little yellow, holds it all up and sees that it is good, then lowers it and turns on the tap of fizzy stuff, and he moves the glass up and down as he fills it with fizz, singing all the time, No, sir, no my baby, puts the glass down for a moment to let the froth subside, then he fills it up again with just soda, no fizz, and at last he turns towards the youngster himself: Here you are, young sir. Enjoy.

God, how much happens in such a short time. Daddy lowers him with the glass in his hand. Daddy feels for the purse in his deep pocket to find a half-piastre, Daddy's other hand does not leave the child's head, the boy thinks suddenly, all I need now is to drop the glass and spill the lot, a strange treacherous thought, and there's room at one table on the corner right on the line between Nahalat Binyamin and Montefiore, and he dips his face in and takes a sip, and doesn't know what to think, it's cold and sweet and makes you want to hiccup, and it's sort of prickly, he doesn't know yet if it's good, and he dips his face again in the liquid whose colour is a mixture, full of angry bubbles, and he takes a breath, and Daddy with a big smile gives him all his attention, Well, Daddy says, and the youngster pushes the glass towards him, Taste it, he says, and Daddy dips his lips and the edge of his moustache and tastes, It's sweet, says Daddy, and makes a face, revealing total incomprehension, seemingly ignoring the special smell, and the winking of the glass, and the prickly sweetness, and the sizzling fizz, mixed with the music, and the dancing in the tummy, then he takes it back and swallows three or four swigs, he's never known such drinking in his life, then suddenly lets out a noisy, surprising, not very polite burp and Daddy and he both burst out laughing and they laugh more and suddenly feel that that's what it's like.

Much later, when the youngster comes back as a man and remembers it all again, he recalls how it was, how it was all around and how it was for the two of them, Daddy and his boy, when they sat and sinned with the soda, outrageously sitting over a glass of multicoloured soda, at one table, facing each other, stranger apparently than all the other customers in the Kiosk, while over everything waved the catchy voice of the gramophone with its stubborn, inescapable insistence

Yes, sir, yes my baby
No, sir, no my baby

clinging to everything, clinging to the floor and the air and the people and even as they walk home, just a few steps across the road, still clinging to their steps, and only when they are close to the steps do they see Mummy standing there, the huddled form of an anxious Mummy, and they feel guilty, sinful and unfaithful, and Mummy can't wait any longer, and she tells them that another two doctors have just come to the poor woman, and She's terribly, terribly ill, Mummy says, she's very poorly, Mummy tells, she's terribly, terribly ill, all she can do is repeat it, adding something in Russian so that the youngster won't understand, but he does.

Allenby

Has he ever been there? What a question, he's been there, he's drunk there, not once and not twice, the big brother, but at all times of the night and day, and he knows people there and he even knows that the man there is called Feldman, that's what everyone calls him; it's not clear where he got so many half-piastres; he explains that it was all from errands he ran, and in case there is still some doubt lurking he adds with a laugh that half-piastres are always falling in the sand and he always finds them, and what's more he also knows a lot about the gramophone records, some of them are tangos and some are foxtrots, some are Charlestons and some are just jazz; he can say new words that haven't been heard before, and he also knows that there's a kind of trumpet that's called a saxophone, although he tires of describing it, because no one has ever seen one, and he can also make his body gyrate and his shoulders, his narrow behind and his lithe back, a straight, slender, joyful youth, tapping his feet and wailing in imitation of that wailing instrument that changes the colours of its wailing, and he sings Yes, sir, yes my baby, almost like the real thing, and Mummy doesn't know whether to laugh or to be terrified at this obscene corruption that has entered her clean house, and Daddy doesn't know how to lay down the law, Times are changing, that's all he can say with a shrug of his shoulders, while to the suggestion that she should come along one day and try a soda she quickly answers, Get along with you, what will you think of next, and Are they sure that the glasses have been washed properly and that they won't catch something, because people are always catching something and falling ill. And the sick neighbour is bad, they say she's going to be taken to hospital, she's very, very bad.

But even Mummy cannot imagine how bad things will become. Because at midday when the boys come home from school and Daddy returns for lunch from the town hall with the water tanks on the roof—all he has to do is to go down Rothschild Boulevard to Nahalat Binyamin, turn sharp left, cross Ahad Ha'am, stare at the new buildings on either side of the street and the still empty plots, and who is going to build on them, and the new shops that even those in Jaffa can't rival for size and certainly not for cleanliness, taste and elegance, lingering to peer into this one or that, wondering if they will open a bookshop here too, with books, papers and magazines from the Land and from abroad in Hebrew and foreign languages, like Mr Krugliakov's shop in Jaffa, or Mr Bulis's in Petach Tikva, and passing the throngs and hubbub of the Kiosk with something resembling regret in his tummy—and already he is climbing the steps when Mummy comes towards him wringing her hands, and whispering, They've taken her leg off, she tells what has been pent up inside her since she heard it in the morning, and when they stop and look around it is plain in the stairwell and all the doors that everybody knows and they are peering secretively at this terrible thing that is known but it is not clear what, or what their duty is as neighbours, or as fellow-citizens, and if they shouldn't go to see the man at the Kiosk, Feldman or whatever his name is, and tell him that today—no. And then, it's not at all clear who said it, if it's just a rumour spread by the children in the yard, or if it was heard from the kitchen of some mother who did not take care to whisper, that that leg, the woman's leg, the one that was cut off, so they are all saying, that the leg that was cut off is lying in that dustbin, and they are waiting for the dustmen to come and take it away, and if you've got the nerve why don't you raise the lid and see for yourself.

Poor woman. Why did they do that to her. It's terrible. And the pain and all the blood from the cut. And how did they cut it. And the bones, how could she bear it. And what will she look like now. And how will she come home. And what will they say about her. And what did she do, for them to do that to her. And that leg. What's it like, a leg without a woman. A leg on its own. The one that's in the dustbin. What's it like, a leg without a body. Like a doll, lying in the sand in the yard. Or on the seashore. It's intolerable. It's unbearable. Why did they tell him. Why did they force him to be full of something that he cannot bear, and now he'll have to go to the dustbin and lift the lid to see it. Because if he doesn't see it he will never be free from it. Lift the lid very slowly take a quick look shut it and run. Why did they involve him in this and what do they want of him. Now it will sink into his soul and he will never be free of it. What does the woman's leg look like without the woman. He doesn't want to know but he has to. He doesn't want to, doesn't want to, he only doesn't want to. Yet he has to, he has no choice. Why do they torment a child who can't bear it. From now on he will be unable not to think about that leg, and he will have to go and lift the lid and see what it's like, a cut off leg without, and how from this moment he is no longer what he was before, and the child who got up this morning and went to school is no longer the child who is hiding his face in a cushion with a cut off leg on him, and suddenly he remembers that there are some tribes in Africa apparently that eat human flesh and they could have had a great feast here today, like the chicken leg that Mummy gives on Sabbath, now he's going to throw up, his guts can't stand it any more.

Is the leg in the dustbin still dressed, with a single stocking and a woman's shoe? Does it fill the whole bin? and why are they waiting for him to go and see, and why does he want to go and see and even touch that terrible thing, and yet on no account, only to run away to the other end of the land, and wash all this out of his head, and wake up as though from a bad dream, as though there's nothing and he doesn't know anything, and why do those savages have to come back and lift the lid and take it out with shrieks and start to take bites from it, terribly disgusting and terribly exciting, and why is he caught in this, unable to be in it and unable to escape, and how can he erase it and how can he wash himself clean from everything he has heard, the way Mummy washes filthy clothes and they come out fresh and ironed and as good as new. He would never have imagined that such a thing was possible, to cut off a woman's leg, or a man's, in their own home, he would never have imagined that they could throw any leg into any dustbin until the dustmen come to take it away, he never even asked what was wrong with that woman and what happened to her afterwards, and how she came home eventually limping somehow, just as it never occurred to him to doubt the story, and that all Mummy said was that they had cut off some woman's leg, and that everything he had heard had just been said by some boy or boys, that the leg was in the bin, and if you have the nerve go and lift the lid and see for yourself, but you don't have the nerve, you don't at all, you can't either do it or not do it, and they expected you to, and that's enough, enough, enough, God, it's enough, and it's a pity he went to drink soda with Daddy yesterday, and before he drank the soda everything was much nicer, and he doesn't want anything, only to throw up, he wants not to exist, he wants to go to sleep, he wants them to leave him alone, you shouldn't put all this on a child, even if he's called youngster now, inevitably he can't either do it or not do it, or deny it and say that he knows nothing about any leg and he doesn't have to do anything, it never happened, or not even to beg for mercy that they should leave him alone, because he will never get out of this, ever, he will never be free of it, he will never be cleansed of it, even when he is grown up, never, to this day.

Did he cry? Did he fall asleep? It seems he did, but he woke with a start, and suddenly there were those masks again, here on Allenby Street and not long ago, at that rotten Purim again, and everyone was going, he too, and when he asked not to go they said to him Why not, it's Purim today and at Purim you have to have fun, that's the rule, and why not, come and see, come with all the others, hold Daddy's hand, you're a big boy now, and he was being dragged along, pulling his hand back while Daddy pulled it forwards, Come, he was saying, come come, see how they all, and the street was filling with people, the whole of Allenby Street from one pavement to the other, even the sand in between, because the road was not paved yet, crowds of people all walking in the sand that had been sprayed with water and now it was dirty sand, and there was a crush that the winter breeze could not cool, and the masks and the gurgling, the balloons and the flags, the rattles and the Purim guns, and all the pushing and shoving, as though there was some place that they were all pushing to reach in the densely packed crowd: maybe somebody was going to make a speech or say a few words or a choir would sing; maybe Mr Dizengoff seated on his horse from which he never got off—he even rode it into the cemetery on the Memorial Day for the victims of Jaffa—would speak; maybe they would put a chair out and old A. Z. Rabinovitch would stand up on it and treat the crowd to a story from the *Book of the Early Rabbis* that he had recently published, and that was where everyone was pushing to go; and meanwhile they were enjoying jostling, talking loudly, shouting and laughing and meeting people and asking what's new, and because they were afraid it would rain there were umbrellas and people were waving them, and sometimes the crush was unbearable, and suddenly your hand wasn't in Daddy's hand, and you were surrounded by crowds of strangers, and they were separated from you and dragged forward and you were separated from them and dragged forward and a moment was occurring that at first seemed to be just almost a minor incident, a little moment that suddenly became an eternal moment, that sweeps you away like the sea sweeping away a drowning man, they were are no longer somewhere where you could can reach them easily or where they could can stop quickly and reach you, and they would just say, What happened to you, youngster, how did you disappear, and you would say Me? You disappeared, and they would laugh and it would all be forgotten, but as it is there is no way of putting it right, whether they went ahead or backtracked or crossed to the other side, and it was clear now that everything was determined and this was a separation with no way back, and you wouldn't be able to push your way on your own through all these people, pushing and shoving and tightly packed together like an impenetrable wall, and there was nothing you could do except to raise your tiny voice and scream Daddy Daddy, until even you couldn't recognise your voice, and the people couldn't hear because they were also screaming with what was left of their voices and shouting on every side, not because they had lost their daddies but because this was the game they were all playing, looking for each other and disguising themselves as things they were not, and Daddy wasn't Daddy and the Arab wasn't an Arab and the British policeman was not a British policeman, and King Ahasuerus wasn't the King and Queen Esther wasn't the Queen, and suddenly you knew for a certainty that everything was lost, and that you were alone and lost. And that among this jostling crowd of a million you had nobody and you yourself no longer existed.

You don't want to scream, you don't want to cry, all you want and it's urgent is to go to the toilet. And this humiliation how they lost you and they don't care. Maybe ask some grown-up to lift you up so you can look for them from up there. Please mister lift me up, but they are all Arabs, they are all Blacks, they are all Bigtan and Teresh, they are all Queen Esther or the righteous Mordechai the Righteous, they are all a British policeman, they are all a brigand with an eyepatch, nobody is what he is really, and even the place has changed and stopped being your place, and become a place that you precisely don't want to be in, or be part of or part of all of them all, and you yourself have no place in the world, you are simply superfluous, being dragged along goallessly, directionlessly, you don't belong to anything and nothing belongs to you, you are surrounded by monsters in disguise and camouflaged people, they catch hold of you and you lack the strength to resist or to flee, and soon they will trample on you and the revellers not caring will tread you underfoot, if only Mr Dizengoff would come past on his horse and a space would clear around him, and then you could go up to him and shout to him, Mr Dizengoff, where is my Daddy?

Stuck in a place you do not want. Stuck in something you

do not want. Luckily there is a little tree there. A tree that has not managed to grow even though they have poured a lot of water on the sand where they planted it, and hammered in a stake next to it and tied it up because of the salt sea breeze, and he clings to this tree, a thin trunk with thin hands, barely protected from the wind, and there the tears burst and he weeps and the tree supports him. But there is no purpose, there is no point in anything, he is alone and only alone, there is no God in the world, there is no Mummy and no Daddy in the world, there is nothing except being alone, and that is that. And nobody in the whole world needs him, and whether he exists or not does not interest anybody. And nobody in the whole world cares. Oh, how sorry they will be when they find out how it ended. How he walked due west from here, simply and straightforwardly, not like going north to the neighbourhood of the homeless at night, but due west straight to the sea and into the sea that is storming now, and overcoming the first fear and going in deep and it will happen quickly and he will become nonexistent, and how sorry they will be then. That will be the end of their little boy. Let them know, they deserve it. How can you abandon a child. How can you leave such a little boy in that mass of monstrous masks, with all the guns and the noise, the Ahasueruses and the Esthers and the Arabs and the British, and everything that they weren't really, it is all a lie, just pretend and not real—only the cruelty is real, and how they dragged him to go, to all this carnival of all these strangers shouting and disguising themselves, jostling one another as though they had somewhere where they should be going, when everything is false and untrue and impossible.

He knows Allenby Street well—after all, it's the way to school— but when it is covered by a dense noisy crowd going in the opposite direction, and it's hard to walk when you're crying, sobbing quietly, and nobody pays any attention because it's surely only another mask and he's only seeming to cry, the mask of the crying child, and it's so sad to cry out loud when there's no one to hear, and he reaches Montefiore Street and turns into it, starting to run because it's not far now, crossing Nahalat Binyamin, before that Kiosk Café was there, and straight ahead two houses and inside to the courtyard the stairs one flight up and the door—it is closed, locked, totally, no tapping, no knocking, no shouting Daddy Daddy Mummy, it's closed and there's no one in, just him outside, and it's locked, and even when you push it hard it's locked, and he has nothing and there is nothing left. And what is left, what's left is to sit on the steps and the crying starts again, openly, but there's no one to take any notice because they've all gone and they're all at the procession in Allenby Street, disguised as all sorts and as stupid as the rest of them, and even if there was someone what are they to him and he doesn't need anyone, only his Daddy, and he will never forgive this Daddy for giving up on his little boy. And later the tears dry and later he doesn't know what to do, and later he knows that if he had not been separated from them he would be in some happy place now where everyone including himself would be glad to be and he would be laughing now instead of crying and with Daddy and Mummy instead of alone. His big brother, for instance, disguised as a brigand, Abu Jilda, apparently, or perhaps as that rioter that everyone was afraid of at the time of the Jaffa riots, now he is the rioter, let them be afraid of him, and he is the brigand who will save them from the wicked rioters; he has been missing since morning and will not return before midnight or the early hours, and no one will know where he has been or who he has been running around with, and he will come home happy and tired and hungry, laughingly telling all sorts of funny things that happened that make Mummy melt, indulging him and his beauty even though she conceals it and tells him off, because only one who hates her child spares the rod.

And he returns from Purim that was in the winter to this summer's day when they put the severed leg of that woman from the flat opposite in the dustbin in the yard, and are waiting for him to get up and do something that he does not want to do and if he doesn't do it they'll brand him a shirker and a scaredy cat, and that someone who wants it, however incomprehensible it sounds, will remain inside him, someone who is tempted to know despite everything, and suddenly it seems as though this unwillingness is not real, and really, inside himself, he does want, he is attracted and tempted, to raise the lid of the bin, to take and see and run, and while running to know that he is different, that something has happened that there is no going back from, that he has crossed some border, shrugged off some old skin, that if he hadn't dared he would have lost something and given up and chosen to remain a little boy and forever.

And then it is all so terribly tiring, he falls asleep curled up in a corner of the sofa with one arm trailing almost to the ground, and when he wakes up he has no idea where he is or what's going on, and Mummy is telling someone casually that the dustmen have been and have taken the rubbish away, not referring to any particular rubbish, and not noticing the boy who is awake now though still curled up on the sofa, not imagining where the child has come from or what a great weight has been lifted from his tiny heart, and what a faraway, lonely place he has to return from, and how empty, how tired and yet how liberated he feels. If only, without asking anyone, somebody would spread a blanket over him and let him sleep forever. From what distance the twittering of birds close by, and the braying of a donkey from somewhere, braying to the very end of all its braying. Apart from that everyone is doing his own thing and everyone is continuing with something. But he does not have the strength to do anything. Only above everything the sound of the gramophone comes from downstairs beyond the corner, not blaring so much, but terribly lonesome and terribly wild, that instrument that's there, which pleads and fades, and wails and fades, as though it knows exactly what one is feeling, as though it can express what none of them can express, both because they don't know how and because they would be ashamed to wail like that in the middle of the day.

There is nothing to do at home. There is nothing to do on the steps. There is nothing to do in the yard. Even the dustbins don't interest anybody now, and the children have all run off somewhere, maybe they are playing in the empty playground at the back of the Herzliya Gymnasium. And there is nothing to do in this Montefiore Street, where nobody comes or goes, while across the street on the corner of Nahalat Binyamin the assistant is watering the pavement as though he has sworn to do this as long as he lives, and the sand in the roadway too, which dries up before it has smelt the water, and only a few people are sitting on the shiny chairs on the pavement, maybe he should try to see if he's lucky enough to find a half-piastre in the sand, but he doesn't feel like doing anything except stay curled up here near the low wall that is unfinished like so many walls where the money has run out before they were complete and so they have been abandoned to the lizards and sad children, to lean their tired back against and soak up the heat that the wall has soaked up all day long from the sun, and sometimes to smell a smell of plaster that stirs you to scrape a bit off and put it in your mouth to taste that stirring taste of plaster, and the sun is in the southwest already, he knows, it's empty to the end of the unbuilt street, and only right at the end stands a single strange building, not like the rest of them, two storeys with a pointed black steeple like in pictures of castles, and with all sorts of corners, exaggeratedly splendid, too wonderful, as though set down in the wrong place, surrounded by a wall with a locked gate, it's not clear how it got there, beyond the wall and the tall green and red plants—he's forgotten what they're called—people say some plague or pestilence, maybe cholera, broke out there and it was put under quarantine and no one is allowed into the garden, you would risk your life, and not do anything except fold your legs underneath you like some Arab in the desert, with your hands between your legs and your back against the warm wall, drawing in the warmth, looking around, there are no people except the people at the café, sitting with their chairs tipped back almost till they fall over, smoking and puffing out the smoke in wonderful ways, doing nothing and not talking, not even drinking the soda that is in front of them, just smoking and puffing out the smoke, each with his own way of getting rid of the ash at the tip of the cigarette, even when not enough has collected, with little taps of the finger, with what skill and expertise, with what languid enjoyment, and it is impossible not to hear all the time above their heads and above the street, as though it is part of it now, the music from the shiny gramophone, wailing to itself with the tunes of that wailing instrument, that is sometimes joined by a man's voice and is sometimes on its own, and when it wails on its own like that it does all kinds of things to the hearer, so sad and also so necessary, so lonely right now this afternoon but it will sound different later in the evening and different again in the night, and it's just a shame that he doesn't know what the instrument is and he's never seen it and has not heard its name, and he has never seen an orchestra even though he does know the name, and he doesn't know what plays in it, apart from the violin that he has heard before and the piano, there was one in his kindergarten and they used to play it on special days, but on other days the teacher Miss Yehudit had a concertina, a kind of hexagon with pointed buttons, opening diagonally one way and closing diagonally the other way in the hands of his teacher who waved it around and added her own shrill voice to the instrument's shrill, frail sound, interrupting herself occasionally for a brief rebuke, All together now, or Sit still there, or even shouting occasionally because of the commotion, the children sitting in a circle at her feet stunned by everything and by her shrill singing, apart from the music that you could always hear in the alleys of Jaffa and from the dark coffee houses there, with a pungent smell of spices and those endless wailing, quivering or endlessly protracted effusions that you could always hear in Jaffa but that were nothing like what there is here, neither this instrument, nor the wide-jawed gramophone, nor that necessity you feel even before you know it to start to move your shoulders and your trunk, and your head too, this way and that, and up and down, as though joining some agreement, without knowing what it agrees to, only that it is necessary and that it makes you suddenly differently sensitive and attentive, so that you almost start to grasp something that you did not know before.

What did all the people in the Kiosk Café do before it opened here? Did they stay at home? Did they go to Jaffa? Did they go to sleep? Suddenly it's as though this is the centre of the Land, a place you could not manage without, and that everyone in the city loves soda and shiny tunes, and the song Yes sir, yes my baby grabs them in their heart, and they are all attracted to the bright lights, and they enjoy a watered pavement and they like sitting there crowded together in the midst of the din—and when Mummy complained to Daddy yesterday about how vulgar that noisy place was and that there was nothing cultured about it and nothing that would arouse deep thoughts in a person, and that song that she couldn't repeat and she wasn't sorry she couldn't, what educational value did it have, Daddy, who always agrees with Mummy and says nothing, just nodding his head, this time replied with a question, not without a secret little smile in his moustache, what was so deep about *Rejoice O Maccabees, valiant in the fight / Be glad and happy day and night*? At which Mummy was very surprised, because that was one of our national songs, whereas this was a totally foreign, *goyish* song, and Just you see how it will uproot our youth and make them look abroad, it was just frivolous entertainment. At which, unexpectedly, her beloved the elder brother intervened, and stood up and sang in front of her and even danced with his hands raised in the air, *Meat balls and borsht, hop hop, goulash and wursht, hop hop!*, and collapsed in laughter, because that was what they were singing these days in the workers' canteens, Get away with you, Mummy pushed her little sweetheart away, that's just because they're hungry and can barely get hold of some borsht. *Like he that sings songs to a heavy heart*, Daddy recalled, in support. From the Book of Proverbs.

But neither the Kiosk nor the owner, Mr Feldman, knows about all this, all they do is water the pavement all the time and make pleasant shade all the time and serve soda with syrups, whoever wants to can help himself and go to a table to drink, or if he prefers he can spoil himself and sit and be served, and above them all all the time, as if that is the whole point, those tunes, no one knows who makes them, or with what kinds of instruments, and how they set your shoulders and your neck dancing, with a clear rhythm that the drums beat out relentlessly, and how they make their hearers, or at least one of them who as yet understands nothing about the world, about life, about music or about anything, and who still doesn't know how to pronounce the word jazz, and among all the things that he didn't know previously were possible he is beginning to see that the world is more than used to be imagined, and there is more room in it than used to appear, and that people can get to know what they did not know was allowed, and at the same time, and this he does know, that there are things that one does need to know how to say more than is permitted, and that you will not go on forever being an unknowing child shut up in only what you are allowed to know, and that you will not always be unknowing and lacking words to say, just sensing blindly that this is the right thing, and with a kind of unruly stubbornness that this is the real truth, and that even when you can see that I am here, at the same time I am not here, and don't belong to any here, not really. I am not of here even when I am here. And that really I am someone else, even when it seems that I am still one of them, just like this unknown musical instrument that plays invisibly and is now wailing and going on playing on its own when all the other instruments have stopped to let it play on its own, and this hoarse wail bursts out, with nothing to stop it or say what it can wail about and what it can't, and as if it too is here to say that it is possible not to be here even when you are, and that I am someone else as well as myself, and that they are all just disguised as what we usually think they are, and they only talk like what we are used to hearing them say, but in reality it is not them, and that is not what they should be saying, but they are left choked, unable to utter a single cheep, now you can hear how it is possible and how it is permitted, and all this wailing, something very wild, something that knows a lot of suffering, that doesn't need any pity or to be told any word but only to get out and be, to get out at last from inside and be heard, to get out of that confinement and be, and that you mustn't give up something that is necessary, even if it is hard, and even if it has no name yet, but inside you know exactly what it is. And that's how it is.

Then the youngster gets up and with his sandals dribbling sand as he goes he crosses Nahalat Binyamin whose west side is already casting a blue shadow on its east side, and turns north, towards Gruzenberg, he walks without taking up any room on the pavement, deciding not to walk on the cracks between the paving stones, which makes his walk into a kind of dance, like in a private ceremony, and meanwhile he studies the differences between the fences and garden walls, those made from wavy iron bars, those made from wooden planks, and those made from stepped bricks, and all the fantasy the owners have not allowed themselves in making their houses as modest as the rest they give free rein to in constructing the fence or low wall, just as people permit themselves a smile and some sweetmeats at the end of a serious meal, and on the other side of each fence naturally there is a private garden, with cosmos, Indian rose, petunias, and all those other flowers whose names he does not know but Daddy does, all apparently bought from the same S. Guzman, Jaffa, opposite the German Colony, in that great depot that has everything that exists in the world, from ploughs to hoes and from fertilisers to plants and seeds, and anything required by farmers, citrus growers, millers, builders, he even has spare parts for automobiles, and for all kinds of factories, only he hasn't moved from Jaffa to this Nahalat Binyamin, and it's high time he did, says Daddy. Some people even grow maize, eggplants and tomatoes in the sand, and every evening when they come home from work they hurry to change and they stand, garden after garden, householder after householder, each one watering his flowers or his vegetables, and chatting in a relaxed way, about what if not about Nahalat Binyamin and its future glories, and from all the open windows that the shadow has already reached and covered the lace curtains that are drawn wide open now to let in the air the housewives peer out and chat in a relaxed way, housewife to housewife from window to window and from window to garden, and housewife to householder, and pointing out to those who are watering the bits they have missed, because the sand swallows everything so quickly that they don't see where they have watered and what they have missed.

And how far? As far as the garden with the climbing roses, those white roses whose name he does not know but Daddy does. They have made them a trellis of strips of wood that form squares painted green to the height of a tall man with his arms raised, and the stems of the roses have twined in and out of the strips of wood and the squares, climbing upwards and growing straight into the air, plunging into that void that is under the azure sky, twirling delicately to the four winds, and it seems as though all their power of growth is concentrated in the upper tips, in tiny nut-like clenched fists, babyish green and pink, that have done nothing yet in their lives, apart from rambling and climbing in the fine air, ready to open at any moment, and from the ground up to the highest height it is all full of flowering white white white, with maybe a drop of green blended in the white white, clusters of crowded white whirls of crowded little white and full white roses, until even those stray blooms that are almost faded have not fallen yet but are inside this great white carpet of white in white on white, white buds and white open blooms, swirling upwards in all their calm whiteness, and you can't see through them inside, you are overcome by the need suddenly to touch them and to feel the substantiality of the projection of their gathered buds, the roundness of their buttons, like nipples or glands, a stiffening of tiny crowded things, full of unfolding folds and close-packed openings, beside the fully opened blooms, and all the white of this single white carpet only frays at the top, beyond the top of the trellis, with the excess growth waving into the empty air, a thrusting of inexhaustible power of growth, with a proliferation of fine thread-like stems clutching at the air, to reach even higher, with a clear firm conviction that there will be something to hold onto eventually so as to climb more and soar up in an abundance of whiteness containing a further infinity of white buds opening out white into the high nothingness beyond, with an urge for more and an urge to open and an urge to give, to be liberated, and to try all the time to discover if it is possible at one and the same time to see the whole of the white carpet and every one of the white details, not first the whole and then the details, but just for a single second, the whole wholeness and the single one, both every single white corpuscle and all the whiteness united into a single whole whiteness, at the top of which, always, more fine fingers are ready like spiders' feet to catch and wrap themselves round anything they can and to climb still higher—in a kind of happiness that you would not have believed possible. Or that such a thing can exist in the world and that there is nothing more than it in any place or time or for ever and ever to this day, I swear it.

Teresh

It starts with the big argument at home, in Montefiore Street on the corner of Nahalat Binyamin, second house on the right, and continues in Nahalat Binyamin and turning right, and in Ahad Ha'am Street and turning left, and in Herzl Street and turning right and in Lilienblum Street, and finally reaches the Eden Picturehouse (founded by Abravanel & Weisser), which is at the end of Lilienblum on the corner of Pines Street; it begins with two children hand in hand walking, it continues with three or four children hurrying, it continues further with six or seven children running, and it ends with ten panting head to head at the ticket desk at the Eden Picturehouse; and it begins with Mummy who as usual says no, and the persuasions of the big brother who skilfully deploys all the most seductive arguments, plus his little brother, whom he calls Teresh (ever since last Purim when he came home alone in tears, hating masks and fancy dress, including the comical costumes of Bigthan and Teresh, the two chamberlains who sought to lay hand on stupid king Ahasuerus), and his calm explanation to his mother that this time it was not some vulgar film about thieves and robbers or a scary film about gangsters and murderers, who place no value on human life and view the death of a man with contempt—the big brother knows how to quote—no, this time it is a film about the international exhibition that was reported in *Ha'aretz* and that everyone is talking about, a film all about culture, learning, science and civilization, recommended by leading figures as you can read on the posters in the street, and what's more—this breaks Mummy's heart—he will take little Teresh, sorry, his darling brother, he will take him, look after him and bring him back safe and sound, and it really is a film for children, really educational, really compulsory viewing, until faced with the older brother's thirst for knowledge and the younger one's big eyes Mummy begins to weaken, she goes and comes back and counts out into his hand enough money, after they have done the sums and done them again, and she gives the little brother a small apple in case he is hungry and a hankie in case he sneezes, and after more warnings, and flying off hand in hand down the steps and onto Montefiore Street and speeding past the Kiosk Café and everything there, and right and straight ahead and as though springing out of the ground two young people join them, and over a fence in Ahad Ha'am another two, and leaping under the little trees on Rothschild Boulevard, that crosses Herzl Street, another two or three join them and by now they are a merry band, and in a noisy crowd they turn right into Lilienblum and pass the Takhkemoni School with its poor religious kids, and burning for adventure they all talk together and laugh horribly, and the biggest joke of all is that the international exhibition is only in the newsreel, and the main item will be the adventures in the mysterious castle, maybe even with Douglas Fairbanks in person and Mary Pickford, maybe, or something, and what's the difference, one or other of them, and it will be a heart-stopping, heart-throbbing festival of suspense and action, and they all press in a body towards the ticket desk which it transpires will not open for another half an hour and is already besieged by fellow enthusiasts, some known to them and others not, some our kind of people and others so scary that you have to watch the money and hold it tight in your clenched fist deep in your trouser pocket.

And suddenly the doors open and everyone pushes to get in at the same time and the doorman tears off the counterfoils of the tickets firmly, shouting, and now they are inside the auditorium all together in a mass, rushing to grab seats, if only they knew which is better, the front or the back, until they all sit down together laughing a great laugh of victory, and Teresh does not know where to look first or what exactly is going to happen. And the most troubling thing is the question of the pictures that will appear on the big empty white screen that is rippled by the breeze from the big door with all kinds of rustling wrinkles that you are not supposed to notice, maybe the pictures are as wide as the screen and they run down some channel in the ceiling and down over the screen and pause for a moment until you've seen enough of them, then go on their way and fold up one after another somewhere in the basement, unless it's the other way round and they emerge from under the floor and move up the screen one by one? He has to understand this magic that is going to happen here, and he doesn't have enough eyes to see all the rest, the room, the children, the hubbub, the movement, and maybe it's already begun and the movements on the screen are the thing only it's a bit fuzzy and you have to get used to it? He is perspiring with excitement, with the need to know, the humiliation of the knowledge of this empty void full of utter ignorance, and the feeling that he is about to enter into knowledge that once he has it will change him forever. Then suddenly all the lights are put out and total darkness falls all at once, and on the illuminated screen the incredible happens, not at all like what he has imagined and pictured to himself, and you discover with astonishment but also with joy some impossible thing that has simply become possible, the powerful beam of light that begins in a hole in the wall at the back, a narrow, powerful beam full of sort of flickering sawdust as though flocks of flies are flitting around in it, and getting wider and wider till it occupies the entire width of the screen that it lights up brilliantly, and already there are kind of photographs starting to move around without making any sound, and it looks so real and the people are as they are only bigger, and all sorts of things in the world as they are only bigger, which seems totally explicable and straightforward and at the same time full of magic, and a heavy weight of anxiety is lifted from his heart because he will not have to invent the cinema because somebody else has already invented it for him and he is freed from the responsibility of inventing it, and completely free to look from above his extended neck between the heads of the big children in front of him, straight at the international exhibition, and it doesn't bother him that he cannot understand anything, either what an exhibition is or what international means or what goes on there, the magic of the existence of what he sees captivates his whole heart, his head, his eyes and his sweaty palms, and the words that interrupt the pictures set in fringed frames do not help him any more than the sounds of the piano that he has just noticed coming from the side of the darkened hall, he only turns his face from the screen to look back at the bright beam coming from the hole in the wall at the back, full of flickering whirls in the flood of light that gets wider as it approaches the screen, and he does not know if he has ever seen anything in the world as wonderful or as powerful as this.

What exactly was in the great adventure-packed film he does not remember, certainly not now, now he is entirely occupied with the success of the existence of the thing projected on the screen, only celebrating the triumph of the invention that casts great big living moving pictures onto the cloth, and by the avoidance of the responsibility of finding a way of bringing the pictures to the screen in whatever wearisome, clumsy fashion he might have devised on his own, and as for the plot of the spectacle that makes everyone else here hold their breath in suspense, he postpones it for the time being and may only come back to it tonight in bed, watching the film again slowly and quietly, but now he does not relent but does everything he can to understand exactly how it is done, and he will not spare his father a flood of basic questions. Meanwhile, between reels (his brother's expression), there is an intermission with the lights on, when the spectators emerge from the silence imposed on them by the excitement of the plot and burst out in unison in a roar of relaxed tension and appreciative enjoyment, with guesses and wagers about how the story will unfold and how the hero will be saved, and shouts of warning to be careful, and then darkness falls again and silence accompanied by sighs due to the suspense of the evident danger, and great laughs of relief when he is finally rescued, and so on throughout another three changes of reels, making another three intermissions with the lights on, until eventually it really is the end and a turbid gloomy light fills the hall and a rapid drying up of the enchantment, and a jostling stream of all the monkeys to the door, and then suddenly they are faced by a sun that astonishes by its powerful presence when just now it was darkest night apart from the enchanted screen. It is a pity to part, a pity to shatter the magical togetherness, a pity to leave the wonderful land and return to this dreary Lilienblum, but they are all bound by the domestic rules and however long they delay must finally go home, not exactly hand in hand, until that terrifying dog that suddenly leaps out of a yard like some bristling wild beast, and the big brother hurries to enfold the little one, and reassure him with words born of experience, Don't be frightened don't let him see that you're scared a dog that barks doesn't bite, and with this advice he turns to the terrible shouting dog, Get away with you, shouts the brother to the beast, *yallah etla'*, shouting in Arabic because that's the only language they understand, and bends down as though to pick up a stone, which stops the beast and makes it drop its tail, Keep walking, don't look at it, it's just a rotten Arab dog, he says soothingly to the little one, whose neck is stiff from the effort of not looking round, and that is how the brother saves his little brother Teresh from being mauled to death, and then, hand in hand now, they hop along from pavement to pavement, until they reach the corner of Montefiore and the Kiosk Café, and here the brother says to his brother, Now we'll have a soda, and he takes a half-piastre out of his pocket, despite Mummy's calculations, and like an experienced grown-up he approaches the counter, Give us a red he says without a please, to the man, that Mr Feldman, who never tires, and he does his magic and mixes the syrup with a jet of fizzy foam, raising and lowering the glass ceremoniously, and pushes it towards the brother who pays and tastes and hands it to his little brother, who dips his nose in and sips until the gas brings out a surprised burp, but then the brother comes back clutching two straws like a habitué, and from either side with their heads almost touching they both suck as hard as they can, and the elder not only drinks like an expert with evident pleasure, but he even says It's good to Mr Feldman, who is pleased and says Sure, and the younger takes one last suck and holds the upturned glass to his mouth in case he can get out one last hidden drop, and puts down the completely clean glass, and only then does the elder turn to the younger, Now then, says the elder to the younger, don't you go running to tell Mummy. Says the elder to the younger.

There are several ways to get to school. You mustn't shame any one of them by not trying it. The simplest way of all is to go straight down Montefiore and turn right into Allenby and right down to the end to the level crossing, and another way is to go down Nahalat Binyamin and turn left at Ahad Ha'am and then right onto Allenby, but you can also carry on down Nahalat Binyamin as far as Rothschild Boulevard and then you turn left and then right into Allenby, and you can even go further on as far as Yehuda Hallevi and turn left and go straight up to Allenby right to the gate of the school, but you can't go any further than Yehuda Hallevi because of the wall of the railway that runs along its cutting and gate after gate is closed in its honour, the Allenby gate comes down and the Herzl gate slides, so that neither man nor donkey is crushed, and they just stand silently before the train's magnificent smoky progress towards Jaffa. But every single route always begins from the Kiosk Café, and every one always ends at the same Kiosk Café. Surely this is truly the centre of the Land and the world revolves around it. It is not the same people who sit there from morning to night, apart from the owner Mr Feldman who is the only one who is there all the time, always smiling and always asking who would like another, always pouring soda wonderfully, and one afternoon a certain youngster finds himself a place opposite, by the half-finished wall, his back to the blocks whose heat is pleasant even on a summer day, his eyes straying to all sorts of eye-catching things, to a bird (what is it called?) on the threadbare, snail-covered cypress tree, so thirsty and wretched, or to the emptiness of Montefiore Street that has not been built yet apart from that mysterious house that is under quarantine, so they say (is it true?), or to that silent movie he saw yesterday with his brother that comes before him only today in snippets (from the top of the cliff straight into the sea...), or lingering on those people who keep coming and sitting down at the café, drinking and talking and drinking in silence and drinking and going off (where to?).

He does not hear every word. Nor does he always understand what they are saying. But, almost certainly, he can always hear the music of their words, when they are just words and when they are real. Even when they are all talking together excitedly or shouting together excitedly or trying to get a word in, although they are always silenced, and in the end there is always one who succeeds and he talks and the others listen—maybe because of his voice, maybe because he is in the middle—and there is always someone left begging to be allowed to say something, and there are also always some girls talking and laughing, but the men mainly talk so that the girls or one of them listens and knows. But what he knows, this youngster, Teresh, with his back to the blocks and his wandering gaze, is not what they have said but when it is wrong, when it's just play-acting, when it's only pretend, when it's not true, when they are saying something just because it's the easy thing to say and not necessarily the right thing, and they generally talk about what's up, are you well, how are your problems, or what's going to happen, but not about what they want to talk about or what he was waiting for them to say, and they have no idea how to say the truth, or maybe they are afraid of everyone knowing what they really want to say, they haven't got the courage to let everyone know what they really want to say, so that only rarely, suddenly, when somebody suddenly comes out and says suddenly something that is right with the right words, they all listen to him in silence, and then they say, He's right, and they say, How true, and there is a moment of silence, and again, So true, for a moment, and then they go back to talking about what it's easy to talk about, and it's only from the music of their voices that you can hear that it's just make-believe, and that they are just pretending to talk when they are actually saying nothing, without noticing that they are moving away, again, and evading, they are all great experts at evasion, even though they know they're just evading, and that nothing will come of all this talking, again what's been happening and again what's going to happen, again what's up and again what's new, in the morning as in the evening, at the café as in the street, there is always something important left unknown and untouched, beyond all the mishaps that always happen, something more important than all this, that he, the youngster, little Teresh, obviously doesn't know, but he just knows that the music with which they talk hour after hour isn't right, and that it's just going around and around. And that's not how you talk when you're talking properly, that's not how things sound. And it's a shame, because apparently that must be the reason they meet and sit and talk to each other and listen and interrupt to say, and silence each other to say, so that the thing will be said correctly, and they don't know it until they finally fall silent from exhaustion; or as though it's just to rest from all their efforts that they sat here, to be served a glass of soda, when really it was simply to listen that they came, in case somebody knows how to speak properly and say what needs to be said the way it needs to be said so that the music of what is said will ring true. And that's the way it is.

When you wake up very early, and listen to the darkness and the silence and the sleepers' breathing and Daddy will get up soon quietly and close the door quietly, after straightening the blanket slightly on the sleeping youngster, without realising that he is watching without giving a hint that he is not asleep, and on the other side of the door he quietly lights the lamp, it is so quiet that even the scratch of the match is audible, and makes tea on the paraffin cooker, and sits quietly at his desk, which is smaller than the one at the town hall but closer and fuller of his own things; and whoever wakes up listens to the cocks crowing all around, as though doing their duty they shout round and round, from that hoarse old one who seems so near, even downstairs in the yard, to that jolly cock across the street, or perhaps even in the house that's under quarantine—isn't he tired of repeating his story over and over again, and sometimes he calls out of turn; and the barking of the dogs, one of whom seems to be stuck on a single everlasting bark, as though he's been given a hammer and he's using it to beat on the brains of the sleeping world; and very soon the birds too, starting to wake slowly, seemingly clearing their throats or tuning their voices to the right pitch, launch into clusters of shrill jubilation until you can't distinguish one voice from another, and all at once you want to burrow under the blanket, turn over and go back to sleep, yet also to sit up and listen more intently outwards to the world and inwards to what last night before you fell asleep seemed like a lot of frayed threads that did not meet, or maybe to get out of bed quietly and barefoot and open the door quietly and sit down quietly at Daddy's feet and not disturb him but just leaf through yesterday's *Ha'aretz*. To look at the shapes of the drawings in an advertisement for women's shoes with laces and without, and the pictures of ploughs that the settlers can buy at Mr Guzman's in instalments, and also to read the story about the British airman who landed his airplane in a field near Mikve Yisrael to buy some watermelons and then took off again, and also to read a notice from the Eden Picturehouse, about a highly praised new film they are going to show, called 'The Last Days of Pompeii', and to ask Daddy once he is allowed to talk.

And one day the Sabbath comes, and young Teresh and Daddy are going on an excursion, and nobody else for all sorts of reasons wants to join them despite Daddy's explanations of how useful and enjoyable the trip will be, because they are going to go to Sarona and possibly on from there to the Montefiore Orchard, which was the first Hebrew citrus plantation in our land, and is the continuation of our friend Montefiore, the street here at our feet. Which being so, the two of them take their shoes and sandals, respectively, one with a hat on and one with his tousled hair, and without a water bottle or a couple of slices of bread and jam, they go down the steps and set off up Montefiore Street, crossing Nahalat Binyamin that splendid street, and cross Allenby Street that at this early hour is all empty, quiet and clean, and keep climbing till there are fewer and fewer buildings on Montefiore Street, as though the builders have run out of steam, and there are just a few houses here and there, and only the sand dunes to join them to one another, and very soon it all comes to an end and so does the whole of Tel Aviv with Ahuzat Bayit, with the Nahalat Binyamin Association and the enterprises of Schenkin, Dizengoff and Bugrashov, and all the bold plans including those that will be realised shortly, so that even people who are short of money will be able to build; it all comes to an end, and what begins now is the place that has never changed and the land that nothing has happened to yet and an immense terrain extending as it has done since time immemorial, and after nations, people, wars, rains and droughts have come and gone it still preserves its integrity, free of all the scratches of times and events, with nothing but sand dunes, vines and scattered palm trees, and a hedge of prickly pear nearby that bears no fruit now except for the terrible prickles on all of its thick cheeks, and Daddy tells a horrible story about how the Arabs once captured the Biluist Hazanov from Gedera and hurled him into the prickly pears, and how he barely escaped with his life, and the pain he was in until they extracted the needle-like spines from his body (so lucky his eyes were not touched) and the millions of fine prickles that went on for ever and the humiliation, especially the ineradicable humiliation, and the vow that it would never happen again, so that the youngster peers cautiously beyond the hedge, no Arabs around for the moment, but naturally Daddy would never have led his child into danger, and yet.

Now Daddy starts to twist and turn, turning this way and that and finally he knows and he says, Here, this is how far Yehuda Hallevi Street will extend; it's terribly important for him and he makes a mark in the sand with the heel of his shoe and stands up straight with both arms extended sideways, indicating precisely the direction of Yehuda Hallevi in its built-up beginning and the imagined extent of Yehuda Hallevi when it is completed, And Rothschild Boulevard will be extended to down there, he points with both hands, in parallel, with the trees they will plant here too, while from here from these sycamores northwards everything is still open for settlement, he explains earnestly. And indeed there is a little raised space among the sand dunes and the vines, and when you look closer you can see clearly the whole ancient story: once upon a time there was the water in the rainy season that washed the hills and then came running down carrying silt down to the place where the water slowed and there the clay gradually accumulated and made the heavy soils, and from the sand that the wind shifted and the dust that it lifted came the fields of brown and dun, and the dark squares of the citrus groves sought out the sandy loam while the light-coloured vineyards preferred the light loam, and the luxuriant vegetables selected the heavy loam, but all together they only cover a patch here and a patch there, so that the whole of human activity over thousands of years, the adventures of their settlements and their doings, their flocks and their herds and everything they were, have left no more trace than a scrape here and a scratch there, a few mounds here and a few tracks there, and a few darker fields, but nothing more substantial, and when all is said and done here it lies over everything, from one end to the other, straight and wavy, compact and crumbly, totally empty, very simple and totally flat, the everlasting earth, totally clean, totally naked, warm and calm and beautiful, easy for the sun to come into and easy for it to surrender itself to the sun, and from when the morning mists dissolve until the reddish haze of sunset everything here is forever continuous, eternal and carefree, with the same quiet equilibrium, the same unweighty lightness, perhaps like the flight of a hawk, when it collects itself for a moment before it comes in to land, grazing the contour of the land, hovering for an instant before being swallowed into its calm being, so that had it not been there it would seem not to exist, there would be just the earth.

They walk on and come upon the side of a small orchard with the usual acacia hedge and inside as usual the throb of a motor in a sort of inverted jar on the end of a pipe throbbing regularly as water pumps do when they are working well, and there is a small deep cistern—you can drink from the palm of your hand that stops a jet from the broad rushing flow which gushes coolly, daintily straight from the darkness of the earth, so pure and full of the first touch of sunlight on its life, flowing cold and amusing itself for a moment with the splashing interplay of water and sunlight, and swiftly vanishing into the blue shadow under the trees—and there is no one to be seen. And now they are walking in the great wilderness of hot sand, and suddenly there is a dried-up field of watermelons that has already been picked, and suddenly there is a pair of donkeys galloping past, one holding on to the other's neck with its teeth, biting and biting while stamping its hooves, then they turn together the biter and the bit and as they turn the one unleashes from its hindquarters something big and fleshy and very long, that reminds you of something but not like this, and it goes round excitedly to the rear of the other donkey and tries to jump on its back as the other kicks out with both hind legs, hitting it full in the chest, and as this one plunges the other lowers its tail and runs with the first close behind, sniffing at its hindquarters, while Daddy is so embarrassed but he doesn't know how to deflect the youngster's gaze from the shameful spectacle, or how to distract his attention, while Teresh doesn't know how to reassure him, and doesn't press him for explanations, and Daddy senses that the youngster understands him and Teresh senses that Daddy senses, and when the donkeys have run off Daddy dismisses it all with 'things like that', the two donkeys, one of which, Daddy insists, was a she-ass (using the rather quaint old phrase), were just misbehaving, and this kind of misbehaviour is something that is shameful to see and shameful to show that you see.

And they walk both of them together. Sycamores here and there, date palms here and there, and vines that have been abandoned—there are only some warm honey-sweet grapes left among the withering leaves, golden-ripe and rusty with sweetness, they don't belong to anyone and you are allowed to pick some and rescue them from the nasty bees, and you can see a long way now, in the shimmer of the warming light, a whole stretch of earth with no additions, as from time immemorial, as though all that has taken place these last years in Tel Aviv and all its glory is really nothing more than a slight scratch or a little heap on the edge of this unchanging wholeness, a mere what-of-it beside the great unchanging, and all the exertions of the builders have melted away inoffensively on the face of the great open space all around, untouched and unaltered alike by the Arabs' vineyards and the Jews' houses. Only a little further to the east, right beneath the sun, you can see some cypresses and red roofed houses. And that's Sarona, says Daddy, the German colony, and beyond, further down, near Musrara, is Montefiore's orange grove, but if the youngster is tired we can sit here in the leafy shade of this fig tree, take off our shoes to tip out the sand, and maybe also find a few ripe figs that have not rotted or been eaten by the wasps, and try a soft one that you can eat whole with the skin on.

Montefiore planted the orange grove on his fourth visit, some eighty years ago, and he entrusted its care to a convert, Peter Ben-Abraham, and it contained one thousand four hundred trees and another six, at a time when there were not more than fifteen thousand people in the whole of Jaffa, and three thousand dunams of orange groves and two hundred Jews. With his chin on his knees Teresh listens to Daddy who knows everything, and so precisely, even though he simplifies it sometimes to suit the level of a youngster in Year 1, who is not soothed by the sight of the unbuilt-on land, on which no one can be seen hurrying and which no one can be seen working, everyone seems to have departed and there is not a soul left, all that remains is this expanse of light soil, totally bare, with the here and there next to nothing on it, all just soaking up the warmth of the climbing morning sun, and where to the side, invisible, there may be all sorts of vague villages, apart from that German colony that can be seen clearly, with its heavy black cypress trees and its very red pitched roofs, it is very well and solidly built, not like our settlements, and soon we'll go and take a closer look at how unique it is, Daddy explains, so clean, so hard-working, and so precise, and you'll be able to see the little church with its little bell tower, and the farmyards where everything is so well arranged and calm and whole, and if you like we can also see some pigs.

And finally, when they are both fairly tired and it is really hot, they sit down on a green bench under a large mulberry tree, and Daddy fans himself with his hat. And there are red geraniums, and behind them there is very tall very green maize, and very green potato plants with heavy moist brown earth piled up around them, all so similar and yet so different and foreign, so familiar and so unfamiliar, always richer and more solid, and the building behind with green shutters seems to be the schoolhouse, even though it is so quiet, and there is no noise or hubbub, maybe they have all gone home, or they are on a trip too. And then suddenly it starts.

Singing. Sudden singing. Suddenly there is singing. Suddenly a choir starts singing. Suddenly there is the sound of a choir singing. From the windows of the school, and suddenly everything is full of the sound of singing.

Suddenly and that. Stunned. He is stunned. No, not he. There is no he. He is now only what enters him floods him fills him full. Once he was sitting on a green bench outside and Daddy was there.

Now he is like a diver who cannot breathe again until he surfaces. It's not that either. But talking and he is without a word, now it is the singing and in the middle the flood that enters him and blows into him and fills him. One moment he knew what and the next nothing but a kind of non-existent thrill. Nothing else, only this thing that he never knew existed. Nothing else exists. Only this, a choir singing.

There is no more to tell. That's all. There's nothing, only this splendour that enters him and floods him with the sound of the choir singing. Such harmonious vocal colours, in such a way, he doesn't know what way. Only this feeling of fullness, only being on the edge of the abyss, and none of all this because it is all just words to explain later, right now he is simply stunned by what is coming over him, coming into him filling him, and it is beautiful, so very very beautiful.

Suddenly with voices filled to the right height for singing voices, with full, clear singing, with many voices singing together fully, not in a single line but with many lines together, wonderfully intertwined, like a pipe they have thickness and bulk and a full roundness, and it enters into him warm and strong and smooth and full and whole and round and rich, or as though lots of horses are suddenly bursting out of a gate and galloping in the open, or like the wind unleashing a running wave over a field, he doesn't know what it is like, and there is no like, unless it is a sudden vast view from the top of a mountain, no, not that either, just that it is beautiful, wonderful, so very, yes so very beautiful.

He does not know that it is a youth choir and he does not know that it is accompanied by a harmonium and he does not know that it is Schubert, he cannot know, how could he, but just that it is beautiful, yes, beautiful, only later he may begin to know, now it is within, with a fulfilment that absorbs you, later perhaps memory will find words and he will know how to tell it true, not now, like blue or green that exist on their own without words to say: he is simply open now and is filled with abundance, he simply chokes back tears from the choking over-fullness—not even this because this is later—now it is just the fulfilment, the knowledge of the fullness that is being filled, the knowledge of more than he can know there is, just opened up to be filled by this filling abundance, for which he seems to have been waiting forever, with all his six little years, closed in by the limits of his little capacity, and suddenly it's as though the sun has risen and he is opening up, ready without knowing it, and the choir of many voices comes into him, and he feels he is becoming lost in what is coming into him. And that this exceeds his capacity and he will never be able to come back from it.

He never knew that such a thing existed or could exist. How could he have known? After all, our singing is always a matter of *Hurry brothers hurry*, or *There in the land our fathers loved*, or the interminable *The journey to Jerusalem, jam and preserves*, with everybody singing as they pleased, and deep inside he always knew that this was not it, the real thing would come one day, and suddenly it has come, it has grabbed him suddenly, and he is still a child, smooth and innocent like sand rippled by the wind. And suddenly, inside in his innermost being, suddenly it exists, and it is beautiful, oh, so beautiful.

It will be ten years before he hears names like Schubert, or gets to know the song 'Rose among the heather'; only later, reading Romain Rolland's *Jean Christophe*, will he discover Beethoven before hearing a note of his music; and later still, on Uncle Moshe's record player, will he start to listen to records of what they will call classical music, and see for the first time a sheet of music held by a strange man playing the violin; whereas music, composition, harmony, counterpoint, polyphony, harmonics, and suchlike do not exist yet at all, or thirds, fourths and fifths, and without all this, without words, without any context, without any preparation, only the essence of this wonderful thing itself, maybe like a desert-dweller encountering rain for the first time, or like an inland dweller meeting the sea, stunned, surprised, delighted, and there is no like, or like suddenly from the top of a mountain, no, not that and nothing ready-made, no things that are ready at hand, only it itself, this encounter, with all its force.

Schubert? 'Rose among the heather'? German folksongs? Chorales? In three voices, accompanied on the organ? Who knows. What difference does it make. Only that it should all be full, that it should all flow, that it should all be like a hosepipe, totally round, and you all open, only that they should not stop, the people singing the children singing the school choir singing. And suddenly there is a world. Suddenly everything. And different from what there was before. As though it's opened up and it simply flows. And it is nothing but so beautiful, this beautiful thing. And everything.

Part four

Tiyyara

Since this morning they have been making a *tiyyara*. Not a kite, but
a *tiyyara*, and not a hexagon, but a triangle, made from three canes
and not bulrush stems, and not fixed in the middle with a stout knot
of string, and not attached by a string that runs round their ends, in
slits so that it doesn't slip—this time it is a huge triangle, with its tip
at the bottom and its base at the top, with strips of paper like side-
whiskers stuck on its two long sides, and the full, firm tail stuck at
the tip; and the innovation is not just the height of the *tiyyara* which
will be as tall as a man, but the revolution of going from a hexagon
to a triangle, unbelievable, a simple triangle that only has three angles
that total exactly 180 degrees, the bare essentials, and you need to
have sufficient competence to make it from three canes tied together
firmly with string, so that they do not come undone in the wind in
mid-air, and it is over this special knot that they are now bent, the
elder brother and his two friends, their three tousled heads almost
touching, as they have been since morning, in the summer holidays,
when they could have been out looking for some temporary job, as
Mummy pointed out persuasively, without taking the bread out of
the mouths of the unemployed who have become more numerous
lately, in this depression that has become more noticeable in the first
Hebrew city, but even pennies can help to pay off the massive debts in
which the building of the new house has plunged us up to our necks,
and why shouldn't a strong healthy lad of fifteen and an excellent
worker help a bit—why, Daddy at his age, or a year later, he was
only sixteen when he left everything behind him and came straight
to Hadera, with Tolstoy in one hand and the Bible in the other, and

all the responsibility for the rebuilding of the Land was in his two hands that held a hoe or a pruning hook by turns, instead of which he and his two friends have been head to tousled head since early this morning, labouring with responsible industry to bring about the perfect accomplishment of an aerial revolution in the neighbourhood of Tel Nordau (named for some old Zionist leader), and they will not rest until this giant triangle takes to the air today, in the afternoon breeze, and soars high above all the pathetic kids of Nordiya with their childish hexagonal kites that rely on rustling strips and ribbons and do not rise above the norm, in a flash of genius transcending the limitations of the common run, and to make it you have to get up early and find canes that are long enough, strong enough and supple enough, because the impact of the wind on the triangular sail that will take to the air this afternoon will be bruising, and the paper must be strong enough but light enough, and the string must be strong enough but not too thick, because the young man who is in charge has a yen for the big and the unusual, and for more than others have, and his eyes are flashing now and his hair is waving, and his bronzed beauty is lithe and from his bare feet to his golden dextrous hands he is all industry and his two friends with him, and on the paper they will stretch over the skeleton of this airship they will stick the face of a smiling sun and around it they will stick a beard made of strips of paper, and below a tail with many strips, which will be a kind of rudder and a kind of counterweight so that the triangle does not turn upside down in the air, or spin round and round, or plunge diagonally to earth and smash itself to bits, and so they had to look for a different kind of string, they could not make do with the usual string that is called *shpugat*, and the choice fell upon the greased string called Samson that is sold in balls in all shops serving the needs of citrus growers, and there is no point in explaining how three balls came to end up here, and now the most difficult and responsible moment of all has arrived, the balancing of the three strings that join the three corners of the triangle to the main knot to which the Samson string is attached, which will withstand the forces of the afternoon wind that blows from the sea, that sea that lies down there just a thousand steps from here, counted and leapt each morning when you run to plunge into it and it is open to you ready for you blue for you with foamy waves for you and it loves you.

The sand dunes stand all around, a building here and there springs from the sand, pure dunes on which the ripples still run as on virgin dunes, and close to the sea they sprout like all the coastal dunes with evening primrose that you can dust your friends' noses with for fun, extravagantly laying bare the bulbs of lilies that have not flowered yet and white convolvulus with a heart of gold, and all sorts of thorns and especially the hidden ones that prick your bare feet like a white-hot burn, and the things that Daddy calls gall bushes, plus all those scurrying beetles and fleeting lizards, and it is as if the builders of Tel Nordau have not come this far, and at night the jackals at the doors of the houses, almighty terror, and sometimes it seems you have been forgotten by the world and sometimes it seems as though you are all good friends, and that in all the houses live children who are all friends, inseparable, and the mothers all consult each other earnestly too, all in the same one shop, and when the day ends for all of them in darkness they all light the lamp in their room and all the world is ended, and they are shut away like a ship on the high seas, and there is no more land until tomorrow morning, and now it is quiet, just crickets, and silence, and the din of the sea, and darkness and a little fear, and silence that sounds like the echo of a huge non-existent bell. He is not called Teresh any more; now he is called Tsi. Because Mikha'ela has a dog, a thin greyhound, lean and tall, with drooping ears and a pointed, wet nose, all aquiver with excitement, and above all he is thin, thin, thin, and the dog's name is Tsi, plain tsi, tsi tsi tsi, and it's not surprising that Mikha'ela, and the others after her, started calling him Tsi, tsi, tsi tsi, and Mikha'ela has two plaits down her back and she is interested in all the boys except him, and at school she talks to all of the others but not to him, because he is Tsi, tsi, tsi tsi, a thin hound, and all this is since they moved here, to Tel Nordau, to Mendele Mokher Sefarim Street, number 22, the second house along from Sirkin Street, that was built on the spot where one of the numerous sand dunes that used to stand here was demolished, that you could tumble down head over heels, and it was easy to dig foundations in it, and easy too to pour the concrete in, and to pour concrete into moulds to make blocks, with Daddy standing over them to stop them pouring as much concrete in as they wanted, because concrete is expensive, so they built with concreteless concrete blocks, as the workmen laughingly said, but Daddy hasn't laughed since then, as he is totally embroiled in debts and demands for payment, he doesn't sleep at night, he struggles to find extra work, he gets up in the early hours to write an article to earn a few more pennies, rumours about pay cuts chase rumours about sackings, he looks for ways of saving money as the house is being built, despite which all of a sudden they are surrounded by a world that is waking up, clean, free, with the sighing of the sea and the blowing of the breeze and the sand, and eventually we'll think of a way out of this, Mummy says, like everyone else here.

Tsi is a short name and you don't need to make a big effort to remember it, and it accompanies you easily all along Ben Yehuda Street when you go to school in the morning, and during all the breaks at school, of course, Geula School in Geula Street, and there are always shouts in the playground, Tsi tsi tsi, but you don't care, both because it's really funny, and also because the hound is really cute, and also because Mikha'ela with her plaits looks at you then, you don't say anything to her and she doesn't say anything to you, and yet. There are only children from good families at the school, only children of teachers, civil servants and writers, only from all the neighbourhoods that have just been built, they all have names evoking redemption, like Yigal, Go'el or Geula, apart from those who come each morning from faraway Mikve Yisrael in a wonderful-smelling conveyance drawn by two black horses, swaddled in coats, apparently coming from a faraway land with a faraway smell, and apart of course from all the teachers who converge from every direction on Mrs Yehudit Harari, the headmistress who used to work in the kindergarten in Neve Tzedek, using the new Montessori method and not the Farber method favoured by the kindergarten teacher Mrs Haskina—Tova Haskina from Yehuda Hallevi Street—and their destinies seem to be intertwined, Mrs Yehudit Harari and the thin child Tsi, tsi tsi tsi, and there is also Mr Riklis and there is Mr Yekutieli and Mr Maaravi who teaches singing, accompanying himself on the accordion and gym, jump jump jump, and in Bible lessons Mrs Harari with enthusiasm and skinny Tsi with wonderment climb up to the seventh heaven, but in nature study when the teacher asked what was the most horizontal line in the room, and they guessed the floor or the ceiling or the desk or the teacher, only young Menuhin, a dark boy with flashing eyes, said eventually The water in the aquarium, and it was so right, and they all saw that there was nobody cleverer in the class, and the teacher praised him to his face, or Zemira, the red-headed girl who can recite the whole of Haim Nahman Bialik's 'To the volunteers of the people' by heart, or Shoshana, the dark-haired, dark-eyed girl who knew who Dostoevsky was, or Avital, the boy with the glasses, who knew what a threshing sledge is and how you separate the straw from the chaff—but that's not clever because in the holidays he always goes to stay with his grandfather in Gedera—or the curly-haired fat boy Ahuvia who can always tell jokes about everything, even though, they say, his father is dead, and all the rest of the ten-year-old Go'els and Geulas gathered in class 5, only to shout during break with a din that no playground can contain, punctuated with noisy tweets in honour of Tsi, tsi tsi tsi, and Mikha'ela, to whom Tsi sends quiet looks without saying anything, also says nothing and doesn't send looks or anything.

This afternoon it will fly, and Tel Aviv has not seen anything like it yet. Beyond the Silicate factory, which is the most splendid enterprise in the world, with its chimney that would scrape the clouds if there were any, because it is hot summer outside and the grown-ups find its humidity oppressive but the children don't remember that it's summer, apart from the grapes in all the Arab vineyards and the figs in all the Arab gardens and the melons in all the Arab fields, which the jackals will eat in a nocturnal frenzy with demented shrieks if they don't pick them soon. They make paste from flour and water, but to make enough paste for the dimensions of the triangle they will need enough flour for three Sabbath loaves, Mummy declares as she chases them away, and they leave through the door but come back through the window, because before this evening the *tiyyara* has to fly in broad daylight and before this great day is up, and if they do not paste it well the wind will come and smash it and tear that great expanse of paper, and it will be impossible to avert the catastrophe and the breaking of three hearts, and the mockery and contempt of all the children of Nordiya, including some from Mendele Street, Sirkin Street, and Shalom Aleikhem Street that literally adjoins this Nordiya that bred these children as brazen as Indians or Bedouin, who destroy everything and respect nothing, who swoop like hungry locusts to snatch whatever they are allowed to and even things they are not strictly allowed to, like that Yigal of theirs who walks barefoot all year round and is always coughing and has a runny nose, who swears as nobody else can or dares; and on the west side beyond Ben Yehuda Street as far as Yarkon Street, near the far end of which lives that naturalist who limps with one shoe made higher than the other, while on the corner lives Peretz, with his pretty daughters who play the piano, and right below which is the surging sea with its foam-capped breakers, and just above which Mr Munchik has just put up his house that was built entirely by a team of women, with baggy trousers down to their knees and big straw hats, and no man was allowed near, a team of women working to contract, with gravel, cement, pouring concrete, carrying buckets up the scaffolding, let everyone know in this land that is being rebuilt that there is nothing a woman cannot do as well, if not better, and they were proud of their handiwork, even if they were exhausted and bruised, as Yigal, Munchik's son, now tells, whose bread and jam which he brought from his house on the sea—which today is the Dan Hotel, apparently—is suddenly grabbed by someone who is hungrier than he, it seems it is Yigal from Nordiya, who is known as Galeguleh.

It seems that everything is ready for the launch, though no detail has been carried through to the end, and when this space triangle flies every defect that has not been put right yet will stand out, and the whole thing will fall apart and smash, and they have to take the tail, which they have stuck together from quantities of newspapers torn into strips, including *Davar*, the new paper that is not saved by its novelty but turns into strips that will flutter noisily above the clouds, with all the advertisements for Maspero cigarettes and Raanan chocolate and Poliakov the modern tailor, and the editorial and jeremiads about the rising tide of unemployment; they still have to check the whiskers that are going to be stuck on the sides of the triangle and make sure that they are heavy enough but not too heavy; they particularly have to see to the knot that joins the three strings coming from the tips of the triangle to ensure that they are properly balanced, and that requires precise measurement and serious calculation, and the circle of visitors who have heard rumours and come to argue don't leave a moment's silence for concentration, and soon this elder brother and his two friends will repel and expel these invasive individuals, besides the fact that it is midday and at midday all the children from good homes have to go home to Mummy's kitchen, before each mother's voice in turn is raised in a shout that carries across the open sands, Yi-i-i-gal, ho-o-o-me, and only those nobody's children, the urchins from Nordiya, will be left, so messages are sent to three mothers informing them that their darlings will be home a little late today, and once more, head to tousled head, they bend over the work in hand, while around them press the Amalekites, clasping their unwashed knees, with only a little bit of shorts to cover their meagre flesh, so little that they don't care if you can see everything, their childish droopy willies, sprawling in a circle as taut as springs ready to run or to snatch, and you can't get rid of them, until on a sudden ruse, *Yallah*, says the elder brother, run and fetch some grapes, and this raises them light on their bare feet to vanish among the shimmering sand dunes, glowing dots and whitening dots, until they are back with bunches of grapes, laughing, they plucked them from under the nose of the sleeping Arab, and they all wipe the sand and the paste off their fingers on their trousers and settle down to pull off grapes that are yellow with honey and rusty with oozing juice.

Only a stranger would think that there is nothing here but a cluster of desolate sunbaked sand dunes, when in reality one round-shouldered hill does not resemble another nor does one curve of sand resemble another, and when you go for a walk on the Sabbath to the Yarkon, for example, everything is full of adventures, and Tsi, the skinny little boy, when they deign to take him along, is not sure how they will know the way out and back again in these rounded expanses, all equally swept by the light sea breeze whose light progress there is nothing to obstruct; when you take the sea path you quickly come to the big Muslim cemetery, and sometimes you happen on a funeral cortège walking along the sea shore singing *La Allah ila Allah u-Muhammad rasul Allah*, which has a monotonous tune and also something hostile and threatening about it, for some reason, as though some evil will break out, and then you leap over the sandstone rocks that are amazing in their interaction with the sea, with their hollow caves and rocky outcrops on which the sea dashes its foam, and then you turn into the area of the fenced-off vineyards and it is best not to meddle with the keepers, and very tired from the long walk you finally reach the sluggish Yarkon, so green and greasy, of which the most fascinating aspect is the boats moored along its banks, beside the tall eucalyptus trees, seagoing boats that came here when the water was still high and the mouth of the river had not yet been silted up with sand so that camels can cross it with dry feet, laden with boxes of coarse sand or watermelons; with their tall masts and arrangements of ropes, painted red, blue and green, this paltry water pretending to be a river cannot match their massive bulk yearning for the oceans, so colourful, so regal, straight out of tales of pirates, now humbled and sunk in the mud; and the mischievous elder brother has climbed to the top of the highest mast to the tip above where the ropes and the flags are tied, from where in a rush of courage and fear he plunges unhesitatingly head and arms first into the water, before anyone can shout, No, no, don't jump, after which one of those in the know said anxiously that the water was not very deep here, and he could have broken his neck, and also that there is bilharzia in the water, which is a terrible disease from Egypt, and if you catch it you piss blood till you die, to which the naked elder brother responds by simply standing up, holding his thing, and shooting his own water in a wide arc into the stagnant water of the river, bursting out laughing and all the others with him, and the water makes ripples for him as far as the opposite bank.

But not only he is surrounded all day long by his busy, scheming friends, even skinny Tsi is no longer a lonely child sitting at home with books and bits of junk serving him as toys. In every street where there is no roadway yet and just a few houses here and there, some of them still being built, giving work to the jobless, friends are already living, some of whom go to Geula School with him while others go to all sorts of different schools, including the educational establishment for workers' children that has opened somewhere recently, and some of whose parents are actually teachers—Zerubavel's father, for instance, a heavily-built, serious man, is always standing cutting letters from coloured paper for his Class 1, while Binji's father, for example, has a briefcase full of high school students' exercise books, and another one that he takes to the publishing house with unpublished writings by Brenner, as Binji himself, an active member of the Defenders of the Hebrew Language and the campaign to buy local products, explained once, and Yigal's father, the one who had his house built by women, is working on setting up an insurance company for the Histadrut, the General Federation of Jewish Labour, though it is none too clear what the project is, nor is it clear what Gershon's father does, but Gershon himself is an amusing boy whose funny faces and imitations are famous from Shalom Aleikhem Street to Yarkon Street, and Avital's father is a delightful teacher who works at school in the morning and gives private lessons in the afternoons and he writes poems for children and is not to be disturbed, and their house on Bugrashov Street is near the sea, and only Ahuvia from Sirkin Street has no father but he has a jolly mother, and he himself is curly-haired and jolly, and he has a very famous friend, and one day they all went to see him because he loves children especially Ahuvia, and he puts him on his lap and strokes his curls, and that day he gave Tsi an illustrated book entitled *A Tale of a Camel Who Went to Look for a Pair of Horns and Had His Ears Cut Off*, and he even signed the flyleaf with a poetic flourish, H.N. Bialik, but alas, the book got lost.

The children have no difficulty running around and coming and going, but for the grown-ups everything is sand that fills their shoes and it is hard to drag them around; they are hot and sweaty, and in the morning and the evening you can see columns of ants in human form picking their way along the kerb in Ben Yehuda Street waving their arms to keep their balance like strange birds, and two black threads of people going in either direction, patiently and uncomplainingly, so long as they do not sink in the sand in the middle, from Tel Nordau to Allenby and back, and the strangest of all are the pair who walk through the sand of Mendele several times a day, talking to one another, one in front and one behind: the one in front has flame-red hair as wild as fire, and he does not look down at his feet but only up at the sky, and his feet drag behind him heavy and forgotten, dragging in the loose sand, literally with his head in the clouds and his feet in the sand, while the one behind has his head in the sand and his feet in the sand, all of him is in the sand, buttoned up in his clothes, and he seems to be grumbling, and those in the know explain that the first one, the one with the fiery hair and the dragging feet, is actually a well-known poet who has just brought out a book of poems, entitled of all things *Great Fear and the Moon*, apparently his feet are in fear and his head is in the moon, and the one trailing behind him is apparently also a writer and an important translator and it is not known yet but will come out years later that he is the one who translated *Jean Christophe* and heaven and earth opened before Beethoven and one way or another there is no child on his own in the whole of Tel Nordau, or in any of the new houses with the sharp smell of fresh plaster that still looks too bright on the walls, all the children are always with all the other children, and when they finish being at one's home they all go off to another's, and only at night when the dark closes in and transforms each house into an isolated boat by the light of the lamp in its cabin, when the silence echoes as though it were the noise of the sea, so much so that if you look up from your book you begin to feel the rocking of the sea, and its waves licking at the hull and continuing to rock in the great darkness, and everything is infinite and there is nothing except the quiet that is not the absence of sound but silence: a moaning silence.

Their house has three rooms now, a kitchen and a bathroom with no bath for lack of money, and in the kitchen there is a larder and a table for Mummy to prepare the food on—apart from the vegetables a pumpkin stew and rice and sugar and cinnamon, *oy*, and hardboiled egg mashed up with fried onions and oil and something else rather revolting, *oy*, and the boiled chicken with potatoes, *oy*, or the fish that she buys straight from the fisherman who goes past in the morning chanting *Yallah* fish, *yallah* fish, after driving him half mad by haggling, *oy oy*, and there is still the omelette with tomato, and the glass of milk, and the apricot jam, for which it's worth eating almost a quarter of a slice of bread—which early in the morning also serves Daddy as a desk for writing his articles, he sits and writes without disturbing anybody's sleep, for without public assistance or the help of a bank how can a worker or a clerk manage to build a house, when a rented room costs half a month's salary, and some people pay three or four Egyptian pounds for a single room, goodness gracious, and the house is empty and bare of any ornament apart from the chandelier that they brought one day from somewhere, made of dripping clusters of glass beads that the slightest breeze sets tinkling with a cheerful silvery sound, and apart from one of the doors that has a glass panel set in it so that if you like you can look at your own reflection as in a mirror or if you prefer you can look through it to the view outside, and one day a camel filled it, and a whole camel was suddenly walking through the house, seemingly looking for somewhere to sit down. But what really fills the house, more than anything else and all the time, is the anxiety whose weight is gradually breaking Daddy; he is always repeating annoying words like debts, IOUs, mortgages, interest, short term, deferred payment, where will I get, God Almighty where will I get, and so on and so forth, like someone who knows he has failed, who has betrayed his family, who has shown himself shamefully weak. What if the boy finds a treasure, what if he talks to Mr Dizengoff and asks him to help, what if he sells newspapers on the corner of the street?

Now a caravan of camels arrives on the plot where they are building the house next door, which will be number 24 apparently, carrying leaking boxes of coarse sand. The camel does not need to kneel because with one blow of a shovel they open the fastening underneath and it all pours out with a rush so that the camel almost overbalances and it grumbles and mutters and fouls the air, and its master runs round to empty the other box—he has strips of transparent paper stuck to his nose and lips against the painful peeling of his skin that refuses to tan, and there is something mismatched about the imported appearance of the man and the primordial appearance of the camel as they both shout at each other, one in plaintive Yiddish and the other in a timeless gurgle—and so camel after camel empties its load onto the heap in this plot that is an earnest of a serious intention to build here, and he goes to the tap to drink from his cupped hands and the camel is left gurgling and refusing but eventually it obeys with its great doe's eyes and its lower lip sagging to display alarmingly huge and yellow teeth, and finally they get into line, the man in front and the camels behind him, waving their tails and swaying from two legs to two legs, ancient creatures in a new place. And now a breeze blows from the sea and it is time to launch the *tiyyara* of the century, the *tiyyara* of Tel Aviv under construction, it will soar over above everything and high above the Silicate chimney that will remain insignificantly below, with the coil of Samson string to the end of which they will tie the beginning of the next coil and the third to the second, so much, to control the faraway flying triangle on which the red face of the sun with a yellow smile has been stuck now, and when the wind gets stronger and the sea that is warmer now than the land now sends those rising currents of air inshore to blow on the sand dunes and trace new ripples on them to stir the few sycamores and the few eucalyptus trees that are there without having been planted, the breeze will catch in the stretched triangle of paper with its impudent red and yellow smile firmly fixed to the carefully chosen canes and accurately balanced on the knot—according to the laws governing lift, which are even mentioned in school books, the wind will have no choice, it will blow and the kite will sway against it like a horse straining against its tether, it will quiver against it as taut and sensitive as a violin, and then one of the friends will carry it backwards with both hands, knowing how to hold its rustling weight delicately, while the other friend moves to the side to give the signal for the launch, and the big brother too will walk back to take up a position from which when the signal is given he will start running backwards, unwinding enough string for the opening manoeuvre, and while one friend lets go and the other shouts and jumps up and down our brother will start running backwards against the wind and give the triangle a reason to rise gracefully upwards and climb up the high wind and then up the higher wind for as long as the string is paid out, and more wind will make more lift and more lift will make more distance and more string released, and then a great shout of triumph will burst over the earth: It's flying!

And almost everything is ready. Where did so many children come from, camping nervously and excitedly all round, one with some advice, another with a question, another with doubts and yet another with admiration, which does not pass by these pioneers of Hebrew aviation, all sprawling in the sand and sifting it from hand to hand excitedly or sinking in the sand as they look for a group to talk to or a vantage point? Some heard and escaped in the middle of a violin or piano lesson, or an English lesson, or in the middle of the washing up, or of looking after their younger brother, or even on their way to the beach, clutching a half-chewed corn-cob, but there are no girls here, not because they don't know—because who doesn't know that the *tiyyara* of the century is about to be launched—there is no doubt that the entire sisterhood has heard and knows but they won't come, it's not proper, the only one to come is Mikha'ela, here she is with her plaits down her back and her hound Tsi with his splendid collar, so there is Tsi the dog and Tsi the boy, one held by her hand and the other holding onto her with his eyes, torn between two sights, moments before the clash between Tel Nordau and Nordiya, or even between Tel Aviv and Jaffa, because this is not an Arab *tiyyara*, despite its Arabic name, nor is it some hexagonal kite with a wavy fringe and a snakelike tail, wobbling from side to side, but a *tiyyara* of invention and revolution, of conquest and breakthrough, of imagination and daring, of the triumph of the Jews and the triumph of progress, there are great expectations, there is breathless tension in all the streets with their few scattered houses, there is suspense, as though the film of films were being shown in the cultural centre, they are all crowded here to be present at the heart of things, where it is happening.

What next? Now a hush falls. Without anyone trying to silence them. The youth carries the *tiyyara* backwards holding the great triangle up reverently before him with its paper whiskers and its mighty tail made from a motley assortment of newspaper and shining coloured paper, and he is hidden behind the bulk of the triangle and you can see that even the slight breeze on the ground senses what awaits it and is straining at his hands as they hold fast, and the boy who is to give the signal, who is responsible for general co-ordination, is walking backwards to get a commanding view, and it would be easy to crawl behind him and trip him up to general laughter but it would not occur to anyone to play such a mean trick now, until he finds the precise vantage point, while the elder brother, the only begetter of the whole performance, its accessories, its actors and the magnificence of its imminent triumph, with the stout string partly rolled round a piece of wood for immediate use and the rest coiled in round balls of Samson string so as not to get tangled kept ready under his bare feet, raises the string coiled round the piece of wood to chest height and stands attentively with the string taut some fifty paces behind the red triangle with its broad smile; the youth who is carrying the triangle and is hidden behind it waits for the signal, and the youth who is to give the signal waits for the right moment, and nobody breathes on the sandhill, not a man or a boy or a girl or a dog, and then it is impossible to wait any longer, and the cry Fly, aimed at the *tiyyara* and its authors, makes everything happen at once, the elder brother runs backwards with the taut string, the other gives a push and lets go, and the whole congregation of the children of Israel cheers.

And it rises, and the wind jolts it and lifts it, and even the tail leaves the sand, after tracing a serpentine line on it, and it flies, and rises, and the elder brother runs and as he runs he pulls on the string so that the wind will find the chest of the triangle and not its sides, and the youth who carried it jumps and jumps as though he has vowed to jump from now to the end of his days, and he cheers too, and the one who gave the signal jumps and jumps and his trousers almost fall down because they are not buttoned up properly and were not made for apelike leaping, and the whole congregation of the children of Israel jumps up and down, and the cheering re-echoes and reaches the Silicate chimney that will soon be left far below, because the *tiyyara*, unlike the usual pathetic efforts, does not rock jerkily, unsure whether to fly or collapse, but it is excellently, accurately and wonderfully made, and it rises catching gust after gust, and it catches the big wind that is above the low breeze and it provokes the wind to hit it with its really big gusts, and now the Samson string stretches, and were it not Samson string it would have snapped long ago with the strain, and now they give it more string, and more string, to make it happy make it rise make it fly, and all because of the absolute precision of the knot balancing the three corners of the triangle at the right angle in relation to the wind it takes in and devours all the string and rises to daring heights and keeps rising and receding into the distance, and now the second ball of string is finished, and the triangle that was so huge on the ground is now no more than a quarter of a songbird in the sky, you can hardly make out that it has a smiling face on it, and you can sense that the thing is too strong to hold, and this queen of *tiyyaras* is pulling so hard that the two friends come and hold onto it with the elder brother and the three of them strain to master it, it's as if down here they have spent the whole morning making a creature that is bigger and stronger than they are, and a tense silence seizes all the hill as they strain with the three children whose six hands are holding onto this mighty celestial serpent that is dragging them up into the sky, so high that the whole Silicate factory is a joke and all the houses of Tel Nordau must look like a child's building blocks from up there, as though there is no trace of human creation left here on the sand dunes, and probably the people picking their way along the pavements of Ben Yehuda Street, who are the best of the builders of

Tel Aviv, its sages, writers and teachers, resemble nothing more than last year's stubble among the sand dunes, and now almost three balls of Samson string have unwound and flown aloft to hold onto the well-balanced knot of that great triangle that has soared into the sky and the wind is blowing it as though it were really a fitting partner for its infinite free force instead of just a few pieces of paper stuck with paste made with Mummy's flour onto three canes, as though the *tiyyara* were some mighty eagle made by God instead of paper stuck on canes by three boys, who are now holding onto the end of the Samson string with the last of their strength and the whole hill is holding its breath with them, it is not clear what will happen now, when suddenly—oh God—when suddenly it is snatched out of their hands, out of all six clenched hands, the string is snatched away and takes flight and starts running, at first on the sand and then it is pulled up into the air and the whole thing belongs to the sky from the end of the string to the highest heights, and they, the three of them, and the whole hill, all start running to catch the fleeing end, running and falling, leaping after it, snatching, chasing and snatching, stumbling in the sand, getting up and falling, but it is flying further and further, light and free and flying, fleeing, fleeing, fleeing, everything, the string, the *tiyyara*, the smiling sun, everything, it flies away and it flees and is no more it has gone away and is no more, is nothing, it has gone gone gone.

Tel Nordau

On brown folding chairs, with pierced seats and backs, sitting on the open veranda, one sipping tea, one leaning back so far he would tip over if the wall were not there to support him, one with his face in his hands and his elbows on his knees, something is weighing on him apparently, and Mummy is pouring them all tea, and there is a little shadow lying on the ground between them and the lit room;

there is no light out here because it would attract the mosquitoes, but this is not the only shadow, because they all have some shadow, the shadow of anxiety, the shadow of mounting unemployment, the shadow of pay cuts and lay-offs, or the shadow of bills, debts and how to pay them, and they drink Mummy's tasty tea, and her home-made biscuits, rather hard and dusted with sugar, and apart from Daddy there is the new neighbour who has started to build to the right of them, who is not called by his real name but for some reason by a nickname that sounds something like Yatta, he is moving in soon with his pale, bespectacled wife and their baby girl Yaelinka and their son Dushinka, and Yatta is known to work in the big co-operative printing works that prints virtually everything that is printed in the country and everything that is worth reading, and he is an expert on everything that is written but never agrees with a word that is printed or spoken, here on the veranda or anywhere else, and there is also Mr Munchik, who here among friends is simply called Eliyahu, and his subject is anything to do with business and economics, he is the one whose house on the seashore was built by a team of women working to contract and his son Yigal is a friend of the shadow lying on the ground near the door, who has enough light to read his book and enough darkness for them not to notice that he is not missing a word of their conversation, which were it not for him would vanish at once and nothing would be known of it, it would remain in the darkness that begins literally at the end of the veranda, because right after that start those sand dunes that are cooling down fast, and from which now, as you look, a vague dim glow comes, as though they have not been completely extinguished.

Does the crisis have to come? That is the topic they are discussing at the moment in the half-darkness. What have they not done right to prevent it, and what can they still do to avert it? Comrade Eliyahu thinks the main thing is the middle class people who have just started to arrive and whose lives are being made difficult, and that no priority given to the working class will achieve what they can achieve, and Yatta of course disagrees, everything is so bad because there is no planning, no prior consideration is given to how to invest and in what, and Mummy thinks it is all because of the terrible waste everywhere and she has examples, and Daddy who is an expert in figures says nothing for the time being but only tries unsuccessfully to hide his repeated sighs of *ach vey*, because he is terribly worried, and if you watch him day by day you can see his temples greying day by day and his moustache too. A little free enterprise, says Comrade Eliyahu, and not having everything decided from above; too much anarchy, Mummy replies, everyone grabbing for himself; while Yatta, with his voice that brooks no contradiction, says that what is lacking today is the idea, and if the big idea has been lost no wonder the everyday reality has gone too. What idea? The Zionist idea, of course, and if they won't agree that the idea takes precedence over everything, the idea and the organisation, the idea and the Party, the idea and making demands on people, and the recognition, too, yes, the recognition that the idea takes precedence over people, over the individual, over supplying people's needs, where do you get, well, you get exactly where we've got. At which Comrade Eliyahu sighs and says that these things belong to the past, they cannot help us now, only initiative, only the middle class will find ways to survive that don't occur to the bureaucrats, What, he says truculently, do the bureaucrats have all the wisdom, don't we know who they are and how they got to be where they are? Mummy thanks him and says he has taken the words out of her mouth, and he takes her hand and kisses it courteously.

But no, Yatta says with his mop of hair and his thick curls in the half-light, we are not people who are out for ourselves, we are people with an idea, we are people who belong, without that we would not be here, people who belong to an idea, a goal and a mission, and if we are all for ourselves what are we? Thieves or exploiters, he says excitedly, and hence co-operatives, for example, collective enterprises, for example, mutual aid for example, he says, and Daddy intervenes now, Like in Nahalal, he says, sighing undisguisedly, *ach vey*, and the banks and the Anglo-Palestine Company, he says, and the interest, and credit that you cannot meet, not if you are an honest man, he said. And Comrade Eliyahu says that insurance against unemployment and insurance against bankruptcy might help, but instead of society trying to find ways, it would be better to let each individual find his own way. Only individuals think, he says, and society can only respond, Amen. But this makes Yatta shout, Eliyahu, Eliyahu, what has come over you? What has become of the principles, the values? And the darkness round about seems to move and withdraw a little.

They fall silent, and sip their tea, which is cold now, and Mummy offers to make some fresh hot tea, but they do not answer her and even the half-dark half-light continues to be silent, if it has not fallen asleep. And now it is time to get up and plod their way home, along dark roads through deep sand, only before that Comrade Eliyahu sums up by saying that you don't need a single brain for everyone, it's better to let everyone find his own way with his own brain, at which Yatta, who will be a neighbour once his house is finished, and who has a long way to tramp through the sand to the rented flat where he lives with his pale wife, his baby daughter Yaelinka and his son Dushinka somewhere at the end of Shalom Aleikhem, shouts again, No, no, and the darkness is startled, you have to have a collective brain, do you hear? That will work for the good of all, without discrimination or favour, do you hear? Mummy asks Daddy what he thinks, but Daddy is sad, nevertheless he says that maybe you don't need to interfere too much but just help the weak, until they are not weak any more, a colourless reply that does not please either Comrade Eliyahu or Yatta, for different reasons in each case, and so they say goodnight and go off into the dark sand dunes, and the shadow who has been watching them from between the light of the room and the dark of the balcony has the feeling he has heard these very same words before, more or less understood, precisely here between the house and the sand dunes, and half in light and half in shadow then too, and everything was wrapped in a great, dreary yawn. And that's the way it is.

Maybe because Ben Yehuda Street is the middle, after all, that's where they always meet, in a plot that has not been built on, between Binji's and Gershon's houses and Zerubavel's father's hut—the plot is empty apart from a rickety hut covered in tar paper, overgrown with some kind of blue-flowered convolvulus that, even though it is green and has flowers, is more than wretched, like an abandoned object, and it only climbs or twines around ownerless huts, or occasionally ownerless electricity poles, and inside the hut there is nothing but a torn suitcase and two mismatched shoes on a broken-down bedstead, with a vague smell of cobwebs, and something scary, were it not that the sun as it revolves round the earth also moves round the hut while its shadow moves round in the opposite direction, shortening then lengthening again, and this puddle of shade is the world's navel and the heart of Tel Nordau, and there the whole half dozen of them sprawl, sometimes huddled together and sometimes spread out according to the progression of the shade, and sometimes they burst out for no clear reason and run wildly one after the other round and round the ramshackle hut a few times with a lot of shouting and inexplicable laughter, then subside all together onto the patch of sand in the shade, and resume taking care of the unending affairs of the world, although school, its teachers and lessons hardly ever come this far, nor do family and family troubles, nor football matches, which are not considered important here, nor the films shown at the cultural centre with their endless wonders shown in instalments, to be continued next week, nor who else is building a house in the neighbourhood, but all the time they are totally immersed in adventure stories of let's suppose, imagine that, what if, that only require a plot and an announcement of who we are now, from *By Fire and Sword*, from *The Mountains of the Moon*, *Treasure Island*, *The Mysterious Island* with Captain Nemo, *The Pathfinder* and *Leather Stocking*, and *The Three Musketeers*, and are we dragoons this time or hussars, or grenadiers, or just plain pirates, or Vasco da Gama's men, or Magellan's men on their way to circumnavigate the globe, or even despite everything some ageless films, like *The Mysterious Maiden*, *The Roaring Lions*, or *The Lost Treasure*, where we never have to do anything except say so, and everything, surprisingly, happens, you only say the word and it comes into being, just say so and this is no longer Tel Nordau, it is more real and alive than the world, you only have to say so and the world exists.

No, they do not talk with one speaking and another listening quietly, but always only all together, and only in this way are things magically transformed from nothing into being, from words to reality, each one on his own could never have become such a magician, and it is only when they are all together in the shade of the blue-convolvulus-overgrown hut that this magic happens, that you only have to speak and it exists, it's enough to sit and talk, it's enough to begin with let's say that, or suppose that, or this time let's be, or you remember how… and immediately it exists, the adventures made of words alone come into being, and the events all made from words that come tumbling out quickly, and the exciting doings that are nothing but word play develop a crust of reality, just by sitting in the sand, in the shade of the hut covered in that creeper, one takes the beginning from the other and runs with it, and one completes the beginning he has received and runs with it, just like football, one dribbles and one shoots, they pass, one kicks forward from the spot where they got stopped, suddenly it is a show they all take part in and everyone knows his lines, like actors on stage, except that it's not on stage but in real life, really, where the parts are written on the spur of the moment, as they happen, and anyone watching from the slips might be alarmed and not understand what is going on, like Zerubavel's father, when he came out of his little house, a whitewashed hut until he extends it and builds a whitewashed house, one day to find the whole gang lying in the sand, 'their sturdy bodies sank in the yellow dunes', no, that's not right, it's 'the sand sank neath the sprawl of their sturdy bodies', he quoted as he told Gershon's mother and Binji's father of the mind-boggling spectacle that had met his eyes, nearly a dozen lads all from good homes lying there in that shade pouring out with incredible speed a complicated, confused, unbridled fabric of words, with animation, strange laughs, with crazy grimaces, total absorption, and a devotion that was not of this world, he said, and he didn't know whether he was complaining or marvelling, and surely as parents and teachers they should get together one day and discuss the matter from every angle, or maybe look for a serious book that would explain, or seek expert advice, or something, who had ever seen or heard of such a thing, and what sort of people would they grow into? And they could only answer his questions with amused or anxious nods of the head.

There he stood, Zerubavel's father, a large, heavy man who had named his son Zerubavel because 'Zeru' means go forth and 'Bavel' means the Diaspora in general, and what a decisive resonance of the rejection of Diaspora this bold name contains, and there stood Binji's father, a man of average build with the face of a genius, whose son Binyamin was the apple of his eye, and Gershon's mother, who had named her son after her father, apparently, with short-cropped round hair surrounding her face and a lot of stripes on her dress, her hands fidgeting with the edge of her apron because she had come straight from the kitchen and didn't know if it was proper to come out in an apron, Where were we at their age, the big man mused, and what were we doing at their age, There's no point in comparing, declared the mother, we went from one world to another, and they are fortunate enough to live in a single world, she said, and the thin man tried to stroke his few remaining hairs back into place on his learned head and said, We burnt our bridges when we came here and they only have to walk on the pavements, What did you expect them to do, said the mother, rebel? against whom? us? Surely we rebelled enough for three generations, said the heavily-built father, enough for the whole of history, none of them will grow up to be a doctor or a lawyer or a businessman, apparently, They will settle in the Valley or the Negev and be tillers of the soil, said the mother protectively, and Maybe, who knows, said the genius, they will be the leaders of the next generation? Life is so difficult, said the mother, and they are still so young, let them be, let them be, and suddenly they felt they had gone too far and revealed something that was too much, when actually all they had meant to do was to come out for a moment and do something and go straight back indoors, which is what they did.

What will we be when we grow up? They never talk about this really, in the shade of the tumbledown hut, perhaps because without talking about it, it is perfectly clear what they will be. And even when they meet years later they will only remember what it never occurred

S. Yizhar

to them they might be, like a sailor for instance, despite all the games, or an aviator for instance, despite all the games, or an explorer or a cavalryman in His Majesty's army, despite everything, or a wanderer travelling light and free with just a knapsack on his back, and that's not all, they didn't even aspire to be, for example, a great writer, or a heart-wrenching musician, or a famous painter, and in fact the one who ended up as a well-known theatrical producer had only one aim in life then, in the shadow of the hut with the blue creeper, to be an agricultural worker in Ein Harod or Beit Alfa, and the one who became an editor in a big publishing house wanted to become a cowman, and the one who became a well-known insurance agent wanted to be a carter, bringing the hay home at evening in his cart, and the one who became one of the heads of illegal immigration and the Mosad only longed to be a farrier at Yagur, and all of them to a man, under Binji's direction, volunteered for a day of films organised by the Jewish National Fund, or an induction day for the campaign for the promotion of the Hebrew language or for the 'Buy Local Produce' campaign, or a tree-planting day in the Ben Shemen hills, or a day of lectures with a magic lantern on the draining of the Huleh Swamps, and soon, one after another, they would all go off to all sorts of places to help their aunts and uncles pick apples or harvest maize or sort tomatoes, nobody wanted to be a leader of the masses or an activist in some organisation or a big fish in some small pond, and nowhere here yet has—only they soon will—all those youth organizations, the *Shomer Hatza'ir* and the Immigrants' Camps and the Working Youth and the Enrichment Sessions, and the Scouts, including the Haganah, sh-sh-sh, that would swallow up the wonderworkers in the shadow of the magicians' hut, and send them off to every corner of the Land bowed with responsibility, clutching briefcases, with tousled hair and blue shirts, as responsible youth leaders or earnest organisers of ideological seminars, or as intermediaries between the great figures of the nation and the militant youth, and they will not have a moment to breathe because of all the responsibility, the explanations, the committees and the camps, whereas now, here in the shade of that tumbledown hut overgrown with sickly blue convolvulus, there was nothing of all this, only Indians, only scalp-hunters, only creating wonderful frothy worlds out of word alone, erecting a flourishing world on the world of the dunes on which houses were springing up between the noise of the sea and the emptiness all around, without demanding anything for themselves or expecting anything. And that's the way it was. Like that.

Other children did not attach themselves to the group. They did not know the roles spontaneously. They came for a moment, sat for a moment and if they did not start mocking they just sat in silent bewilderment. And once Yigal, the drippy-nosed kid from Nordiya, came and was so fascinated that they could not get rid of him, until it transpired that he was hungry so Binji went to fetch him some bread and halvah, but then he was embarrassed at the thought that they thought he was hungry, and he said they were all arrogant and weren't worth his spit, and he left. And what about the girls? You must be joking. They have places of their own to go to, and what girls get up to when they are on their own is their own affair, who knows what they do, sometimes it seems as though girls are just like boys only a little different, and at other times it seems as though they are totally different with just a few drops of similarity. And Mikha'ela? Just her name means confusion and an urge to flee, with those plaits of hers down her back, her brown (is it?) eyes, and her arrogant walk and her indifference towards his whole being. And they say she plays the piano. Suddenly they become aware that it's evening and terribly late already, and it's time to go home, and that it's sad, and a shame, it's not clear about what, and they get up from the sand, which has heard a lot all day but it has left no trace, and start to go home and as far as Sirkin with Ahuvia, and they feel the need at the same time, raise a leg of their shorts and pee side by side until there is a little hole below them, they don't speak whether from tiredness or sadness or because that's the way it is, and on the corner of the two streets they stand for a moment as though to say a last word and Ahuvia says, Look how everyone here designed his own home and yet they have all come out the same, and Tsi says, Right down to the larder built into the kitchen wall, and Ahuvia says, Yes, and the little hatch between the kitchen and the veranda, and they linger for a moment and notice that the new people have already moved into the house that has just been completed, and people say that they are really Revisionists, even though they look just like everyone else, and apparently one of the children is called Neri, or Amihai, or something, and so now another hill has been wiped off the sum of all the wild hills that were here once. And that's the way it is. Ahuvia turns and goes his way, plump and curly-haired, and Tsi goes his way, skinny and floppy-haired, and the day has passed, and something, it's not clear what, seems to be missing, or something like that, and it's sad.

Mummy is in the kitchen, Do you want something to eat? Or a glass of milk? He smiles and says nothing, but curls up in the sand next to the veranda, resting his back and watching what is going on in the sky. Not much is happening, there is just an ordinary sunset, with no special performance, just an ordinary summer sunset in an ordinary empty sky with nothing on it. But now this empty sky is seen to be filling with something that is coming into being. The sun has set but the sky is still full of light. Not a burning light, but a gentle, calm light that fills all the western half of the sky and seems to be spread out evenly. And suddenly you see that the sky is higher than you thought and very smooth, and full of a special presence that you cannot name, nor can you name its colour, that is not a single colour but a kind of whole smoothness of a single whole thing, and it is really completely white or colourless, but all the dust of the day, which is still warm from the sun, has absorbed transparent colour or is reflecting back cooling echoes of colour, but you only know this, you don't see it, and all you see are different degrees, beginning with a little pink at the bottom to yellow-green further up and deep blue right at the top, with all the shades of orange in between, and also a kind of green, not a yellow green but the green of a ripe lemon, so that you can almost smell its lemony smell, and the sky is higher now than it seemed to be, or maybe it's not high but deep, so deep and far away, turning to a definite orange now, or even light blue, a very delicate light blue that has not been eliminated by this long furnace of a day, very blue and smooth and totally silent, and it all remains so high and distant and so far beyond all known dimensions that are within the limits of your power, these ready-made dimensions that are easy to say, because whether Tel Nordau is built this way or that way, quickly or slowly, calmly or painfully, it was there before and it will be there afterwards, it always exists, this sky, with its deep heights and its colours that cannot be described, just a detail here and there, but not its greatness or its unchanging sameness, and you can't leave before you have found a way of saying how the orange spreads, leaving the green only on its edges here and the pink on its edges there, above the invisible line of the sea, and above it, right above the line of the sea, the red yet remains, still red, so red that suddenly it changes and looks dark blue, totally and precisely blue, beyond any possibility of error, and only the infinite extent of this dome, lit without the sun, which has long since set, is wholly bright and smooth and arches up into the heights above that apparently have no end or bound, as if it really is the dome of the infinite orange height, without any connection to our presence as we watch it, or the tininess of our contemplation of it, or the ungraspable miracle of the possibility of its being, with the same certainty, this same wholly full greatness, at one and the same time near in all its details and wholly distant with no details at all, that produces a kind of knowledge in you and also an uninvited partnership in the exalted height, if such a thing may be said, and that from moment to moment, without your being aware of the transitions, the whole spectacle is becoming cooler and being extinguished, and that it is a shame, such a shame, if you only knew, a terrible shame.

Daddy comes home from work, the whole length of Allenby Street and the whole length of Ben Yehuda, tramping through their sand and waving his arms on the kerbstones, the older son comes home from all sorts of unknown places where he has been since morning, for the evening gathers in even those who have been roaming the sand dunes and shore of the great sea, from all their useful or useless activities, according to whether we consider such work as the building of a *hasaqeh* on the seashore as something worthwhile or the work of idle loafers who grow up in a home where hard-working people deny themselves even what they do not have so as to make this new house which is built entirely from scrimping and saving and low-cement blocks, and too many loans which no one knows, even when they can't sleep at night, how they will ever repay. Next year, soon, he will go to Mikve Yisrael to study agriculture and become a useful worker, and he too will become one of those young heroes with a khaki woollen beret pulled down over one ear, and he will sing with all the others what he sings already, *I'm a hard-working lad from Mikve Yisrael and I am as proud as he-e-e-ell, They give me an apple when I'm feeling tired, and that is a wonder as we-e-e-ell,* and meanwhile, unknown to anyone in Tel Nordau or Nordiya, and certainly anyone at home, he and a couple of friends are building a wonderful *hasaqeh*, in which they will sail away to, God, he can't say and they mustn't even get a whiff of it. The darkness is gradually severing all contact with the world, and concealing the world, as though it is extinguished and no longer exists, and around the single paraffin lamp Mummy is patching something, and Daddy is pretending to read *Davar* but is really fast asleep and is even snoring slightly because he is so depressed, and the brother has some illustrated paper with a small map of the eastern Mediterranean that one looks at while suppressing any sign of excitement, and there is someone else, who is sorry that the day has passed, because spending the whole day with the other children around the hut covered in blue-flowered creeper leaves a feeling of not having done anything, and there is something you would have liked to do all alone and it is being put off, from day to day, and you do not know how not to go to them or how not to be sad about something of yours alone, that is coming but never arrives, and another day has passed.

Because even when they are all together there is always one who is left on his own. And even when he is surrounded by them there is always one who is left on his own. And even when they all belong there is always one who does not entirely belong. Or let's say he belongs yet doesn't belong, or not wholly, or not all the time, even if he is with them all the time. And not because he likes it like this but because that's the way it is. And even though it's sad being on your own there is always one who doesn't entirely join in, who doesn't entirely belong, who is always slightly not. And how can someone like that rebuild the Land when you all have to rebuild the Land together, and one on his own cannot rebuild anything? Or it's as though he's only there to watch, from the sidelines, watching, seeing, saying nothing, but writing it down as it were in a notebook that doesn't exist yet, and, since it is so, it's as though all the time he is required to explain something about himself, to make excuses or apologise, instead of admitting, leave me alone, friends, let me be and don't wait for me. Even though, at the same time, strangely enough, wait for me, I'm coming too, wait for me I'm coming too. A single lamp and everyone in the dark room around the pit of light, and beyond the lamp there is nothing and nothing can be seen and beyond the house there is nothing and even if you want to you cannot see anything because there is nothing, the darkness has closed in.

Mummy is very tired, washing all day in the zinc tub outside over a fire of building wood that has been gathered for her, rubbing, rinsing, ringing, hanging out, in her own phrase she's falling off her feet; Daddy is very tired, from getting up before dawn till now with the accumulating debts without complaining apart from his sigh *ach vey*; and the older son is very tired too, both from what he has been doing all day long on the seashore in the sun and from the effort of keeping the wonderful plan secret, because if they make the *hasaqeh* a little bigger and if they make it a biggish sail, and if they practise every day at sea, and if they have the courage, how far away after all is Cyprus? And Tsi is among them, reading the ads in the paper, the Bank Hapoalim is generously offering loans on favourable terms, maybe he should show Daddy, and the newly-opened Toelet co-operative sandal factory is making everything better and more cheaply, apparently unaware that people go barefoot in the summer, and Mr R. Ish-Sadeh has a shop selling spectacles, watches and compasses, maybe he should show his brother, and all the time he knows that he ought to be thinking more about what he has been putting off all day long, when he heard in the morning by the hut with the blue creeper that Mikha'ela, who lives down Ben Yehuda Street where the curtains flapping in a certain window must be familiar with his watching form by now, and remember him, assuming that it really is her flat, and who plays the piano not badly at all, she may become a pianist, assuming her flat does not face the other way, onto the courtyard and the still unbuilt-on sand dunes, and whom he has not seen since the holidays began, except the day the big *tiyyara* was flown, when, so they say, she stood there and wiped away a tear when the *tiyyara* broke free from its makers' hands and disappeared, and may even, so the experts claim, have reached Jerusalem, high and excited, trailing its Samson string, and if the string didn't catch on David's Tower and keep it swaying up there, caught, with the sun smiling on its face, maybe it managed to continue on its way and may even have flown over the Temple, and onward over the Dead Sea, and further over the hills of Transjordan, and further over the deserts, he can't remember what there is there, he should ask Daddy or look in his brother's atlas, and he should ask him what Revisionists are too, and who the writer Asher Barash is, who they say has moved into a house in the extension of Sirkin, so that we'll have a writer too, and what does a writer look like, and is it true that across the road, right on the site of the huge dune, they are going to build a new school, Tel Nordau School, right across from their house, nobody knows if it will be built on top of the high dune or if they will clear the dune away first with wheelbarrows and another dune will be wiped away and they'll build on the level area left when the dune has been taken away, that will replace the splendour of the dune, and perhaps they'll go to this school instead of Geula School in Geula Street, and Mikha'ela too?

No, he should have been in Nahalal, he would be in the middle of the establishment of the farm now, in the middle of its development, farmers never go broke, their feet are always firmly planted on their soil, he would be in the middle of everything growing, in the middle of knowing that everything he did was right, and that it was what he had been striving for all his life; she is here, but she should not have had to be reduced to this wretchedness, and to the fear of his being sacked by the Tel Aviv Municipality because of the cuts, and why does Munchik earn twenty-five pound and even Yatta the printer brings home twenty, when he only gets fifteen because he sits shyly in the corner and everyone exploits his figures, maybe they'll let a room, another three or four pounds, and she can be more involved in culture, more involved in community affairs, after all everyone speaks so highly of her 'practical wisdom', and the fact that she always has real-life examples of everything; he is here, but the behaviour of the sea currents and waves, navigating out of sight of land, even though the ancient mariners, so he heard from a teacher during a lesson he had not been expelled from or skipped, even the Phoenicians and Sidonians and Philistines and all the rest of them, who after all were only a kind of Arabs, and if all those Arabs were able to sail and even to arrive, why can't he, because what does it involve after all; he is here, but only his other is sitting with them, the I inside him doesn't exist when he is not alone, among other people he is one thing but on his own he is someone else, and he is sorry for his father who is gradually becoming a broken man, and he is sorry for his mother who is becoming embittered, but he is not sorry for his elder brother, even though he runs risks and always tries to do things that are beyond his strength, and seems to be playing with his life, all of it not just a bit, and if they would only let him be on his own, to read, wander, listen, and one day, maybe, also, and from close up, listen to Mikha'ela playing, they say she's not bad at all, and also, how does she look, when she stands, one leg straight and the other slightly relaxed, resting on the tip of her shoe, a light girl's shoe, like a boat, bending her knee slightly, with a sort of freedom, that it's very hard to describe exactly, just that all of a sudden you don't know what to do.

It's night and they are beginning to go to bed, they are shutting everything up and locking it well then checking to see whether they've locked the whole house properly, because of what? Burglars? In Tel Nordau? Because of the darkness? The excessive openness? Or in case some hungry jackal that doesn't care enough to be afraid of humans breaks in? Or simply because one doesn't go to bed without shutting everything up and checking, because indoors is not outdoors and you have to have a locked door between them. And a moment before everything is locked and barred you go outside to take a look at the darkness that remains outside, and at first you can see nothing but the myriad stars some of which are amazingly bright, and then you start to make out the big patches of darkness, and that the darkness is not all that thick and not all that absolute, and that you can still see, if you open your eyes, something of the shimmering remains of the day that even now have not yet been erased to the west, and one can hesitantly imagine that they still contain something of that orange colour left over from the sunset, and that parts of the dome are still glowing, almost green, while other parts, thinly scattered with stars, are just like pitch, or like infinitely deep holes, and it is impossible to say a single thing that will be true of all the sky, apart from this hugeness, which is the only unchanging thing in all of it, and if only he knew more he would be able to locate all the constellations with their names that his father has often pointed out to him and always been able to name, and tell him stories about them from Greek mythology, but they immediately became muddled in his mind, and he is not even sure that he can identify the Pole Star or the Great Bear or the Little Bear with that absolute certainty with which someone sailing on the Great Sea sees and knows and aims for and steers by, and that is his lucky star, that will guide him on the straight path, amen, goodnight everyone, goodnight.

Sycamore

There are three of them, very old apparently, and from a distance, in the midst of the sea of dunes and its waves they look as though they are a single mass rising like a solitary green island above the tawny dunes, and only when you get close do you see that the huge hemisphere is actually three mighty masses on three massive trunks which separate into branches and boughs and crowded masses of foliage, climbing thickly to the ultimate limit of its height, and only up there do they join to form a single vaulted canopy, which starts above a man's height and extends upwards to reach, without exaggeration, the height of a three or four storey building, if not higher, while the heavy shoulders of the lower branches are thick with those crowded clusters of fruits called *jumez*, some unripe and hard, others soft and ripe, which nourish wasps and flies, and changing from dull green to a loose pink, so squashy and soft as to rot in gentle pinkness, and when one day the whole gang from Tel Nordau arrive, having uprooted themselves from sprawling in the puddle of shade of the blue creeper-covered hut and found the courage to venture into the desert, and fling themselves down after using their sandals to wipe and sweep clear each shallow depression inside and out of the whole sluggish carpet of squashed fruits within this dense deep blue shadow before lying down in it, but without losing the sweetish sickly smell, and above everything is closed by the thick leafy canopy, which still allows some gently swaying coins of light to filter through with otiose cobwebs of brilliance, without distinguishing where the first ends and the second or third begins, and somebody is already explaining, probably Binji, who is a good pupil all round, with Very Good all the way through his report card, including in music, gym, behaviour, effort and neatness, never late or absent, who, above those lying in blessed supineness, can explain that the fruits without seeds are the unripe ones and the juicy ones are the ones called *jumez* and that to make them ripen earlier they used to cut into them, like the prophet Amos, in Bible class, and he also knows that beams of sycamore wood are excellent for building, and have been used since the times of our forefathers, but he does not finish because it suddenly transpires that our skinny friend Tsi is not there, there is only a hastily abandoned pair of sandals, and anyone who wants to know where he is has to make an effort and raise his head laboriously, supporting himself on his elbows so as not to tire, and look up and search among the thicket of branches, as in the poem 'rings of gold descended through the thicket of branches', and up there at a height of three or four storeys, on the finest of the last fine boughs, unbelievably, a faint silhouette is hovering, and apparently that is all that remains of the

substantiality of what was Tsi's body when he was with us down on
the ground, before he evaporated into the void at the end of the
green, and he is walking around up there now from tree to tree on
the outer circumference, and he seems to have a need to rise higher
above the roof of the canopy, until it chills their heart and they are
tickled by a fear of witnessing the terrible inevitable end, and they
cannot understand what has stung this quiet boy, except that as some
are good at singing or swimming or team games he, this skinny child,
is good at climbing, and he climbs climbs climbs, and here he is now
floating on the circumference of the canopy of sycamores, on boughs
so slight that even a tiny bird would take care not to alight on them
without a frantic fluttering of its wings.

Why is he like that? What is he looking for? Or is it really just
because he too has to excel at something? No, it's simply that he is
stricken with a wild urge whenever he encounters something he can
climb, a pole, a house, a tree, or something else, an urge that cannot
be curbed or explained, a fizzling urge to hold onto nothing and to
grasp a non-existent projection, to climb beyond anything solid, firm
or swinging, a stronger urge than the ordinary urge to smell lime in
the earth and lick it, for instance, or to play a tune with a stick on
any railings, or the frequent urge to pick up a stone and throw it at
any dog he sees while shouting *kishta*, or *pista* at any peaceful cat, or
if he suddenly comes upon a low smooth wall, if it is slanting enough,
the urge takes hold of him to accelerate and run along it like a car
on a steep winding road, to enjoy this running attached by the force
of Earth's gravity, and likewise show him a fine hosepipe suspended
between two buildings, whatever the height, and he floats along it
with the walk of a tightrope walker, with outstretched arms and an
entranced smile on his face, or if he comes to a tall building then at
once from window to shutter and from cornice to railing and from
gutter to eaves, and there he is already on top of the ridge of the rooftiles, none of which crumbles under his feet even if they are short of
cement, and of course a tree, a eucalyptus even if it is as smooth as
the legs of a slender girl, and before he knows if he has decided the
urge has carried him up to the top, like a chirping bird.

And so, smitten with an inexplicable, irresistible yen, like a monkey except for the tail, holding on here and holding on there, swaying and swinging himself, he throws his body into the air and catches hold and flies from branch to branch right up to the top of the tree, almost transparent, apart from those eyes of his, and it happened once, and has often been told throughout Tel Nordau and the surrounding neighbourhoods, that a certain teacher, in a science class, not long ago, having difficulty explaining the human body and its skeleton, and having no skeleton handy in the science room to present to the young seekers of knowledge, produced a chair and beckoned to Tsi, and while she continued her lesson she pointed to the chair and got him to stand on it, in front of them all, surprised and somewhat alarmed, ready to burst out laughing and to hold their breath at the same time, and with her practised mother's hands—for her darling son had the same name as her skinny pupil—with a single movement she took hold of the hem of his shirt, which his mother had made a little too large for him, pulled it off, and in the same movement folded and draped it over the back of the chair, with her skilful mother's hand, and without interrupting her lesson for a moment she demonstrated on the bared body, with the help of a gold-ringed finger, touching each several rib, and even indicating what was visible inside the ribcage, because it was all so transparent and whatever was known about the human body was there revealed and displayed to view before all those viewers eager for instruction, then she turned him on the chair as Mr Poliakov the modern tailor turns his dummy before a customer who is tempted to buy, and her fingers were cold, the rings were hard, and for some reason he was also suddenly choking back tears, and Mikha'ela was there too.

What is it like to stand there over the void at the top of all that swaying swinging height? You can see how the whole plain crawls on its belly, so misty brown in the distance, and how it turns to pale blue before it solidifies into those hills, and you can also see how very open it all is, totally and without any obstacle, open and totally untouched by base, troublesome human actions, and how the faint patchwork of green made by humans here and there, now and in all generations past, is all rendered of no account by the calm forward movement of the element of earth, on which the whole of history, both written and oral, has not etched the most tenuous trace, and you can see that the earth is just like the sea, including the hard, red earth and the brown plough, and the powdery soil that flies away, and the slightly green here and there, and the smoky at the far edge—they are all like the sea, unchanged and unscratched by human deeds, and like the sea it is at one with its being, needing no justification in respect of the utility or comfort that it offers, it simply extends peacefully, and everything it is is there, big and visible, and even when it drapes itself in distant mists, as far as he can see from his miraculous crow's nest on the outermost rim of the treetop with his feet on a few frail leaves, this hand holding onto a few frail leaves, the other shading him from the brilliance of the sun, and truth be told not without some fear and some knee-knocking, but the fear actually belongs to this stance, this swinging stance on nothing firm, insecure and unsustainable, on this less-than-a-place that is not a place, with neither the branches of the tree nor the density of the air under his feet, and nothing solid supports him, but he is between, literally betwixt and between, if that is comprehensible, however contradictory or even irritating it may seem, standing between the fear of a bone-crushing fall and the confidence that spurns any fall, between the end of the solid and corporeal and the lure of the nothingness beyond, and perhaps, again, it resembles standing on the seashore, between the fleeting fluidity of the water and the solidity of terra firma, moved by the ability of the unsolid water to bite and pluck at the solidity of the land, and seeing in practice how everything always remains at the end in its very beginning. It is wonderful and also hard to explain to someone who has never in his life stood at the frightening top of a sycamore as though suspended over the abyss, what it feels like to stand there, how full he feels then, how exactly he feels then, he can't explain how he feels, but that's exactly how he feels.

He doesn't want to climb down yet he can't not do it. And there is one more moment to continue to absorb the moment, until it comes into you all full, a moment of absorption perhaps like the moment of the knowledge of fertilization at the moment it takes place, and then, calmly, from branch to branch and from bough to bough comes the descent, calmly into the midst of the others sprawling there, who for some time have been tired of looking up at that crazy Tsi, and are deep in stimulating talk and even deeper in taut listening under the branches in the deep blue shade, in the dampness of the infected smell of the rotting *jumez* fruits, and it is Binji who is talking again in his turn, and saying that the aim is to turn ourselves into men of the commune, when the time comes, so he says, and he believes in every word and they all believe in every word he utters, and We must learn to give up, he says, What? he asks, the private will, In favour of what? he asks, in favour of society, he says, and in favour of the New Jew, he says, and What is the New Jew? he asks, it is the Jew who obeys the imperative of history, he says, and builds the new Land and the new society, he says, and to work for the establishment here, he is saying now not asking, a just society with no exploiters and no exploited, he says, and they are all breathing with him, and to become people for whom the community comes first, ahead of themselves, and who, of their own accord, he adds, place themselves at the service of the community, and in the preparatory training that we have to go to, quite soon now, we'll have to learn to place the communal good ahead of our individual desires, and even ahead of our individual talents, and they don't argue with him, not only because what he says is right, even if not every word is understood, but also because all this will not happen overnight, To be a member of a preparatory kibbutz, he continues, talking quietly but emphatically as though he has a hidden interlocutor, is to weigh our own petty concerns against the needs of the commune, he says, and again not every word is clear, but it is clear that he is right, and that is the way it is. And he also says, A man lives so as to give himself for a great cause, and he speaks as though he is remembering to say precisely the thing that matters, and not only does everyone here know that he is right but even the sycamores know he is quite right, So, for example, Binji says, if you are a pianist you don't play the piano but you make hay, for instance, because that's what's needed right now, and if you are a scholar, for instance, you don't go to study, you work in the cattle shed if that's where they send you, Binji says breathing heavily, and they all breathe with him, because it's right, it's all right. And that's the way it is.

What is each of them thinking at this moment? Or are there moments when you don't think at all but you simply exist? But now somebody begins, for no reason, to hum something, some tune, quietly, and they listen to him because it's so right just now. Then someone joins in, and someone else follows, and then they are all humming the same tune, under the shade of the dense sycamores, which are not one but three together covering together the song they are humming together, and it may not be nice to say that it is beautiful, but they feel that it is, really. Then they stop humming and they sing, quietly, they sing and they listen to the others singing, quietly. And then that stops too, of its own accord, there is no more need so they don't sing, soon they must get up and go home. To tell the truth there is a sudden embarrassment, it's not clear why, as if they have overstepped some mark, or perhaps they are hungry and tired, it is not clear from what, or as if they are suddenly in the presence of something that is beyond their power, or perhaps they are remembering how they forgot the child Tsi up in the treetops, he might have fallen and smashed his little bones, what sort of friends are we, and one way or another they get up and start tramping through the red-hot dunes that scorch the soles of their feet deliciously, not before they feel an urgent need to pick a few rotting fruits of which there is no shortage here and hurl them at each other with reckless abandon, these good children, if only they were not so revoltingly squashy, hitting you like wet spit.

Mummy is in the kitchen preparing fish, he has to get out, does he want something to eat or a glass of milk? The room is shady even though it is hot, and on a corner of the bedspread he tucks his legs under his tummy, pulls towards himself and how good that it was waiting here for him all the time at the right page, and in an instant he is totally absorbed in *Michel Strogoff*, and only the occasional tinkling of the chandelier testifies that there is a world and that a slight breeze outside can set the chandelier aquiver inside. Then his thoughts travel to all sorts of places, and then, from an endless sweet weariness, everything goes foggy and the boy drops off to sleep clutching the book, and then, perhaps because of the faint tinkling of the chandelier quivering at the touch of a fickle breeze, he knows that he sees exactly that this is her white, her very white dress, a very smooth white, dotted with very blue coins, in some light summer fabric, spreading out bell-like over the knees and narrow at the waist, with a round neck and puffy sleeves, a little girl's summer frock, very smooth white with very blue sequins, very blue on very white, with a kind of shininess and a kind of necessity, it's not surprising that no dream can contain her, and the way she walks away, with a way of walking that looks ordinary while it is also a restrained dance, paying no attention, with her light flat white shoes, her little-girls' shoes, without turning her head with those plaits on her back, without paying the slightest attention, she walks on, leaving behind her a sense of loss, with that wonderful summer dress, light white printed with blue coins, is it linen or silk or what, you can feel the taste of that pleasant beauty in your mouth, something as smooth as petals, totally simple totally wonderful and totally out of the ordinary, and suddenly everything is lost, destroying rest, what is this lying, she walks away in those flat white shoes of hers, little-girls' shoes, and you will probably never be able to say exactly what it was like, or how mysterious it was, there is no other word, and you will never ever be able to get close to her, she walks away, inaccessible, unapproachable, lost, and you have a lump in your throat, and you don't know what.

Your friends are here, Mummy calls from the kitchen (why do they catch fish, who can eat fish or open them up with their guts and everything else they have and scrape off the scales, and haggle early in the morning with the Arab fisherman with his two baskets and his scales—two pans hanging from a stick and stone weights that he swears are accurate in kilos—get away with you, Mummy shouts at him for his prices after picking up every fish in his catch and peering into its gills and grabbing hold of her catch, even though a fish is so disgustingly smooth, and the fisherman knows the game and he picks up his baskets and his scales and gets ready to leave, *isma'*, Mummy calls out to him, *isma'*, and as though by prearrangement she takes a piastre and a half off the price), and Ahuvia and Gershon come in, and Mummy offers them all white grapes and dried watermelon pips, and they sit down on the edge of the veranda where they can dabble their feet in the sand and feast their eyes on the dunes that are beyond the few houses that have been built on them. They talk about *Michel Strogoff*, *By Sword and by Fire*, *Treasure Island*, *The Mysterious Island* and Captain Nemo, will he save them in the end, and they are full of praise for the Omanut publishing house that brings out a new gem of literature each month, in a red binding with two white stars in the middle, printed with the vowels and with a glossary at the end of unusual words that are not properly understood (jungle: waste land; falcon: kind of bird; antelope: kind of animal; penguin: kind of bird), and they are not printed in Frankfurt am M. any more but right here, at Omanut Typesetters, Ha'aretz Printers, T. A., and there's a rumour that soon they are going to bring out *Conquest of the Pole*, they are impatient, and they also talk about the film that is being shown at the cultural centre that's worth sneaking into this evening, *The Last of the Mohicans* (what is a Mohican?), if they haven't changed it, and they also talk about a play that Gershon wants to put on with his friends, based on a story called 'Oded the Wanderer'.

Now somehow drippy-nosed Yigal from Nordiya has turned up, perhaps he heard the sound of the watermelon pips, at any rate the plate of grapes is clean now without a pip or a skin, and he listens to every word with shining eyes, and they discuss what Binji was saying under the shade of the sycamore trees, and about the Jezreel Valley and the Jordan Valley, and the Golan perhaps one day, and the Horan which is beyond all that, and Mount Hermon and when will they be able to climb all the way to the top, two thousand eight hundred and fourteen metres above sea level, skinny Tsi declares, although he doesn't know how it was measured, and suddenly, apropos of nothing, this Yigal stands up and starts to wail some kind of tune that nobody knows, and he stretches out his arms and starts to prance around as though he is dancing, singing and dancing, gesturing with his hands, with movements of his head and shoulders, and it's not at all funny or ridiculous, on the contrary, something they would never have expected, it even has a certain beauty about it, the soft sand does not trip him, he is barefoot and wearing nothing apart from his shorts, a thin, lithe boy with cinnamon spots on his shoulders and a lot of freckles, and suddenly he starts dancing, in earnest, like a dancer, and he has a lot of strength, he uses his hands and moves his shoulders and hips, his head moves from side to side and his legs leap and raise his hungry body that weighs nothing at all, and he has some movements that look girlish and others that look like a bird about to take flight, as if he too wants to take off but everything is against him, and one moment he seems to give up and drop down when suddenly he spins dizzyingly and starts to go up, in front of their eyes, to rise higher and higher, and he is a tall boy suddenly and good-looking with his curls that no comb has ever touched, and everything—and then, as suddenly as he began he stops, and lies helplessly on the ground, and they don't know what to do exactly, they only know that it was something special and out of the ordinary, and that it is sad to use such words. Beautiful, they say, that was really beautiful, and they see that Mummy, who is suddenly standing behind them in the doorway, is wiping away her tears with her apron, and she goes to fetch them some water with her home-made lemon juice.

And it is sad. Ahuvia announces that he and his mother are moving from Sirkin Street and going to live in Allenby, where his mother is going to open a pension, a kind of restaurant, and they already know that one of the customers will be the poet Tchernikhowski, but that does not make up for the separation, and Tsi knows that they are going to take a lodger too to bring in some extra money, and the lodger will take his room and he will sleep at the foot of his brother's bed, and they say the lodger is someone who writes songs for the Workers' Theatre for a show about Jacob and Rachel or Jacob's dream, or something, and it will be ancient music, Gershon says, because he knows everything about plays and shows, music from the time of our ancestors, from the time of the Bible, he knows, or like Arab music, or something, and Yigal listens with shining eyes and the sun is clearly sinking fast and getting ready for its evening dip in the sea, and the sadness does not diminish. Ahuvia is leaving, and soon someone else will go, and everything will break up, and where in the world will you find friends like these. And plump curly-haired Ahuvia, who knows everyone including Berl Katznelson, is thinking now and says that there are some places you can only get to only as a group. Individuals, he says, can't get there. What is so great about Tel Nordau, he says, is that there is a group that is growing here that will go together and arrive together, where? Obviously to preparatory training. Who decided that? Obviously, reality, the situation, that's how we breathe here and that's how we do things here and that's what will happen.

They sit in silence sitting and thinking facing the sinking sun. Everything here, the good houses, the good people, the good children and what they do every day, everything is working towards the good society. That is growing and moving confidently and with dedication, towards what? What a question, towards preparatory training. And not one by one or one here and one there, the ten-year-olds will become fifteen-year-olds, and the twenty-year-olds will already be bearing the burden, or else what? That's it. A man grows up to bear the burden, the burden of the commandments, the burden of duty, the burden of work, the burden of life, the burden of family, a life of burden. What is the burden? It is like the yoke that cows wear when they plough. As simple as that: people are born to bear the burden and they live to bear the burden, and that's how it is. Ahuvia goes on to mention that there are some words that always bring on specific emotions, the word building brings trembling, a word like 'plant' brings trepidation, and an expression like 'only a path' or 'only a plant' brings trepidation and trembling, and more than all, he says, a word like 'conquest', conquest by toil, conquest of the wilderness, conquest of man, conquest of the spirit, conquest of the Jew, Conquest of the marshes, interjects Yigal who has been forgotten, and We have no more powerful words, Gershon agrees, than conduct, conquest, consecration, he laughs so hard that his slightly slanting eyes close, as though his parents were Chinese or something, make a campfire, sit children round it and burst into song, conduct, conquer, consecrate, here are tomorrow's troops, all these Go'els and Geulas, marching forward with a mighty song. And they all laugh with him. Though what's so funny.

Now someone arrives. Not someone we know. A young man with shoulders and a white-toothed laugh. I am Eliyahu Hershkovich he says, with a laugh, from Ekron, in the south, he is going to Mikve with the brother, where is he? Mummy, who has come out to see who has come, appraises him and asks, And what have you come to tell us? at which he laughs, No, he hasn't come to tell us anything, only to see her elder son, as they have arranged, if he's not in Nicosia or Larnaca, hungry, wet, possibly in prison, he laughs, What are you talking about, Mummy shudders, what have you come to tell us? Nothing, laughs Eliyahu, he is on his way, he'll be here soon, we arranged to meet here, there is no news (he does not know, how could he, that he is not the man who will bring the news, on that day, when the messenger comes to Mummy, on that terrible day, not to be counted among the days of the year), laughs Eliyahu, a strong, healthy lad, of peasant stock, with creases round his eyes, strong hands, square shoulders, he is going to Mikve too, and to the Haganah, to teach the use of rifles and guns (and naturally he does not know that he will become one of the greatest arms purchasers, from the British and the Arabs and others, a smiling young man, you can trust him, a hundred percent. And he knows nothing as yet about the 'Brigade', he has not heard about Italy and how he too will… alright, not now), they all watch the sunset that is beginning to change pinks in the sky, and everything around is still so small and useless among the dunes, so much at the beginning and the beginning of the beginning, and very soon the brother will come and Daddy will come home, and what's this suddenly about Nicosia and Larnaca, and where are they, and when they arrive Eliyahu and the big brother are going to Beit Ha'am together because they're changing the film tonight and they're going to show the film to end all films, *Ben Hur*.

And what are you doing, Eliyahu sits down with the three of them who have just been examining, beyond their powers, the current that is drawing them ineluctably towards preparatory training, We study, but it's the holidays now, Ahuvia replies drily, Yes, says Eliyahu, you study and you study without any holidays, and what do you learn? He pauses for effect. You study one thing, how to bear the burden. As though he heard what they were saying before, and as he speaks he laughs and his eyes crease, because here that's all you have to learn, to bear the burden. There is a burden, he says, and it is heavy and hard and young shoulders have to be taught to bear it, and they don't want to, they shirk it, but there's no point, it doesn't help anyone, and there is no choice, for anyone, and to Mummy: Isn't that right? And then like a silhouette before the sun that is almost touching the invisible sea, appears someone tall and strong, with a curly mane framed by a halo from the sunset, radiating a quiet youthful strength, the impatiently awaited brother, Ah, Eliyahu, he greets him, is there anything to eat, Mum, Get along with you, Mummy says, I was so anxious, Mummy makes a fuss of him, come and let me give you a kiss, my darling, what's this about Nicosia, what was Eliyahu telling us? Eliyahu, the brother shakes himself, is from Ekron, and they're all liars there, and simple-minded too, and now they can see that he has brought a box with him from which he produces one by one the prickly pears he has picked on the way and rolled in the sand to get rid of the prickles, and with the curved blade of his pocketknife he makes two cuts, one at each end of the fruit, and another cut along its belly and digging in his thumbs he presses out the pulp which emerges all golden in the twilight, and he passes them round generously, and each in turn takes one and licks the sweet and sour juice with all the pips, except for Mummy who says it gives her constipation, excuse me, and Yigal from Nordiya who takes two and swallows them whole straight from his palm and then takes a third to hold until he has finished swallowing down the other two, if he does not choke first, then the big brother wipes his hands on each other and beaming at Mummy, Put out something to eat, Mum, Shouldn't we wait for Daddy? says Mummy, which is a kind of hint to the three youngsters to take their leave and vanish, although Yigal lingers for a little in the hope of being invited to stay, then vanishes as though swept off under the great crimson canopy, which glows as though everything else is insubstantial, and Daddy also floats in quietly from the wings and says Good evening quietly, and to Eliyahu he says that he knows his father, Hershkovich from Ekron, very well, but that's irrelevant.

Even Daddy cannot refrain from smiling and laughing occasionally, a slightly twisted laugh as though he has not laughed for a while and has forgotten how to do it, and Mummy gives her usual shriek, Get along with you, at the sound of this mischievous young prattle around her table, and her fish is soon devoured along with the salad and her fried potatoes, she takes pleasure in feeding people like these who know how to eat and enjoy every mouthful, take plenty of bread, she encourages the owners of these youthful appetites, and the jug of cold water circulates freely, stopping mostly in front of young Tsi, because he can't stand the rest of the food, only pretending to nibble with his front teeth so they won't notice him, and the meal concludes with blancmange, a yellow pudding that Mummy calls *kissel*, and they finish off all the *kissel* intended for the whole week with a single big gulp, those two future Mikve students, for whom the future holds in store only jumbo-sized rissoles and whatever they can pinch, not counting the bread. But their generosity does not end there, because they invite the youngster, who has eaten nothing, to come to the film with them, no need to sneak in, and to sit comfortably on the bench with a hot corn cob instead of squatting like a frog in the sand for fear of the ushers who track down freeloaders, as befits the princes of Tel Nordau and their guests, and Daddy stands up to watch them go, more stooped than he was once, with a twisted smile under his greying moustache which has bits of fish caught in it, and Mummy wipes her hands on her apron, her eyes still wet from laughing, and from suddenly remaining without the youngsters, while the two big ones almost dance along and the skinny one leaps after them not to get left behind, and he only listens as befits a youngster with his elders; they go down Sirkin Street among whose completed houses a lot of golden sand remains, responding to the crimson of the now fading sunset, and turn right into Bugrashov, and at once left into Ben Yehuda, just a few more dance steps and here is Beit Ha'am, and the film, *Ben Hur*, when something happens to stop one of them, the youngest, and a short time passes before they notice that a fine thread has snapped and he is no longer trailing behind them, What happened to you? asks the big brother, Don't you feel like it? asks Eliyahu from Ekron, relieved no doubt, because he has plans for after the film and has already arranged with a certain Adina and a certain Bilha that they may meet here, in the brightly-lit foyer, and this fine thread is not necessarily useful for this knot, You go ahead and I'll come in a moment, chirps the youngster, and they don't insist, they have two good reasons to hurry, while he has one good reason to stay where he is, some notes from a piano coming from one of the buildings on the left of Ben Yehuda, the very notes he has been thinking about for many days without knowing how or when, and in a flash he is assailed by certain knowledge, and an echo of excitement answers it.

Yes, it's here, he exults, yes it's here, he knows with dizzying certainty, and this is the sound of her piano and it's her and it's here, not at the front of the building but of course overlooking the back courtyard, and as though he has been here before with one leap he is there, and there is a slight sand dune that has not been flattened yet, and the space between it and the building is filled by a young mulberry tree, he takes flight effortlessly and here he is up in the tree, at the height of your window, it must be your window, just reach out, there is nothing more in the way except the fine muslin of the curtain, and if you stood up your silhouette would fall on its waving fineness, and it's clear that she has finished what she was playing, now there is talking there, her teacher or her mother, and soon, pray God, she will start again, and now she really has begun again, three notes and quietly, and again the same three notes quietly, a little more and she stops again, perhaps she has made a mistake and the teacher is correcting her, although why should she suddenly make a mistake, then the same three again, like this, pa pa pam, pa pa pam, and again pa pa pam, pa pa pam, and she continues with notes that are similar but slowly change, as though very slowly they learn to say more, and suddenly it touches you so deeply that you hurl yourself down from the tree to the sand and fly up again with excitement, quiet notes she is playing now, without knowing that there is sheet music in front of her and that it is not she who is inventing what she is playing, without knowing or imagining that there is anything to imagine, about some year 1801 for instance, and a certain Beethoven, and two respectable ladies, Countess Theresa and her sister Countess Josephina of Brunswick, and at one time he was madly in love with one and at another time with the sister, and each time that one was his only great love, and eventually of course both of them married lords who had nothing in their heads except horses, drinking and money, certainly without knowing that you ought to know more about some Opus 27 in C sharp minor, because such things mean nothing to you and don't begin to mean anything, you are just an ignorant boy from Tel Nordau who is only open to the sounds of the music, without any connexion to anything else, sitting in the mulberry tree outside Mikha'ela's window without the slightest idea about that thirty-one-year-old who once sat and wrote for some sixteen-year-old, ever since when every sixteen-year-old, wherever she is, plays and hears how he is speaking specially to her, and only sixteen-year-old girls can play the Moonlight Sonata properly, with depth, no nine-year-old can, even if she has plaits down her back and is quite proud, but now you are only listening to her and it is she, just scales rising and quickly falling before you, with sudden claps of bold echoing thunder, that you do wonderfully now, so joyful, running up and down, so filling, that it is hard to believe that there is no more than a flimsy muslin curtain between us, and you have no idea that I am hiding behind it in your mulberry tree, just as you never noticed me even when you were almost touching me, just passing me as though I didn't exist.

Three light beats and then another three, softly, then another three and another three and softly, and then they are replaced by longer phrases that gradually change and seem to be playing on the first statement, and then suddenly the moment comes, and they set off at a gallop like horses and they are as beautiful as galloping horses, and underneath, all the time, there are two low, deep, thick notes, and there is no need for someone to come and talk about an enchanted lake at night and a bobbing boat and two lovers whose breathing is all that disturbs the reflection of the moon in the water, it is all so easily understood, it is all so close and so moving, and who can know now what he will only begin to know in another seven years, that the pa-pa-pam that he can hear from the mulberry tree is simply G-C-E, or more precisely G#-C#-E, and that the bass notes underneath are rumbling in tones and semitones and it will transpire that even then and always this sonata has three separate movements, and each one has a name, *adagio sostenuto*, a brief *allegretto* with a rondo, and *presto agitato*, unashamedly fast, unashamedly emotional, indeed unashamedly excited, unashamedly singing aloud, unashamedly unconcerned for what people will say, when suddenly a lively barking bursts from the room, it must be Tsi inside, woken by the emotional thunder, barking at Tsi in the tree, and Tsi to Tsi would that I were in your place, and he is sharply ordered to calm down and he does, a good dog from a good home, but the Tsi in the mulberry tree cannot be calm, hidden and unknown except to the now quiet dog, and unaware that not far from this very spot, at this very moment, right here in Tel Nordau, the strange man, the second strange man who is always walking behind the first strange man—the one whose red hair has caught fire and whose legs drag forgotten behind him, who does not want to know about the sand and never looks down at it, and who were it not that he drags his feet in the clinging sand would long ago have flown away in flames forever—this second man who always follows him, always buttoned up, always mumbling and grumbling, his head always bowed towards the wearying sand, is at this moment sitting in his room translating *Jean Christophe* for him, which was written precisely for sixteen-year-olds listening to a thirty-one-year old yearning for them, trying to approach their beauty, sick with love and disappointment, tossed from storm to storm, and there is one chapter in *Jean Christophe* that begins with the cry 'I've a friend', 'I've a friend', just like the pa-pa-pam pa-pa-pam that we heard here, and it is impossible to stop and not to sob when you read it so intensely and you suddenly know how right, how accurate, and now when you are hanging here in the tree outside the window, but beyond everything that is here, between what is completed and built and what is desert-like and wild, with the constant sound of the sea, you know clearly that I shall also, you'll see that I shall also, I shall also do something great and beautiful like that, just wait, I'll do it too, maybe not on the piano but saying it right just like the piano, something exactly as great as you feel it, and as true and fluid and singing, I don't know what it's called, but it will be just like this and it too will be called, unflinchingly, unashamedly, *presto agitato*, just wait and see.

Part five

Dagon

It is the Rabbi's House. They get up in the morning in the Rabbi's House. When asked they explain that they live in the Rabbi's House, and the others reply, Oh, the Rabbi's House. Whereas the truth is that there is no rabbi in this house, there is no trace of a rabbi's house, no shadow of a rabbi's house, maybe a rabbi lived here once, it is not clear which rabbi, and his name has remained attached inseparably to this house, like a landmark, a signpost, instead of a house number, at the end of Jacob's Lane, near the cemetery, on the flattened hill, elevated a little above the ground on foundations of red and white sandstone, and limestone rubble of friable white and dull red, so that you have to climb a few steps to reach the front door, and there is always a deep silence all around, especially at night, when you can hear nearby the night jackals coming hungrily to hunt and crunch, and all the dogs barking furiously, and you can hear the throbbing of the motors of the water pumps in the orange groves, throbbing regularly like a heart, although with different-coloured sounds, and of course the lowing of the cows in the cowshed of the farmer Yehuda opposite, whom the cowherd Attiya calls by name early each morning with an unvarying cry like the creaking of a gate that opens at a fixed time, Hawaja Yuta-a-a, to untie his cows from the empty mangers and let them stomp along with the heavy dignity and self-importance of big red Damascus cows, swinging their swollen wet udders as they press in a mass to the gate to join with a rubbing together of big bodies the other cows that Attiya the cowherd has already gathered in his progress along the waking road, and he will continue with the gradually swelling herd from farmyard to farmyard and out beyond the cemetery and on towards the citrus groves and vineyards on the eastern boundary of the settlement, to the meadows of grass which is dry now at the end of the summer that lies hot, tired indifferent on all the open land beyond the tilled, from which they will not return until evening when the herd will separate once more into little groups of cows that know their master's crib, again with that creaking cry, Yuta-a-a, and they get fewer and fewer as they go from farmyard to farmyard until the final one, where the cowherd disappears as though by magic and is not seen again until early next morning; and then, in the evening twilight, when they are tied up again at their mangers from which the smell of crushed carobs comes wafting to our nostrils, in the close heat that has built up dully in the heavy close cowshed with all its pungent smells, the jets of milk will start squirting into the pails with a musical tzzzz sound, that always arouses all sorts of accompanying feelings one way and another, not all well explained, while the milked milk squirts into the pail with a steady rhythm and a layer of froth on the top, feelings that have something that ensnares the heart, and after that there will be silence all night apart from the occasional mournful lowing, and the continual rounds of cockcrowing all night long, and the endless throngs of crickets monotonously sawing the darkness with untiring industry, now as though to cover things that are being done in the darkness, and now as though, really and truly as though, they are choirs singing, and far beyond all this, faraway, dimly, the sudden sound of the sea, that the night brings sometimes faraway and uncertain and sometimes clear and close, although never as clear or as certain or as close as it was a few months ago, at the end of the winter, when it used to roar and moan almost within touching distance, and whether it growled or whispered it was always as though you could really see its flattening waves fawning and licking with their hot salty tongue with that lacy foam, right underneath the veranda of Yigal's house that his father Munchik had had built by a wonderful team of women, but for some months now, since the winter, it has gone far away and its moaning can no longer be heard except when the silence is full and the sea is full of moaning, and then only by someone who is tossing in his bed and cannot sleep, when it is joined by the mournful creaking of the wooden ceiling of this Rabbi's House, a high ceiling with no glass chandelier quietly tinkling, bringing another portion of grief to the sleepless heart, and at the same time comforting, as though nothing is final, including the disintegration of this old house which continues even more forcefully at night, without denying or confirming anything, and this too maybe is a certain relief, and perhaps indeed the evil is not yet determined, when you lie sleeplessly tossing and turning all night long in this alien house where you now live, the Rabbi's House.

He is not called Tsi any more, either, nor do they know here that this is his generally acknowledged nickname, just as it was generally accepted that Zerubavel should be called Chipaf, thus correcting the lack of foresight with which his parents had provisionally named him, or that Yigal should be called Galeguleh, even though it made him angry, and he used to throw stones or pebbles or sticks or whatever came to hand and even kick anyone who persisted in using the nickname, or only seemed to have done so, but it was of no avail, for such is the way of the world, so now he is called Dagon and that is what he is called at school, too, not in honour of the Philistine god who dwelt precisely here in olden times, in Beit Dagon to the north, in Ekron to the south, Ashdod to the west and Gath somewhere else, and to whom the Philistines burnt incense and before whom they danced and whirled with all their might, and with all those emerods and golden mice and all the rest of it, nor after the diminutive fish known as *dagon*, which dart around in huge numbers among the green rocks near the shore, disappearing and reappearing in the water by turns, like clouds of tiny things so transparent that you can almost see the insides of their lithe little bellies, and they never managed to catch one of them because they were so elusive as they raced around in shoals in the shallow water, even in the emptying rock pools, not because they were merely a mirage in the imagination of the fascinated observer, but because they moved so quickly and elusively, showing their bluish bones through their tiny transparent bodies, but once again because of a dog—strange, isn't it?—another greyhound, belonging to a certain Tzila this time, Tzila from his class that only has three girls in it, Tzila, Shlomit and Batya known as Bashke, Dagon, another slim hound, thin-legged, long-eared, wet-nosed, so lean and skinny that it is hard to understand how such a tall, sensitive creature can be so insubstantial, with no body but just such slender sticks of legs and such big black sad or maybe wise eyes, staring out of nothing but the black smudge underneath that is his sniffing, ever-sensitive nose; and so he circulates in the world outside as Dagon, although he does not circulate and is only rarely outside, and wants to be outside even less, he stays indoors as much as possible, with his head between his hands and a book pressed to his chest, he rarely leaves the Rabbi's House, and all alone, his friends from Tel Nordau have been cut off at a stroke, like turning off a tap, and there are no children around him now and you don't go to visit other children, he is all alone and on his own, and even when they go to school and come home among the other children he is not with them or part of them, whatever he is does not interest them and whatever they are does not include him. And that's the way it is.

The school is a single storey under the eucalyptus trees and dusty casuarinas, and each classroom has two windows with tall shutters looking onto Jacob's Lane, and in Class 7 there are only three girls and the rest are boys most of whom are manly youths, three Binyamins, the red one, the dark one and the burly one, Dov, Arie, Tzvi, Moshe, Aharon and Yehoshua, Yigal, Go'el and Yiga'el, and Rehavia, Petachia and Amatzia, and that, as far as can be recalled, is all, and the three Binyamins are as strong as wrestlers that you see in the cinema (if the machine that makes the electricity does let us down that evening and if Amram the projectionist has finished translating the words and copying the translation onto the strip that is projected next to the film, and no one minds that it sometimes goes too fast or too slowly, unless it gets completely out of synch and then they whistle with two fingers and even shout out 'Wake up Amram!'), and they say that one of the Binyamins once grabbed a horse and lifted it up by its forelegs and the horse was amazed and confused to find itself standing on its hind legs, and another of the Binyamins lifted the cart with his hands to take a wheel off to be repaired, and one of the Binyamins, they say, demolished with one blow of his fist a thief who had broken into his father's vineyard, before he could even make a squeak, let alone steal a grape, and these stories arouse general laughter and admiration and also caution, in case they challenge you to a mock-match, and they are bored most of the day and do not hide it, not only in class, except when playing football, or working in their fathers' orange groves, because they are afraid of their fathers, despite their savage strength, and out of boredom they spit four or five yards and piss in long arcs in front of an audience, or except when they flash white-toothed smiles at the girls and joke with them in coarse hints, and with a comb they keep in their pocket they improve their gleaming black, blond or brown hair, and an endless stream of stories follows them around, their details unchecked, and not intelligible in detail to this new arrival, about each one of them and the daughters of the Arab guards in the citrus groves here and there, whether it is a story or wishful thinking, or all sorts of suggestions based on experience of how to secure cheaply with a little force forbidden but very attractive things, and for some reason they fall silent when he approaches, as though they have to take him into account, even though he is just a little worthless Dagon, good for nothing except maybe to tell tales to some teacher or someone, they care nothing about the *Carters' Jubilee* that the teacher Bekhor Levi reads to them with excellent diction, or the tales of I.L. Peretz, each of which they find more boring than the last, and they find it hard to fill half a page when they are asked to write an essay, until the break comes and they can smoke a cigarette and talk freely in Arabic and Hebrew with some Yiddish and a few gems of Russian, isolated words surrounded by impressive silences, words carved in stone, so that to dismiss someone absolutely they will say contemptuously that he is 'absolutely useless, totally *binfa'esh'*, which is the negative of the Arabic verb *nafa'a*, meaning to be useful, and the most dismissive expression imaginable, and this is the term they have decided to apply to that skinny runt Dagon, who is totally *binfa'esh*, were it not for his brother, the great football player, the right back of Maccabi Yehuda, who with one kick from goal to goal delivers such a crushing blow to Maccabi Rishon and Maccabi Nes Tziona that they are totally annihilated and retreat from the field in disgrace and don't dare show their faces again till Sunday night, and on his account they lay off his useless younger brother, even though the useful brother is in Mikve Yisrael and only comes for the occasional weekend, dressed in the finery of *a lad from Mikve Yisrael who's as proud as hell*, surrounded by sweet forbidden stories that are silenced the moment the useless one wanders up innocently to listen.

In another year they will finish their schooling and stop wasting their lives in lessons, here as at Tel Nordau, except that there they will go straight to the Haganah for preparatory training and to the youth movement, each summer holiday from the Herzliya Gymnasium, whereas here they will work all year round in the citrus groves or the Pardes depots, and two will even go to Beirut to 'do lawyer studies'—apart from the girls, who will go off to learn to be kindergarten teachers, or study piano in the big town, apart from Batya nicknamed Bashke, whom even the teachers call 'iron-brain', partly because it's true, and partly because her father is the mighty blacksmith, with the mighty moustache, with the resonant Russian, and a mighty farrier, and she is already ready to marry—and apart from another one, Petachia, who already knows that he is going to London to study business, and that riding a donkey will give way to riding a horse and then a motorcycle, and finally a more comfortable and dignified ride in an American automobile, a Chevrolet or a Ford, soon when the citrus business achieves 'prosperity' (using the English word). And where will Dagon go? He has been cut off from his friends who will go on as a single band to the Haganah to preparatory training and to the youth movement, just as he is cut off from the transformation of the existing reality into the correct reality that is achieved by means of incantations and the magic of wonderful words alone, in the shadow of the hut with the green creeper, incantations that came from the red-covered books and the conflagration of their rich imaginations, just as he is cut off from the group that used to surround the individual and make him into just another pip in the great many-pipped fruit, like a watermelon or a pomegranate, from now on no one will go anywhere alone but only together as a gang, always together everywhere, and eventually they will ineluctably end up in Kibbutz Maoz or Kibbutz Beit Hashitta or Kibbutz Hamadiya, or to Kibbutz Beit Alfa and one or two other places, and also to a moshav or two and in the Haganah and the Palmach all of them, whereas he is unable to form any friendships with these tough boys, they do not need him and he does not need them, and the stories told with such splendid sloppiness and such splendid contempt for complete sentences, each word coming with difficulty because that is stylish, and it's stylish to wait for the next word to come out with difficulty, because that is how useful people speak, even when they tell stories about a certain Malkele, short fat and stupid, that you can do anything you like to, even get her dress over her head, and see her and show her, in exchange for some sweets, and all they need are some gestures to describe generously all the well-rounded advantages her body possesses, Malkele who is always laughing and dribbling, or stories about wonderful tricks they have played on some old woman who cooked a meal for her old man and they pinched it from their kitchen and fed it to the dogs and the old folks are still looking for it, or they gave it to the Arab cowherd and then informed on him so that he was caught, or competed to see who can pull up the new gate post that so-and-so had worked so hard to put in, uprooting it with a single heave and throwing it away like some contemptible twig, or on Sabbath in the courtyard of the synagogue, waiting for the service to finish, in their best clothes, waiting for the afternoon to come so they can play football, waiting for the evening to come so they can put on the electricity in Amram's cinema and show a film, and swinging to and fro on the corner of the street under the feeble lamp, only because they are so big and strong, and rocking backwards and forwards on their feet and going out and splitting sunflower seeds and with amazing elegance lighting cigarettes and flicking them away half-smoked, painfully telling laborious stories and somehow it is midnight and they go to bed, and that's the way it is.

Because the crisis came in the end, despite the best efforts of Uncle David, that clean and good man, who was a member of many associations of good and beneficent people, and despite the good will of Mr Dizengoff there was no alternative, Mr Dizengoff even tried to sweeten the bitter pill and promised that at the first opportunity and as soon as things got better, and that everyone appreciated, it was just the hard times we were going through, there was nothing for it, all the budgets were exhausted so they were closing down dismissing releasing locking up and there was nothing for it, it wasn't out of malice but simply the hard times, and that's the way it was. What else was there to do? Nothing, only to turn to Uncle Moshe, the angry-looking uncle who ever since his accident had a somewhat battered face and wore dark glasses with leather side-flaps, he was never easy to talk to and all the more so now, and if you did not come on a good day you found him remote, censorious, taciturn, and he sometimes spoke a harsh word that was hard to get over or forget, and even if it was his own flesh and blood and his own brother's son with whom he had undergone all those hard beginnings, ever since they had come and rebuilt this hard land together, nearly thirty-seven hard years, hard years in a hard Land of Israel, one his own way, as a farmer, a citrus grower, a public figure, a farmers' leader, a writer of articles and books, whom many sought out, hoping not to catch him on one of his less good days, and the other in his own way, a worker among workers, more often by the roadside than on the road, doing every kind of work where the Hebrew worker needed to prove himself, a tiller of the soil, a blacksmith and a farrier, a kindergarten teacher and a teacher of workers, spending his nights researching the economy of the Land in a comparative context, never talking in public, bottling it all up, refining it sevenfold and writing it down accurately, and eager to go with all the friends with whom he shared all the hard tests of friendship, all deeply scarred by the hardships of this land, eager to start with Nahalal, precisely as he had always dreamed of finally doing, with Ben Yishai and Ben Barak and Natan Hofshi and all the rest of them, and when it didn't work out he had gone to Tel Aviv by way of Neve Shalom and built a house in Mendele Street that was beyond his means, and set up that statistical department that enjoyed such a great reputation among economists that there was no new investor who did not come to study his figures, such a modest man who did everything on his own, so that he was almost forgotten in his little corner, they had only remembered him in time to sack him, in the middle of adding up his neat long columns of figures; one day what he feared most had happened, and the dark vision of those terrible sleepless nights finally came true, the city was hit by crisis, depression, shortages, hunger, emigration, suicide, lay-offs, public assistance, soup kitchens, sackings, sackings, sackings, coming home one day and that was that, empty-handed, with debts beyond all hope, with nothing, one day coming home and that was that, they had had to sell the house, for less than nothing because of the depression, and to look around quickly, if not for his own sake, because he could have dropped everything and died, yes, but for the children, and he was a broken man of fifty-five, his body broken his frame broken his stature broken dragging himself through the day with difficulty and surviving the night with difficulty, the only thing that was left for him to do was to pull himself together and go and see Uncle Moshe in his settlement and talk to him, God only knew he didn't want to go, nobody knew how little he wanted to, and what a difficult man Uncle Moshe was, on a bad day he was capable of letting fly a word that would make it impossible to continue, but Uncle Moshe just happened to have good news for him that day, it's funny how things work out, because a group of English Jews had just made an agreement with him, Uncle Moshe, to plant some big citrus groves, seeing that Jaffa oranges were suddenly in demand in that foggy land that craved this orange-coloured fruit not only for its special flavour but also for its effectiveness against scurvy, colds and other afflictions of the body and the soul, there in their eternal downpours, they would invest and Uncle Moshe would be their agent, purchasing the land, planting nurseries of hushhash and sweet lemon, ploughing the plots deeply with huge ploughs driven by huge motors, 'employing the best and most modern agrotechnical advances', as the advertisements put it, marking out the terrain with wonderfully straight lines of posts like a never-ending row of soldiers, joining up with straight lines going off in all sorts of surprising directions, oblique and straight, and he would come and plant the two plots, one near Qubeibeh that he had bought from his friend the great effendi, the king of real estate between Ramleh and Ashdod, namely Abderrahman Beg al-Taji, whose palace and harem on a high hill eventually became a mental health utility for some of those who had immigrated and settled all his properties free of charge as abandoned property after he had managed to escape with nothing but his sack of gold among the other refugees who had nothing, the other near Zarnuga, overlooked by a high hill that was soon to be planted, and given the name Givat Brenner by a group of very serious young pioneers who had recently prepared themselves on German farms somewhere in Saxony apparently, in the snow and the cold, so they would fear no hardship.

For this mighty enterprise, the special characteristic of which was that it was not a gift or an offering or charity, but an investment by realistic moneyed men desirous of making money, because they believed Uncle Moshe when he explained to them with honest common sense and figures, and the Book of Isaiah, and Ahad Ha'am, of whom he was an admiring disciple, and because they had made enquiries and done their homework like any businessmen contemplating an investment, and planting citrus groves to make a profit, and therefore Uncle Moshe needed some hard-working and experienced assistants, right now, of the sort known as 'managers' or simply 'supervisors', to keep an eye on the workers and make sure they worked well and weren't paid for doing nothing, and according to Uncle Moshe's firmly established principles half of them would be Arabs and half Jews, fifteen Egyptian piastres for the former and twenty for the latter, seventeen and a half for Yemenite Jews, precisely, because this was a land in which Jews and Arabs both lived and that was right and proper and that was how it would be, and one lot would not dispossess or drive out the other, and the supervisor would have to know who was going where and why, who was to hoe and who was to prune, who was to measure and mark out the plot and who was to dig holes, and make sure all Uncle Moshe's orders were carried out faithfully, precisely and promptly, and that nobody got yelled at, overseeing everything from under his cork hat that comes a long way down and his very dark very protective sunglasses, every morning, when he sighs deeply as he gets down from his carriage, sighing for the sake of sighing, the carriage that has already replaced the donkey that was sufficient until yesterday for riding to his citrus grove near Zarnuga but cannot manage the journey to both groves that are a long way apart, and which will soon be replaced by the Studebaker he will buy to be driven by his chauffeur Gross, while the workmen will be transported on the big new Witt truck, bought from an acquaintance of Uncle Moshe, engineer Levinsohn in Tel Aviv, a big strong vehicle with no fear of sinking into any sand, driven by Yirmiyahu known as Emma, a sly, resourceful man, and he will have to make a note of the workmen and what they do and how much they are paid and how many times they are absent or late for work and whether they are lazy or work hard, and report any incident and solve any problem, and make sure that they do as they are told and look after the new well that will be worked by electricity supplied by a friend of Uncle Moshe's, Pinhas Ruthenberg, that apart from its clean, very effective power will not sing day and night or throb noisily or make a sound like a flute that paints the place, and go to work when the morning bell rings and work till the midday bell, which takes no one by surprise here because the train from Egypt goes past every day at a quarter to twelve and whistles, and there are some experts who will shirk that quarter of an hour if he does not keep his eyes open, and ring the bell again at four o'clock in the evening, when everything suddenly empties, and the silence descends that has remained hidden here since the days of the desert, when everything here was just sandstone and only the old sheikh Abu Hattab would suddenly appear galloping on his noble mare from where to where.

This is what Daddy learnt that day from Uncle Moshe, who also deigned to ask him whether he had eaten and how the children were, and it looked as though he had been saved at the eleventh hour, so why does Daddy look so glum as he tells Mummy all about it, and also that he'll get seventeen pounds a month, and that they can rent the Rabbi's House, and that the school will take the boy, so why is he so miserable? It's not only because of failing in Tel Aviv, or having to sell 22 Mendele, or being shown to be a man who can never succeed, a father who cannot be relied on, a husband whose wife does not respect his weakness, but also, and perhaps mainly, because of Uncle Moshe, a man whom it is not good to have as an employer, and also, and this is perhaps the hardest part of all, because of becoming a supervisor. Because Daddy will suddenly become a supervisor, supervising the workmen, making sure that they work, they will be the workmen and he will be their superior, the workmen will work and he will supervise them, he will oppress them, he will be tough with them, he will be their exploiter's man, the boss's man, the capitalist's man, the man who represents the owner of the citrus groves, the one who converts labour into capital, the man the workers are afraid of, they will stop talking at his approach, the other side of the class barricade, the supervisor is the creation of the exploitative economy, he has no equivalent in the collective or the co-operative system, or in a worker's society or a working team, and not even when he sat at his little desk in the great Tel Aviv Municipality, now he will have to supervise workmen, he who used to explain that a plantation belongs to the workers more than it does to the owners, and that eventually the workers will run it instead of the owners, how a man can fall, and all his smashed gods fall down upon him, how his faith caves in and everything that he has sacrificed himself for in the past, everything that was high above the hardships of this hard land, a worker, a Hebrew worker, a Hebrew worker in the Land of the Hebrews, a worker on the Land, admired and respected, workers' settlement, workers' party, workers' newspaper, workers' culture, workers' library, workers' theatre, the worker, and now he will be supervising workers, so what is left to a man of all his faith, of the purity of his ideals, his hair, his moustache are white now, not grey, he is a drooping, grey man, it's no longer the crisis, the depression, the situation, the worries about the future, it's see what he looks like now, see what is left of Daddy, that man who raised this hard land and suddenly it eludes him, the ground has fallen away under his feet, there is nothing underneath him now, there is no firm ground under his feet, why dwell on it, he gets up each morning, he goes to work each morning, taking the wicker basket with his lunch wrapped in newspaper and his flask of lukewarm tea, and in the evening he comes home, he reads the paper, and he doesn't sigh, sometimes he even smiles a twisted smile, at the boy. And that's the way it is.

And Mummy, in the kitchen, when he came home barely alive, How could the Tel Aviv Municipality have treated you like that, and Daddy, Just like everyone else, and Mummy, But you were bringing this land into being back in 1890, you of all people, without you what would there be here, what sort of people are they, and Daddy, The situation, and Mummy, What do you mean the situation, they didn't fire everyone, there were some they kept on, and Daddy, The crisis, and Mummy, The crisis didn't throw everyone out, they are shameless, if only people knew, and Daddy, They're all like that, all of them, and Mummy, You should have gone to Berl Katznelson, you should have written about it in *Davar*, to let people know, and Daddy, Everybody knows it all, and Mummy, Aren't they ashamed of themselves, look who they are throwing out, and Daddy, They threw everyone out, and Mummy, And all our friends, where was my brother Yosef, and your brother David, what's going on here, and Daddy, It's a collapse like there's never been before, and Mummy, No, not everyone, not everyone, plenty of people carried on working as normal, Munchik for instance and Yatta, it's just you, you shouldn't keep quiet you mustn't keep quiet, what's going on here, what's becoming of this place, and Daddy, That's the way it is, and Mummy, What do you mean that's the way it is, it shows lack of respect, not just lack of respect for you, lack of respect for all the old-timers, all the pioneers, all the founders of this land, and she was unable to continue, her shoulders were shaking, so they stopped talking. There's nothing more, that's the way it is, and Mummy can't be calm and can't find a place, and Daddy doesn't want to be. And that's the way it is.

When you go down the steps from the Rabbi's House into Jacob's Lane and turn left you are among the houses of the settlement, which are small and built of unplastered sandstone shards, with red tiled roofs and lots of eucalyptus trees, mulberry trees pruned into a round shape, casuarinas and also gravilleas, with the cowsheds and stables at the end of the yard; but if you turn right when you leave the Rabbi's House there are just three or four houses and then the whole settlement stops abruptly, and the whole east is open, with the citrus groves, vineyards and almond orchards that surprised them when they arrived in the middle of the winter, with those clouds of unbelievable blossom, and now in the middle of summer they bring in sackloads of almonds to shell under the mighty unpruned mulberry trees in the yard between the house and the cowshed, like in a forgotten story, *The Cockchafer-Hunters* or something like that, and the vineyards from which they have started to bring in cart-loads sinking in the sand from the ripe weight of grapes that have already begun to ferment and are a little intoxicating, and with the unplanted fields that were ploughed in the spring until the wonder-ful red colour that is in the soul of this clay soil burst through, that red that is the foundation of the world, the same red soil from which man was created, and further east to the sycamores on the border, and the olives, beyond which can be seen the Judean Hills, always bluish always as though a faint smoke hangs over them always with tattered shadows of clouds sailing over them as though that is as far as they can sail (and if anyone wants to know more details for some reason, they can find them in the stories of someone who published them once, and it's a pity to repeat them, and there is no spare time today, because who knows how much time we have left, how for instance the children used to swim in the pool under the grevillea trees in the old orange grove that belonged to Miller or Jacobson; or the little trains for instance that they once used to race under the canopy of orange trees deep in the shy groves, deep in the deep blue shade, cutting drowsy spiders' webs with their noses; or the fragrant acacia hedges that closed the sandy paths beneath them like a tunnel, dotting them with crumbs of capering light; or the purchasing of manure, for instance, that they used to buy in the autumn, early in the morning, from the Bedouin who used to gather on their camels that gurgled in anger or fear coming from the vast expanse of the south, and they had to finish everything before the sun was too strong in the bright sky, leaving behind at the end a huge heap of manure and the promise of a fine crop of Jaffa oranges with a reputation on the markets of Liverpool and London).

But all that sounds superfluous today, like exaggerated sentimentalising of a glory that is gone, or like trying to delay something that is doomed to vanish, or boasting before the newcomers who were not here then, or preferring what is not to what is, a well-known lament for what has been, which like any lament merely repels its listeners and is suspected of distorting reality and of dismissing a priori whatever exists today, and one way or another there's not much patience with all that, we are not the Society for the Preservation of Nature, nor are we the Society for the Protection of the Land, nor the Society for the Archaeology of Yesterday. Nor is it worth expatiating here on Uncle Moshe, not because he isn't worth writing about, he is a very special man, a farmer and a poet, an idealist and a practical man, devoted heart and soul yet with a torn soul, sensitive, sentimental, remote and also crude, the prophet Isaiah no less a determinative reality for him than the APC, he purchases land from the Arabs and does not allow them to be expelled, he is hostile to the workers' movements with their class struggle yet favours the involvement of the Hebrew worker in the settlement of the Land, a man of peace and a man of war, so taciturn that people shun him yet capable as an orator of expressing the innermost feelings of all, considered a successful farmer yet always stressed, concealing his true feelings yet weeping suddenly among his brothers like Joseph in his day, and that house of his, with those cool floor tiles, and the eucalyptus tree that is the tallest in the Land and perhaps in the whole world, in whose shade he played quietly with Yishai, and for all its height it merely rustled quietly overhead, with the wise rooks' nests in its topmost boughs, and neither they nor it can imagine what is going to befall them a few years later, when they will attack that tree that is the tallest of all and topple it and uproot it and not rest until it is no more and cut it into pieces, until there is no sign that it ever existed, and nothing remains of it but the housing development that was built on the place where it once stood, unaware on the site of what it stands, and on the site of Uncle Moshe's house with its thick walls and its red tiles and the ring of eucalyptus trees pressing against its windows all around, a house firm-built that cannot be moved, happy is the man who dwells in such a house, it too blotted out like all the rest as usual, and the housing development encompasses the house, the cowshed behind and the stables, which at the end were empty apart from Uncle Moshe's she-ass, about which we shall have a thing or two to tell before we are done, and the hen-houses and the vineyard at the back, and the lemon trees where we were always being sent to pick a lemon or two for Auntie Tzila in the kitchen, the housing development devoured and destroyed it all and left no trace that it was ever there, and that's the way it is, such an old story, falling from the treetop apparently, touching some of these things, but there is no point in expatiating.

As for Uncle Moshe's trips to the new orange groves, that has already been written about too, as well as his venerable carriage which was replaced, with the passage of the years and changing times, by that Studebaker with the chauffeur Gross, and how Daddy, very faded, wandered around among all the innovations and all the successful citrus plantations, all green and lush and promising a good return, and how, above all, and apropos of nothing in particular, like a forgotten truth that turns out to be the greatest truth of all, when everyone had gone home and the evening silence fallen, there in the furthest west, somebody touched by things could see, even from the edge of the settlement, how the sun as it went to sink among those hills, above the citrus groves, in a rounded valley between two round hills, clearly defined on the horizon that was beginning to turn pink with the weariness of summer, how the sun turned into a big red wheel, shamelessly stripped of all the pallor of its dazzling heat, and a moment later, in all its blazing majesty, it descended beautiful, light and naked into that hollow between two hills that seemed to have been prepared for it since time immemorial, gradually entering it, slowly and all the time more and more, gradually entering it, into the concavity that opened up to receive it to gather it into its prepared embrace, and a moment later the entire wheel was inside, in that depression between two hills which enfolded it entirely and it entered it entirely all red and hot and entirely entirely, and then there was a fullness than which nothing is fuller.

She-ass

No? You don't remember? Abdon the son of Hillel the Pirathonite? And he had forty sons and thirty grandsons, and the land was in turmoil when the thing was known, how all seventy rode forth upon seventy ass colts, and that is all that the Good Book sees fit to recount about this judge who judged Israel for eight successive years, no further stories, no greater exploit than this, no victory and no defeat, only that wonderful procession when in a single line forty sons rode out in front and thirty grandsons behind them, mounted on the seventy ass colts, and this was his glory and his praise, and there was nothing more to add, or Jair the Gileadite, who sounds more familiar, and he too had sons although only thirty of them, and no grandsons for the time being, and what did they do, these famous men, but ride out again in a single line, the thirty of them on thirty ass colts, and after this singular act of valour the Good Book is silent and does not add a word either about this illustrious man or about his thirty heroic sons upon their thirty ass colts, although we might have expected a little more, and how eventually after the twenty-two years that he judged Israel he too was gathered unto his fathers, like many of the great ones of Israel, and was buried in Camon, apparently a place in Gilead.

And what of all those she-asses that Saul son of Kish was sent to find, and he did not rest until he had found the kingship, or the ass of Abraham our Father who walked bowed to Mount Moriah, or Deborah the Prophetess whose heart went out to those that rose on white asses, or the Prophet Zechariah, the son of Iddo, who is still awaiting the righteous king who will come riding upon an ass and upon a colt the son of she-asses, not to mention that she-ass that once opened her mouth and spoke good sense, What have I done unto thee, that thou hast smitten me these three times—although everyone knows what an ass is, after all, and how there is nothing more wretched or humble than an ass, and nothing more miserable or cheaper than a she-ass, and an ass colt is nothing but a *jahsh*, and that for twenty pounds and a little haggling you have an ass, who will be satisfied with what the horse leaves and with kitchen scraps, and you ride him with no saddle between his back and his rump, and that apart for some terrible braying that cannot be quieted until they cease slowly this wretched creature will carry any burden in silence, and you do not even speak to him but it is enough to make a sound like *nts nts nts* or a long-drawn-out guttural grunt of encouragement, or to give him a humiliating jab with a stick in a humiliating place, and you urge him on with a *zar-r-r* to make him bray or mount a female, but he does not listen, he only lowers his big heavy head and sinks into meditation on the words of Ecclesiastes, he is all grey, neither white nor black, except perhaps the most honoured asses in stories and the most precious of the sons of she-asses the most exalted among them and those that make mares bear a mule to their deep sorrow, whereas the one who was the sole survivor here was just a mousy grey all over, with a white belly, a black stripe along her spine, a pair of black rings around her nostrils and that is all, and what has been said is already too much.

Uncle Moshe, as has been said, had a she-ass. At first Abdul Aziz, who was in charge of the yard and the running of the house, a respectable man of gracious mien, with a clean turban wound round his head, a grey moustache and sad eyes, would put the clumsy saddle on her back and fit the redundant bit in her mouth, and Uncle Moshe would sigh as he climbed on a stone, swung his leg over the saddle, held on tight and settled himself comfortably, and then he would address her briefly with the command *yallah*, then he would sigh again and the she-ass, whose lower hind legs were always placed so close that they almost rubbed together as she walked, with a black mark above her right hoof on the inside, would shake her big head and set off, there was no point in encouraging her to go faster with the well-known devices, no need for stick or whip, she plodded briskly and found her own way to the orange grove and she halted by the post she would be tethered to, with a bucket of fodder already prepared beside it, but she never hurried except on the way back when she caught the smell of home, and then she would suddenly break into a mighty run as though she were a racehorse on the home straight, and then no power on earth could stop her, the wise would sit tight and the fool would take panic and fall, he would fall flat on his face and even were the road empty of all human presence a salvo of mocking laughter would erupt, and not for the first time, and it is clear who the unfortunate faller in question was.

And so, in a world where everything was beginning to speed up suddenly and to change fast, when they no longer lit oil lamps in the evening but switched on the electric light, when they no longer drew water by hand in the orange grove but pumped it electrically, when the piping of flutes in the orange groves at night became rarer, and there was no more need for pools to store the water and to serve also as swimming pools for the urchins of the settlement, many were exchanging their horses and donkeys for automobiles, and not a Model T Ford but a real Ford or a Chevrolet, and Uncle Moshe replaced his she-ass with the famous black carriage, which in turn was replaced by a Studebaker with the chauffeur Gross, abandoning the she-ass to her sorrows in the empty stables in the yard, eating straw and doing nothing, apart from short outings with young Taleb, the son of Abdul Aziz, when he was sent to Padova's grocery—the grocer had violet-tinted spectacles, he measured oil into a bottle, and sliced halvah with a big knife, and from the gaping sacks to the balance with its weights in rotls and okas he was meticulous in filling brown paper bags with rice, split peas or buckwheat, and he added some bars of chocolate wrapped in pictures of faraway places—and from there to the bakery or the post office, and the disrespectful boy tried to make her gallop without success until on the way home she smelt her stable and broke into a surprising frantic rush, and he fell off shamefully, spilling the groceries all around him in the sand, and so the ass was left as though out of fashion, just as a boy was left then without the gang from which he had come, he was not constantly surrounded by them and going everywhere with them, and he had not found a new one yet, they were not for him and he was not for them, small wonder then if these two useless relics found themselves spending more and more time together; hesitantly at first, with the permission of Abdul Aziz who was in charge of the household, who almost always agreed to lend her, and even Uncle Moshe on a day that was not one of his bad days agreed one day, eyeing him gravely though also with that smile that is used with children, and asked the fateful question, Whither shalt thou go? to which he replied promptly, in the immortal words of Ahad Ha'am of whom Uncle Moshe was a fervent admirer, To the crossroads, at which Uncle Moshe smiled and said Well, well, and sighed, from which time on he more or less had permission from the highest authority, and the two of them, the boy and the ass, whenever they were both forgotten by the world and were not sent on some futile errand, would ride out together, fully intending to see the world, starting with the nearer parts around the settlement, then to the orange groves, and after that deep into the empty regions beyond, and the vineyards and the olive groves and beyond the sycamores on the border, and even beyond the border of the farmed land, either towards the sycamores of Ramleh or towards Tel Batikh in Satariyeh, and right up to the beautiful empty hills above which are suddenly revealed, in an almost smoky blue and with shadows moving upon them, the mountains towards an invisible Jerusalem.

And there are hours of silence. Suddenly she stops for something that seems to her worthy of tasting, suddenly he stops for something that seems to him worthy of examining, a lizard worshipping on a dilapidated wall, a snake that has disappeared in the sand after writing a winding message, or a kingfisher standing on a post watching a foolish frog, or both of them stopping for a drink in an orange grove, he cupping his hand, and finding a pail or an abandoned saucepan for her, there are hardly any people to be seen, everyone is busy somewhere, only the unseen turtledoves scatter monotonous strings of cooing three and again three and again three and three, as though they have an infinity of three and again three, as though someone wants the riches of their squandered three and again three, and sometimes she stops, hollows her back, and empties out a thick yellow jet as donkeys do, and then he gets off discreetly, remembers, raises a leg of his shorts and emits a thread of pee as boys do, and sometimes he does not ride and she is not ridden but side by side she will not run away and he will not chase her and in perfect accord on six thin legs they pick their way on the sand and the clay soil and between hedges of acacia, and the world offers itself with a suspicious serenity, with indifference and total couldn't-care-less, the earth is simply lying on its back compactly exposed to this brilliant heat that cannot be disturbed either by the waving of an artichoke nymphet's wings or by the flight of a stray warbler from hedge to hedge, and they are not eager to find shade, what is wrong with the sun, nor to pause for rest, what is wrong with walking, what is each of them thinking about, the she-ass surely about Ecclesiastes and the boy apparently about the silence of the clay, not that it makes much difference, until suddenly they realise that they must turn back, and she, that mousy she-ass, knows how to get straight home from any place however far, taking short cuts to her manger in Uncle Moshe's stable empty now of horses where only a musty smell of fodder and a smell of old cobwebs remain of all the smells, and it is for there that she breaks out at the last moment in a frantic race that must also be accepted. And that's the way it is.

And what was there before the walks in the world with the she-ass, surely the world and its wonders did not begin with the ass—now it can be told, even though with somewhat lowered voice that until the she-ass turned out to be available to walk with in the world, and she was, after all, a living creature, he used to walk in the world before too, entire afternoons, with or without a sufficient excuse to Mummy, and not on his own but with a little wooden wheelbarrow, on two wheels, because a man always needs someone else to walk with, even if ostensibly it is only someone made entirely of wood, just so as not to have to talk to himself, something that in any case there was no escape from, all sorts of sentences and conversations, even quite fraught at times, though it is embarrassing to tell how stupid it must have seemed, when it's revealed how a grown lad walked on his own with a little wheelbarrow and talked to it silently, he talking and answering on the wheelbarrow's behalf, and the wheelbarrow understanding everything down to the most hidden roots of things, there was no one like it; embarrassing too to recount how he had made it with such devotion by such ingenious means, with two orphan wheels collected from somewhere, and two smoothly sanded handles, and a wooden receptacle shaped like a boat, Robinson's boat probably, all really well-made without any carpenter's tools, and you could take it and walk it on the paths, so obedient and well-oiled, revolving noiselessly and fast, to leave its traces in the traces of imagined famous travellers of bygone days, winding with it from side to side on this straight flat path, totally sleepy, unused and unsought-out, if we except the ants that never rest or a startled lizard frightened in its afternoon rest, winding along the flat path as though descending a dangerous steep slope with a sheer drop, narrowly avoiding hidden crevasses, being the first to conquer unexplored lands, the most astounding invention of all being undoubtedly the brakes he had fitted on that little barrow—that was so light that it could easily be carried on one shoulder, while it itself could carry nothing, except perhaps once that puppy he found by the wayside abandoned and shrieking wretchedly, which he had to unload apologetically before coming home to Mummy, not only because of the terrifying flea that was crawling on him but because of the shrieking that nothing would silence, not even a little condensed milk in a squashed tin that he opened with a nail and a stone—wonderfully perfected brakes, which with a single little squeeze jumped out with the power of a strong spring and stopped both wheels with a single triumphant braking action, but why, in heaven's name, did a little wheelbarrow pushed by hand need brakes, that was precisely the point, brakes for their own sake, art for art's sake, for the victory of progress no doubt, because surely a wheelbarrow needs brakes the way a bird needs a gangplank to board a plane, a prank that would barely suit a six-year-old and is strange to the point of uncomfortable suspicion when it is a youngster of twelve, think about it, perfection for perfection's sake, with this unique, perfected wheelbarrow, for entire afternoons, they voyaged among the orange groves and the open fields exposed to the sun, one murmuring crazy secrets to the other who did not reply, catching its words and speaking its lines in the conversation, and walking on and on, conquering the world no less than Vasco da Gama, although perhaps with a measure of humility, nevertheless, for if the world did not need them to discover anything more in it and did not care if they did or did not, for the sake of truth, they would walk and discover more and more in it every day, and that no one could deny.

Whereas now everything is changing fast and only a few people lag behind, as though they have been granted a truce between times and who knows how long it will last, and no one can guess today for instance what will happen tomorrow to these heavy orange groves with their dark green and the fruit that conquers the markets, or to these vineyards that now conceal in their bosoms some sweet young grapes, happy those who will eat them ripe, or to these fallow fields on which the world breathes in and out slowly, hot and unmoving and unchanging except slowly from season to season, with all the poppies and camomile and the dense clumps of spectacular lupins that give way to various kinds of hare's tail and all those other rustling plants, what will take their place, because they will not survive, as though the flat plain never existed here but it was a sheer cliff that everything is sliding and moving and slipping away from, another moment and it will disappear completely, perhaps it is lucky that nobody knows and that no wise man can see the future, and that meanwhile it is possible, while the summer holiday is at its height, for a certain boy and a certain she-ass to continue to go out every day without anything being demanded of them, without serving any purpose, without being sent for anything, plodding along the paths of sand, sandstone and clay, learning that the minerals of which the world is built are sand, sandstone and clay and their combinations, not talking to man or ass, without arguing with any, and sometimes when they pass along the flank of an ancient orange grove that is still irrigated by water from a well pumped by an ancient paraffin motor with an ancient glass jar pressed down on the exhaust which rises above the roof of the generator shack, secured by an old wire that the mechanic has wound round and waited until he directed its angle towards the exhaust gases in such a way that they played on this flute to his pleasure with a regular beat and the selected tone of voice, and the ancient water still collects in the forgotten cistern, and the youngster in two moves peels off his few clothes and plunges headfirst into the water, and it is shameful to relate how good it feels, truly, and then he comes out almost frozen and stretches out as he is on the hot, crumbly, sweet-smelling yellow sand, pressed and caressed in it, his back to the hot sun and his tummy in the softness of the hot sand that tickles hot both here and there.

And how is it that there is not a soul in the whole of the hot wide world, and how is it that nobody asks what or which, and how is it that every day a new secret place that they neither knew nor imagined discloses itself to them, and they don't need to ask anyone how to get there or how to get home, it's simple, that's the way it is. In a certain packing room a forsaken workman with his old hammer is repairing crates for the coming season, and he cannot imagine either that soon they will be packing in an automated packing room near the railway station and that he and all the crates will be sent home, no more crates, no more patching up, no more hammer, no more workman, the fruit will be transported en masse in huge containers straight to the moving strip that will carry them in a flash to the washing trough and the cleaning brushes and the automatic sorting and the packing almost without being touched by hand, those precious oranges that all the workers have been warned time and again not to and they must take care and those oranges are like eggs, anything more than light pressure or any touch stronger than a caress can cause a slight defect that is sufficient to cause a tiny barely gleaming drop of moisture to bud and then a million aphids and spores and other hellish creatures rush towards it and then decay sets in and spreads through one fruit and then through the adjacent ones and finally the crate travelling over the wide stormy sea to England, by train by boat and then by train again, when it is opened will turn out to be rotten and so on from crate to crate and soon the whole consignment will rot and it is not enough that the farmer will do badly and won't get a penny but the whole market for Jaffa oranges will fail, and great famine and unemployment and terrible despair will break out in the Land, so now watch how to pick the fruit and toss it into the container without any unnecessary twists and turns, and the hoist will come and lift it easily onto the lorry that goes easily with a thousand more containers heaped right up and empties the fruit into the huge hopper with a single swing, and on from there to the end of the whole journey not in wooden crates made by a skilled carpenter with his old hammer and with expertise learned over the years, but simply in cardboard cases folded by machine with no smart wrapping or tissue paper, but as naked as the day they were picked, and simply sprayed with some kind of smelly abomination against those hellish creatures that make a man's work turn rotten, and from the moment they leave the tree they become an industrial product that is sold partly in the skin and partly in tin cans and bottles.

Last winter, right after they arrived from Tel Nordau, did he not stand gaping in the doorway of the packing room in Uncle Moshe's old orange grove, and remain astonished at what went on there endlessly, because the packing room was not, as it might appear at first glance, just a depot of corrugated iron and cement blocks with big recessed windows, but incredibly it was a veritable temple, dimly-lit, serious, quiet, softly padded, with soft mats and screens on the walls, and sleeve-like sacks filled with softness, and with all the Levites and temple servants sitting around in a circle and in the middle the cross-legged high-priest, the packer, and no one must say or do or want anything without a sign from him, the open crate was set at an angle in front of him, lined with tissue paper and divided into two compartments, and he picked the fruit he wanted from the heap of wrapped oranges in front of him, and placed them quickly, expertly and with ingenious skill in such a way that the layers in both compartments were of equal height and the rows were of equal number, if there was a gap he made it up with a little one and if there were too many he swapped them nimbly with his fingers with their smoothly filed nails, his agility was nothing like that of the women wrappers whose hands fluttered as they picked up the fruit and wrapped it in tissue paper, a composite action comprising several smaller movements that were swallowed up in one rapid one, working so fast that they bent forward and straightened up rhythmically, tossing without tossing each fruit as fragile as an egg onto piles graded according to size, and the naked pile from which they snatched each fruit to wrap it was prepared by the sorters who picked up each fruit in their fine feminine hands that were smeared with some ethereal dampness emanating from the fruit despite all the precautions, making them black and sticky, and they rolled each orange around, turning it to see if there was any blemish in it (which would spoil the crate and the consignment, and inflict famine on the Land), throwing any doubtful ones out ruthlessly for the Yemenite from the market who would come in the evening to fetch them, and when the high-priestly packer who was surrounded by an important silence that no one dared break by speaking singing coughing or sneezing finished and the crate was filled with wrapped oranges neatly ordered in rows, he slapped the palm of his hand against the side of the crate and the carpenter instantly bowed and lifted it, concealing the grimace caused by its weight, went out clutching it to his apron and placed it on his bench, then darted inside already carrying an empty crate already lined with tissue paper, then came out again and laid thin strips of wood on its open mouth, spacing them at the right distance, took a nail from his mouth and tapped it into place with a single blow and with a precise stroke of his hammer he closed the crate and bent the willow bands, soaked to make them more pliant, fixing them unerringly with nails, for it would be enough for the tip of one nail to pierce one orange and it would rot and the crate would rot and the consignment would rot and famine would break out in the Land, and when the crate was reinforced and banded ready for its long journey the 'lifter' would come and lift it, tottering a little under its weight and carrying it carefully, because oranges are like eggs, and to the pile of crates that was growing all the time without teetering, not before fetching the stamps and carefully stamping it with the number of fruit, their size and the name of the producer (otherwise who would get paid?) and whether they are 'large' or 'medium', crate after crate clearly stamped, until the camel caravan arrived and the time of the great gurgling, the drivers beating and shouting until the beasts finally knelt and settled down correctly, not before trying to snatch a stray orange and chew it with their scary yellow teeth, to be punished for this by the ancestor of the camels' ancestors and their god, if camels have a god, and when it was all loaded upon them and tied on well four crates on either side and another in the middle on the saddle, they began to protest against having to get up with this great weight on their backs, and one tied behind the other with a driver at the front and another at the back, they set off for the railway station to tramp along under the acacia hedges in the soft yielding sand that their feet were made not to sink into, the leader making his big bell ring, like the image printed on the tissue paper wrappers and on the crates under the emblem of the Pardes company, a laden camel ringing his bell, and every camel in the picture had a ringing bell, when you were suddenly seized by a fear that could not be gainsaid that everything was going to be destroyed had to be destroyed and there was no escape.

But if anyone still wants, for some reason, to remember some more about the temple with the high priest and the throng of Levites around him in the service of the sanctuary, he will not have much difficulty finding some stories, some like the story of Uncle Moshe's carriage that has already been mentioned, or the story of the little train, or the cockchafer-hunters, and other suchlike that appeared once like fireflies that light up and go out, or if anyone insists on knowing what there was between the orange groves and the vineyards and the fallow fields between them where those two never tired of roaming on their own, at a time when everyone was busy working and making themselves useful, and why only they roamed between heaven and earth between trees and grasses between the colour of the clay soil and its special smell, not like everyone else who prefers to roam among people, or alternatively among donkeys, it is hard to supply a good answer, except that that was what they liked apparently, except that heaven and earth and trees and grasses and the colour of the clay soil and its smell apparently had a way of touching the inside and the life juices of a certain child, and except that the she-ass, without intending anything, kept him company in an unburdensome way without doing anything more than any ordinary she-ass, indifferent to anything except some grass here or there, which she apparently preferred to the dreary fodder in the close air of the empty stable, and that this child, when he was restless sitting still, or when he was searching so that he too could have a friend or two and in the meantime having none, made friends wordlessly with absent listeners, and said to them, to the nothing that was before him and the open space that was before him, importuning the ass's ears as though continuing or resuming a conversation, many things that needed to be said, some of them ready-made and others in the process of becoming, and asking questions too and replying to questions that no one had asked yet, but the question why he was like that was a pointless question, who could answer it, perhaps it was simply because that was the way he was, and that something inside him seemed to be being filled, it felt good that it was being filled, he didn't know what it was that was being filled, but something that was being filled was being filled and longed to be filled more, and to see, and to see well, and to see the details, and to look for words, seeing is like touching and touching is like being and being is like doing and doing is like saying correctly, without giving up, like for example sitting in the corner of a field and soaking up, as the leaves of a plant soak up the light that makes the chlorophyll in them, as is well known, without which there is no life, or sitting on a high branch, with the ass grazing beneath and there too soaking up, or to stop in a bend of the road and soak up how it bends, or soaking up how the roofs of the German farm near Beer Yaakov under those eucalyptus trees suddenly make a quiet corner and for some reason remind you of a choir singing, even if the whole time a sort of low murmur, or perhaps a sort of hidden threat, has not stopped, and to tell the truth under all this heat of tired late summer there is continuously a coldness under the imagined heat, even when the heat is really hot there is a coldness underneath it. As it were.

But suddenly one day, with no prior warning, Mr Miller's library suddenly appeared (has this also not been told about somewhere?), one day suddenly, without remembering any particular reason, and he was invited in, and up the wooden stairs to the upper floor of that special house in Menuha ve-Nahala—Rest & Security—Street, also known as Millionaires' Row, just because this house was special, rising to the height of two storeys, and surrounded by Washingtonia palms swaying on their supple trunks, their boughs always seeming to be damp, always shaking with their height exposed to the wind, and surrounded by a rose garden and a flower garden that were watered abundantly and were always damp and fragrant, and upstairs too the tiles were red and cool and the ceiling was high and painted white, with a fundamental silence: he was invited to enter through the tall white door and to wait a moment, and this was easy and calm to do and it seemed right to walk on tiptoe only and quietly here, because that really was the right thing to do, when suddenly, inside, it's hard to say, because your breath suddenly stopped, because there, big and all round was the library with countless shelves of which all you remember is the black of those horizontal lines, above and below which stood the bindings of those books, hundreds, thousands, tens of thousands, more, books and more books most of them dark and the few that were red or blue or green only emphasized the darkness of the rest, thousands upon thousands bound, upright, one beside the other, in this vast room, that looked like a hall, like the whole upper storey, as though it was beyond human power to estimate its size, O God, books up to the ceiling and books all round the walls, not in piles, not sloppily or casually, and not closed, cold and distant either, but warm books that were read by those who loved them, and suddenly in that wall there were also windows that faced west to judge by the sun and the tops of the palm trees, and the way the curtain was blown inwards by that sea breeze, and also east, to judge by the open view of the Jerusalem Hills in the distance, and you also noticed a black rocking chair in a corner and a huge table with books on it, when suddenly there came into the room—impossible to recall who or what and it was not even important at that moment—apparently this was Mr Miller himself, a shortish man with a little beard, a big citrus grower, whose sons rode horses, that big pool was in his orange grove, he did not talk much, but he was a close friend of Uncle Moshe, and sometimes they shut themselves away together and it was forbidden to disturb them, it was forbidden to breathe even, and if only it were allowed he would have asked permission to crouch on the rug here, and if they gave him a little water because he was parched, and let him relax and take a closer look, with all the silence that was required, something that he was not allowed to do on this shock encounter, he returned home weak and weaving like a drunkard, unable to explain to Mummy or to Daddy, he just went straight to bed, and it was only after a while that they let him with a smile, and Mrs Miller was quiet and sweet, only Don't touch or disturb anything, something that he himself would have killed anyone who dared to do, and even though he knew now what he was going to see when he opened that tall white door he entered on tiptoe and his heart was pounding again, and it was not on the rug but of course on that black rocking chair, on the edge of his thin behind, and he merely looked around and round and round he looked shelf after shelf bookcase after bookcase, there were too many to count or number, like looking from the stage at the audience gathered for a big ceremony waiting for it to start, they looked like a crowd and there were so many of them, another and another, endlessly, most of them naturally not in Hebrew, he could barely make out a few large words on the large spines, dictionaries apparently, or encyclopaedias, or big atlases, all in the same binding, with gilded edges, and above section on section, more and more, and to each side another section and another, and more and more books, who had read them, who had opened them, who had leafed through them, who knew every one of them, these were not questions, not for then anyhow, and suddenly there were a lot of old acquaintances standing together in the same section, bookcase after bookcase, all

sorts of Talmuds and Mishnahs and prayer books and other books
he had never seen close up because Daddy had no books like these,
and also Bibles, whole Bibles and also the Pentateuch and Prophets
and Writings separately, row upon row and books in Hebrew about
the Land of Israel, and about explorations and excavations and dis-
coveries, and collections of maps, and beyond that were friends from
publishing houses like Stiebel and Mitzpeh and Moriah and other
names he was familiar with, and further on were books about agriculture apparently and plants and science, and it all suddenly made
him dizzy, the room was revolving, the books were revolving, and
suddenly without any warning he was sobbing there sitting on the
edge of his bottom on the edge of the rocking chair, and unable to
hold back his tears.

Were the bookcases made of mahogany? He did not know what
mahogany was and had never heard of it, were the books arranged,
as became clear much later, in sections on sociology, psychology, phi-
losophy, natural science, agronomy, Judaism and literature, and so
forth, he could not imagine and had never heard, nor did he have
such words or such knowledge, he had never read anything that
was not in Hebrew, he was only a child in Class 7 in the settlement
school, he would not be bar-mitzvah for another year, but he knew
that this was a separate kingdom from everything all around, a hundred miles around if not a thousand, yet joined to what was around
by two big ever-open windows, one that brought the sea breeze from
the west and one that sent it on its way eastwards, a kingdom on
its own made by Mr Miller the citrus grower because that was the
way he wanted to live, surrounded by books, which never stopped
multiplying, so he learnt later, and new boxes of books kept arriving and whenever he travelled abroad he sent more boxes of books,
and there was no end to it because there really was no end to it, and
every day despite all his work he sat in his rocking chair with books
in his hands and more books on the table beside him and his glass
of tea getting cold among the piled-up books, reading for enjoyment
here, leafing through another book for pleasure there, pulling down
a third book for comparison over there, remembering and opening

a fourth for further comparison, taking a gulp of tea, and it was so much precisely what had to be done and so precise and so necessary, and above all so beautiful, this very living existence of these books all around him and in the midst of the world that could be seen through the windows, without the world having any need of the treasure he had laid up for himself (as would become clear years later when his heirs did not know what to do with the mortal remains of these endless books or how to get rid of their finely bound but unwanted quantity), and which nonetheless made there to be in the world some sense that it actually was worthwhile, and even suddenly made there be a decision that books by him too would one day stand in this library, that he too would one day be among those admitted to these bookcases, and short Mr Miller sitting comfortably in his rocking chair, caressed by the sea breeze that stirred the curtains with his glass of tea in front of him, would turn with his thin fingers the pages that he would bring into being, that would be beautifully and necessarily written, no less beautifully and necessarily than all the other beautifully and necessarily books here, and it was hard to say how much, because everything here was again so exciting, so open, so breathing and so very full.

And only when he went home somewhat shocked, dragging his sandals in the hot sand down Millionaires' Row and turning under the brown yellow-leaved gravilleas into Jacob's Lane, realising suddenly how unfair it was that Daddy, his Daddy, did not have such a library, even a smaller one, when it was only right that he should have one, a library where he could sit and work, after all Daddy had prepared himself, prepared and prepared himself, with hard work, with honest work, work of perfection, for thirty or forty years he had prepared himself to go to Nahalal, in fact he had spent his whole life preparing himself to get to Nahalal and he had never got there, he had only got to where all his life he had wanted not to get: to supervise workmen, and even without Nahalal he could surely have sat in this library, sat quietly and worked, that hard-working Daddy, who never sat down to leaf through a book or to enjoy books but to work, and suddenly he could have returned to himself, and begun to flower again, a flow-

ering working man, and suddenly he could have truly been there, all
of Daddy could have been there again. Look at him now, like those
boats on the Yarkon, condemned never to sail again, lying on their
sides, at the water's edge, bodies with no souls. And now it was clear
that Nahalal was not just an agricultural settlement, it was also a social
order, that made a man feel confident that he would not be allowed
to fall, that people would support him in hard times, that they understood that things in the world only happened by chance, and that no
will could force the world to behave as one expected, and that people
only reached the place in the world that they reached, so that at best
all they could do was to try to justify whatever they had produced,
strange to think it was so but apparently there was no mistake, and
that was how it was. And suddenly it was hard to go on, better to
stop and sit down suddenly, here close to the Rabbi's House, on the
hillock in the empty plot, and just watch the setting sun.

Now you can see the great wheels of the world in action as
they start to slow down and stop or seem to start to lose height on
the approach to landing, as half of the sky is entirely preparing for
the sunset, above everything and totally unconcerned one way or the
other, it is fully occupied with spreading its sunset above everything,
there is nothing corporeal about it, it is all just reflection or refraction
of light and just nothing, a kind of vast nothingness that is gradually spreading above the world, caring about nothing but gradually
spreading silently above everything, turning upwards not downwards,
just one colour blended with another, all the time, with the same
peaceful, indifferent illumination above the world, so indifferent and
beautiful, supremely beautiful, not sad, not not-sad, just beautiful,
not promising anyone anything, just beautiful and totally clear, just
one clear nothing turning gradually pink, orange at the bottom and
almost green at the top, a sort of clarity made of nothing, a sort of
clear beauty made of clear nothing, only the shades of pink turning
in absolute silence from one pink to another, with a proud superior-
ity towards themselves, not to impress anyone else, as though there
is some necessary and superior truth in them that makes this indifference totally complete in every way.

Squill

Dostoevsky, *Crime and Punishment*, in his innermost being; Moka, one day, said that in his father's house too there were endless books, always being added to, and yes, why not, he could come with him, no problem, why not right now, yes, to see what there was, they would leave him on his own, he could look at whatever he liked, he could even have some grapes, yes, why not, as soon as his father woke up from his siesta, which was sacrosanct, and among the many shelves, with no comparison to Mr Miller's library, and without that height going up beyond the tops of the tall constantly bowing palm trees, but in his father's study, his father was a big dealer in building materials, paraffin, petrol, oils, chemical fertilisers, agencies, telephones, everything, with heavily laden shelves all around, books and books and no room for more, the new ones squeezed in here and there betwixt and between, and among them, suddenly, in an instant, by its appearance, its smell, the spaces between the lines, you know that this is the book, Dostoevsky, *Crime and Punishment*, with no beating about the bush, Can I borrow it? and Moka, Why not? Just for a day or two? Take it, Till after the weekend? It's fine, really, Can I? No one reads here anyway, not Amikam, not Azrikam, not Matitya, not Efratya, not the kids, not the grown ups, who has time to read, take it, take it, show me which one you've taken, *Crime and Punishment*—what is it, a detective story? Is it worth reading? Tell me when you bring it back, great, see you, that's fine, don't mention it, and now, in his usual place, at the end of his bed, curled up with his knees under his tummy and his head in his hands, only his eyes running ceaselessly, into the steadily thickening gloom, there's a lot he doesn't grasp, there's a lot he doesn't understand, words, places, events, deeds, there's a lot the fast-moving reading doesn't let him catch, but the desire that rushes on from one page to the next grasps the depression that gets worse and worse, the hard place in which they are more and more entangled, that power that grasps a man and closes him more and more tightly in its grip, like the fangs of a wild beast closing on its prey, that grasp from which there is no escape, even into the necessity to commit a forbidden act, even into the terrified will to get out quickly and be purged, even the knowledge that there is no way to get out or to be purged, and that you will never again be simple, innocent and small, as you were before or as people thought you were, and it's such a pity and yet so wonderful, and there is a something in everything that comes and goes all the time, with no retreat, and it is frightening and true and just as one has been waiting for it to be finally.

And it awakens in an instant what he does not yet know what to do with, both a decision to wash and cleanse himself from the knowledge of what he saw and curiosity to know more and from close up—a few days ago when he came out of the Rabbi's House and climbed the huge fig tree in the yard of the farmer Yehuda opposite to taste some figs almost bursting from their discharge of nectar, purple blue and thin from dark ripeness, and not be stung by those buzzing yellow things, and he was still up in the smooth grey branches when he saw them coming out of the thick thuja bushes, she was unmistakably fat Malkele, shaking herself and straightening and pulling at her tattered dress, her face red and with her thin hair and her strange laugh, and he following her, still pulling up his trousers, and going straight to the tap in the yard to wash his loins and his privates in full view of anyone who was watching, and splashing frothy water from the tap on his face, from which the big Australian hat had not been removed—he was the new vineyard man, the king of the grape-pickers—and without drying himself he hoisted up his trousers and fastened them with the wide belt, concealing his hairy belly and all his gleaming male nudity above the thick black hair, Run along, he grumbled at Malkele, filling his cupped palms with water and wetting his face again and again, Run along, he grumbled at her, as she stood by the gate and went on laughing red-faced, fat and short, but not moving, and suddenly he was seized with dread that they would see him, that they would know that he was here and that he knew, knew something he didn't want to know and that he was suddenly choked by a wild urge to know more and more, but also angry at the knowledge of the humiliation that was ahead of him, and shame at knowing something he was not supposed to know, and wished he didn't, and how the man had washed his privates at the frothy tap, and also the curiosity that it was shameful that he had such dark curiosity inside him, what had he done to her in there, and how he was inside her, and all those things that the bigger boys stopped talking about when he came near, because he was the way he was, and how could he put it all away as though it had never happened, if only he had not been here and hadn't seen and didn't know, and it wasn't like that, he shouldn't have, and what he had seen was so dirty that all the water in the tap could never wash it away, and that big thing of his that he had held to wash, and that fat girl it had been done to, with her stupid laugh, the wrong that was done to her, if only someone had come and beaten him up, her brother or her father or someone, so he'd learn his lesson, and if only it could all be wiped out as though he had never seen it, what would he do with what he knew now, and all that disgusting stuff, and the protest that was surging up inside him against something bad, something that wasn't right, and how could he ever rid himself of that indecent forbidden thing, and from the excited curiosity to know more, everything, and how easy it was for any boy here who felt a pressure in his loins to go and unload himself inside her, while she just laughed and dribbled, then got up and straightened her miserable dress and went off with a handful of sweets and Run along, when they grumbled at her to clear off.

It's getting complicated. Where should he go exactly. Everything that was possible just before seems empty and bleak now. Talk to somebody. Ask somebody. If only it were possible. If he were a carpenter he would go and make a chair or a table, with all his energy and making it as beautiful as he could, if he were a blacksmith he would go and make horseshoes, smiting the iron with all his force, but a child who doesn't do anything and doesn't know how to do anything? Incidentally, now, from time to time, in a notebook made up of pages that he has bound together quite clumsily, he writes poems, always in rhyme, in four-line stanzas, with beautiful words the choicest of beautiful words, about nature, the sunset, sadness, and suchlike, he is sure they are not good but he is sure they are beautiful, the rhymes are beautiful, and the words are beautiful, and the images are beautiful, but now it's all boring, and sometimes he writes out a beautiful line from memory but continues it with a line of his own, why is that wrong, like *How long will thy tormented spirit sigh?* which he rhymed with *And whither will she send her mournful cry?*, whereas Ibn Gabirol wrote *She moans aloud and seeks to rise on high*, he found the poem in a book in Mr Miller's library that he was leafing through, excited by how right and how accurate it was, and immediately knew it by heart, *How long will thy tormented spirit sigh?*, both with the pronunciation of the words and with the knowledge of this torment that afflicts the spirit, which is too much, too much to bear, and not expressed with an outcry but in measured words, with the repeated *s* sound, and he only made a small change and look how it comes out, *How long will thy tormented spirit sigh, And whither will she send her mournful cry?*, very beautiful, very poetic, pity it's not all his, after all, and suddenly Mikha'ela was here with him too, in the night, apparently, presumably in a dream, and he doesn't remember except that it was she, and she was dressed as though for the winter, in a long grey warm coat, a soft grey coat, with her plaits over the back of this long soft grey coat that enfolded and enclosed all of her, till he woke, so full of longing and excitement, so pointless, nothing will come of it, but so unforgettable, standing there, in that grey coat, that long, warm, soft coat of hers.

It's cold again in the middle of the heat, and in the small hours of the morning you look for the sheet to wrap yourself in, the chill before dawn and the cry of a crow, and in the distance you can hear what sounds like the faraway weeping of the congregation reciting penitential prayers, there in Shaarayim, a dim faraway mournful chant, whereas in Jacob's Lane there are no Yemenites, except for Kadia, Hamama and Masouda, who come every morning to help the women and leave again every evening in their long red trousers worn under their embroidered dresses and with scarves round their heads, and except for the Yemenite men who go past in the morning on their way to the orange groves with their baskets and their long, curled sidelocks, so thin and nimble-fingered, but they earn less because they are Yemenites, and there are no Sephardim in Jacob's Lane either, except maybe Mr Bekhor Levi the teacher, and the barber Habibi who comes from Persia, apparently, and all the rest are called Rabinovich or Kantorovich and all sorts of names that end in 'ski' or 'ov' or 'stein'; Daddy showed him the penitential prayers in the prayer book, prayers like *Forgive us O our Father* and *As a father has compassion on his children*, hymns like *May our prayer come before You and turn not away from our supplications*, and all those alphabetical acrostics, *Ancient men of faith | Assailed by mighty waters | Attend to my supplication*, and *Assuage your anger*—some day he must study them closely, and find out what it is that suddenly responds in you so to these convoluted words, something enclosed in them, something in you that opens up to them. But not now, he is so empty now, what can he do to make it be different, suddenly there is no goal, there's nothing that's worthwhile, so alone, alone that is nothing but alone, cold, boring and empty, and he doesn't want anything.

The murmur of the bulbul is muted now, songless, as though he has had enough, all he has left is his end-of-season muttering, he is just hanging around, and even the yellow wagtail whose arrival always seems to bring good news, as though with the onset of autumn the year is turning, everything has finished, change is on the way, steps like a yellow dancer with too many wiggles of its tail, and it's sad to watch, there is nowhere to go, for anyone, and autumn will come of its own accord anyway, and anyway no one cares, and if Raskolnikov came here he wouldn't know what to do or where to go, the people in Jacob's Lane are all citrus growers, or citrus growers and wine growers, or citrus growers and wine growers and almond growers, apart from a few shopkeepers, and a few people who sell equipment for citrus growing, and the saddler on the corner at the bottom of the lane: nobody here will murder anybody, and no old lady, no matter how mean and rich, will be murdered here, the most that happens is that the vineyard man, the king of the grape-pickers, drags Malkele into the thuja bushes, it's not clear exactly what he does to her there, or how he does it, he doesn't want to know even though he's desperately curious, and it's impossible to be rid of that irritating excitement, between revulsion and attraction, and there is not a soul right now in the whole of Jacob's Lane, even the crows in the tree are quiet, those wise crows, even they are sick of everything, even Yehuda's big mangy dog is fed up and is sleeping like a bundle of rags in a hollow in the sand, or perhaps he should climb to the top of the eucalyptus and scream I don't want to I don't want to I don't want to, without knowing what he doesn't want to do, just not wanting, not wanting, not wanting, run away warbler, no one is interested in you, joyless wagtail, joyless bulbul, pointless Jacob's Lane, worthless, useless, it was like a big white worm, his thing against the hair at the bottom of his belly, and he held it under the splashing water from the tap and washed it so shamelessly, even with an indifferent pride, like someone who'd done a great deed, something so frightening, so abominable, and it was such a pity, such a pity he had got involved, and he didn't know how to disentangle himself, what did he need all this for, and what did everyone want from him, and with his other hand he gestured to her to leave, Run along, he grumbled at her.

The farmer Yehuda in the farmyard across the way from the Rabbi's House comes out and looks up and down Jacob's Lane, waiting for someone, What are you doing right now? he suddenly turns to Dagon, Young lazy-bones, would you mind, Yehuda's wrinkled face suddenly lights up but his thick moustache is smooth and grey, would you mind very much, he sharpens his request, taking this cart here and going to the vincyard, they're waiting to load the baskets of muscat that we're keeping for the festivals, and when you get back I'll give you a shilling, would you, you've driven a horse and cart haven't you; he must have been sent by the gods, Yehuda the farmer, who doesn't even suspect what they got up to on the edge of his farmyard under those thuja bushes, and even though he's never driven a horse and cart in his life, only wanted to, why not start now, after all there's nothing grander than driving a horse and cart, an old dream that will come surprisingly true, driving on his own along the dust track between the orange groves to the vineyard that the farmer Yehuda is trying to explain to him how to get to, with many waves of his arms and a rapid sketch with his shoe in the dust, saying that he can't go wrong, and that they're waiting for him there, and that they will all come back together with the loaded cart, and he will get a shilling, if he's willing to do it. So they go into the farmyard, and there is the horse and cart all ready, and the horse is a roan, with reddish flecks, and a red mane and tail, and when he waves his tail it looks like flames of fire, and he is already harnessed and standing between the shafts, tossing his head in impatience to be off, and here he is sitting on the board that rests crosswise on the two boards that lie longways, holding the reins in both hands, he doesn't need to choose the word of command or the cry to be off, because the horse has already started drawing the cart behind him effortlessly and he's out of the yard in a rush, turning sharp left and missing by a hairsbreadth scraping against the gatepost and catching it with the end of the axle, without a worry as he crosses the empty sandy road, then breaking into a trot, with a pounding of hooves, as though this is the moment he was waiting for, resolutely ignoring his diminutive driver sitting on the board, clutching the reins in both hands, and it is lucky there is no one around to see what a novice he is at driving a horse, rushing along now as if the devil were on their tails, not saying a word or pulling on the reins, letting things come as they will, and there is no need of a carter for them to come as they have to, as though the horse's big muscles were only waiting for this freedom, his tail raised like the red flag in the assault, and the trot turns into a canter and then a gallop, suddenly everything changes and seems less like playing at driving a cart and more like a wild adventure, and a certain anxiety about survival, grasping the comforting thought that he can always jump out onto the soft sand, and that white and red beast can run on as crazily as it likes, and you haven't got the nerve to turn back and see if the farmer Yehuda, as at this furious gallop they pass between the acacia hedges and the lemon grove, is watching from his gate, bursting with peasant laughter, or terrified what will happen to the child, regretting entrusting him with the final part of the harvesting of his muscat grapes that will make a killing on the pre-festival market, but either way the sand has become deeper, on the way to the cemetery, and their progress is being slowed by the sinking sands, and the big fallow field of red clay is all naked except for a little tickle-grass and some centaureas covered in snails, and, oh God!, the stalks of the new squills are beginning to peep through, if only there were time to look at anything, and only the depth of the sand that has collected on the road is now slowing the speed of the empty cart and its unacknowledged driver whose blazing horse is triumphantly doing whatever he and his freedom-seeking muscles like, and it is only now thanks to the restraint of the deep sand that the child is beginning to hold the reins more correctly, to breathe more deeply, to regain his self-control and to become a man, and although he forgot to ask Yehuda the horse's name, he is beginning to call him White, not without an intention to make friends with him, and also Whitey, and as the wheels sink in almost up to the axle something that was very clenched inside him opens up, and as the trot changes to a strained effort to get out of this clinging deep sand he starts calling the horse Whitey-white, and the sand is not yellow but frankly red, without any of the glistening little shells you find in sea sand, a powdery clean mass of shining redness, until the top of this gentle rise, where the hard clay is exposed again, the horse strains his freedom-thirsty muscles again and flicks up his red tail, and his big muscular hindquarters push forward the irresistible onward rush, which becomes a joyous gallop, cart and carter and all the rest cancelled as though they were no more than a light feather at his heels, and again tossing his red tail he runs free, while Dagon, that child, too late now to stop him, opens his mouth and sings, unbelievably, all kinds of *ho* and *hi*, all kinds of I don't care, and there is nothing in this open field but a single open rush and a single lark-like song.

Why did Yehuda the farmer need a driver, and why did he bother to explain the way and even draw a plan in the dust with the toe of his shoe, when this horse knows the way and draws the cart in a single rush, now racing like the wind and now straining every muscle, so young and waving his red tail, and he seems to be in business with the farmer to go quickly and come back quickly with the baskets of grapes before they start to ferment in the sun in those big baskets, and because of that experienced partnership he needs neither reins nor anyone to hold them, neither bridle nor bit, but just a slap on his muscular flanks wrapped in smooth sensitive silky skin, white flecked with red, and he would race straight to the vineyard and stop by the baskets where without so much as an *ahlan* or a *sahlan* he would join the pickers and load up and turn round and race straight back to his master's stall, so that the driver can slacken the reins and look around, and see how the orange groves end and the vineyards begin, and they do not need a special well, and they are the last vineyards before the edge of the settlement, after which you can't see much but you can smell the danger and the mystery that lie beyond, and these vines, they say, will not last long in these changing times, soon they will be dug up and wells will be sunk and oranges will be planted here instead, just as they dug up the almonds to plant vines instead, just as they dug up the tobacco they used to grow here to plant vines instead, just as they abandoned the barley they used to sow in the winter for a summer harvest, and maybe the only thing that always remains is the earth that changes its clothing according to the cost of outgoings and the value of receipts, that clay soil that is sometimes covered in reddish dust that trips you up as you run, and sometimes bare and hard so you rush insolently on, and sometimes covered in almost dried up turf on which the cows that Attiya the cowherd brings every morning graze, and sometimes simply exposed to the sun, with no covering at all and the sun can see everything it has and the wind caresses everything it has, and suddenly, in a corner of the field, there is a group, a crowd of squills, standing on their naked stalks gleaming with the pure starry whiteness of their inflorescences, and these are real heralds of the approaching autumn, hail to you autumn.

And we seem to have arrived because the horse the farmer's ally suddenly stops and stands still, on the edge of a vineyard with withering leaves, although there is no one here and no sign of baskets, he stands pawing the ground with one of his front legs, which seems to be a pre-arranged signal, because an Arab suddenly pops up with a scarf wound round his head and smiling says *ahlan* and *shalom* and *kif hilak,* and *ta'al inzil,* and after taking the horse's bridle in one hand and stroking his sweat-covered neck with the other, he gathers up the reins and hangs them on the saddle-horn, because there is no need to tie up this horse that as a partner will not do anything that does not contribute to the partnership and certainly not run away suddenly just before the loading, and insubstantial Dagon descends and joins the substantial man; in the doubtful shade of a splendid vine in a sooty depression in the dust is a tripod made of clods of earth, because there are no stones to be found here unless you run to the foot of the hills, and a blackened pot and a smouldering fire and bubbling coffee, and *tishrab nitfat qahwe* says the big man and the skinny-legged guest in his wide shorts nods acceptance although he is not a coffee-drinker, folds his legs beneath him and carefully holds the scalding little cup that was washed before his eyes in water from the *libriq* or *ibriq* with the application of a thumb that removed no previous traces, filled precisely one-third full with the best of well-brewed coffee, as is the custom in places where good manners have not yet died out in these changing times, and then the man gives a practised sigh and the boy gives a less practised sigh and the man explains that they are coming, the basket-bearers from the depths of the vineyard, because they have been picking young grapes and they have to go along all the rows picking a few grapes here and there, like beating young grapes when the harvest is ended, two or three clusters on a vine and four or five on its branches, as the Prophet said apparently, it is warm and good in the world and only the crickets are talking now and with all their might.

A little clump of squills is bowing right over his shoulder and if he turns towards them they smile back at him except that they pay him no attention whatever, and only the stem, or the smooth stalk, grey green and brown, rather cold and marble-like, stirs slightly as though towards him, and piled up close-packed and not yet open on the inflorescence at its slightly stooped head are tiny pearls enclosed in green, while at its base there are already some green triangular pods in ovaries that have already been fertilised, while high up in the middle part, between those further down that have faded and those above that have not yet opened, in their full radiant splendour stand masses of white open stars with greenish-gold stamens, buffeted by squalls of bees that are drunk on pollen and nectar, and every day the flowering flame rises one stage higher, extinguishing closed pods beneath and lighting opening flowers above, six brilliant white membranous petals with a green line running up the middle of each, and the stamens that bear the green or gold in their midst, all ranged by order of generations, faded, flowering and then closed, high up on these five tall flowering stalks, with another two or three little ones just peering out of the ground, they may yet rise up or they may have been born to remain dwarfs, here in a corner of the vineyard, marking from generations back apparently the limit of the plot, dark green when the field is ploughed and bursting into a blaze of white flowers at harvest time, and until they are uprooted with changing times they are unchanging and immovable landmarks or boundary stones, and it's a pity he doesn't know what to do exactly before the sadness comes down again.

But now there comes a bustle and a rustling from among the rows of vines and the basket-bearers arrive, stooping on either side of the black wicker basket, full heavy and dripping sticky black juice through the wickerwork, one man on either side half-dragging and half-lifting, and with a stomach-wrenching effort they swing it straight up onto the cart, and only now do they turn to look and see, and only now does it transpire that who is one of the two but the king of the grape-pickers, sweaty weary hot and breathless, and from close up you can see that he is not a youth, he is not young and he is not shaven either, and his sweat smells sharp, and his big Australian hat seems to be stuck to his forehead, he does not utter a word, and nobody speaks, but knowing their allotted task they turn back into the rows of vines to fetch another heavy basket, and now the browning leaves part and another black basket arrives but this time it is carried by two Arab women with a teeth-gritting effort and wordlessly they summon up all their strength and raise it first onto the rim of the wheel and then with another effort they heave it over the side and onto the cart, and lightened they let out a sigh, dressed in black down to their feet, ageless with white headscarves that they now adjust, and wordlessly they too turn back into the vines with a rustling of their long black dresses that catch in the fading leaves and trailing a sour waft of sweat they vanish, and a moment later the two men are back kneeling on either side of their heavy black basket that is dripping sticky juice and they hoist it onto the cart, and now they turn to the water pitcher the *libriq* or *ibriq* and swig one after the other wordlessly, then the two women return and raise the basket onto the wheel and then with another effort into the cart, which of course says nothing, nor does the horse, nor does anyone of those standing around, their arms drooping, breathing heavily, and it is hot and quiet and empty all around and that is all.

How will one horse be able to drag all this through the yielding sand, and where will all the workers sit on this full cart, and what will happen when they break their silence, it is not clear, but one after the other they kneel and sit around to take a break, sitting under the sun, and as though everything there has ever been to say has been said they all sit in silence, the two women slightly apart, as is right and proper. And a crow suddenly caws, as though to say if you have nothing to say I do, long-drawn-out rather hoarse cries, which can be interpreted in different ways. And perhaps it really can see further, and perhaps it knows what others do not or do not dare to know, but even it does not know that this man, who is as he is now from close up, was completely different in the morning, and just as under his hat his face now is withered, unshaven, smeared with sweat and tired, so then under his clothes his body was young, hairy, bright, male and shining beneath the splashing water, powerfully potent, and his flesh fresh just come out of her white flesh, while his other hand dismissed her, Run along, it's as if he's not the same man, what does the crow, the wisest of birds, know about him, and is he not even here reaching out to touch those black-robed women who carried those heavy baskets with the last of their strength and wordlessly, and who might also conceal a surprising nakedness under their robes, who knows, and who knows how he suddenly has thoughts that he never knew he would have, not because it's forbidden but because he never had them before, he is only becoming more deeply embroiled in what is too heavy for him, three men, two women and a child are sitting and a horse is standing and they do not say anything and only the crow as though it knows something proclaims from time to time and with deep feeling and stops, and then you can hear the crickets and beyond them the silence that goes all the way to the sun, and upright beyond your shoulder stand the columns of the flowering squills, with squalls of bees on the nectar that fills the membranous insides of those white flowers between the extinguished fertilised flowers and the virginal flowers that have not opened yet.

But suddenly, in the midst of all the silence and non-speaking, whether from tiredness or dragging or something, suddenly he knows with certainty, without having any certainty, for how would he suddenly know with certainty, or who could know, and now as he moves his gaze over all those seated figures, sitting heavily and silently without any shade over them, suddenly he knows that soon, almost imperceptibly, none of this will remain, neither this vineyard nor this sandy path, none of this will remain, and even Yehuda the farmer, who sent them all here to pick the late-ripening grapes from his vineyard, is not particularly attached to this vineyard or to any other vineyard, or to the muscat grapes that will make a killing on the market, or to any other grapes, or even to this particular horse or to any other horse, or to these particular workers or any vineyard workers, and he really is not attached to any vineyard, or to any grapes or vineyard workers, not because they are not good, because they all work as hard as they can, the horse and the people, but because everything here is provisional, with no necessity to exist like this particularly, the vineyard that will be replaced by an orange grove, and the building plots that will replace the orange grove, and the houses that will be built on the plots, and this place is not like all those other places where year after year and generation after generation the olive harvest comes regularly in its season and year after year and generation after generation the time of threshing comes regularly in its season and year after year since time immemorial you simply wait and the squill and the wagtail appear at their regular time, and you bathe your heart in the certainty that everything will turn out well, and every year at this time there are sunsets like this, and the days always get shorter as they always have done, and the rest, none of that will exist here, because everything here is provisional, and that ancient cycle of the year has no binding force here, it does not enter into the bloodstream of existence here, the eternal existence of this place, there is no necessity that is always confirmed again in the cycle of the year, that is reconfirmed each year with a necessity that seems more solid than everything that is transient and provisional, but everything that is here is all temporary and they are only pretending to be farmers, only temporary vineyards and temporary orange groves, it's only temporarily that they sink in the yielding red sand or speed over the hard bare clay, they all exist but not in the blood, not firmly grounded, nothing is solid here, the vineyard has no solid basis and the late-ripening grapes for the festivals have no solid basis nor does the farmer and it is not clear if his sons will, and all the solidity of whatever seems solid here is just the ethereal solidity of existence here, and the who knows, maybe yes and maybe no.

But who really knows that it is so, and that this vineyard has been harvested for the last time and Yehuda the farmer is going to replace it with an orange grove and sink a well, and send off crates of gold to earn him silver, no man here is a prophet and even a prophet would not know, a child might perhaps, with his unspoilt innocence, as though he has listened and heard and knows without any confirmation that the vineyard will not remain, but that even this boundary between the settled land and the threatening silence of the dangerous mystery beyond the boundary will not remain, and these Arabs will not remain, the men and the women, and that Zarnuga will not remain and Qubeibeh will not remain and Yibne will not remain, they will all go away and start to live in Gaza, woe for them, and the orange groves both old and new will make no more gold and earn no more silver, they will all be dried up because the value of land will be greater than the income from orange growing, and only another generation or two, or two and a half at the most, will hold on here, only one generation of farmers or two, or two and a half at the most, one day they will all go and they will all change places and the place itself will change places too, as though it is just a changing stage set, and this world will go and be completely mixed up, nothing solid will remain solid, nothing clear will remain clear, and nothing unimaginable will remain unimaginable, and even the squills will not remain because they will be built over, and the clay soil will not either because it will be built over, and the red dust tracks will not because they will become paved roads, and the horse will not because first they will transport the containers of fruit on carts with tyres and then on trailers pulled by tractors and soon after that they will not transport anything to any big automated packing room because there will be nothing to transport, and only people with memories will tell others who refuse to listen how there were orange groves here once upon a time before the flood and they will bore their hearers stiff, what does that wise crow on the tree know today, what can it see, what can you know about that man sitting here if you see him as he is now, tired, withered and not speaking, and how this morning he knew and embraced a woman's flesh and thrust his big thing into her with all his might, and sowed a terrible curiosity in a certain unwilling person, only now everyone knows that the time has come to go home, and without saying a word, because if they do something may come out that is better left unsaid, they beckon to the child to get up on the board, and they take their leave by looks alone of the man who is staying in the vineyard, and all the rest of them, the two men in front and the two women behind, grasp with one hand each of the four sides of the cart and accompany it to right and to left and walk with it in the sand, and when it sinks they hold it with both hands and push with all their strength, together and without saying a word, and the cart sinking in deep under the four black wicker baskets full of grapes bursting with juice and almost split by must, as heavy as a load of lead if not heavier, now it is moving and stirring and the horse hollows his back with effort and there is no need to urge him on because he is a full partner and understands the whole business of extricating the sinking cart from the sand and on to the firm clay and slowly along the paths of soft sand and firm clay, with or without the hedges round the orange groves, and here and there more clumps of flowering squills, eagerly returning to the farmer Yehuda who is waiting for them in his doorway, looking like a lighthouse.

On the steps of the Rabbi's House facing west to the approaching sunset, and the long day is gradually moving away and dissolving and two steps below him his friend Moka is sitting hunched up, he has come to visit for a moment before he and his friends go to the cinema, the moment after Amram the projectionist starts the electric motor and the lights go on in the entrance to the cultural centre, and they are just chatting, and Moka is thoroughly intrigued by his friend who is two steps above him, because among all his friends there is no one else quite like this Dagon, because he and his friends are always together, with one another, always together they know what they are going to do all day and in any case they won't waste time on reading, apart from what they have to read for school, and barely that, apart from a bit of sport in the paper or stars of the silver screen or news of a murder or a robbery, their eyes never lap up the printed word, they go to football together on Saturday and they go out with girls together on Saturday night, and they go to Tel Aviv together for shopping or to stuff their faces, and together on horses or donkeys sometimes to Nebi Rubin on the seashore to watch the Arabs dancing at the camp they have every year at the end of the threshing, shrieking, singing, killing sheep with rice and cinnamon and folk dancing and belly dancing and a few other forbidden things that they do there apparently that they don't tell him about they stop talking when he approaches, and together they always know everything and together they learn all about life straight from life and about the work they will do and their parents' business successes, and about racehorses, and motorcycles too, and the exchange of useful information about girls in general and one or two in particular, and there are always experts among them who know more about girls and about things to do with girls than have ever even occurred to anyone, and now here he is on the lower step because he finds this friend who is not with the rest of them strange, and it is just because he is so kindhearted that he has come to see him, to exchange a word or two, to be surprised and amazed by things he hears him say, and it is his kind heart too that has made him bring Dagon a little present in an old shoebox, both of them know what's inside, a book from Moka's father's library, that no one has ever read or will ever read, both because they don't read and because the very title of the book is so ridiculous and doesn't compel you to read it and because the book has fallen apart into separate gatherings that the binding could not hold together so it broke up into lots of sections, only when Dagon saw this dismembered packet he burst into the cries of a true collector, Oh what a pity, oh don't throw it away, let me bind it together for you, and various other equally weird exclamations, and kind Moka promised that if his father didn't object, and why should he, books keep arriving all the time ever since he signed when the bookseller came to the house and pressed him to sign up for subscriptions to Stiebel and Mitzpeh publishing houses, and support culture, and pestered in all sorts of other ways so that his father soon gave in and forgot all about it on the spot so that the books continue to arrive regularly, they unpack them, glance at them and push them into the almost non-existent space left, until this book arrived in its two volumes and fell apart in their hands and was hastily thrust to one side to be disposed of before the mice sniffed it, and now here it is in this shoe-box, lying there quietly and inoffensively for the moment in no particular order, and Take it if you still want it, he takes off the lid and there it really lies revealed, the title page which reads in this order, Charles Dickens, *The Posthumous Papers of the Pickwick Club*, translated by Y. H. Taviov and B. Krupnik, Stiebel Publishing Co., 1929, not too many words, but enough to scare off any young man with healthy feelings, and containing nothing useful for a useful person, in fact just plain *binfa'esh*.

Do you really like books like this, Moka asks innocently, and are you going to read all of it? Sure, answers Dagon, of course, What does it do for you, Moka inquires, and what do you need it for? Why, Dagon replies, because it's simply wonderful, which Moka's eyes do not accept as true, You see the world, he tries to explain, but Moka doesn't accept this, the world for him is not in any book, because here is the world right here outside as it is, not like an image, which is not the world, Moka insists, and why read a book when you have the real thing, he says, Take girls for instance, he adds suddenly, which is better, to read about them in books or to do it to them in real life? to which Dagon has no reply, but he suddenly remembers Mikha'ela coming to him in a dream, wearing a warm winter coat, a thick grey buttoned up coat, and so soft, so very soft, and then he woke up, And don't you want to come to the cinema with us? he asks when suddenly the lamps come on outside the cultural centre further down at the bottom of the road, handing over the shoe-box with the treasure inside it, and Dagon does not admit that he hasn't got three piastres, and he won't ask his mother because she hasn't got the money either, but he thanks Moka and thanks him again and says it was very nice of him, to which Moka says warm-heartedly with a kind smile, It's nothing, but you always stay on your own and never come along with the rest of us, he asks, Are you really happier like that? he asks, and Dagon has no answer to the question are you really happier like that, so they say goodbye and Moka gets up and goes down the steps, then turns and smiles and waves goodbye, a tall figure with broad shoulders, and as he goes away the reddening sunset receives his silhouette that sways a little as he walks, from youthful vigour apparently.

One to watch the film one to watch the sunset, which is changing colours and becoming like a glorious war story, mighty forces of which there has been no knowledge all day are going forth now above anything known, and creating a great spectacle in the west, greater than anything you could expect, greater than anything you could dream, like another truth that is more true than any known truth, gradually taking form and amazing every moment with another possibility that you would never have imagined possible, such a pity that it will all collapse in a short while and be shown to be false as though it never was. And then the darkness will thicken, and they will eat supper, each with their own worries, each at the end of their day that has passed, beyond a few words here and there, and then he will go to bed with the lamp, because here in the Rabbi's House there is no electricity yet, and he will carefully lay the sheaf of pages down, everything exactly as he likes it, the colour of the paper and the printing and the stretched letters to justify the lines, and the announcement after the title of each chapter of what will happen in this chapter, and the smile that begins at the beginning, and the way the story is told, and that from this evening on there will not be an evening when he does not pick up a sheaf of pages to read before he goes to sleep and he won't read without his laughter suddenly scaring the softly creaking ceiling, and Mummy and Daddy in the next room will look up and know the child is laughing, and he will discover the sayings of Sam Weller, such as 'Oh, quite enough to get, Sir, as the soldier said ven they ordered him three hundred and fifty lashes', or the father who cut off his son's head to cure his squint, and said 'Now we look fine and dandy', or 'Come and call on me, as the spider said to the fly', and many other such gems, and Mr Pickwick, Mr Tupman, Mr Snodgrass and Mr Winkle, and the mail coach, and all those persons who do insignificant things which are recounted with great importance, and suddenly without the grim seriousness of life, oh life, and of the world, oh world, and without the constant soul-searching, and the tears of all those lonely, rootless and always disappointed people, not in Dostoevsky's attic or cellar, people always swearing oaths and contending with God, and always bearing some dark guilt, guilt and despair, despair and heartbreak, and men who cannot relate to other men and even less to women, everything but everything about them is uprooted, broken, their hearts are broken, and their souls and their lives and their loves, the mire and the spitting *tfu tfu*, suddenly everything appears different, recognising that there is more folly than wisdom in the world, and folly that one can laugh at without condoning it, and that villains only appear to be villains and everyone is punished in the end and what are they employed in all the time if not in essence folly, and they become embroiled in foolish things and in other human weaknesses and pretensions, which are more ridiculous than dangerous, and here nobody expects some tortured and tormented young man to get up one day and murder a stingy, mean old lady, and eat out his own heart and that of his hearers, and you can also see that there is always another side to things, a little foolish, a little pretentious, deserving of laughter and cleansing of vision, and that anyone who writes should write like Dickens, moving the action along not by hatred but with perceptiveness and indulgence, not reforming the world but passing through it, the sentences not violent and aggressive, not ripping off masks or uncovering crimes, but like here with a musical stream, with a stream of sentences happy to stream, a flow happy to flow, recounting all the details that it is a pleasure to narrate correctly, everything in movement everything boisterous everything coming more and more and full all the time, and it is beautiful to write like that, and so every evening he takes a sheaf of pages out of the shoe-box that from now on will always accompany him everywhere, until it disappeared somehow or other, perhaps it really was the mice, and Moka was right, curling up every evening to read and finding out how beautiful it is to narrate the spate of things that exist correctly and with enjoyment at putting one right colour next to another right colour, then taking two steps back and knowing, yes, that's right, that's exactly the way it is.

Since

And one day before the festivals Daddy came home with fewer wrinkles and the wrinkles that there were had less darkness in them, and Daddy said to Mummy, and he was overheard, that the thing they had talked about a while back would be possible apparently, and they could, and they would build a new house in the settlement, it had just emerged that Pardes would offer a loan on Uncle Moshe's recommendation, and that Uncle David, that good man, had got the benevolent society of which he was a prominent member to put in twenty-five Egyptian pounds as a philanthropic gesture, virtually at no interest, and a little of the money left over from the sale of the house on Mendele St, and a mortgage from the Loan Fund and fifteen years' savings at eight percent, in all two hundred and forty Egyptian pounds, underwritten by Uncle Moshe, Uncle David and Uncle Yosef, and a little more from here and there perhaps, some articles or a room to let, and by skimping and saving every penny, at the weekend they would go and see the designated lot, a dunam and seven hundred square metres, making exactly two Turkish dunams, with nothing on it at present except an abandoned sandstone quarry full of crumbling bits of stone, because of which Esther and Nehama Dondikow had agreed to lower the price of the lot, also because it was an isolated plot beyond all the built area right on the edge of the orange groves, and you would have to walk through sand and clay to reach the centre of the settlement, and because jackals peered through the windows at night, and perhaps even a crazed hyena, and the plot would have to be levelled off before it could be built on, it was as though they were trying to get a foothold again, Mummy and Daddy, and to take their places again, and hold their heads up again, and pretend that what had been had been, and that a fresh start was always possible, even though the game was well known, and next week they would contact their friend Ben-Tzion Hurwitz the man from Solel Boneh to sign an agreement for the house to be built on Plot 260 in Block 16 in Ramleh Sub-district, three rooms and an open veranda, a grey house with low-cement red rooftiles, skilfully designed by the architect Teiner who had just arrived from Prague, and the middle room would protrude from the façade on three sides, like a tortoise sticking its head out of its shell, and that was how the house would stand and rise above all the nothing all around, on the edge of the orange groves, the last house at the end of the built settlement, not a large house at all, after forty years of roaming as a valiant pioneer over this hard land, and on the edge of this dense dark blue-green sea of orange groves, immediately beyond which were the Arabs with their villages of Zarnuga and Qubeibeh and Yivneh, and beyond them Nebi Rubin and the sand dunes and beyond them the great sea, invisible but audible in the full nights, and once it was built they would grow round it a purple jacaranda and a red poinciana and an araucaria that every year would produce a new generation of round brush-like leaves, and cypresses dotted here and there along the fence, one of which would grow bent, and a mighty mulberry tree that would grow magnificently even though it was a male that would not produce fruit, which was just as well as it would not attract flies, and some citrus trees and vines, and a chicken coop and a stable for the donkey, and possibly even a goat, and all sorts of vegetables and flowers, flowering or fading according to the seasons, the price of water and weariness, a new house that would stand proudly through sixty-four good and not-so-good years until it was sold for demolition, and thirteen years after it was built the brother aged thirty, and fifteen years after it was built the father aged seventy-three, and forty-nine years after it was built the mother aged eighty-seven, would be carried out of it on their last journey to the old burial ground, but all this, now on the eve of Rosh Hashanah, when day and night are approaching equality, when the sunrises are marvellous and the sunsets are splendid, is still of course unknown and doesn't occur to them, happily, innocently and with no gloomy thoughts, roaming no further than the first mortgage repayment, or the end of Mikve Yisrael next year when those tough young lads will suddenly be sent off on guard duty to Kfar Tavor and Segera, including Eliyahu Hershkovich, and they will return with photographs of themselves with girls of the Lower Galilee, those wild apples or wild roses, embracing enough, radiant enough, and entirely youthful, and here, one night in August, half the eastern sky will suddenly be lit up by the terrible red fire of the burning of the barn at Hulda, and for his bar-mitzvah the youngster will be given a Kodak box camera, and perhaps also a watch, each thing in its appointed time in the coming year, may it be a blessing for us, amen, and on this new plot on the edge of all the orange groves the house is going to be built, and from now on it will be called simply Moskovich 14.

Summer 1991

About the Author

S. YIZHAR (Yizhar Smilansky, 1916-2006) was born in Rehovot, Israel, to a family of Russian immigrants who were members of the Zionist pioneer intelligentsia. He fought in the 1948 War of Independence, was a member of the political parties headed by David Ben Gurion and held a seat in the Knesset, the Israeli Parliament, for 17 years. Yizhar was professor of education at the Hebrew University of Jerusalem and professor of Hebrew literature at Tel Aviv University. He started publishing in 1938, writing fiction for both adults and children. Yizhar was considered Israel's most illustrious writer. He was awarded the Israel Prize for his masterpiece, *Days of Ziklag* (1959). He also received the Brenner Prize, the Bialik Prize (1991) and the Emet Prize for Art, Science and Culture (2002). *Days of Ziklag* is included among *The 100 Greatest Works of Modern Jewish Literature* (2001).

The fonts used in this book are from the Garamond family

Other works by S. Yizhar available from *The* Toby Press

Midnight Convoy & Other Stories